..., London and
...ing career as a professional
...dy the Romantics. Since then he
has taug. ...nool English, edited a left-wing cultural
magazine, and written essays, stories and reviews for,
among other publications, the *New York Times*, the
Guardian, the *London Review of Books* and the *Paris
Review*. His novels include *The Syme Papers*, *Either Side
of Winter*, *Imposture* and *A Quiet Adjustment*. Markovits
has lived in London since 2000 and is married with a
daughter and a son. He teaches creative writing at Royal
Holloway, University of London.

Further praise for *Childish Loves*:

'A satisfyingly rich and challenging conclusion to the tri-
logy.' *The Times*

'A striking mergence of biography, fiction and memoir.'
Daily Telegraph

'Elegant work of metafiction . . . full of provocative inquiries.' *New Yorker*

'The historical novel reinvented for postmoderns . . . All
three [parts of the Byron trilogy] are beautifully written

and reel you in to a disturbing world of fictions and a genuine attempt to answer the question about the essential unknowability of history . . . If the postmodern "revival" of the historical novel is, as [Perry] Anderson argues, about "a desperate attempt to awaken us to history", then few can have done it as entertainingly as Markovits.' *Scotsman*

'This novel is full of life, moving, at times disturbing and a terrific read.' *Jewish Chronicle*

By the same author

The Syme Papers
Either Side of Winter
Playing Days
Imposture
A Quiet Adjustment

Childish Loves

BENJAMIN MARKOVITS

faber and faber

First published in the United Kingdom in 2011
by Faber and Faber Ltd
Bloomsbury House
74–77 Great Russell Street
London WC1B 3DA

This paperback edition first published in 2012

Typeset by Faber and Faber Ltd
Printed in England by CPI Group (UK) Ltd, Croydon CR0 4YY

A CIP record for this book
is available from the British Library

ISBN 978-0-571-23337-3

FSC
www.fsc.org
MIX
Paper from
responsible sources
FSC® C101712

2 4 6 8 10 9 7 5 3 1

To Caroline

If I could explain at length the *real* causes which have contributed to increase this perhaps *natural* temperament of mine – this Melancholy which hath made me a bye-word – nobody would wonder – – but this is impossible without doing much mischief. – – I do not know what other men's lives have been – but I cannot conceive anything more strange than some of the earlier parts of mine – – I have written my memoirs – but omitted *all* the really *consequential & important* parts – from deference to the dead – to the living – and to those who must be both.

Lord Byron

Two years ago, on my way through New York, I called Steve Heinz and left a message for him on his answering machine. Could he meet me in the city in the next couple weeks, for lunch or coffee or an early drink? I suggested a few places convenient for the train to Westchester. Heinz had just been promoted to principal at the high school where I used to teach, and I expected to learn from him a certain amount of insider gossip about former colleagues and friends. Ten years had passed since I shared an office with him – my first real taste of working life. I drew from it a pretty general picture of what adulthood was like, what New York was like, what my own life *might* have been like, and then quit. How much curiosity could I decently show about the characters of a place where I spent nine months a decade before? Still, this time I wanted to ask him a few questions about one of those characters, and I guessed he probably knew which one.

It was the week after Labor Day, when traffic and business suddenly return to the city, as bright and colorful in their way as the onset of fall a few months later amongst the trees of Central Park. The school year had started, and Heinz made some difficulties about finding a time. I wondered if something I'd written had offended him. One of my books was set on a campus very much like the one he presided over, and the school's reputation had suffered recently, in the gossip columns, for the way it handled the firing of another teacher who had based a novel on his experience there. (In my day maybe half the English department, and a quarter of the history department, were working on novels; I was just one of a crowd.) It's not always easy having for a local paper the *New York Times*. Such incidents get blown out of proportion, and the angry back and forth between the supporters and opponents of this guy's book had filled the Metro section for several weeks and had even made its way onto the cover of *New York Magazine*. Heinz might have thought I was hoping to stir up the same kind of publicity – not for my old novel, which had passed into silence painlessly enough, but for a new publication, which I had come into town to promote.

But I'm getting ahead of myself. A few years previously, a man named Peter Pattieson, a colleague of Heinz's – an old colleague of mine – had died. (There's no real point in covering up the name of this school. Anyone who lives in New York will recognize it at once, and anyone who doesn't won't care. It's the Horatio Alger School in Riverdale, known familiarly, to much of the faculty if not the students themselves, as Algiers.) Peter was one of Algiers' true eccentrics. In the first place, his real name wasn't Pattieson, it was Sullivan. He was the only teacher I ever heard of who taught under a nom de plume. By the time I came on the scene, he had more or less stopped talking to everyone in the department office. He occupied a little spare room next to the utility closet, which contained a desk and a chair and a small couch and used to be called the Winter Palace by ironic English masters. It was a place they could retire to, to read during a free hour, or catch up on sleep, or meet quietly with a student. But once Peter took it over, everyone else stopped coming – out of respect, I would like to say, but respect isn't quite the right word.

Many of my colleagues, especially the older ones, treated him the way you might treat a homeless man on the subway. Not unkindly, but with the deference you show to someone who isn't particularly clean. Cleanliness, in fact, was never Peter's strong suit. He always wore the same black chalk-stained smoking jacket to class; and his beard, which was both wild and sparse, was larded in the morning with the crumbs of his breakfast and stained in the afternoon by the grease of his lunch. But if he smelled of anything, it was the sweetness of pipe tobacco. For his part, Peter tended to avoid other people as systematically as they avoided him, and for the whole of my admittedly brief tenure at Horatio Alger, I never heard Steve Heinz exchange a single word with him. They were both very popular teachers, and once or twice I saw the strain between them showing up among their students in the cafeteria. Peter's followers were easy to spot. They dressed like him, both the boys and the girls, and tended to carry around in their back pockets those pretty Faber editions of whatever poet Peter happened to be preaching from at the time.

At one point, very late in the spring, I took advantage of the privilege accorded to new teachers and sat in on one of Peter's classes. After that a sort of friendship grew up between us. We used to go for walks during our free period around the wide shady neighborhood in which the school was located, and quote poetry at each other. Nothing could embarrass Peter, least of all pretension. He had

3

an extraordinary gift for recitation, which could be set off by the slightest of associations. I remember once, on our way back to class, seeing a young history teacher (who had managed to annoy him) walking in high heels across the uneven ground of the football field to her car. Something absurd about the way she moved made Peter whisper to me:

Oh fat white woman whom nobody loves
Why do you walk through the fields in gloves?

In fact, the teacher in question was slender and rather pretty; but for the rest of the year, whenever I saw her, I heard in my mind's ear Peter's hesitant soft Irish accent, which sounded more like a cough than a voice, repeating those lines.

He died in 2006 and I didn't make it to the funeral – one of the things I hoped Heinz could tell me about. Later, a package arrived for me in London from Peter's estate. It contained a phonebook-thick slab of manuscript papers, typed (on a typewriter) and Tipp-Exed by a careful hand and printed on a mishmash of stationery. I took them into my study and arranged them as I do my own papers, on my knees, laying them out against the checked covering of a fold-out sofa. My daughter had recently been born and served as my excuse for missing his funeral – her crying reached me through the Victorian floorboards. But then I began to read, and Peter's voice returned to me, 'mumbling, reluctant, low, compelling,' as I had heard it for the first time a decade before in the quiet of his classroom. I remember thinking, with a half-smile, oh, he's talking

4

about Byron again, and being touched by his consistency. It was hard for me to imagine him reliably dead.

Within a few hours I had separated the manuscripts into two complete novels and three large unconnected sections of a third. I figured Peter had probably bequeathed them to me because he had seen my name in the *New York Times*. (By that stage, I had begun to publish a little, two novels, a few short stories, some reviews.) There was something flattering about the whole business. Look at me, I thought, with my wife and daughter a flight of stairs away and my own books, bearing my name, on my own shelves. Peter, so far as I knew, had never married and had never mentioned to me the existence of any lovers. One of the reasons I let the correspondence lapse when I stopped teaching, one of the more shameful reasons, is that I suspected his affection for me had a sexual element, which I never pretended to classify or define. But it seemed easier, when he wrote me, not to write back. The guilt of that was mixed in with everything else. Anyway, and for whatever reason, I decided to do what I could for his novels and felt suddenly flushed with the conviction, unusual in a writer, that I might be in a position to help somebody.

My editor, Lee Brackstone, is much more of a Romantic, in the old-fashioned, capitalized sense of the word, than I ever was. The idea of a dead, neglected New York private school teacher appealed to him at once. We argued a little about the books themselves. *Imposture* appeared to be the earliest piece. Peter didn't date his work, and the copies I inherited had clearly been typed around the same time. You could practically see him wearing down the ribbon as he went, page after page. (I once saw him type, finger by finger, his end-of-year student reports. It couldn't

5

have taken any less than three months of eight hours a day to produce the wedge that had come in the post.) At any rate, *Imposture* struck me as immature – clever in a first-novelish kind of way, but too plot-heavy and conceit-driven. The kind of novel a young man might write during his free hours, on weekends, and over the long summers, both as a respite from the grind of high-school teaching and as a way of launching himself clear of it. The kind of novel you write when you still hope that writing is a way of making money.

Lee agreed but wanted to publish it first anyway. He had rescued my own first novel from the 'long grass of neglect,' and the misery of endless redrafting, shortly before my thirtieth birthday. He was not much older at the time; it was one of the first things he offered for. I have sometimes felt in his company like nothing but a kind of middleman between a certain mild strain of private, comfortable disappointment and the public appetite for it, such as it is. Whatever 'star' quality the business of professional writing depends on is possessed by him. In Peter's case, middleman describes my role exactly. As soon as Lee got his hands on the papers, I discovered how little real control I had over their publication. He insisted on bringing out *Imposture* first, in spite of my hesitations; and followed it up a year later with *A Quiet Adjustment*, the second and final completed manuscript from the stack I had inherited on Peter's death. The best I could do was leave the novels alone and let them stand or fall according to their strengths. But a part of my resistance to publishing *Imposture* first was the fact that *A Quiet Adjustment* would be judged in its light; it needed to be judged in its own light.

Something had happened to me since Peter died, and the task of publishing his unpublished work deepened the effect of it. I had a mortgage and a daughter, and the pressure to support the cost of each persuaded me in the end to accept the kind of job I would once have despised myself for doing. I began to teach creative writing. I stayed up at night correcting other people's manuscripts and commuted in the morning, an hour each way in the car, to an office, where I sketched out new ways of inspiring my students to do the thing I wasn't doing any more: creative writing. Then, sometimes twice a day, for two-hour sessions, I stood in front of a room full of kids and talked about it. Of course, the burden of Peter's inheritance didn't help, a burden that seemed larger than just the bundle of loose pages I had somehow committed myself to transforming – into books, those magical things. I had a duty to him, not only because he was my friend, but because I had gotten published and he hadn't, and there wasn't any difference between us that could justify this fact.

Imposture came out while I was staying with my in-laws for a few months. Our house had a leaky roof, and we were taking the chance to renovate the kitchen as well. I remember feeling surprised at how nervously I opened the papers each Saturday morning – maneuvering my way to the review section before anyone could offer it to me with a significant air. It wasn't my book; the guy whose book it was was dead. But still I suffered the familiar heartache of anticipation until I had gone through all the papers looking for his name. Then I spent the rest of the day arguing in my head with each reviewer, the sort of protracted internal conversation teenage boys have with girls they haven't yet dared to talk to in real life.

'Well, we got through that time,' I said to Lee, when the final review was in. I meant, no one had noticed the book's obvious flaw; that it depends on a ridiculous mistake, the sort of mistake that in life would be cleared up in a minute, and which only in bad literature is allowed to fester and produce a plot. Peter grounds his story on the resemblance between its two main characters, between Lord Byron and Lord Byron's doctor. It sounds like the beginning of a bad joke, but none of his reviewers challenged Peter on this central conceit. Some of them even referred to their resemblance as historical fact. We were sitting over our pints in one of the florid crude Victorian pubs on the fringes of Bloomsbury, near the Faber offices. Pressed tin ceilings; cut-glass mirrors above the bar. Lee looked at me curiously, began to say one thing and then changed his mind. 'It will get easier,' he said.

I don't know that it did, but then, my hopes for the second novel were so much higher. If *Imposture* was meant to make money, *A Quiet Adjustment*, by contrast, has the air of a book written entirely for its author's own pleasure. Peter manages to trace in it a history of nineteenth-century sensibility. He shows how the age that began with Austen produced in the end a Henry James. An argument he makes not only through the style of the novel itself, evolving from one to the other, but through the life of its central character. Lady Byron was caught up in the most famous scandal of the Romantic age. She presided over that scandal into a ripe and sanctimonious widowhood and became the perfect symbol for Victorianism. Reading Peter's novel, between the soft covers of the

Faber first edition, I missed him – with a fresh pang of baffled friendship. Not the man I knew, who could never have written this book, but the man I didn't know, who had.

*

Which brings me back to New York: the American edition of *A Quiet Adjustment* was being launched. My publicist, a perfectly sensible woman named Anne, prepared me for the absence of reviews with the usual laments about the current state of literary fiction in America. I refused to believe that the story of a dead high-school teacher, survived by nothing but the unpublished manuscripts on which he had spent his private life, wouldn't arouse the imaginative sympathies of every books-page editor in the country. But books-page editors aren't in the business of imaginative sympathies, Anne said; they are in the business of filling advertising pages. What I *could* do was 'reach out more directly to the readers.' You mean blogs, I said. No, not just blogs: reading groups. But she didn't really mean reading groups, either.

I had my first experience that fall of an ancient and sometimes respectable form of human association: the Literary Society. The Byron Society of America had an obvious interest in Peter's work – Peter himself used to be a member of it. They met occasionally for lectures or meals or drinks, in New York or Boston or Philadelphia, at restaurants and private clubs. Mostly academics, of course, but schoolteachers, too; booksellers, housewives, doctors; gentlemen of independent means; grad-school drop-outs suffering from intellectual nostalgia. One of the reasons I had come to New York was to find out more about my author. His two completed manuscripts were already in print. There was nothing left but a strange uncomfortable collection of chapters, which couldn't be published without some kind of context. The best context would be Peter's life – it was the thought of what I might learn that made me uncomfortable. I had come to realize just how odd his silence in the school halls *was*. Try spending a week or even a day refusing to talk. You would need a certain amount of resentment spurring you on, but also a few things worth keeping quiet about.

For two weeks I traveled up and down the eastern seaboard. The Austen Society met in Philadelphia at a building belonging to Penn. Seven people showed up: the president of the Austen Society, the treasurer of the Austen Society, three junior professors from the English department, and two friends of mine from college. I read some of the love letters from *Imposture*, which Peter had cribbed almost word for word from Claire Clairmont's correspondence with Lord Byron. Afterwards I stole a bottle of red wine from the refreshments table the English department had laid on and ended up spilling some of it on the futon where I spent the night. The Henry James Society in New York was slightly better attended. A family friend arranged the meeting at his club, and by force of, not will, exactly, but a kind of whimsy, managed to persuade a number of the members to take their cocktails into the club library where I gave my talk. I read the anal rape scene from *A Quiet Adjustment*. At the Club of Odd Volumes, in Boston, which admitted only men, I chose a passage from *Imposture* in which Peter describes the home of the bookseller Henry Colburn – the shoes that line the stairs leading from the shop floor to his private quarters.

My lectures were often followed by dinner of some kind. Members gathered in the club dining room or a nearby 'pub' and talked quite childishly about what is after all a rather childish love: I mean, the love of books. The oddest, saddest reading I ever gave was at something called the Society for the Publication of the Dead, one of those vague grand titles that shows up just what it's meant to conceal. Humbleness, obscurity, insignificance. The Society was run out of the home of the club president, Mike Lowenthal, a tax lawyer who lived in Queens. Once a quarter the members got together in his living room and ate unidentifiable stews and talked about their 'progress.' Progress was a big word with them; I heard it again and again.

Lowenthal had founded the society, he told me over the phone, 'in order to bring into one boat people who could be of mutual support and service to each other.' He meant, people who had inherited unpublished manuscripts: the children of memoirists and closet novelists; the parents of precocious suicides. So far, he said, there had been a lot of support but not much service. They were very excited to have a speaker.

'In this business,' he said, 'there aren't many success stories.'

'Is that what I am?' I asked.

I was staying with my sister in New Haven and got the commuter service into Grand Central, then transferred to the 7 train and rode it all the way out to Flushing. For some reason I found this journey especially dispiriting. To come into Manhattan and go out of it again – to feel yourself diminishing on the way to the suburbs, into a different kind of anonymity. Mike's enthusiasm for my success had touched a nerve. Since taking up Peter's cause, I had published little of my own work. Nothing but *Playing Days*, a quiet memoir of my first long year after college, which I spent playing minor-league basketball in Germany. It came out in England first; my American publishers were still undecided about it. The book had received a more muted critical reception than Peter's novels, and I found myself struggling, on the long train ride to Queens, against the inevitable comparisons. A dull overcast late summer day, as pale as December, and in the course of my journey the street lamps came on without discernible effect on the general whiteness.

After five years in the fiction business I should have learned my lesson. Writers get rewarded according to their exaggerations. This explains why, compared with the real thing, most novels seem so vivid and unnatural – the qualities by which critics and readers tend to recognize 'good writing.' What I aimed at in *Playing Days* wasn't vividness, it was the mildly unusual, overcomplicated quality of the story you tell on coming home from work. Our lives are governed mostly by technicalities; literature ignores them because they are boring. We stopped at 33rd Street, 40th Street, 51st Street stations. I'm inventing the numbers but the impression they made somehow reinforced my case. The streets below us, viewed sidelong from the elevated tracks and partly obscured by window-shine, seemed more or less indistinguishable. Sometimes I even saw the same shopping chains reproduced in slightly different order. The variations in people are hardly more significant. After an hour of self-justification, I had the stuffed-up, hungry feeling you get from eating too much of the same thing. So I rested my head against the glass and closed my eyes.

Flushing was the last stop. There was no danger of overshooting, and I was plenty early in any case to be at Lowenthal's house by seven thirty. Drifting off, I played over again a sort of internal dialogue, which originated God knows where, but had become familiar to me over the past few weeks. It's what I thought about sometimes instead of sleeping; maybe it was the same thing as sleep. Someone said, Do you find this passage of time acceptable? A voice not exactly my own – maybe my father's or brother's. Yes, I always answered. After a moment it spoke again. Is there anything you have to do? No, I said. There is nothing I have to do. Then why not accept it? said the voice. Then other people intruded themselves. I could hear them like you hear your parents' guests arrive while you lie upstairs in bed. Is this where you get off for Shea Stadium? That's why they call it Shea Station, lady. I beg your pardon, that's not what they call it, and so on. By the time I woke up, the artificial light of the subway car was sharp enough to hurt my eyes. It was dark outside, and I felt oddly intimidated by the hurry of the commuters going home.

*

Mike Lowenthal lived in a gray clapboard row-house about ten minutes' walk from the station. His wife and seventeen-year-old son had died in a car accident five years before. This is one of the first things he told me as he showed me inside. There was a woman he called his

13

Super Maid hustling around the kitchen, a middle-aged Polish woman named Marte, bulky, sweating, with the wide shoulders and hips of a Matisse or a Henry Moore. 'Don't introduce me,' she said. 'I don't have time to talk. My hands are dirty. Don't shake my hands.'

'My wife was the only one who could get her to do anything,' Mike said. 'Now she bosses me around.'

'Look at me, bossing,' she called out.

'Listen, you're a little early. Before the rest of this crowd arrive, why don't I show you something.'

I followed his back up the staircase running through the center of the house. He had the ordinary, loose-skinned face of a middle-aged working man, but from behind he looked like some strange vegetable, with all its weight gathered in the middle and tapering away to the top and bottom. When he reached the landing, he turned towards the rear of the house into a boy's bedroom. Pinned to the door, a large official-looking sign: Beware of the Teenager. There was an unmade single bed in the room, under a window that overlooked the backs of the row-houses: porch lights glared as regular as street lamps. Mike sat down at his son's desk, wheezing a little from the stairs. There was nowhere for me to sit but the bed. Something about it, however, made me hesitate, and the awful thought crossed my mind that the sheets hadn't been changed in five years.

He lifted a thin sheaf of papers from a drawer, cheaply bound and covered in clear plastic, and laid it out carefully on the leather of his son's desk. It looked like a senior essay and was titled: NOT THE FIRST LOVE STORY IN THE WORLD, BY STEVEN LOWENTHAL. It cost him some effort to rise to his feet again. 'I'm going to get out of your hair. What you don't need is me standing over your shoulder.' Then, in a sudden change of tone: 'What are we doing here. Let me get you a drink.' He put his hands quietly together, an effeminate gesture; it struck me that he was waiting for me to make room. At that moment the doorbell rang and Marte called up to him something unintelligible. 'They're playing my song,' he said and moved awkwardly past me to the head of the stairs, where he stopped and turned again. We looked at each other for a moment and I felt strongly the need to add something. Then the bell rang again, the quick double-ring of social, light-hearted impatience. 'Take as long as you want,' he said. 'This crowd is good for nothing till the food arrives.'

Once he was gone, I closed his son's door and spent a few minutes looking over the bedroom, which still smelled of sleep. It struck me that Mike probably used it as a guest room or slept in it himself when his marriage bed seemed too large for one. The desk, square and old-fashioned, crowded out a corner of the window and seemed like a recent addition. Maybe Mike used the room as an office and napped there when he got tired. On the wall over Steven's bed was a poster of Norm Duke, a big-eared, red-faced grinning young man, stuck on with Blu-Tack. The poster said, Winner of the 2000 PBA National Championship, Toledo, Ohio; and I noticed on the top shelf of the narrow bookcase a row of bowling trophies, several honorable mentions and a 2nd place finish in the father/son category. The books were mostly the books you'd expect to see on the shelf of a high-school senior: *A Tale of Two Cities*, *The Great Gatsby*, *The Norton Anthology of Poetry*. There were also a few more personal touches: *The Big Lebowski* on VHS, and a series of fantasy novels, with women on the cover entwined around swords, etc.

I sat down to read NOT THE FIRST LOVE STORY IN THE WORLD. The opening paragraph was a single sentence: *They say that grief is transient.* As I skimmed the rest of it, the doorbell continued to ring. A young man, who seems to be unnamed, falls in love with a girl from his high-school chemistry class, Laura Salzburger. He is a very nice young man, in most public ways, a good student, but he imagines doing all kinds of unspeakable things to her. Because of his terrible imagination, he breaks out in a sweat whenever he sees her and can never manage more than the most perfunctory conversation. Eventually he decides to announce his feelings for her 'in prose.' He writes a story about a beautiful girl named Laura Salzburger, who dies tragically and mysteriously and is mourned for the rest of his life by the awkward young man who never had the courage to 'express his feelings for her.'

A short story, then, or a novella – fifty-odd pages long. I wondered if he meant to suggest that the protagonist himself had been responsible for the girl's death. This is the kind of thing teenaged writers like to hint at. Regardless, the story was more or less unpublishable and contained many of the simple flaws, easy to spot but awkward to correct, which had become familiar to me in my teaching. Sudden shifts in tense and point of view. False oppositions; grammatical carelessness. A tendency to rely on the first phrase or thought that comes to hand, which is usually the phrase or thought left lying around on the surface of the imagination by bad movies and books: 'Laura Salzburger had a beautiful smile that lit up not only most rooms but her own blue eyes.' It's common, in creative writing seminars, to talk about the difference between the reader's truth and the writer's truth – in other words, about the

16

gap between what you see in your mind and what you can put on the page. But this difference matters little in practice. Most young writers put on the page exactly what it is they *do* see, a world of bright, textureless, unconnected parts, some of it borrowed from other books.

Then I thought, and he's dead, and he's been dead five years. And it's quite possible that this story is basically 'true.' That Steven Lowenthal had a crush on a girl from his chemistry class, his first real sexual crush; and that he imagined doing all kinds of perfectly acceptable things with her, which he felt terrible about from the point of view of his decent, daylight, pre-sexual personality; and that he never got the chance to reconcile himself, as most of us do and should, to certain aspects of his human nature. One of the things I had learned after three years in teaching is that my training had taught me to distinguish between good and bad writing, but not between what was true and what wasn't. I'd had kids handing in stories about their alcoholic mothers you could have sworn were lifted from the plots of daytime television until you saw them shivering in your office, holding themselves by the arms to keep from crying. What's happening to these people, you think, that it comes out so badly written? Don't they suffer too?

For a minute I sat at Steven Lowenthal's desk, calming down. Saying to myself, what are you getting worked up about. Below me I heard Mike's voice, not the words themselves, but the muffled shape of the words, diminishing as he moved away from the stairs in the hall. More guests. And the feeling returned to me that I was lying half-asleep in my parents' house and listening to one of their parties. Another minute, I thought, another minute.

Then decided I was probably angry about being somewhere I didn't want to be and doing something I didn't want to do; and at that point I stood up and went downstairs.

When I walked into the living room, there were nine or ten people sitting down, haphazardly, with food on their laps. The oldest was in his eighties, bald and straight-backed, with thick rolls of skin on his forehead and the back of his neck. I learned afterwards he had recently lost a great deal of weight. Henry Pantolini. He offered to make space for me on the piano seat.

'There's not much of me,' he said, with a kind of pride. I sat down for a minute beside him. 'I don't play any more because of my hands,' he added and held up his hands. 'When I was your age I used to work nights sweeping floors at the Harry Eichler School in Richmond Hill. They kept a little upright Mason-Hamlin in a corner of the gym. Sometimes, when I had the place to myself, I played whatever they had on the stand, like "Bandstand Boogie", that kind of thing. For ten, twenty minutes. Very spooky and loud. This was my second job, and the rest of my free time was taken up with an accounting degree. It's amazing how hard you can work when you have no choice. Now I get tired rolling out of bed.' I could think of nothing to say to any of this, and he took pity. 'Why don't you get some food.'

The youngest was Sarah, in her mid-twenties; an undergraduate at Queens College. Permed hair; an accommodating blouse; and a dark skirt made of some synthetic material that clung to her thighs when she stood up. She told me within a few minutes of conversation that she was a single mother with a two-year-old child at home. 'I come here to meet men, that's what I tell people,' she joked. 'This is my fifth meeting, and you're the first one I've seen. Age-suitable, I mean.' Her father, before he died, had written her what started out as a long letter about the year and a half he spent as a teenager in Birkenau. The reason she started school so late is because he needed taking care of, and also because of her daughter. The letter by the time he was done was a hundred and fifty pages long. 'Some letter,' she said. She didn't even look at it before he was dead, but by the time I met her she had read it 'five or six times over, and always with tears in my eyes. The old bastard. If he does this to me, who had every reason to resent him, what will he do to people he *didn't* annoy?'

Marte had made two kinds of stew, one with meat and one without, which bubbled thickly in the kitchen, still in their pots. I moved vaguely towards it, through an arch in the living room. Next to the pots were bowls and slices of cheap white bread. 'I don't know you,' a woman said to me, ladle in hand – middle-aged, round-bellied, with a girlish, unpretty face. She wore her red hair in a bob. 'You're the new kid.'

'Do you normally know everybody?'

'It's a pretty good crew,' she said. Crowd; crew. They had found odd, affectionate ways of referring to each other.

'I'm sure it is.' I stood waiting for her to finish serving herself. 'I don't know what the thing you say here is. To new members, I mean.'

'You mean, who died? My sister. She didn't have any specially awful story, except she wanted to be a writer and couldn't get published. I teach high-school English in Forest Hills. What she wrote is not bad. I don't have any illusions about it, either. She died last February, not this year's but the one before. Forty-five years old. You know how many manuscripts she left behind? But what do you care; let me ask you. Who died for you.'

'A guy I used to teach with. In Riverdale. I was also a high-school English teacher.'

Mike interrupted me, with a hand on her shoulder. 'This is our distinguished speaker,' he said. And then: 'Can I have a word?' He led me to a sidebar in the sitting room, where the drinks were kept. The house reminded me of my grandmother's house and suggested a touching Jewish faith in material quality. I could hear her commenting, 'the best of everything,' and meaning, the most expensive. Thick white carpets; club chairs; the carpet still white and the chairs recently re-upholstered. All of which struck me as evidence that either Mike Lowenthal was doing okay or Marte was more helpful than he pretended. The television lived in a mahogany wall-cupboard, which was built out of the fireplace and matched the piano stationed prominently in the bay window. So passers-by could look at it and admire. It was also a fact about my grandmother that she played beautifully, with real feeling.

'I don't know if you had a chance to look at . . . what I showed you,' Mike said to me. His voice had dropped.

'Do you mind talking about your son?'

'Believe me, that's one thing you *do* get used to. I understand your concerns, though. So far as I know he was no kind of sexual pervert. But then, he was a seventeen-year-old boy: what I don't know about him could fill a much bigger book than he wrote. Such a vocabulary. In conversation, you were lucky to get a yes or no.' He picked up a lemon and began to cut. 'Gin and tonic? Isn't that what you English types like to drink?' He handed me a tall glass, and we shifted slightly into a corner of the room. 'I can guess your next question,' he went on. 'My wife was literary, that's where he gets it from. When I was a young man, just in practice, I joined what has since become, so people tell me, a very fashionable kind of association. I mean, a book group. Mostly I was on the lookout for girls. Whenever I made any kind of comment about wouldn't it be nice to clear up this point with the author, you can't believe the grief they gave me. Now everybody I show it to, these publishing guys, want to know the same thing. There was no Laura Salzburger in his high-school graduating class. But was there a Meira Schulzman, a Rachel Littman, a Deborah Leibowitz? Of course there was. More than that I couldn't say.'

I wasn't sure if he was angry or enjoying himself, or both; his voice had risen again. 'Next question,' he said.

'Can you tell me anything about how he died?'

'Like I said, a car accident. This isn't an interesting or dramatic kind of death, not like cancer, which seems to get so much press these days. I mean from you people, the writers. (You see, I've been reading your books.) There wasn't even some drunk running a red light I could devote myself to putting behind bars. My wife hit a patch of black ice coming off the White Stone Expressway five years ago last December. Nobody's fault but dumb luck's; she was going about forty miles an hour. They had just been to visit her mother in Florida – *she* had the cancer, and outlived them both to see the funeral. Somebody, I think it was Delta, used to run a very reasonable shuttle from Fort Lauderdale to La Guardia. I came back late from work to nobody home, but you know how it is with flights; there's always delays. Even if the flight comes in, they lose the luggage. Till about midnight, I was perfectly calm and sensible. I brushed my teeth like a good boy; I went to bed. First I can't sleep and then, after twenty minutes of fighting the sheets, my heart begins pounding and I start making calls. It turns out when I stopped being sensible I was more or less on the money, but I didn't invite you here to talk to you about this.'

'No, you wanted to talk about publication.'

He looked up at me and waited. Eventually, I said, 'I can anticipate several difficulties about publication. Let me add, this is a line I've heard myself in one way or another more than thirty times. You see, I keep count. Also, I'm not a publisher, I'm a writer, and what I know about is the trouble I might have selling my own work.' It seemed to me that people were listening in, so I continued as quietly as I could. 'Here is the first problem. Nobody wants long short stories. Nobody wants short short stories, either, but at least they don't take up much space.'

'What I was thinking of was somebody might write some kind of introduction and bulk it up a little. Like you did.'

'Who did you have in mind?'

He stared at me, with a conscious smile, and lifted his hands. 'Look, I'm no writer.'

'It's not just a question of length,' I said. 'There's a problem with the ending. I know what he meant to do, but he hasn't done it, and even if he had it wouldn't have worked.'

'Listen, don't worry about the ending. That's what I expected you to say. You mean, in real life, it's the boy who dies, not the girl. Am I right? That's what seemed to me the problem, too; I mean, if you want to sell this kind of thing on context. I'll be honest with you. Publication for me is just a means to an end. What do you reach with your books, if you don't mind me asking, by way of audience? Fifty, sixty thousand? If you're doing well. Look at the box-office results they print in the Monday papers, after the first weekend of business. Even the flops take in a few hundred thousand, *in two days*. Publication for me is just a stepping-stone to the movies, and in the movies you see this kind of thing all the time. Right off the bat the hero dies, and then they show the rest of the picture to explain why. In this case there is no why; that's what breaks your heart. What this kid went through for puberty every boy should see. God knows the difference it might have made in my life. It took me four years of college before I had the nerve or opportunity to stick my prick in anything other than my own hand. That means about ten years of unnecessary shame and frustration, but I didn't have the words to describe them. You can imagine what I felt when I first read my son's story. I discovered it a few days after his death on the computer I bought him for his bar mitzvah. Probably what you felt just now, only he wasn't your son and he hadn't just died. Shame on top of grief on top of loneliness. But I've been living with that story every day now for five years, and every time I look at it I see something else. This was not a bad kid. This was a kid going through a difficult transformation, who had the talent and the emotional maturity to step outside of himself and put it into words. But the girl he falls in love with doesn't get it, and people in my personal opinion will happily pay out ten bucks fifty, or whatever it costs these days to go to the movies, to see if at the end of two hours she

23

understands what it means to be a young man.' Then he added: 'Look and your food's gone cold. While I've been chewing your ear off.'

The girl from Queens College called out, 'Let's get started here. My sitter is costing me ten bucks an hour.'

Mike stepped forward, taking up space in the center of the room, and introduced me. I chose to read my preface to *Imposture*. For two reasons – it's what they wanted to hear, and I had written it. This preface tells the story of my inheritance: how I came to know Peter during a stint teaching high school in New York; how we lost touch; the resentment I felt at being saddled with a stack of manuscripts he hadn't had the energy or the luck to see into print himself. Afterwards, in the Q and A, Mr Pantolini asked me why, since I didn't know Mr Pattieson well, I had gone to so much trouble to get him published? 'Since you seem to have little personal feeling for the man.'

'Personal feeling doesn't come into it. I might ask all of you the same thing. Why do you want these manuscripts to be published? It won't bring the people you loved back to life. It will only mean that others can see them more coldly and clearly than you see them yourself.'

'Is that what happens when you publish a book?'

'More or less.'

No one asked me about Peter's novels. There was a smattering of applause, and I was allowed to refresh my drink at the bar. Mike pulled out, from under the piano, a small box of books my publicist had sent along and began to arrange them on the piano itself. 'I almost forgot,' he said. 'These came for you.' I told a joke I like to tell after readings, a line from a Dawn Powell letter about the difficult build-up to publication day, the anticipation, the waiting around. She used to call this period, I said, 'the calm before the calm.' A few laughs. But none of them cared about that kind of calm; they had another kind of calm on their minds. 'Okay, since nobody's asking, I'll ask,' said the woman with the short red hair. 'You talk a lot in this preface about receiving the manuscripts, but you don't say much about getting them published. That's what we want to know. How did you get them published?'

'I'm a writer,' I said. 'It wasn't so hard for me. The truth is, people publish the people they know.'

Mr Pantolini said, 'Does that mean we know you now?'

'I'm not an editor.'

'Well, how did you get to know your editor?'

'He was the friend of a friend of a friend.'

'I have friends of friends, too,' Mr Pantolini said. 'But it doesn't help me.'

Afterwards, in spite of anything I could say, they approached me with their manuscripts. Most of them bound, like Steven Lowenthal's, with a cheap black spine and plastic covering. The queue took on an oddly formal shape: I might have been selling tickets. Only the red-haired woman had shown up empty-handed. She was on the edge of tears. 'I didn't know there would be a chance for that,' she kept repeating and asked me for my card.

'I don't have a card,' I said.

'Then where are you staying in the city?'

'I'll be leaving in a few days. I'm flying back to England.'

'A few days doesn't matter. I can drive down tomorrow after work and drop something off, if you tell me where you're staying.'

'Please don't drive down,' I told her. 'Not for my sake.'

25

'Who are you kidding. It isn't for your sake.'

So I gave her my address in London, and she promised to send me 'only one or two.'

Novels, I supposed. 'How many are there?'

'I won't tell you. I don't like how many there are. It makes me unhappy, to see them piled up. I'll send you the best.'

Mike looked around for a bag I could carry the manuscripts in. I had eight in all, some of them hundreds of pages long. Too much for a paper shopping bag, even when we split the load in two. We gave the bags a trial run in the front hallway and on my second turn back to the piano one of the handles broke. The whole party had gathered round me, making suggestions. I felt like a sergeant on parade; my mood had lifted. Eventually, someone proposed the box Peter's books had come in, which was made of stiff cardboard and about two feet deep and wide. But what should I do, I said, with all those copies of *Imposture* and *A Quiet Adjustment*, which were lying untouched on top of the piano? And Mike, with the sudden enthusiasm of a man rallying his troops, began very efficiently to auction them off – by naming names. 'Sarah,' he said, 'one book or two books? How much dough you got on you?' And so on, going all the way down the line. I ended up with something like two hundred and sixty dollars in my pocket, in cash and checks. Also, a few books left over, though we managed at last to pack the manuscripts around them.

Then it was just a question of making it to the subway: with both arms stretched out underneath and my elbows propped against my ribs; with several brief stops along the way, every few hundred yards. I always dress up for readings in jacket and tie and could feel the sweat gathering on my neck and staining the collar. Mike had said to me something like Go forth. A number of the others stood in the doorway to wave me off – as if I were catching a boat, a long-haul steamer. Instead, I made it breathlessly to the train, which was standing at the station with open doors. There were three empty seats in the first car and I set my box down gratefully on two of them. Then the train continued stationary for another five minutes, and I could feel like a blush the heat coming off my neck and through my shirt. But nobody looked at me. Most people traveling back towards the city at the end of a long day don't have very sociable reasons.

It was almost midnight before we reached Manhattan. Steve Heinz had finally gotten in touch and invited me to lunch at Horatio Alger the next day. He had also apologized for his silence. There was nothing behind it but the fact that his wife's sister was staying with them. She wasn't very well. He had reached the age, Heinz said, of medicalization, and most of the people he knew suffered from one kind of unmentionable disease or another. Anyway, this woman was a very *simpatica*, strong-minded, independent woman but at the moment the most important and noticeable fact of her personality was that she needed a lot of attention. His wife gave her the daily dose, but in the evenings he had also been on call. All of which was a roundabout way of saying could I come up to see him at work. He promised me 'impossibilities: a free lunch.' And it occurred to me on the long train ride that I should have some questions to ask him, about Peter, the right questions, the questions he wouldn't mind answering.

Why couldn't the guy get himself published? I knew

27

first-hand the luck involved, the almost willful persistence. Liking a book is like liking a human being: you need a good introduction. People publish people they know, not because editors are corrupt, but because there's a big difference between spending two minutes on the first page of a manuscript and five minutes on it. Novels are only good or bad at certain speeds. I knew this, along with all the other excuses an unpublished writer thinks up to explain why nobody buys his work. After ten years of rejections, I had a lot of excuses. But I also knew, from the other side of the business, that if you can spell, and put one sentence after another, and tell a story that seems both unpredictable and inevitable; if you can do these difficult things and don't mind the humiliations of self-promotion, you should find a publisher in the end. Especially with an income to support you and a life untroubled by dependents.

It's not as if Peter was stuck in the foothills of Appalachia. He had a position of influence and authority over wealthy New York kids, themselves the children of influential people in diverse fields. I couldn't help thinking, if he wants to get published, he gets published – he wasn't Mike Lowenthal's son or the redhead's sister. Unless he decides that the humiliations of self-promotion are worse than I think they are, or he has other reasons for keeping a low profile.

When I reviewed novels, for a half-living, I used to spend weeks going over the backlists of particular authors. Lying on a couch to ease the pressure on my spine, which had been badly reorganized by years of basketball. A cup of cold tea on the sofa arm and a heap of books on the floor. I remember being struck by the fact that most writers write the same novel again and again. Not just on the grand scale – they also repeat phrases, ideas, characters, events and places. So what? So the imagination even of gifted fantasists is limited, who cares? But it occurred to me that if you could somehow map these elements onto a transparency and lay them on top of each other, then the repetitions would solidify into a landscape of sorts – which might more closely resemble the literal truths of the author's life. The houses he has lived in; the things his wife says; what his father was like.

At Woodside a man in slovenly tied work boots came on with what at first glance I took to be his daughter, a child of darker skin, maybe twelve years old. But the way he put his arm around her arrested my attention. He wore the kind of comfortable red plaid jacket that remains fashionable both among people who care a great deal about their clothes and those who don't. The girl was in tights and a short soft skirt; she might have just edged seventeen. I felt a certain amount of disapproval concentrated on them – she drowsed in his armpit – and before we reached Manhattan they got off again. An old guy a few seats down from me said, 'What do you think that was about?' To no one in particular; one of those old men who voices general concerns aloud because they have few people available for private conversation. Nobody answered him. Eventually, to prove he was uncowed, he added, 'I'd like to see her mother, that's all.'

'What's he done to you?' someone called out.

'Piqued my curiosity.'

Then the car settled into silence again.

I began, in my mind's eye, gently to lay Peter's books on top of each other. Mothers and fathers both featured in *Imposture* and *A Quiet Adjustment*. He didn't flatter them, but they offered nothing consistent, either, to suggest the presence of real figures in his life. One mother was an alcoholic; another so faint a personality she was almost invisible. The fathers were either kindly and ineffectual or pompous and ineffectual, but not both at once. Grand houses occasionally appeared: Halnaby Hall, where the Byrons honeymooned; his apartments in Piccadilly; various mansions in St James's and Mayfair. My personal knowledge of such historical details is poor, but I assumed he had borrowed them from fact. (As I thought these thoughts the warehouses and factories of Queens, lit from below by street lamps, rushed past, surrounded by tracks.)

The literary influences were easier to trace. I could imagine most clearly from his life the books on his shelves. Byron, of course. James is prominent, too, especially in the second novel. Jane Austen. One reviewer mentioned the Silver Fork school, which I had never heard of and spent a few days in the British Library looking up: writers like Bulwer-Lytton and Disraeli, and novels like *Tremaine: Or the Man of Refinement*, many of them published by Henry Colburn, one of the villains in *Imposture*. But there seemed to me also a distinct American influence: the super-rational prose of Edgar Allan Poe, the clause-addiction of Melville. Of course, the greatest influence on any writer's work is what I sometimes think of as the IKEA of his imagination, which disassembles the cheap materials of his reading and experience and puts them roughly back together. With some screws loose, others left over. Veneer effects, bad hinge-work, unbalanced feet. A few standard devices for solving the problems of construction.

This line of thinking suggested to me what his novels

really have in common. They both turn on sex-acts involving dubious consent. In the climax of *Imposture*, Polidori deflowers Eliza, who thinks he's Lord Byron, at their Brighton hotel. She shrieks at him childishly after he reveals himself: 'This is not what I wanted at all!' And he can think of nothing else to do but leave a handful of money on her bed and run away. In *A Quiet Adjustment*, Annabella gives herself up wholeheartedly to marriage only after Byron has sodomized her in his sister's house. She realizes that she has become involved in a species of sinfulness that can corrupt even her own cold virtue; there is no way out. And on top of these examples, the unpublished stories. What was darkening into shape was something unhappy in the bedroom. I thought of Peter's famous reserve, how much it had to do with shyness or arrogance. His silence might have been the silence of the victim or the exploiter; silences sound alike. And I recalled my own sexual discomfort around him. Some instinct had warned me against Peter, but if it was just the stupid, red-faced, heterosexual suspicion of gay friendship, or something sharper, I couldn't be sure.

In Manhattan I transferred at 42nd Street for the number 9 train – the same train I would take in the morning up to Riverdale and Horatio Alger. I was staying for a couple nights at an apartment on the Upper West Side. When I lived in New York, I lived east of the Park and rarely had to navigate the platforms, alleys, stairwells and ramps of Times Square. Even at that hour, the station was full of its New York types. Under the sign for the uptown red line, I saw a short, tired man in a suit trying to undo the knot in his tie; his elbow held a briefcase against his ribs. As he tore it loose, I felt suddenly unencumbered –

worried and unencumbered, and realized I had left the box of manuscripts in the subway car. It was too late to go back for them. The only novels that reached me came in the post several weeks later, from the red-haired school-teacher. Out of guilt, I looked them over more carefully than I otherwise might have. The first ten pages; a middle chapter; the endings. She was right about her sister's work. It wasn't bad or particularly good, and there was nothing I could do for her.

***

Around eleven o'clock the next morning, I made my way up the hill from the subway at Van Cortlandt Park – a broad flat green at the foot of Riverdale, just across the river from the warehouses of northern Manhattan. Sometimes in the spring I used to see cricket played there on Friday afternoons. Friday was the only day I didn't take the school bus. A few of the teachers met at Dorney and Malone's, a bar underneath the elevated tracks, and drank beer (rarely more than one) and ate popcorn from wooden bowls, before taking the train into town and beginning the weekend. Students passed by us on their way home and sometimes caught us going in. It pleased them, to see signs of ordinary life in their teachers; they felt they had something over us.

The hill is steep enough that I paused at a bend in the drive to catch my breath and look back. Van Cortlandt expands as you rise above it; the dirty industrial face of Inwood appears over the treetops. The last time I walked up that hill I was twenty-three years old, and most of the things that now define my life had not yet occurred.

I was unmarried, daughterless; I had never published a book. But as I approached the school gates, the strong original sense of my first impressions returned to me – including the dread I always felt each Monday morning on re-entering a world of children.

Peter and I, whenever we could, used our free periods to wander the streets. 'Shuttered with branches,' as he once put it, and away from *them*. We stopped sometimes in front of the gabled houses, set back behind driveways and driveway hoops; looked at the expensive cars, the lawns maintained by men in overalls, filling the daylight hours with slow work. Peter had the trick of falling in step with the kind of conversation I might have had with myself. We described the weather or talked about some of the kids. We also discussed the deep restlessness of a schoolmaster's life: the things we thought about while we lectured or looked at out of the classroom window. Teachers are sometimes granted a second chance at the friendships of youth, which are based on the small intimacies of people bounded on all sides by unwanted tasks.

I entered the grounds through the parking lot (Peter always stood just outside the gates to smoke his pipe) and climbed over a low wall. Two or three concrete steps led to the back door. Classes, at least, were in session; most of the halls were empty. Only a few of the older kids had gathered around their bags in the corridors. I used to reckon up in the first few years after teaching the number of students who would remember me if I came back. Diminishing year by year: teachers and students alike pass slowly through the bloodstream of school life after they leave and then disappear altogether. It was actually a relief when my youngest class graduated, though

33

I still dream sometimes about entering a room full of kids whose names I have forgotten, about losing my way in the halls.

At reception, I asked the way to Heinz's office. The bird-like Irish woman at the black phones, smaller than she used to be, blinder (her pale staring blue eyes were fading into the whites), remembered me. 'Sure I know you,' she said, 'tall as you are. You were Mr Pattieson's great friend.'

'I knew him a little and liked what I knew.'

'A very amusing man. A great one for impressions.'

'I never heard his impressions.'

'Well, I suppose he didn't intend them for the upstairs.' Most of the department offices were on the second floor. The ground floor housed administration, and that's where she directed me now, back the way I had come. 'To the door with the window in it,' she said. I stopped a moment at her desk; she worked in a little cubicle just off the main entrance, with an old-fashioned switchboard over her head that hadn't been used in years.

'I hear he died a few years ago. I was very sorry to miss the funeral.'

'You weren't the only one who was sorry.'

'I hear he wrote a few books.'

She gripped me confidentially on the back of the wrist and said, 'I wouldn't bother with them. I had a look at one of them – one of the teachers brought it in, for show, you know. It looked sad stuff to me. He was much more amusing in life, but then, most people are.'

When I walked in Heinz's office, he called out, 'Ah, the famous Markovits.' Whenever old students came to visit him, this is what he cried: 'Ah, the famous so-and-so.' He

34

had taken me under his wing for the nine months I taught at Horatio Alger. I had been warned by other teachers that he liked to play the father-figure, but I didn't stay long enough for any strain to develop. Still, it disappointed me mildly to be greeted with the stock enthusiasm he showed to everyone else. People who play the father-figure usually find replacements for the young men who leave them behind. Also, in my case he might have meant a dig about the way I had given up an honorable profession to make a name for myself.

He was a short, round-shouldered man in his early sixties, with a short white beard that covered his cheeks and the loose skin of his neck. I should add, it was one of his jokes that we were distantly related, through a cousin on his side and a married aunt on mine, who had roots in the small close-knit community of Pittsburgh Jews.

'Look at you,' I said to him. 'You've got a fish tank.' Fish tank, mahogany shelves, a new Persian rug. The chair he sat in rotated effortlessly between the two wings of an L-shaped desk. Which had a view, across it, of the baseball field – itself brand new and bright with fresh chalk and turf.

'It's what they give you when you reach higher office.'

'To see if you can keep something alive?' And so on. This is how we talked.

'Listen,' he said at last, 'I got a class to teach. Why don't you come along and we can get lunch after.'

I followed him into the hallway, suddenly filled with students (the noise of them like the noise of ugly birds). The school board didn't believe in bells; it was one of the illusions of the place that this traffic was voluntary. At the beginning of class, he introduced me as 'the famous writer,' but mostly what I felt, as I leaned my head against the back wall, was sixteen years old. For the next forty minutes I sat in a gray plastic chair beside an opened window and listened to a discussion of *Bartleby the Scrivener*. Heinz was a good teacher; he had the gift of reviving at will his passion for a familiar book. Teaching is like marriage, he once said to me. 'After thirty years of Shakespeare you got to figure it takes a certain effort of the memory to get it up.'

Outside I could see the kids with early lunch finding a spot at the edge of the baseball field to sit and eat – the regents were particular about the diamond. And I remembered another conversation I had had with Heinz about marriage. He rarely joined us for a beer at Dorney and Malone's. At the time he was head of the English department; maybe he liked to keep a certain distance. But shortly before the end of the spring term, he asked me between classes if the young guns still liked to hit the bars on Friday afternoons because he wouldn't mind tagging along. I said sure; in the end, nobody came and it was just the two of us, which probably suited him.

There was something on his mind. A son from his first marriage was graduating (cum laude) from Rutgers in a few weeks' time, and his ex-wife was making difficulties about the weekend arrangements. But he didn't want to talk about these disagreements, which were equally petty and painful, and more boring than anything else. He never thought when he was young that he would invest so much of his energy and intelligence on administrative detail. Not only at work but at home. It should be clear by now that I spent most of the afternoon on the listening end of this conversation, though he paid for my two beers and his own modest ginger ale. The popcorn came free. I kept eating and drinking, out of embarrassment. This was the first time someone from my father's generation had opened up to me.

No, what he wanted to talk about was something else. His second marriage was much happier, thank God, a fact that had a great deal to do with the character of his second wife, which he had recognized almost immediately. But it was also true that he had learned a few things from his first marriage, which might prove useful to me. By this point he knew I was leaving for London at the end of the year. 'To become a writer,' I had told him – though, of course, what I became first was a sponge and a part-time tutor; subsequently a book reviewer and assistant editor, and finally, etc. What upset him so much about the current round of stupid negotiations with his ex-wife was the fact that all he could think about, even while fighting his own corner, was, This is what I have done to you. You are the way you are because of me.

'Look, I'm not trying to beat myself up here with self-hatred. For some situations I got plenty of hatred to go around. And in this case, when I feel these things, partly what I feel is also, listen lady, when did you get to be so unreasonable, selfish, vain and deliberately hurtful? Because when I met this woman she was none of the above. This was a sophisticated, curious, warm-hearted, pleasure-seeking human being. Most of the first five years of our relationship she had to drag me along, intellectually, socially, emotionally, you name it. Sure, we fought a lot of that time, nobody likes being dragged, we fought like hell. But then we entered a patch of clear water, which lasted long enough that we both came to believe it was the new rules of the game. So we got married. And it was only after five or six years of marriage, after the kids were born and we had started to sleep again and return to some kind of acceptable human existence, that I realized why we had stopped fighting in the first place. It became clear to me that I had created an atmosphere, I don't know what else to call it, in which all of the qualities I originally admired about this woman had become blighted. The sexual creature I had fallen in love with had more or less withered and died in front of my eyes. Partly because of childbirth; I take a healthy enough dose of self-loathing without blaming myself additionally for biological facts. Partly because of what's required to keep two kids fed and clothed, to get them to sleep at night and out of bed in the morning, even to hand them over every day to the people you pay huge sums of money to in order to take such problems off your hands. But I'm convinced that what was essentially lovable about this woman – and let me be clear here, this is no longer a lovable woman – would have survived these traumas if I had not created an atmosphere around her that was basically poisonous to her best nature. Not deliberately, I won't go as far as that, but out of some instinct for survival that has everything to do with who I am. I beat this woman down for ten years, with conversation, with argument, by insisting on certain pleasures and opinions and denying her others, and at the end of those ten years I looked at her and thought, Why don't you get up, God damn it, why don't you get up any more?'

What should I have said to him? I was twenty-three years old. With two weeks left in the school year, the only thing on my mind was how to get through them. But I asked him dutifully why his second marriage had turned out better.

'Look,' he said. 'Before you get married you have to judge in cold blood two people you're unaccustomed to treating with any detachment. It requires a cold-blooded decision. Maybe you think, one thing I know about myself is that I'm a bit of a social climber; and this girl here is something of a snob. Not attractive qualities, in either one of us, but they could play to our advantage. I mean, in forging the kind of life we need to forge for us to be comfortable together. I'm old enough to know a few unpleasant things about myself. I like to have my say. To have a wife who is curious and receptive, a natural student, who admires me and lets me talk – this, for me, is no disaster. Of course, if she were nothing besides these things, God help us. But in addition, she is patient and stubborn and maybe even a little passive-aggressive. I'm a blowhard; mostly she gets her way.'

He seemed ashamed of talking too much and excused himself to take a leak. And coming back, with wet hands, he lifted his jacket from the round shoulders of his chair. 'I should let you go,' he said. 'I should go myself.' But even on our way out, he couldn't help himself. 'I'll tell you the real trouble with Barbara' (his first wife). 'She knew me when I was young and stupid and couldn't believe I had grown up to be anything else.'

'My mother likes to say that the secret to happiness is love and work. And children. I'm not sure you're right, though, about the importance of cold blood.'

'Prodigious youth!' he said.

'I suspect she would think, you're better off being too

much in love. Then you've got time afterwards to work out why.'

'I had much love for Barbara. Like Othello for Desdemona. But listen to your mother.'

A few months after this conversation, when school was out, I got a letter from Heinz in London. I was living for free in the basement of a house in Hampstead, which belonged to friends of my parents – the use of this flat was one of my inducements for going abroad. He wanted to see how I was getting along, Heinz wrote, though the real point of his letter was the apology he offered at the end of it for his 'outburst in that tacky bar. Real bar talk, too, full of wifely complaints. I should be ashamed of myself. I am.' The fact is, he said, he was more upset than he knew by his negotiations with Barbara about their son's graduation weekend – which went off almost harmlessly, he added. 'I mean, I knew I was upset, but I wasn't completely clear on what I was upset about. I thought I was angry with Barbara, but I was even more angry about other things that weren't her fault, and which, you might say, she suffered from equally. The way life turns out. But let me stop here before I embarrass myself again with further confessions.' This was the last letter I ever got from him; he didn't answer the note I sent in return.

*

Of course, I had other things on my mind besides these memories. His lecture; the late summer weather, making its way by air and light into the classroom. There was a girl sitting three rows ahead of me in the sunshine of the next window along. She wore a knitted cap, even indoors, even in September; her short brown hair pushed out around the edges of it. Afterwards, I asked Heinz about her, and he said, 'You mean the second Kostadinovic girl. The first was a delight, a real wit; at Brandeis now. But this one I don't know what to do with. Won't say a word.' When she looked out the window, as she did from time to time, her face had the full dark coloring of a breathless boy's – she might have been running all day in the sun. Something about the atmosphere of Heinz's classroom had reminded me of the qualities my own used to bring out in me. The sexual self-consciousness; the boastfulness. The pretense of detachment. Peter once said to me, passing Heinz in the hall on the way to one of our walks, 'The uncle with a special gift at Christmas.' A charge just vague enough I could excuse myself for failing to stand up for a friend.

At lunch, the Kostadinovic girl sat down just across the glass partition separating faculty and students in the cafeteria. I saw the wires of headphones emerging from her knitted hat; she wore a printed dress over jeans. With a pang, I noticed her pull the earplugs down against her cheeks – a boy had set his backpack beside her. And the feeling returned to me, familiar from my teaching days, that I was on the wrong side of some divide. That what was happening to other people mattered more than what was happening to me. But I also took in a number of other impressions. The noise of two hundred teenagers at feeding time. The really distressing atmosphere of disorder (napkins on floors, being kicked about; spilt drinks, dropped books), which requires months of habituation, and even then becomes only tolerable. Such scenes were once the staple of my daily life. 'What is it about these kids they wear their wooly hats indoors?' I said to Heinz, waiting in line with our trays.

Lunch was taken up with re-introductions. A number of people I once shared a faculty lounge with had stayed put. Even their names revived old sympathies: Peasbody, Beinstock, Bostick. Politely I showed an interest in my old life. Politely they responded with curiosity about my new one. But after lunch Heinz led me on a tour of the new grounds, and we had a chance to talk.

The board of regents had raised a great deal of money in the past ten years. The school I had taught in was more or less a Victorian jumble of buildings, complete with cracked-tile hallways and steaming pipes. It had since become a modern college campus. A science observatory, built mostly of steel and glass, offered views across Manhattan of the Chrysler Building and the Empire State. Below it, on the steep slope leading to Van Cortlandt, stood the new theater, surrounded by freshly planted woods. From inside the building you could see the architect's intentions: tall narrow windows let in the silvery birch-light. We might have been anywhere, in the rural wintry depths of a Pushkin story. Even on a warm hazy September day the sunshine came through coldly. Heinz showed more pride in these developments than I would have expected – partly, no doubt, because they contributed to the status of his new position. But, eventually, in the resonant quiet of the theater, he himself brought up the question of the Byron books.

'So how long you gonna keep this game up with Peter Sullivan? My wife says I shouldn't ask you, so I'll ask you.'

He had pulled two metal folding chairs from the wings of the stage.

'What game?'

'Come on. Nobody's buying this business with the manuscripts. I knew Peter. He couldn't write an end-of-year report unless you held his hand.'

'He didn't like writing end-of-year reports. He liked writing novels.'

'So you plan to keep a straight face about this whole thing?'

Heinz had put me in a false position. What I wanted was to find out more about Peter. But people have a bias for certain confessions over others. For a minute I considered telling him about the Society for the Publication of the Dead. 'Look, these are the people I waste my time with . . .' I wanted to make clear that the past few years had been difficult for me, from a professional point of view. What I needed from him was a little information about Peter, and then I could wind up my responsibility towards his literary remains, such as they were, and begin again.

'I'm telling you, my first novel cured me of any interest in historical fiction,' I said. 'The people who matter don't respect you for it. Besides, you know yourself I'm a lazy bastard and have no head for facts. The kind of book I like to read, the kind of book I have been trying to write, is a straightforward but textured account of a mildly interesting experience. Like *Playing Days*. What do I care if Byron slept with his sister? I'll tell you something else, if Peter had lived to push his own books he'd have got sick of such questions, too. All anybody wants to know about is how much is true.'

'So what are you coming to me for?'

'I want to know how much is true.'

'You mean, you want me to tell you what I know about Peter.'

'That's it. You see, there isn't much left – of his work. A few unpublished stories. And the character of these stories . . . raises certain questions. If you need any more convincing: these aren't the kind of stories I could have written myself. In me, the shame of the human being is still stronger than the shamelessness of the writer. There are subjects I won't touch, and Peter did not have my scruples.'

'Oh, the shame of the human being.' He lifted his hand. 'But you want to know why Peter stopped talking? To me and everyone else. This is a dramatic declaration of character, don't you think? And childish, too. Someone who takes himself with a sense of humor *has* to talk; it isn't the kind of thing you can choose to do or not. Even when those rumors started spreading about him, he kept quiet. That he used to play minor-league ball, or gigged with the Ramones. I found all that bullshit deeply off-putting – this about a guy who never did anything more adventurous in his life than feel up some kid.' After a moment: 'Is that what you were expecting? I voted to hire him, let me say that. He was a good teacher. He came to us out of Beaumont Hill, outside Boston. They fired him for fiddling one of the boys, but the evidence was weak; there was a lot of family pressure. I said, if the guy's innocent, you got to hire him. Or un-convicted. Anyway, these boys' schools. There's a kind of perfectly reasonable human being who can't help himself at an all-boys school. Just look at the Catholic Church. They're not all bad men. In different circumstances, with different temptations, some of these priests would have healthy, decent appetites and attitudes

44

towards sex. As far as I'm concerned, that's unquestionable. So out of principle I vote for Peter, but by the end of the first year I already regret it. It's clear to me this is not a man with a healthy attitude towards sex.'

'I didn't know there was such a thing.'

'Listen,' he said, 'how old are you. Thirty-three, thirty-four years old. Been married a few years, there's a baby on the scene. Don't blame yourself too much for lecherous thoughts. This is also a phase you're passing through. But someone like Peter; natural to him isn't natural to you or me. He was a sick man.'

'Then why didn't you fire him?'

'It wasn't anything he did. At least, not that I know of. But the whole presence of the guy. The dirty clothes, the beard. We went out of our way to make ourselves sociable. It was suggested he change his name for publicity reasons: the case in Boston attracted a certain amount of press. But who's he kidding with this Pattieson business? You think I don't know who Peter Pattieson is? I run an English department, for God's sake.' (Peter took his new name from the narrator of Walter Scott's novels – which is how I managed to break down his reserve. I found him out.) 'It's insulting, to the boy involved as well. As if this whole thing were an excuse for dressing up. And then stories started getting back to me, things he said.'

'Like what?'

A boy came in from the wings, dragging a plastic container behind him across the floorboards. He looked up at Heinz and me. A boy already with the stamp of the theater on him, the pallor and pimples, the narrow expressive structure of face and limb. He wore a collared shirt buttoned up to the top and tucked inside his tight-legged trousers. 'Mind if I set up?' he said, gesturing at the stacks of folding chairs to the side. 'Dr Schwarz lets me out early to set up.' Heinz considered him. 'Give us five minutes, and we'll be out of your hair.' So the kid sat down on one of the folding chairs with a patient expression, until Heinz repeated, 'Five minutes. Out of *our* hair. This is grown-up time.'

'Like what?' I said again, when the boy was gone.

'At lunch Peter's overheard telling a story about a friend of his. The punchline goes something like this. Anyone who considers a high-school girl sexually immature has never gone down on one.'

'You heard him say this? I thought his preference ran the other way.'

'It was reported to me. His *friend* supposedly said it; Peter was just repeating the joke.'

'So on the strength of something somebody tells you about something somebody once told Peter, you turn against him. You hired the guy because he wasn't convicted, and you convict him on that?'

'I don't convict him. I quietly have a word with him, about what we consider acceptable lunchtime conversation in this school. And by the way, I'm perfectly capable of hiring a guy according to the presumptions of the law and at the same time thinking he's a sick son of a bitch. Afterwards, Peter refused to talk to me, and pretty soon after that, when the sympathies of the rest of the faculty became clear, he refused to talk to everybody else. What are you looking at me like that for?'

'Ten years seems a long time to live in purdah.'

'He could have broke out of it whenever he wanted to.'

'By doing what? These things get to be a habit.

46

Probably he thought, by speaking to him the way you did, you showed your suspicions about the Beaumont case. Let's say he really is innocent. That's a hell of a thing to live with.'

'Maybe he didn't fiddle the Beaumont boy, I'm willing to believe that much. But this was certainly not an innocent man.'

'Even if he never did anything? Even if he only thought it?'

'Let me tell you something about sexuality. Nobody only *thinks* it. Not with the opportunities Peter had. Now answer me a question. The story about going down on high-school girls, does it sound like him or not?'

'Yes, it sounds like him. It sounds like the kind of thing he would have mocked you and me for, mature, healthy, heterosexual men. For thinking about in class.' But I wasn't sure. Both of us at this point were aware of the way our voices carried, across the stage and into the empty rows. It also surprised me how angrily I had taken Peter's side. My sympathies with Heinz were basically stronger and deeper. He seemed to feel something similar and asked, more gently, 'So what are these stories about then, the unpublished ones?'

'Fiddling boys,' I said.

Afterwards, he walked me as far as the school gates – through the birch wood, then up a flight of stone steps, expensively set into the sloping earth, and along the parking lot.

'What's in this for you?' he asked me, with a hand on my shoulder. 'Why don't you get back to your own work? Honestly, I'm glad the Byron isn't your responsibility. It means I can be straight with you. Yes, I've read them, or

47

near enough – read over them. A little *goyish*, to my taste. A little blue-blooded, with all that that entails. Country houses, sexless marriages, Continental tours. Okay, two hundred years later we have our own tours, called cruises, from which God defend me in my old age. But that Peter should have lost himself in these fantasies doesn't surprise me. He had no *people*. You and I – perhaps we don't make it to synagogue as often as we'd like. And I understand your personal history is a little complicated, but this also is the Jewish experience. We have people. The man who wrote these books has ink running in his veins. Everything is *books* with him. I thought maybe something had happened to you after ten years in England. *A Quiet Adjustment* is three hundred pages of repression, of a particularly English kind.'

He wasn't finished, and I felt rising within me the counter-arguments I wanted to get off my chest. We stood on the curb of the school drive, which winds along the side of the hill, downwards and outwards, to the subway station. A late September day still warm enough to make me feel the heat of my ideas in my armpits and smell them, too. Certain conversations also involve a form of arousal.

'I'll tell you why I didn't mind that novel you wrote about the school,' he said. 'Perhaps you were expecting more resentment from me, maybe even hoping for it. The teachers are all inverts or perverts. I don't mind that. But in the end, what the girl learns is, she is the child of love. That was the phrase you used – I have a head for quotation, too. There is no love in these Byron books, and I thought, something has happened to the young man I knew. It's a relief to learn you're not responsible. Maybe you had obligations to his friendship I don't understand.

48

Whatever they were, what you've done must be more than enough. Leave him alone; he was no good. Not that I blame him entirely. At his funeral, I introduced myself to his mother – a short, red-faced, real Irish-looking woman, whiskery with drink. Everybody else pretending that what had happened to this man of advanced years is not that he killed himself. Except her. "It was only to spite me," she says. "As a boy he said he'd kill himself to haunt me. And now he has." A real piece of work.'

There was more along these lines. Maybe fifteen minutes later I kissed him goodbye on both cheeks, a habit we had somehow fallen into because of his insistence on the blood kinship. And in fact, walking to the station, I felt very strongly (mixed with nostalgia and less sentimental regrets about the course my life might have taken) the passion of our former friendship. His beard was still short enough you could feel it redden your skin. But it was a relief, as it always had been, to escape the school grounds and turn my back on the world of children.

*

I was staying with some friends of my parents, and when I got back to their apartment, it was empty – one of those grand old New York apartments, with high ceilings and interconnecting halls and rooms, whose large windows overlook the cheaper, newer buildings all around it. Their rooftops seemed to be covered in aluminum foil. Hatches and vents and pipes occasionally broke the surface; there were deckchairs, too. A long way below, you could see a slice of Broadway, crawling with traffic and people. In my head, I was still carrying on the argument with Heinz.

49

After sitting down to a glass of cloudy water in the kitchen, I stood up again to get Peter's last manuscript, which I spread out carefully over the kitchen table. It was hand-typed, loose-leaf. I'd been schlepping the pages around in my backpack from Boston to Philadelphia and felt a little guilty about the state they were in.

The manuscript was divided into three chapters. Peter had written the titles in black ballpoint on the front page of each: 'Fair Seed-Time,' 'Behold Him Freshman!' and 'A Soldier's Grave.' As if he came up with them only afterwards. There was also a cover page, with the words CHILDISH LOVES typed in capitals across it; underneath, Peter had added the quote from Byron that serves as the motto to this book. I started reading, to see if what Heinz had told me would change my reaction to the story. 'Fair Seed-Time' begins the summer after Lord Byron turns fifteen. He's just come home from Harrow School to stay with his mother. Home is Southwell, a provincial town a few miles east of Newstead Abbey, the Byron family estate; but Newstead's in bad shape, the Byrons have no money, and the young lord has been forced to rent out the only habitable part of the Abbey to another nobleman, Lord Grey. All of this I remembered more or less from my Masters in English lit. It was hard to see any personal angle, anything that reflected Peter's own life. But by the end I wasn't so sure, and I sat in the quiet kitchen staring at the last couple pages for several minutes – until I heard the front door opening, at which point for no good reason I quickly put them away.

Early the next morning I caught the all-day flight to London out of Newark. I sleep very badly on planes. In response to this problem I try to reduce all activity, mental and physical, to a minimum: drinking water, staring at the seat in front. I lie dormant, as if eight hours occupied by the upright tray-table will pass more quickly than the same stretch of time taken up with random impressions. It doesn't, of course, and besides, I don't have such strict control over my mind. Even when my eyes were closed, I thought about Peter. On our lunchtime expeditions, our escapes from the school grounds, he used to walk holding his hands behind his back. Probably he thought me not much older than one of his students. When I spoke, sometimes he stepped towards me, leaning in to listen. He also seemed very pleased to be talking himself. Once he confessed, quite seriously, that he'd never read *Tom Jones*. This is what passed for intimacy between us. Was there really anything I could learn about him from what he had written? All the way to Heathrow, I drifted in and out of this question, and got nowhere.

Fair Seed-Time

It seems to me very cruel that a boy should be sent away to school for much of the year, where he is regularly abused and made to feel painfully any inferiority of station or person, and then, when he is sent *from* school between terms, should be shut out from his ancestral home. For ten years I was kept out of Newstead by an accident of birth – and death. My cousin had not died, and my great-uncle had outlived him. But now they are both dead. Mr Hanson, who advises me on these matters, has explained that the estate is entangled, and I have seen for myself that it is in ruins. You must be patient, he says. God help me, but I am not.

My mother tells me I have a home, that it is called Southwell. I have been here a week and we are both heartily sick of each other. Yesterday we had a small party to welcome our tenant at Newstead, Lord Grey de Ruthyn. My mother invited the Reverend Becher, and Mrs Pigot, and her daughter Elizabeth – who, with her brother John, make up the only tolerable society in Southwell. Most of the afternoon, I refused to give up my room and was only persuaded to come out when I overheard Lord Grey offering 'to the young Lord the use of his Park, for shooting in'.

'If it is shooting you have come to talk about,' I told

him, when he repeated the suggestion, 'you will find the society here very agreeable, for no one talks of anything else.'

But I thanked him for his kindness. He is a fair, lively, *acceptable*-looking young man, who will if he wishes it turn a great many provincial hearts. About the average height and dressed very properly according to the fashion. My mother says to him, with her hand on my hair, 'I was scarcely eighteen at his birth,' which is a lie – she is out six years.

'Well,' he said to me, on his departure, 'I am not one of those men whom it pleases to promise hospitality for its own sake. I shall spend the summer in Caernarvonshire, in the mountains with my cousins. You are welcome to all that's mine, my bed and table, etc.; after all, they are yours. I have them only on lease.'

When he was gone, Elizabeth declared, 'He looks as if he means to marry one of us.'

'And I wonder what you mean by that,' Mrs Pigot took her up. 'He distinguished nobody so much as Lord Byron, which is just what he *ought* to have done.'

'Perhaps that's just what I *do* mean,' Elizabeth said. Her manner is pretty and arch, which conceals effectively the narrowness of her face and eyes – it is the Pigot face all over, stretched thin and dark. But she wears her brown curls low across the ears and cheeks, to fill them out.

'His lineage is poor,' my mother broke in, understanding nothing but that the question of marriage had come up. 'I have looked into the de Ruthyns and cannot find their title in the peerages of England, Ireland or Scotland. I suppose he is a *new* peer.'

'At least he has a handsome name. Lord Grey de Ruthyn *sounds* very well.'

Our drawing room overlooks the Town Green, through two great French windows, against which my mother has placed a table each, with pots on top and flowers in them to receive the light. She now began to pull one of them aside to improve her vantage. Reverend Becher protested – he is perhaps becoming too much the clergyman. But Elizabeth assisted her and they pressed their noses to the glass.

'He is mounting his horse, the boy has given it him,' Elizabeth said. 'He believes he is observed – there, in a single great stride he is on. Shall he look up to make sure? He will. Oh, he has seen me.' And then, with a giggle, 'He has saluted. What a fine young man he appears, with the addition of a horse. It is a great shame, we have no such advantages to set us off.'

'Oh, you do very well, my dear, as it is,' my mother said, sharply enough, and restoring the table to its place. 'Perhaps you *have* made a conquest. A new peerage is better than none at all.'

She fears very much I will marry Elizabeth, because we are so comfortable together. But I will never marry, I tell her, and least of all for comfort.

*

This journal, in fact, *is* a comfort to me and a great relief, for in it I may complain as much as I like about my mother. Even Elizabeth grows tired of the subject, especially as I admire so much her own. Mrs Pigot is kind, plain and sensible, whereas Kitty is only plain. 'Why do you sometimes call your mother Kitty?' Elizabeth asks me, and for the rest of the afternoon (as the weather is fine, we have decided to walk a part of the way to Newstead, upon the promise I have made her to return even before she absolutely demands it), I consider this question. 'Because she is a widow, I suppose. It is what my father called her.'

'Do you remember your father?'

'He died before my third birthday.'

'But do you remember him?'

'He died in France. For a short time, I believe, he lived with us in Queen Street, in Aberdeen. And then he moved a little away from us, to the other end of Queen Street, before he moved away altogether.'

'But do you remember him?'

'Kitty says I mayn't but I do. He used to kiss me on the – on my foot to make me laugh, so whenever he approached I sat down suddenly the better to lift my leg, and sometimes hurt myself and cried, which made *him* laugh.'

'Poor little Byron,' Elizabeth said, 'from Aberdeen.'

'I remember enough of both of them *together* to inherit a horror of matrimony.'

The headmaster at my school, Dr Drury, has told me that I have a fine memory and might make a name for myself as an orator. My future, I am sure, lies in politics. Indeed, I have a great interest in histories of all kinds and wish to set down as distinctly as I may, merely from the recollection, a record of everything I have said and heard and felt. This seems to me an admirable plan. Novels I have read, too, for which I rather despise myself. It is quite a joke with the Pigots that I always have a book in hand, and Mrs Pigot has put aside a chair in a bright corner of their drawing room, pleasantly secluded beside some drapes, which she calls Byron's Chair, and refuses to let anyone else sit in it. And there I may sit and listen as much as I please.

Elizabeth accuses me sometimes of speaking only with her. She says there are a hundred others, even in Southwell, worthy of my confidences and reflections. For example, the Reverend Becher. Anyone would suppose we was always making love, she says, from the way they startle us together.

'You know I mean never to marry,' I tell her.

It amuses us both to be the subject of so much gossip, especially as it makes my mother anxious. In fact, I confide in Elizabeth less than she imagines, and she isn't quite as pretty as she appears. Kitty, to warn me against her, once reported what she had heard: that Elizabeth, being teased about our intimacy by some ladies, had put them off by declaring she could never marry a *Scot*.

My mother means to poison all of my affections, and not just the filial.

At the moment she coughs incessantly, which is her own fault. Last week she took it into her head to berate Flossie, the maid-of-all-work, for throwing the kitchen scraps into the street instead of giving them to the pig, and she stood on the doorstep in the wet gloaming, looking on, while the poor girl gathered them up. Now the weather, as she says, has got into her lungs as well, on top of everything else (there is a bucket of drips on the landing by the stairs). It was as much as she could do 'to give us respectable *airs*', but at present even this exceeds her 'little strength'.

Yet only yesterday I received proof of strange affinities. I walked out in the morning to inspect a horse Reverend Becher had offered for my use, since I mean to ride to

Newstead in the coming week. It was a clear bright cold morning, which looked like warming in the course of the day; but on my return, out of a clear cold sky, a shower of rain fell. Afterwards I stood in front of the fire in our sitting room, rubbing and blowing against my fingers, when I had a strong impression of my father, taking my hand in his own, and performing the same function. Perhaps I was one or two years old. I believe the house in Queen Street was very cold; that my father used to complain of Kitty's economies.

As I stood there, Kitty remarked to me, 'Your father hated the cold very much. You are a Byron all through. I used to tell him, it is quite the worst thing for a boy to be too warm all the time.'

With all my heart, I wish it were so, only I sometimes feel the mark of my mother's family. Kitty has a great appetite for sweets of all kinds, which she considers becoming in a woman. 'Your father liked to see me eat,' she told me once. 'To eat and laugh. It was said he married me only for money, but my fortune wasn't large – he ran through it quickly enough. At Bath in those days there were a great many beauties, and fortunes. He might have had his pick. But I liked to laugh and eat, and as he liked both laughing and eating, he said, we got on very well.'

It pleases her nearly as much to see me indulge myself.

My mother keeps a locket in her dressing-table, with his picture engraved within. Several times I have asked her for the gift of it, that I might take it with me to school – and sometimes she says, 'Perhaps I will give it you, after all, if you are very good,' or, 'I mean tonight to make up my mind about the locket.' And then in the morning she forgets. If I press her, she resorts to tears, and as her caprices disgust me I have given up asking. It matters very little to me one way or another, only I don't like to be made a fool of.

A few days ago I stole into her room and took it from her dressing-table, to show Elizabeth; Kitty never missed it. I intended to give it to Lord Grey, in return for his kindness to me, but Elizabeth dissuaded me, and after all, it is a mean act, for if I meant to be honourable I would claim it openly. It should be mine by rights, as his son – for a man may abandon the duties of a husband but can never forsake the title of father. Elizabeth said Lord Grey don't want it but admired very much my father's good looks and cheerful air.

I believe Mr Becher is in love with Elizabeth (I can't always call him Reverend), for he speaks to me often of her. She is a kind of cousin to him, which gives him, he supposes, 'a right to advise her'. But he does not dare to, and so he advises me. He considers me capable of taking a part in great events and clearing the Byron name of its association with misanthropy and vice; he upbraids me for my idleness. Sometimes, even, he urges me to fall in love. He considers this necessary in a nature such as mine to the establishment of certain habits of feeling: gentleness, but not only gentleness, he means a kind of chivalry.

'My lord,' he says to me, 'I believe you might accomplish out of *love* what you should never, for your own sake, attempt from ambition.'

I am inclined to laugh at him, for love in my humble opinion is utter nonsense – a mere jargon of compliments, romance and deceit. 'I suppose you mean that I should fall in love with Miss Pigot?'

He looked at me a moment, a little unhappily. 'In her case, I'm afraid,' he said, 'there is the question of rank.'

The Vicarage at Rumpton, where he presides, is being 'done up'; he is staying for the summer in a small cottage on Burgage Lane, and Lady Hathwell has provided him with her barouche. This is the reason he can spare his horse. Mr Becher has literary ambitions. He means to write a history of penal reform, and his parlour, where he keeps a fire lit, is covered over in loose pages and opened volumes, on which he spends most of his unsociable hours. When he rises to take your hand, you may observe him, for a minute or so after, just perceptibly continuing to unbend until his top and bottom halves are aligned.

I asked him his opinion of Lord Grey.

'I knew him at Oxford a little,' he said. 'And others of his kind. He was mostly drunk and always in debt. But at seventeen or eighteen, tolerable enough. There is a kind of freshness even in debauchery. But age does not improve men of his type; their *methods* harden into habits. I should dislike it extremely if you came under his influence.'

*

I spent this morning riding over to Newstead and have only just returned – a two hours journey each way. The impression it made was very strong. As soon as I came upon the lake, and the sky opened up within it, I felt the beat of my heart as if a hand lay against it. And beyond it, the Abbey itself rising greyly out of the lawn. That some part of my destiny lies within those walls strikes me as certain – if only that I wish to be buried in its vaults.

And yet the mansion itself, or its habitable portions, looks common enough.

Owen Mealy, the caretaker, answered my shout and opened the door to an undistinguished hall with dirty boots in it. A wired box (for keeping chickens) lay on its side by the door, propping it open. The weather, at least, has improved and the house had the dusky, watchful air of a hot day indoors.

He has changed very little – he has been away a great deal – and yet I felt Lord Grey's presence in each of the rooms. Mr Mealy left me to speak to Joe Krull, the gardener, so that I had the upper rooms to myself: the bedroom, a study, and a long hallway that Lord Grey has converted into a dining room, since it has a fireplace at one end and windows that overlook the lake. In the bedroom I found a half-dozen pairs of his shoes ranged against the foot of the wardrobe, and a few clothes within. Two silk cravats, hung up by the middles, which looked rather dirty; a waistcoat; a shirt – such are the remains of an English gentleman. As we are about the same height, I tried on a pair of his shoes, which fit snugly enough. But then, a fear of Mr Mealy prevailing upon me, I took them off again and looked in his study, to examine the books – of which he had only a few, and most of them novels.

I half expected at any moment to see Lord Grey stalk in, in his riding boots. The study was windowless and the air inside it very close. In fact, it was little more than a dressing room. I suppose I fell asleep for when I woke again, I had the odd, childish feeling that Kitty was looking for me; and for a moment or two took a kind of pleasure in the idea that she wouldn't find me. Then I remembered myself and went downstairs. Eventually I discovered Mr Mealy in the garden, attempting to untangle the nets of a currant bush; the crows had been tearing at it. The gardener was nowhere to be seen, he complained, so it was left to him to attend to every man's job but his own. I asked him if Lord Grey intended to return soon.

'If I need something or want to know something,' was all his answer, 'I apply to Mr Hanson, who pays me.'

'Oh, we are all the servants of Mr Hanson. He is a great dispenser of moneys.' And then: 'I suppose Lord Grey must find it very dull here, if he is away so often.'

'I don't know what he finds it.'

Once the nets were restored, I told him, 'In a few years, I mean to take the estates in hand myself.'

What clouds there were hung low over the ground. The heat seemed too heavy to move in the long grasses, which wanted cutting. A great swathe ran from the hall to the lake, where they blended themselves among the water-reeds. The ground around the bushes looked purple and trampled. There were also raspberry bushes, gooseberry bushes, a potato bed and a low plum tree. I had tethered Mr Becher's horse against this tree; the fruit was too green to tempt even a horse. But Mr Mealy stood watching her with an air of disapproval.

'Did you know the old Lord Byron?' I said. 'They say he drank very violently.'

'I did not, it was Mr Hanson that hired me.' But then, relenting a little: 'I worked for Mr Chaworth at Annesley Hall. You may imagine what opinion they held of him, or any of the Byrons, for that matter, at Annesley Hall.'

'You mean, because of the duel? It was all a great many years ago. I suppose you know *Miss* Chaworth. She is said to be very pretty. I met her when I was ten or so – she, a few years older – but I believe I have changed a good deal. It was a kind of joke that we would marry in time, like the Montagues and Capulets. Does Lord Grey often ride over? It isn't far to Annesley.'

'Lord Grey often walks; he prefers it to any other exercise.'

I coloured at this, but perhaps he intended no allusion. I told him I meant to bathe before returning to Southwell (the sun had become intolerably direct). But he should see to it that a bed was made up for me the next day, as I proposed to take up Lord Grey's offer and use the house in his absence.

'It means more work for me,' he complained. 'I shall write to Mr Hanson.'

There was nothing more to be said. I walked through the long grass to the edge of the lake, stripped off my clothes, and then slowly pushed my way through the reeds to the open water. After striking out briskly, I lay on my back and let the sunshine warm the water on my head. The light of noon was very strong; I closed my eyes and felt my heart beat against them steadily as waves. When I opened them again, Mr Mealy was still standing by the currant bush where I had left him, but after a minute or so he turned away.

*

Kitty has only reluctantly agreed to let me go. We had a scene tonight. I am so often at the Pigots in the evening that she has requested me, on coming home, always to look in on her, regardless of the hour. And so, very dutifully, at a little after eleven o'clock, I knocked on her door.

When she called out, I took the lamp in with me, and she sat up in bed rather crossly and complained that she had been fast asleep and that the light hurt her eyes – did I mind at all turning it out of her face?

Not at all, I said. I should be only too happy to retire to bed myself and take it with me. It was at her request that I looked in. I should be much happier in future – but then, it hardly mattered, as I intended in the morning to avail myself of Lord Grey's generosity and remove to Newstead for the rest of the summer, or until he should return.

By this point, she had got her wits about her and found her spectacles, and she sat with her hair spread wildly against the cushions behind her, looking frightful. 'What do you mean?' she said. 'You have only just come home.'

'Southwell is not my home. If you were a Byron you would understand. I mean to spend the summer at Newstead.'

'There is a jug on my dressing-table and a glass beside it. Give me a glass of water; thank you. It is too hot to be always arguing – we can discuss it again in the morning.'

'In the morning, I shall be gone.'

There was more of this, on each side, which I don't exactly recall – I never *can* remember what sets off her tears. She complained of her loneliness, with a kind of simper, but then, growing in voice, began to abuse my father and me and everything else. I had no notion of what she suffered as a *widow*. There were houses in Nottinghamshire, she said, from whom she could expect an invitation only as the mother of a *lord*. But in these cases, it was understood, she must 'bring the article with her'. She had supposed that my obligations to the Pigots, if nothing else, would keep me here. But this involved her in contradictions, for she could not help scoring a point off Elizabeth. 'She sets her cap at you,' she said. 'Perhaps it is just as well you should spend the summer at Newstead.'

I have learned it is best in these cases to let her talk and stood with the lamp growing warm in my hands till she was quite talked out. At last she said to me, 'You harden your heart against me. You harden your heart.'

'On the contrary,' I said, 'no one can feel for you what I feel.'

*

I don't suppose I have passed so solitary a week, as this past week, since I was four years old and my mother, having the ague or some other Scottish affliction, in the summer, too, demanded the full attentions of our maid, who consequently let me run rather wild. The Abbey itself is full of wonders. The great hall and refectory are given over to the storage of animal foods, for the use of the farmers, and cats, bats, foxes, crickets and mice have made their homes inside them. But besides hay bales, grain sacks, cobwebs, droppings, and bones – fox skulls, mouse skulls and the like; a hundred feathery skeletons of dead crickets – I have discovered a halberd, blunt with use, an iron pot, a leather boot, and a Bible. Mr Mealy has been telling me stories about my great-uncle. Before his death, he lived and dined and slept in the great hall and used to let the crickets run races over his body. He had been very wicked in his youth and killed a man, for drink; only he repented too greatly and despised everyone for his own sins, preferring creature-company to the company of men. 'For he could kill them as he liked.'

Mr Mealy has employed Alice, the gardener's daughter, to provide my meals. Her father is square-built, dark-set, a little humped with work; and there is also the beginning of a crook in the line of Alice's neck, where her apron is tied. I believe her father beats her. Her face and arms and shoulders (for I have seen her shoulders) are covered over in red marks. Of *me* she has no fear, but when her father sees her speaking with me, he shouts at her until like a dog she runs away. Mr Mealy warned me this morning against her, or rather, against Mr Krull. She is his natural child, he said, or he, her unnatural father – he remained ominous and vague and accused me at last of 'curiosity'. But they are not to be trusted; Alice is a thief. I asked him why in this case he did not dismiss them at once.

'I suppose you mean I should attend to everything my-self?' he answered.

Besides, he said, the house was sufficiently plundered at my great-uncle's death; there is nothing of value. He hinted also that Lord Grey has a 'weakness' for the girl, though I have seen him casting his own eye at her. Alice herself appears to be one of those creatures formed, in all stupidity, for suffering; she can hardly feel anything else. Today I gave her an earring, plain and dirty and a little green, which I had discovered in the great hall. She took it without saying a word and concealed it in her dress.

I mean tomorrow to ride over to Annesley, if only to acquaint myself again with good society.

*

Annesley Hall is a pleasant-looking house, extensive rather than grand. I approached gradually enough, riding up Diadem Hill and descending again between the trees. Another hot day, cloudless and almost windless; the greens of Annesley are becoming yellow and the browns grey. In fact, they have left much of the estate to pasture, and where the grasses have begun to seed, the stalks stand glinting and withering in the sunshine. Through the carriage gate, between the avenue of chestnuts and the mounds of wild flower, the house appears as grey as any ruin. But it is solid and modern, and inside it is dark and cool.

Miss Chaworth was out, so Mrs Thomason led me round. Her mistress had made up a sketching-party, with her mother (Mrs Clarke) and several ladies, and Mr Musters of Colwick Hall, and they had driven to the top of Leivers Hill and made a picnic. They were not expected to tea. I am sure there are many fine things at Annesley, but Mrs Thomason, relenting at last, offered me the key to the churchyard and a piece of currant cake. I said to her, she must be sure to tell Miss Chaworth I had called and would come again the next day. Then I spent an hour among the graves in the long grass and fell asleep. It is a habit with me to take a book whenever I ride out, but I could hardly read a page amid so many interruptions – of crickets and church bells; swallows, sparrows, crows; windows opening and doors closing; trees shifting.

I awoke to the sound of horses and sat up to see, between a church wall and the side of the dairy, the return of Miss Chaworth's sketching-party in two carriages. I recognized Miss Chaworth, in spite of her bonnet and parasol, by the slope of her neck, which is long and handsome. Five years have passed since I saw her last; I was not observed, and then they themselves disappeared behind a wall. Since my horse was tethered at their stable door, I might have encountered them in retrieving it, but delayed ten or fifteen minutes, reading or attempting to read, until they were sure to be gone. There was nothing in my book that suggested what I felt: a slight depression of spirits.

When I left, I took with me the key to the churchyard gate – stealing like a thief into the courtyard and mounting Mr Becher's horse. But the sun warmed my neck as I rode and all around me the wide barren hills glowed, the air thickened with evening. There is a kind of freedom in loneliness, which accounts partly for my reluctance to be introduced. Besides, nothing is more tedious on such occasions than making up lost ground.

*

This morning I rode over to Annesley again on the pretence of returning Mrs Thomason's key. Another fine day, cloudless, etc. though cooler than yesterday, and consequently still more deeply blue. Miss Chaworth had requested a small fire to be lit in the drawing room, where I was introduced to her again, amidst the remainder of her house-guests: the two Miss Wollastons, and their father, a widower, whose wife was a great friend of Mrs Clarke's. Mrs Clarke's husband died last year, in a hunting accident; she is still in black. Miss Chaworth is her daughter by a first marriage, but presides quite naturally (as the house belongs to her) and presented me very charmingly as her 'cousin George'.

'I am glad you have come,' she said, 'I have been feeling out of temper all morning, and nobody knows what to do

67

with me or say to me. Be warned: whatever you do will offend.'

She lives up perfectly to my boyish recollection. Her nose is a little too full at the tip, and suggests still the stubborn child; but her mouth is good, lively and expressive, with a strong under-lip; and her eyes, though set a trifle wide, are brown and soft and deep. Her chin is excellent.

'I am only happy to be called your cousin,' I said, 'when there are unkinder names you might have given the family connection.'

'Oh, please don't talk history to me. I have no patience for history, unless it be in novels. Haven't I told you that I wish to be amused?'

In the end it was decided that we should walk out into the morning, as far as the fish-pond, and return to lunch. And then, in the afternoon, she'd be much obliged if someone would read to her, as she had a headache.

'Maybe what you suffer from is too much pleasure,' I said to her outside the garden gate, as she took my arm. I dislike walking in general, but we went along slowly enough and I surprised myself by this sort of agreeable talk. There is nothing that makes me more awkward than the duty to be pleasant, but Miss Chaworth's manner was so sharp and intimate, that I forgot the slightness of our acquaintance. 'And so now it pleases you to suffer.'

'Don't be clever,' she answered, 'until lunch; and then, when I have eaten something, you may be as clever as you like.'

I said, 'You wish me to be amusing and stupid.'

After lunch, which was a simple affair, a fish dressed in rosemary with new potatoes, we returned to the drawing room. Annesley conveyed generally a sense of happy

68

regulation. The contrast with Newstead was striking and made me feel almost savage as I took my place at a window, where the light was brightest. The fire had been refreshed and a bottle of sherry and some macaroons arranged around a gilt tray. Miss Chaworth (Mary) had asked me to read to her, and I dutifully suggested a volume from her favourite author, Mrs Radcliffe.

'Did she have a preference, among her works, for a particular novel?' I asked her.

'Oh, she loved *The Romance of the Forest* above everything else. Indeed, she had read it twice through almost entirely from beginning to end. Nothing could be so fine as *The Romance of the Forest*. She never saw the use of going to the trouble of reading two books, when one will do. It is bound to be the same thing as before, only a little worse.'

I felt stupidly dejected returning home. All society disappoints you, until you become accustomed to it. Sympathy is a great illusion; there is only sometimes a coincidence of manner.

*

Yesterday, after returning from supper, I discovered Alice in my bedroom. The lamp was unlit and nothing but the green of a summer's evening made its way through the covered windows. She had in her arms one of my silk shirts; the buttons are silver. The closet stands beside the door to the study, and since I had come up by the servants' stairs (sometimes I like to sit in the garden after dining, and it is the nearest way), I practically tumbled upon her.

Surprising us both; by instinct I reached for her with my hand, and she stood so stiff I almost fell over her.

'Let go of me,' Alice said, in her thick accents.

'Owen Mealy told me you were a thief,' I said.

She looked at me so stupidly that I struck her.

*

Mary softens upon acquaintance. In the course of a week, she says, she has come to depend upon me. There is so little society at Annesley that sometimes she finds herself wandering into the kitchen to look for Mrs Thomason, and then she sits there until positively dismissed. I have yet to make up my mind about her. She is very restless and impatient. Even when she tries, and she *has* tried, to enter into a sense of my situation, the effort bores her, as she admits herself.

'Dear Byron,' she said to me once, 'it is very tiresome I am sure to have such a mother, but it is also tiresome to talk about her, and to think about her, too.'

'You are as bad as Miss Pigot. You only wish to think about what is pleasant.'

'And yet there are very few things, in my experience, that are entirely pleasant.' After a minute: 'Who is Miss Pigot?'

'The daughter of Mrs Pigot, in Southwell. Her brother is a great friend of mine.'

'And she herself extremely pretty, I suppose?' etc. and we descend again into pleasantries.

John Musters (of Colwick Hall) is sometimes present during my visits and sometimes not. He says he knows Lord Grey; they have been hunting together. Mr Musters is handsome and reserved, with a face both broad and fine – a statesman's face. His father was High Sheriff of Nottinghamshire. Mary complains that she never knows what he is thinking, he is so quiet, and gives me to understand that I at least afflict her in a different fashion, which surprises me, as I think myself very awkward and silent.

Once, when she left us alone together, Mr Musters said to me, 'I like them to have long necks, for they bend easily.'

The younger Miss Wollaston, who lives in Kirkby, is also a frequent visitor. Her sister has gone to London to stay with an aunt and we hear continual reports of her progress. Last week, for example, she attended a ball in Hanover Square and was introduced to a nephew of Admiral Jervis. This is the kind of thing. The younger Miss Wollaston is short, fat, lively, and shouts. She calls me 'Lord It-grieves-me-to-say' – apparently this is a phrase I am much addicted to. But is otherwise good-natured enough, and hardly seems to mind that her sister, who is taller, more timid, and more accomplished, makes her way in society without her. She is determined to amuse herself regardless and is constantly proposing balls, parties, expeditions and other amusements. Mary is indolent, but has at last agreed to the use of the carriage for the purpose of visiting the caverns at Peaks Hole, to be followed by a dance at Matlock Bath. A good day's journey; Miss Wollaston has written already to reserve rooms at the Old Bath Hotel.

Neither of these prospects interests me particularly, but I have agreed to go. It is just as well, for the days are increasingly taken up with making plans, and I should feel foolish and unnecessary without a role in the business. Mr Musters is coming, too.

*

Yesterday, I rode over to Annesley in the afternoon and found Mary alone in the dining room. She wished to hang a picture, which lay on the table; she was considering where it might show to best advantage. The dining room at Annesley is a low, dark, panelled hall, fifty years out of the fashion, with two small windows set rather high and commanding a view of the hills.

'It is strange,' she said to me, while we both cast our eyes over the walls. 'By the accident of my father's death, everything you see has come to me; and I have arrived without the least striving or contrivance into the possession of the very thing I was taught all my life to seek out, a home and station.'

The picture, lying on the table, showed a modern, cream-coloured mansion and the level grounds before it. A groom led one horse by the rein, while a gentleman in a cloth hat sat astride another.

I asked her where she had acquired the painting and she said Mr Musters had given it her; it was a view of Colwick Hall by George Stubbs. His father had commissioned it. His father was the gentleman in the cloth hat. She had expressed her admiration for it, on a recent visit to Colwick, and a few weeks later it arrived in the gardener's cart.

'When I was there,' she said, 'the housekeeper spoke only of "Carr of York". The architect, you understand; though Mrs Dawes repeated his name so often I thought she must mean a public house. If Annesley wants improvement, she said, you could do worse than asking Carr of York. Bless me, I told her, isn't he dead? But he isn't dead, apparently; not yet.'

'Does Annesley want improvement?'

But instead of answering, she directed my attention to the horse in the picture, which was led by hand.

'Look,' she said, 'do you see?'

The clouds above its back had a sort of freshness, though they were heavy and dark, as if a storm brewed or a fire burned in the house behind.

'She has been painted over – Mrs Musters, I mean. She was unfaithful and deserted both husband and child, and John's father employed another painter to paint over her, which is why the clouds look ugly and thick. I had this from Mrs Dawes' own lips. She returned some years later, while John was away at school, and was taken in again. But I suppose he doesn't like to be reminded of her; she died last summer. The picture is handsome enough.'

'I expect he means to marry you,' I said.

She moved a chair to the hearthstone and climbed on top of it, in order to replace the painting over the mantel: a dirty view of a canal, and two men plying a boat along it, done in the Dutch manner. The square of panelling behind looked dark and dirty, too. I rescued the picture from her and gave her my hand, and she descended again, with a sort of curtsey. This was my first touch of her hand.

'I expect he means to marry you,' I said again.

'I expect he does.'

Shortly after I took my leave.

I know nothing of painting, unless it reminds me of something I have seen or think it possible to see. Of all the arts it is the most artificial and unnatural, and yet I was

73

never more struck by anything *in* a picture than by the absence of Mrs Musters.

*

There has been some difficulty about the Peaks Hole scheme. Mr Wollaston will be away on business in London, and Mrs Clarke refuses to travel so far in the heat of summer. We are unchaperoned.

Miss Wollaston declines to believe in the seriousness of this impediment. There can be nothing improper, she says, in satisfying our curiosity about the caverns; she has no intention of marrying at present; Miss Chaworth and Mr Musters are practically engaged. I am a *boy* and might be spared the suspicions even of the slanderous. What they have in mind is nothing more odious than a day-trip, with a dance appended to it, in a respectable hotel.

But Mary refuses to set forth unsupervised. Mr Musters is announced and the whole business is gone over from the beginning. Upon reflection, he offers to resign his place in the carriage – leaving, hc says (bowing at Miss Wollaston) 'two cousins and a lady'. But this, Mary objects, seems to her a sad sort of summer party. It would hardly be worth the trouble to the coachman – which makes me brighten a little, feeling it in my face.

Miss Wollaston says, 'We must petition your mother again. Once she knows how much we depend on her, she will not stand in our way. The carriage may be covered at least half the journey, if the sun is strong; and I shall write the hotel directly and request a foot-bath for our arrival.'

'Her constitution is not equal to yours. It is always the way – no one can imagine the sufferings of others.'

'I believe a great deal of our sufferings are *entirely* imaginary. The women in this respect being more to blame than the men – we are always suffering, we are always imagining. It is my conviction that afflictions, like manners, deserve to be corrected from time to time, even in mothers.'

Mrs Clarke at that moment entering, exclaimed, 'You are very hard on us poor mothers, my dear Julia, but there are reasons I *must* leave to your imagination. It is no use describing them, and you will discover in time very good reasons of your own. A day's journey in a hot coach in the midst of August, with nothing more to do or see at the other end than a hole in the ground and a dance at an hotel –'

'Oh,' Miss Wollaston broke in, who was cheerful enough in spite of her disappointment, 'when a woman hints darkly to me of her age, even I know enough to keep quiet.'

In truth, Mrs Clarke looks not at all well. Her eyes are rheumy and she limps in one of her legs whenever she has sat down and stands up again. She bustles about in spite of these things so insistently you feel the impediment more sharply.

'Still, it is very distressing,' Miss Wollaston continued. 'I have heard that the caves are as wonderful as the moon, and since we have at our disposal a carriage, and not a hot-air balloon, and it is only thirty or forty miles to Peaks Hole, I had rather go there.'

'I have no objection to your going,' Mrs Clarke said. 'It is only my dear daughter who insists on supervision.'

'That is because, in the absence of a father, it has been

left to me to determine what is proper to my position – of which, dear mother, you have very little sense.'

'Oh, your position. When I was a girl, we thought more of uniforms and less of positions. Besides,' she added, 'Annesley Hall is your own; you have no need of a husband.'

'It is because I have no need of them that they are all frightened away. Even Mr Musters, who is practically my only visitor, hardly dares open his mouth.'

'Confess it, Mary,' Miss Wollaston said, 'you are only too lazy to go. With your cousin to read to you and Mr Musters to stare at you, you are content to remain on your sofa all summer.'

'If I stare and keep silent,' Mr Musters said, 'it is only because there is so much worth looking at and listening to.'

This is a fair sample of how we passed the time. Sometimes I am rather ashamed of playing a part in such scenes, of falling in line so completely with the women. I sit at the edge of my velvet chair and think of Newstead and the ruins surrounding it – the fields uncropped, growing yellow and brown in the sun, and the broken monastery walls, which I have climbed. The lake I have swum in, leaving my clothes in the reeds. Alice – her father – Owen Mealy, appearing by turns. But then, after too long a solitude, I grow strange even to myself, and it is a relief to put on my cleanest shirt and ride to Annesley.

'Perhaps,' I offered at last, 'I might enlist some of my Southwell acquaintance. Our vicar, Mr Becher, though young *looks* respectable, and the Pigots are a good, lively, decent county family. Is not that what one calls them? I have heard there is safety in a large party. And then, Mrs Pigot alone would make us safe enough.'

'Is she so frightful?' Mary said, but it was agreed I should write to them at once.

*

It is all settled; the Pigots are coming. Elizabeth wrote me herself in a state of excitement. Mr Becher is to accompany them in Lady Hathwell's barouche; the box-seat is perfectly adequate for John, which he would prefer in any case if the weather is fine, 'as it positively *must* be'. Elizabeth is longing to meet Miss Chaworth. My silence, she says, on the subject of my 'inveterate cousin' has been particularly interesting. 'What was it you called her once, your little Miss Capulet? I mean to hear all your blushing confessions. It will be curious to see you playing the flatterer with a lady, when we used to have so much fun at their expense – at the flatterers', I mean. Lord Byron in love, who would have supposed it possible?'

There was more in this vein. I don't believe I ever referred to Mary as my *little Miss Capulet*, but it is no use protesting. I begin to have some doubts as to whether introducing these two women will be at all comfortable to my self-opinion. But it is too late, everything has been decided. I rode to Annesley with the letter in hand as soon as it was decently light and was rewarded, for my trouble, with a fried chop and a boiled egg. Miss Wollaston's preference for a cooked breakfast is well known, and she had been staying the night.

Mary, for her part, could hardly contain her curiosity about Miss Pigot. Was she dark or fair? Tall or dumpy? There was always a kind of pause in my breath before I spoke her name. I could never call her simply Miss Pigot.

It was always, You know, the sister of my friend from Southwell, or the daughter of my mother's near neighbour, with whom we have a great deal to do.

'She is as dark and as tall as you,' I said. 'That is, equally fair and dumpy.' And then, in all honesty, I added, 'But not so pretty either, though rather more cheerful. Perhaps it will comfort you to know that she teases me, too, about you; I am mocked on all sides.'

'Oh, I have not the least claim to being original.' Later, she returned to this theme more seriously. 'You say she is like me; I do not believe it. Young men, when it comes to women, have eyes only for the general, they lack any sense of the particular. We are tall or fair or dark or dumpy, as you have said, but nothing more. There is no discrimination, no fineness. You differ only in the words: gentle, sweet, lively, and so on.'

'And yet you have lumped me happily with the rest of my sex. With John Musters, for example.'

Breakfast was finished, and Elizabeth's letter lay on the table before me. We sat in the relative gloom of the dining hall, with a candle lit, in spite of the fair morning. Another long day stretched before us – we could see it through the windows, as far as the crown of elm trees on Miskin Hill, under a blue sky.

'I believe, Mary,' Miss Wollaston said, without any ill-humour, 'it is only you, and others like you, who are *gentle* and *sweet*. Some of us must be content with *cheerful* and *good-tempered*. Though, in truth, I am no better-tempered than you are gentle – we have only the appearance of it, and no one seeks farther than appearances.'

'Miss Pigot is cheerful and Miss Wollaston is cheerful. Everyone, it seems, is cheerful – excepting me.'

Miss Wollaston meanwhile had taken up Elizabeth's letter. I tried to reclaim it, but her strength surprised me, and there was a certain disorder of movement, tilting of chairs, clatter of cutlery, and upsetting of cups, before I was finally persuaded to give up the attempt. Afterwards, she read the letter silently to the end, and I could think of nothing to do or say until she was finished. Phrases like *my little Miss Capulet* and *Lord Byron in love* drowned out every other in my head, and I was conscious of a kind of noise, like the noise of a kettle, growing more insistent all the time.

'She writes a very fair hand,' was all Miss Wollaston said, on returning the letter to me.

'Of course,' Mary added, 'she is perfect in all things. I long to meet her brother.'

*

I have been staying occasionally at Annesley in what Mary calls the nursery, for she played there as a child; but the room has been re-fitted since, with a canopied bed and a side-table and a basin. Her old school desk is still pushed against the window, which overlooks the stables, and sometimes I sit with my knees pressed under it and continue this journal.

Mrs Clarke herself suggested my use of the nursery, when a thick summer rain set in one day after tea. We have all become quite comfortable. Even the presence of my cousin has declined for me in its intensity till she burns no brighter than a household fire. Yet I am constantly warming my heart against her. Whenever she leaves a room, it grows cold. Miss Wollaston has never mentioned to me the suspicions expressed in Elizabeth's letter. In fact, we get along very well together, in a kind of alliance against Mary, and mock her for her charms quite as if we were equally indifferent to them.

Mr Becher has said that I should fall in love and perhaps I have done no worse than follow his advice.

There seems to be a sort of family understanding, according to which Annesley and Colwick Hall shall be united in marriage – and Mary and Mr Musters are merely the instruments of this intention. That she feels his attractions, I have no doubt. He is a proper, mild-mannered, able gentleman, with an income of fifteen thousand, a large estate, and a house on Wimpole Street, but her attraction is mixed up with a deal of fear, which he does nothing to dispel. Once or twice I have been on the point of repeating to her what he once said to me, that he liked them to have long necks, for they bend easily; but I hesitate to contribute to the awe with which she already regards him.

Once indeed I mentioned to Miss Wollaston that Mr Musters was very charming, but one never knew what he thought – so that, in consequence, one imagined all kinds of terrible things.

'I believe I know very well what he is thinking of,' she said. 'I suppose you have thought it, too, or *will* think it.'

We were sitting in the garden, on the gravelled walk, on a bench positioned between the windows leading into the drawing room. Mary was reading on the sofa inside; at least, she had a book in hand. I believe she was asleep. Nevertheless, I kept my voice low, and as the summer's day was loud in other noises, there seemed little danger of our being overheard.

'Is there an engagement? I cannot be sure; sometimes he acts as if there is.'

'I believe there is an understanding,' Miss Wollaston said.

'I cannot understand the need for secrecy. Their fortunes are equal; the families both respectable, and disposed to the match.'

'Yes,' – for the first time, she hesitated. 'Perhaps there is no secrecy. It has been spoken of so long, perhaps there was no occasion for making it explicit.'

'And yet, if there can be any doubt . . .'

We sat like this, companionably enough, enjoying the heat of the afternoon. Miss Wollaston sometimes let the shade of her parasol fall over my face, before withdrawing it again. A kind of game, I supposed, but when I looked at her, with a smile, she appeared unconscious of it. So I said, 'Sometimes I believe she is almost frightened of him.'

'You have been reading too many novels,' she said. 'In life, in Nottinghamshire at least, there is still such a thing as a good match, a comfortable engagement, and a happy marriage.'

'Then I see no reason for so much secrecy and hesitation.'

'It may be,' she said, after a minute, 'there is always a little fear, in such cases, which accounts for much of what you say – on both sides.' Then, with a laugh: 'You look very serious, my lord. You need not worry on *her* account. She has a great gift for doing exactly what she pleases. But I believe you are not, you speak mostly on your own.'

'I do not think you understand my cousin as well as you pretend to. She seems to me not at all happy.'

'Oh, it is the novels again; you see everything through

novels. And pray, why is she so unhappy? With ten thousand a year, and Annesley Hall, and the prettiest eyes and figure in – perhaps she is unhappy because of her eyes. You mean, I suppose, that she is too pretty to be happy? Though as for that one can't be *always* happy. Even I, with five hundred pounds to my name and a hook nose, am not always happy.'

'What are you conspiring about?' Mary called from within. 'I have been having most unpleasant dreams; I keep hearing my name.'

'We have been talking about you, of course,' Miss Wollaston said, turning round.

*

Lord Grey has taken up residence in Newstead. I returned one afternoon for the sake of a few books I had left in his study and found him quite naturally installed in my former bedroom. I came up the back way, through his study, through the dark. 'Alice,' he said, as I pushed open the door; but he received me very hospitably and offered to send for her and bid her make up a bed in a corner of the great hall.

'I suppose old Owen has been telling you stories about the crickets,' he added, on seeing my face. 'I have no objection to sharing my own – we get used to bed-fellows quickly enough at school.'

But in the end I decided to take my luck in the hall; and after a sleepless night, returned in the morning to Annesley. Lord Grey and I breakfasted together. He had caught the sun, as he said, in his mountains, and looked for once quite happily indifferent to his own appearance:

very brown and red in the face. I invited him to join our expedition to Peaks Hole and was rather relieved when he declined. He had travelled enough for one summer. But he inquired pleasantly into the arrangements. Miss Chaworth was a wonderfully pretty girl, and he knew Mr Musters slightly at college – he had the reputation of a 'Man of Method'. I asked him what this meant. Most of his college set, he said, had a touch of the Method – it signified very little, but then he broke off to ask if by this stage they were decently engaged?

'You mean,' I said, 'Miss Chaworth and Mr Musters? Nobody will say, though it is generally presumed.' I added, 'Mr Musters claimed your acquaintance. He said you often went hunting together.'

'A kind of hunting,' Lord Grey replied.

*

My mother has written again and again, complaining of my absence. She wishes to know when I intend to return to school. She has had a letter from Mr Hanson about it, who had a letter from Dr Drury; and now she is threatening to come to Newstead herself. But I am hardly at Newstead these days, with everything in preparation for Peaks Hole. I will make up my mind about school on my return. The dance at Matlock Bath has been put off, owing to a small fire in the kitchens. There was some talk it would be abandoned altogether, but a new date has been fixed, and we have arranged ourselves accordingly. But the weeks have passed. August is over, and already the chestnut trees, which run either side of the approach to Annesley, begin to lose their leaves – they have withered in the heat. After a wet beginning, the summer has had no rain, and the farmers almost despair of it. But the great day is here at last, which has been looming so large. Tomorrow morning the party from Southwell arrive at Annesley, for a hasty breakfast, before we dispose ourselves in the two carriages and continue our journey into Derbyshire.

***

Mr Becher and I have been given a room together, at the Old Bath Hotel; but his bed is empty, he is still at the dance below, the sounds of which make their way up through the chimney and boards of the hotel. And I have lit a candle and sat down to the only table at hand, and pushed the washbasin aside, to write – in order to relieve my feelings, which are strained to bursting.

The breakfast party went off well enough. The duty of introductions fell by necessity to me, which was painful to my diffidence, but I acquitted myself tolerably. There was only one awkward moment. Mr Becher, mistaking John Musters for Lord Grey, reached out his hand and said, 'We knew each other a little at Oxford.' But in fact they had not met and Mr Musters gave him rather a puzzled, cold stare.

Elizabeth and Mary professed themselves greatly pleased with each other, and I had the occasion to compare them *in the flesh*. It amazes me now that I ever considered her pretty. Her face is too narrow and brown and her complexion not at all good, though she makes up for this by the liveliness of her expressions. She is also perhaps a hand's breadth shorter than Mary, which I had not suspected, and carries herself in an under-bred comfortable way. But they claimed each other instantly as friends. Elizabeth said to me, as we left the breakfast table and disposed ourselves again in the yard, 'I am glad she is pretty; she is really very pretty. I should not have liked you to fall in love with a frump.'

And Mary, when she sent me in again for something she had forgotten, Thompson's Tooth-powder, which she could not at all do without, whispered in my ear, 'I like her immensely. She is not so pretty as I.'

It was agreed at breakfast that *Southwell*, as the Pigots were called (with the addition of Mr Becher), and *Annesley* should intermix – it only remained uncertain to which party I belonged. In the end, Mr Musters took us all in hand. He accompanied Elizabeth and her brother John, along with Miss Wollaston, in Lady Hathwell's barouche, leaving Mrs Pigot, Mr Becher and Mary to me. This occasioned the first little drop in Mary's countenance. But we set off in high spirits. The weather, as Elizabeth promised it *must* be, was perfectly blue and clear. There was just a shadow of autumn in the sky, which prevented the sun from scorching and robbed the fields and the hills of any garish brightness. Mary attempted to flirt with Mr Becher.

When we passed through Kirkby, on the half-hour, the bells of St Wilfrid's tolled, and even Mary fell quiet because there was something to see. If only the usual sights. A dressmaker's, showing a dark red dress in its window, with the hems undone; a tea shop; a baker's – at which Mary called quickly for the coachman to stop and sent me out for a currant loaf. Then Mrs Pigot wanted another, and John emerged from Lady Hathwell's barouche on a similar errand. I asked him, as we waited with our pennies in hand, what he made of Mr Musters.

'I don't make much of him,' John said. 'We had an argument about sitting in the box. He strikes me as one of those men who won't have a favour done him. But I won out at last. I said, I can't be sitting with my sister. But Lizzy finds him amusing enough. At least, all I can hear is her laughing. Miss Wollaston, too.'

When I gave Mrs Pigot her loaf, Mary complained, 'It is really shameful of Mr Musters to have put us in the post-chaise. I had much rather travel in a barouche, in this weather. Are you not intolerably hot, Mrs Pigot? Perhaps we may have the hood down, a little; the sun is not *very* strong. I apologize for Mr Musters, but it is always his way, he always takes the best plum for himself.'

A bell marked the quarter when we set off. There was in fact a shout of laughter from the carriage ahead, as we cleared the graveyard and followed the turn of the road towards Sutton. Uphill and down again, with a view of the spire at Kirkby, on one side, and the spires of Hilcote and Huthwaite showing by glimpses. Between the towns, the wide green fields bending to their hedgerows – fields where nothing distinguished itself but a few odd cows and trees.

Mary said, 'I often find that the spirits of a party of people sound much higher at a distance. I can't think what Mr Musters might be saying. He can never think of anything to say to me.'

My heart sank at all this, for it showed Mary in the strongest light; and if I had planned, as I half intended, to confess my feelings to Mr Becher the opinion he must be forming served as a sufficient check. He could not understand her. But it pained me also to see Mary jealous; it made *me* jealous. Lady Hathwell's barouche, which preceded us by twenty paces, had such an elegant, spirited air. There are men whose worst suspicion is that they belong always to the gloomier half of any party, and I seem in a fair way to becoming one of them.

Mrs Pigot asked Mary why her daughter called us always 'the inveterate cousins'. The phrase meant nothing to her, but she supposed there was some scandal attached to it.

'A little scandal,' I said, 'but briefly told. My wicked great-uncle killed Mary's grandfather in a duel. My uncle was very drunk at the time, and Mr Chaworth, I presume, not very sober either.'

'Was this not all a very long time ago?'

'A long time ago, but it is still remembered. In towns, Mrs Pigot,' Mary said, 'you have the great fortune of involving yourself in any dozen little quarrels you wish to. You may pick and choose, and they are all quickly resolved by their own rapid succession. But the Chaworths have only the Byrons, and the Byrons have only the Chaworths, to be disagreeable to; which is why we prize the memory of it so greatly.'

'And was he hanged – your great-uncle, I mean?'

'He was not. He was tried in the House of Lords and acquitted at last, whereupon he retired to Newstead and went mad. It is just what all Byrons wish in their hearts to do – to retire to Newstead and go mad. I have been attempting it myself this summer.'

'Nonsense, Mrs Pigot,' Mary said. 'He is not nearly so strange as he pretends and has been living at Annesley, more or less without interruption, since the beginning of

August. We all feel it as a great betrayal of principle, but his presence is otherwise acceptable to us.'

*

We dined at Castleton. There was some talk of visiting the ruins of Peveril Castle, but Mary has not the least interest in ruins, and Miss Wollaston was eager to see the caverns and be gone – it is two hours by coach to Matlock Bath. This was a great disappointment to me, as there was nothing else that interested me half as much as the ruins. Mr Musters' sympathies surprised me. He took me by the arm, out of the coaching-inn, and led me along the street and around a corner, until we could see, at the top of a green hill, a square grey turret and a low grey wall. Crows settled and unsettled against the walls, and a few herring gulls wheeled above them. A half-hour's good walk might have brought us to the summit, but then, I should have preferred a horse.

'We are all the slaves of female pleasure,' Mr Musters said. 'We do what they please and not what pleases us.'

For a minute we stood arm in arm, looking up, with the sun behind us. 'And yet there is in their presence,' I told him, moved for the first time into a kind of confession, 'a comfortable *something*, which I cannot at all account for; and *their* pleasure pleases us, too.'

It was left to me to propose our return.

'Where have you been?' Mary cried when she saw us. She had come a little way down the road to meet us, which was all dust and pebbles, and looked rather ghostly under the shade of her parasol. 'We have been waiting this hour at least. The horses are all in harness.'

We disposed ourselves as before and returned to the carriages. Mr Becher had brought along a volume of Jonson's containing a masque, which he proposed to read to us, as it was set in Derbyshire and included some reference to Peaks Hole. But he read a little way in and then gave up the attempt; there was too much indecency in it. It was entirely unsuitable, and he spent the rest of the journey turning over the pages and sometimes shaking his head.

Mrs Pigot sat at his right hand. 'Oh, let me look,' she complained. 'I have seen a great deal more of life, young man, than you. There is nothing that shocks me so much as propriety.'

'I thought it would please you,' I said to Mary in a low voice. 'If Mr Musters is to become your – particular friend. I thought, the least service I could render you is to make him *mine*.'

'Oh, the least service . . . I suppose you were talking all the time about me.'

'This at least may be read by a *clergyman* without a blush,' Mr Becher said at last, bowing towards Mary.

He began to recite, until Mrs Pigot interrupted him.

'If it is decent or not, I should not like to say,' she said. 'But it is certainly nonsense.'

'That is not the bit I meant, I have lost my place.'

'If you mean to marry him,' I said to Mary, 'I should like to know him better, because he has always appeared to me uncomfortably mysterious. He frightens me a little. When I am alone with him, I feel something very much like fear.'

'Who said that I meant to marry him?'

'I thought it was generally understood, and Miss Wollaston confirmed it.'

'Miss Wollaston takes a great interest in marriage without the least intention of marrying herself. I should not credit Miss Wollaston with anything besides a wish to amuse herself – often at my expense.'

'I think she meant you no harm. Perhaps she meant to protect me.'

Mary said at last, 'Am I very terrible?'

'This is better,' Mr Becher said and began to read again, in what Elizabeth always calls his *sermony* voice.

'Now I *am* offended,' Mrs Pigot afterwards declared. 'I suppose you mean, because I am old myself, it should please. I confess that the rest meant nothing to me, but I recollect the beginning very well, which ran, To the old, clutch not so fast to your treasures, or something of that sort.'

I said to Mary, 'You mock me. You think of me always as a boy.'

'I am not so easily kidded as that,' Mr Becher replied. 'I know when I am being teased. But this is not what I had wished for at all. I had hoped there should be some fine description of the scenery, but it is all in his humour.'

'For shame, Mr Becher, that when the hills surround us in the sunshine, as they do, when there is a beautiful lady to be looked at, and talked to, you should seek your pleasures in books.'

'You must not blame Mr Becher, Mrs Pigot,' Mary said. 'Lord Byron gives out that it is generally understood I am *spoken* for, which has frightened away every other gentleman. At least, this must be my consolation. But indeed, the view of these hills is very fine, and the ascent not very rough.'

We arrived at last at a station a few hundred yards distant from the caverns, where there was a small cottage with a hut attached to it and a hitching-post in the yard. Mr Musters, who had by this stage thoroughly taken charge of the party, gave Saunders the coachman instructions regarding the horses, and the rest of us arranged ourselves in no very great order around the yard and stretched our legs. It was now three o'clock, and still cloudless and windless, but not excessively hot; the shadows had begun to stretch in the sun.

Elizabeth said to me, 'Mr Musters is quite charming and exactly the kind of man my brother dislikes.'

'Why do you quiz me about Mr Musters?' I said to her. 'He is nothing to me.'

'I believe he may be something to Miss Chaworth.'

'That is their own affair. I am not in the least in love with her.'

'Perhaps I won't tease you,' she said. 'You look very solemn. It ruins the sport.'

The cottage belonged to a farmer, who offered us one of his sons as a guide, for not much money; and after a brief negotiation, in which I played no part, he led the way up a steep single track with grass growing in it. This son was very tall and already a little stooped. He said nothing but walked in long strides, carrying across his shoulders a kind of sack; the rest of us pursued him at a short distance. Mr Musters gave his arm to Mary. They were followed first by Mr Becher and Elizabeth, and then John and Miss Wollaston. Mrs Pigot and I trailed a little behind the others, which suited both of us – as she is a thin, frail, weak-winded woman, and we could 'scramble up' (as she put it) at our leisure.

'You are much missed in Southwell,' Mrs Pigot said to me. 'And much talked about. All the ladies pine after you.'

'I think you don't mean Elizabeth. I think you mean my mother.'

'Oh, Elizabeth talks about you, too.'

There was a short general pause while we turned to look at the view, which had expanded beneath us until it included much of Castleton in a fold of the hills. The sound of the Peakshole was already becoming louder, and we could see the water falling and making its way, by fragments, perhaps a hundred yards ahead of us; and then, appearing again beneath our feet, more sluggishly and silently, as it approached the village.

'I have an idea,' I said, 'that I am always happiest among hills. Flat lands oppress me. I was raised among hills in Aberdeen; perhaps that accounts for it. And there is a view from Harrow Hill I am greatly attached to.'

'Your mother complains that you have no notion of returning.'

'Confess, Mrs Pigot – my mother is always complaining.'

'I will just say this much, that she shares with you a passion for *opposition*.'

'I have no such passion. It is just because I wish to live peacefully that I mean in future to keep my distance from *her* and Harrow. There is a master there who abuses his rights over me. It must come to blows in the end, and as I have no particular liking for scrapes, or for myself in a rage, it seems only sensible to put myself out of the way of temptation.'

'But where will you live?'

'At Newstead. Lord Grey makes no objection.'

'There are certain objections a mother might make to Lord Grey,' she said. 'Besides, I think you mean Annesley.'

We continued our ascent and said nothing for several minutes. Mrs Pigot had grown quite pale, and we both laboured somewhat against the loose stones of the path. Peak's Cavern eventually made its appearance above our heads, like a great faceless cowl, all black within, in spite of the afternoon sun.

'I must say,' she said, 'I have never understood this appetite for nature. I have come along to be pleasant, but left to myself I had much preferred a good provincial town, with a church not too far, to be walked to and looked at, before you return quite pleased with yourself to dine at the hotel.' And then, 'Miss Chaworth is a very pretty, spirited sort of a girl.'

'She appears not at her best in company. I believe she is not very happy.'

'That is because you are in love with her. We always suppose that someone must be miserable, if we are in love with them – probably because it makes us a little miserable ourselves.'

'Oh, Mrs Pigot, I had rather you *mocked* me, as your daughter does, because then I should be less inclined to burst into tears. Perhaps you mean to, after all; you are smiling.'

'My dear, sweet child, not for the world,' she said. 'It is only because, for a moment, you sounded so much like the boy from Aberdeen Lizzy is always teasing you for being. Och, Mrs Pigot. But it was not a smile; indeed, I did not smile.'

And with that, we reached the top.

The others had arrived already. Our guide struck a light

and then distributed the torches he had been carrying in his sack to each of the gentlemen in turn. I received mine, too. The entrance to the cave looked mean and dirty, but the view was very fine across the valley, broken up into fields, with the shallow grey glitter of Castleton to the east. Above us, a high forehead of limestone reared itself covered in trees and mosses – I grew quite dizzy, leaning back with my hands on my hips to glimpse the top. The path had broadened towards the cliff-face, and the entrance itself was as wide as the clearing in which we stood. But the colour of the cave-mouth had lightened from black to dreary. Mr Musters and John had already advanced some distance, torches in hand, to examine the walls. Most of the women followed uncertainly behind.

Mrs Pigot left me to join her daughter, and for the first time I became aware of the fact that Mary stood some way apart, with her back to the entrance – as if her attention were entirely taken up by the view. I remembered she had been walking with Mr Musters. I called to her, approaching, and she turned around with a smile and took my arm, but said nothing; and together we followed the others into the cave.

The air was much cooler inside, and damp and stony.

'It smells of Newstead,' I said, 'where the river has got into the cellars.'

And my words changed as we walked, first diminishing, and then growing again in volume as they found their echo. Gradually the light of day behind us was replaced by the uncertain glow of our torches, and the cold deepened. Miss Wollaston's voice reached us, doubled and redoubled by the cavern walls. She had found something to laugh at, and then her laughter frightened her, and her fear amused her again. Ahead of us we could see, by torch-light, Miss Wollaston on the arm of Mr Musters; Elizabeth and her mother, walking together; and John and Mr Becher arm in arm. The first chamber gave way to a second, and here indeed a perpetual fall of water curtained one of the walls and disappeared again, into God knows what depths. The sound of the water was loud enough to absorb any other, and we all stood silently for a minute – there is an intensity of noise that acts with the force of a blow.

After a hundred paces the path began to taper. The walls of the cavern encroached upon the ceiling, and the space in which a man might walk upright narrowed, as I heard Mr Becher saying, 'to a shoulder's breadth, look out, look out'. The farmer's son crouched by the side of the wall to let us pass, then stuck a torch into the ground. It had grown dark enough by this stage that the light of day behind us had become indistinguishable from the mineral glow and vague aqueous gleams brought out by our own lights, and since the walls of the cavern to either side gave way in many places to several smaller passages and false fronts, he wished, I suppose, to mark the path of our return. Kindling another torch against the flames of the first, he crept alongside me again to the front of the party. Mary, who had begun to shiver against my arm, said, 'I don't want to go on. I can't go on.'

'It is only the cold,' I said, 'it is nothing worse than the cold.'

'I have begun to feel very strange. I have begun to feel that you are all strangers to me.'

'It is only the strange sounds.'

'That none of you can be trusted.'

'What do you mean,' I said, feeling her panic suddenly myself. 'I am only your dear little Byron.'

This struck me almost as a confession of love, and perhaps it struck her in the same light, for it seemed to calm her, and she said nothing in reply.

By this point, we could no longer hear the others. There was a glimmer of light reflected ahead of us, and then that light disappeared. I gave Mary the torch (she was most unwilling to take it) and walked ahead for fifteen or twenty paces, where I was stopped first by an overhang of rock, and then by the body of slow-moving water beneath it – the source of the reflection, and also, of renewed noises, echoing along the surface. I could hear the slap and glide of a boat, and more distantly, the sound of human voices. But then, Mary's cries interrupted them and forced me to retrace my steps, for she was calling, 'Do not leave me, Byron; Byron, Byron, come back.'

I returned to her and took the torch from her hand again; and after another minute, another torch appeared, and then, in its light, the face of the farmer's son. He was dripping, and wet through from the waist. 'Are you the last?' he said. His accents were not at all rough, but sensible rather than kindly. 'You'll have to lie down in the boat. You'll get a knock if you try sitting up.'

'There isn't room for you in it,' Mary said when she saw the boat, a shallow wooden punt, which was tied to a post by the shore of the river – if one may speak of shores in those dark spaces.

'That's all right. I'm used to pushing.'

And with a strange sort of obedience, she lay down in the boat and I lay down beside her.

The journey lasted no more than a minute or two, but

I don't know that I have ever passed a minute of such intensity in my life before, and perhaps never will again. All the time we were conscious of the farmer's son at our feet, pushing his way through cold water, with bowed head; but we could not see him or anything else for that matter. The rock bore heavily down upon us, and I could hardly have turned over to kiss her had I wanted to. Indeed, I could think of nothing else. The punt was so narrow the length of my side pressed against the length of hers, and I could feel, against my hip, her sharp little bones. Water in the boat sluiced up occasionally against the back of my knee and the small of my back. Once one is a little wet, one only becomes wetter. Also, the caverns were very cool; I began to shiver. After about a minute, the weight of the rock over our faces grew truly intolerable – it might just as well have been the weight of the world – and I could only refrain with difficulty from letting out a great shout, when Mary took my hand blindly in her own, and pressed it so hard, and we pressed them together, finger upon finger, which gave some relief. I discovered at this point that the darkness was owing in part to the fact that I had shut my eyes. I opened them again, and the sense of *sliding* helplessly in space struck me for the first time. Torch-light exposed above our faces the growing roof of the cavern, covered in calceous streaks and wet broken gleaming stony teeth, and then the rest of our party appeared at the far shore (by this time we could lift our heads in the boat). My hand almost ached and I suppose she felt the same, for she let go of mine as soon as the punt touched ground and sat up.

'You are very cruel to have left us,' she said to no one in particular, in her own natural teasing petulant voice.

'The inveterate cousins!' Mr Musters cried. 'You see, I mean to adopt Miss Pigot's excellent phrase.'

He gave her his hand, and she stepped delicately from the boat.

'I don't like this cave,' Mary continued. 'We thought you had all gone. I don't see what is so wonderful about a cave. It is like going to a great house and making sure to visit the cellars or the pantry, or any other dark, dirty corner. It is a low taste.'

'I agree with you entirely, Miss Chaworth,' Mrs Pigot said. 'A low taste, and what is worse, it requires *lying down in a boat*, which I mean to do once more, on our return, and then never again as long as I live.'

'For shame, Mother. There is someone here who must do justice to this cave. I have not come all this way, to see so little (I quite agree with you about dirty and dark) without at least some elevating reflection, on the nature of eternity, or anything you please. But Lord Byron is silent. He has been struck; he suffers what cannot be spoken of – and what we, who speak, have not the sense to feel.'

And in this way we passed through another succession of caverns, all dripping, all dark, and made our way back out into the sunshine at last.

*

Mary had considerably recovered her spirits by the time we returned to the farm. The farmer's wife came to greet us, with cakes and tea and fresh cheese, which we consumed standing up before disposing ourselves again in the two carriages. Mary claimed Elizabeth for herself. She didn't care who joined them besides, but she was determined to sit in the barouche. It was now just after five o'clock and the sun declining cast a strong level warmth against our faces. I rode with John and Mr Becher and Mrs Pigot and pretended to fall asleep. There were still two hours ahead of us to Matlock, and then I did fall asleep and awoke to the echo of hooves between the walls of a village street; and five minutes later we pulled in front of the Old Bath Hotel.

Mrs Pigot put her hand to my forehead. 'You are hot. I believe you have caught a chill.'

'It is only the side of my face; it is only where I have been sleeping.'

'Your mother would never forgive me. It was that dreadful cave.'

'He isn't a child, Mother,' John said, stepping out.

Mr Becher and I had been given a room together, and we made our way upstairs to wash and change. I thought he might speak to me of Mary, but instead, as he sat on the bed (there was only one bed) and pulled off his muddy shoes, he asked my opinion of Mr Musters. He dressed again with more attention than I had supposed him capable of – standing for a long time before the mirror and combing his beard in place. Meanwhile I told him what I knew: that he lived at Colwick Hall, which was generally supposed to be a very fine residence, and had perhaps fifteen thousand pounds to his name. Miss Wollaston said he was engaged to Miss Chaworth, though Miss Chaworth denied it. Lord Grey knew him slightly and described him as 'a man of method' but was very strange altogether on the subject and would not explain himself.

'He paid Miss Pigot a great deal of attention,' Mr Becher said, fixing and un-fixing his cravat, 'but that is often their way. I should not like to see my sister married to him. Any man who has been to a public school knows sufficiently the nature of certain temptations to judge no one harshly who yields to them. But there is a season for such things, and I should guess that in his case he had *outlived* it.'

'I have no great reason for liking him,' I said. 'But I don't suppose you have any better reason for *disliking* him than that he flirted with Miss Pigot.'

Mr Becher looked at me with a sudden smile. 'Is not that enough?' he said.

We could already hear the orchestra tuning and went downstairs to find the dining room being cleared of tables, which were all pushed to the side. A light supper was then laid out upon them, and a punchbowl produced, musical with ice, to great acclaim. Guests had already begun to arrive; our own party made its appearance in little groups. Elizabeth and Mary and Miss Wollaston; John and Mr Musters together. Mrs Pigot descended at last and took a plate to herself, and a glass of punch, and sat down at one of the card-tables in the adjoining room. She looked very small, in a puffed dress and a large blue turban – like a bird with a nest on its head. Mary wore a green satin gown covered in strings of leaves. Her hat was also crowned with leaves, in gold and silver. When I took her hand to kiss it, her glove had nothing of its heat and was cool as silk.

She had already engaged herself to Mr Musters for the first two dances. Even John Pigot had managed to inscribe his name upon her card. But she promised me another dance later in the evening. 'I suppose we shall all be forced to make do with each other,' she said. 'I cannot imagine, in this town, there will be a very splendid choice of partners.' Then she added, with an air of relenting, 'Poor little Byron. You have not much heart for these games, have you?'

'I flatter myself that I have seen you in earnest – and like you better for it.'

'When I am in earnest, I am most *unlike* myself. I had rather you liked me for anything but that.'

'There are men enough who will care for you when you are happy.'

'I believe you positively *wish* me miserable,' she said, sharply. 'To be as miserable as you.' She turned on her heel, and I did not see her again until the dancing began.

As I was partnerless, I found Mrs Pigot at her card-table and sat down.

There is often a sort of hesitation at the beginning of these country balls, for the first dances are claimed by acquaintances, and no one is yet very *warm*; and it is sometimes awkward, after the usual exchange of pleasantries, to touch hands suddenly and begin to 'put it about'.

I said as much to Mrs Pigot. 'It is almost as good as a play, to stand aside and observe.'

She had left a little ham on her plate, and I picked at it. The first dance finished, and I noticed Mr Becher bowing deeply to Elizabeth. He was unused to the exercise, and the skin of his neck beneath his beard had reddened. But he was a fair dancer, though he did not smile.

'Have you no partner?' Mrs Pigot said to me. 'For shame, Lord Byron, at your age. Don't think of asking me at mine.'

'I should ask Elizabeth, but she seems happily engaged.'

'Do ask her. I am sure she had much rather dance with you.'

'I have also Mr Becher's preference to consider.'

'No, no. It is all one, at a dance; one may do as one pleases. And a reverend who sets himself up as a beau can expect no special consideration.' But after a minute, she added, 'Though I suppose you had rather dance with Miss Chaworth. Perhaps you are waiting for Miss Chaworth.'

'Mr Musters claimed her for the first two dances, and your son had the jump of me – and has engaged her for the next.'

'Oh, she is cruel, is Miss Chaworth. She knows very well what she is about.'

And yet, as we watched her, she seemed less sure of herself. There were about a dozen couples, and between passes, Mary and Mr Musters had a great deal to say to each other, of an intimate, urgent, disagreeable nature. Whenever the music brought them together, they began talking at once and separated again with an air of impatience – as if they could not wait to be disagreeable again.

We sat quietly observing them until I said, 'Has he no expectation of success? Mr Becher, I mean.' I did not want Mrs Pigot to believe my thoughts were entirely taken up with Mary.

'He is a kind-hearted, respectable young man; and my Elizabeth is a good sort of a girl, with some beauty and not much money to her name. It is an acceptable match, but I do not think she has much appetite for what is acceptable.'

'She struck me always as a clear-headed, well-judging person.'

'You mean, because she judges *you* well enough. But

for herself, I fear, she wishes for something more than her deserving. I have told her, you might look a great deal farther, and do no better, than Lord Byron. Lord Byron in time will cut a very fine figure, and Newstead is a handsome estate. But I'm afraid she thinks of you only as a brother, and it may be, even on your end, the attraction is wanting – that you wish for nothing better than a sister.'

By this time, the room itself had grown hotter, and the women, between reels, permitted the gentlemen to cool them with their fans. Elizabeth and Mr Becher stood together, and there was *that* in his face I almost envied him – not satisfaction exactly, but a kind of intensity. The master of ceremonies was a florid ageless sort of man. He began to make his introductions, in a loud voice; he was one of those men who mistake embarrassment for good humour. Then John claimed Mary for the next dance, and Mrs Pigot pushed me on my feet, in the direction of Elizabeth. Mr Becher, meanwhile, had found another object for his exertions, a red-haired girl in a lace dress, and I found myself at the end of a row.

'You must begin gently with me,' I said to Elizabeth. 'I am not at all a good dancer.'

'I know very well what you mean. You wish to escape me, for Miss Chaworth. But my brother has claimed her now, and I have claimed you.'

'You know very well that is *not* what I mean.'

I danced one dance with her, and then sat out the next – not with Mrs Pigot, but on my own. The music had begun to irritate me; it was like being pulled along by the ear. Also, there is nothing so oppressive as the happiness of other people. Perhaps that accounts for what followed. I mean, there are moods in which one is peculiarly susceptible to a certain kind of injury. I had seen very little of Miss Wollaston since breakfast at Annesley. She had been amusing herself with the members of our party more inclined to amusement. But she found me between sets, looking red in the face, and breathless, but not quite so cheerful and ironical as before. She asked me if I had seen Mary or Mr Musters. She had not seen them these several dances, she said, and wondered if I had claimed my engagement with her. I told her that I had not – that I had neither seen her, nor danced with her, nor cared to very much any more. 'Oh,' says she, in her old way, 'you mean, she has slighted you, and you mean now to stand on your ill-humour.' There was more of this, and after a minute or two, she persuaded me to find Mary and claim a dance with her – if only so Miss Wollaston would let me alone.

There is something shameful in being compelled to do what you already wish to do, and I felt very childish as I began to search the floor. But I do not think Miss Wollaston meant me any harm. I do not believe it was her idea of a joke. Mary and Mr Musters were not to be found, and I looked in the adjoining room, where Mrs Pigot was sitting. But she had not seen them either. Then Elizabeth joined us for refreshments, with a few hairs on end that stood out wispily against her forehead – she had been dancing uninterrupted since nine o'clock. I asked after Miss Chaworth and she answered, simply enough, that she had seen them go into the garden. Someone had opened the doors to the garden, to let a little air in, and she had seen them go out. These were the French doors at the back of the dining room, away from the musicians, so I pushed my way alongside the dancers to reach them. The day had been cloudless and the night was cold. The Old Bath Hotel was a fine provincial hotel in its way, and the gardens included a terraced walk with a stone balustrade and a set of steps leading to a lawn. I could see at some distance the reflection of a pond, or a fountain, and beyond that a row of trees or a brick wall. There was not much moonlight, but a hundred bright stars.

Two small trees in pots stood either side of the entrance, with gravel at my feet that might have given me away, but I could hear Mary speaking as soon as I stepped outside. There were benches beside the door, half-hidden by the trees, and Mary and Mr Musters were sitting on one of them. So I stayed where I was for the moment, in the doorway, in the shelter of a tree.

Mr Musters sat with his hands on his lap and his legs crossed. I could see that much through the branches of the dwarf pine. Mary herself was partly obscured by the leaves, and by Mr Musters' back, but her voice came across perfectly clear. This is what she was saying: that she had seen him in the kitchens with one of the waiters, laughing. It gave him no pleasure to dance with her, she had seen it in his face. He was longing all the time to be away from her; he always looked much happier when he was away from her.

It was because, he said, she had set out deliberately to make him jealous, and he was old enough, and had suffered enough for such nonsense in the past, never to permit himself to become – but he became instead a little entangled and could not finish, and Mary interrupted him. What could he possibly mean by *nonsense* when he made such a point of dancing with Miss Pigot? When she had been his particular companion, both on the road to

Castleton and afterwards in the caverns, and when he had spoken to her exclusively on the journey to Matlock Bath?

'That was only because you were flirting with your cousin,' he said, 'when you know very well he is in love with you.'

'What, do you think I could care anything for that lame boy?'

'It is him I pitied, for the way you lead him on. I remember well enough what young men suffer for such things.'

So I crept back quietly into the hotel again, which was noisy enough to preclude any need for quiet, and made my way unobserved through the length of the ballroom to the stairs. It is now after midnight. I can still hear the music below me, through the boards, and *feel* through the whole house the effect of the dancing feet. Mr Becher is not yet returned and will probably wake me when he comes to bed. But since there is nothing left to write, I will try to sleep.

*

I slept very badly and was almost grateful when Mr Becher retired at last, with a loud sort of quiet, and climbed into bed beside me.

'Are you awake, Byron?'

But I kept my eyes shut. I could no more speak than one can speak in dreams. And after a few minutes he turned over on his face and fell asleep.

In the morning we most of us had a kind of shame-faced air, except Mrs Pigot. It gave her great pleasure to appear cheerful, and after breakfast she enlisted John and me to walk with her as far as the church. Another sunshiny Septemberish day, cool at first but growing warmer. John and I waited for her in the graveyard, and threw stones in a field, and lay down in the long grass of one of the graves. By the time she came out again, the horses were ready, and we recovered our spirits somewhat for the sake of bidding farewell. Southwell was returning to Southwell and Annesley to Annesley. Elizabeth and Mrs Pigot and Mr Becher installed themselves in the barouche, with John in the box. We followed them as far as Sutton and stopped a minute in the road, for a second set of good-byes and currant buns.

'I suppose you had rather return with them to Southwell?' Mary said to me.

'What do you mean?'

'I think you find us rather . . . dull, in comparison with the Pigots. What was it you said of me, that I am always complaining. I am perfectly aware that my temper is very indifferent. Miss Pigot is less disagreeable. She has besides the advantages of a town; it keeps them lively.'

'I have so little appetite for what you call liveliness that I intend, as soon as we reach Annesley, to ride to Newstead. I wish to be alone. It is very trying, to be always in company; I am quite talked out.'

'You mean, you have tired of me.'

'I have tired of nothing so much as *myself*, a subject I am continually reminded of by the presence of other people.'

After a minute, she said, 'I thought Lord Grey had returned to Newstead.'

'He does not mind me in the least. I am only a boy.'

At Annesley Mrs Thomason had set out a cold collation, just a little cold salmon, and fresh bread, and a pigeon pie; but I took my leave at once and went to re-trieve Mr Becher's horse from the stable. As I led him into the yard, to be saddled, Mrs Thomason met me with a cloth in hand, in which she had wrapped a little bread and cheese and a piece of the pie. All of which I accepted gratefully from her – she waited in the doorway to see me ride off.

I had said it would be a relief to be alone again; in fact, it rather surprised me to find that it *was*. The first few leaves of autumn lay on the ground, or rather, the last of summer, which had withered off the trees, and the paths between the woods were as dry as dust. When I reached the lake, I hitched the horse to a tree and sat in the reeds and ate. Afterwards I picked a few plums from the tree, now purple and ripe and beset by birds, and ate them, too. Then I fell asleep in the sunshine. On waking, I stripped and swam out past the reeds and lay in the water on my back until I began to feel cold, though my head was hot. By the time I reached shore again and was thoroughly dry, the sun had begun to thicken against the trees.

Owen Mealy met me at the door; he supposed I would be wanting supper and a bed. I asked him if Lord Grey was at home and said I would dine with Lord Grey.

'I like that,' he said. 'But you may do as you please; it's nothing to me.'

But Lord Grey heard us and called up to me.

'I have the advantage of you,' he said, when I came up the stairs, 'by a bottle or two, which are easily made up.'

He had in fact an indistinct, suspicious air, and looked not nearly so *acceptable* as he did at first – a little fatter, and less clean. It was the worst of these country after-noons, he complained; there was no possibility of keeping track of time. He found himself going to bed with the farmers. It was very shameful. Then he slept till noon. But he slept poorly, and often wondered whether he slept at all. I listened to him in this way for an hour, when Alice brought us dinner. He was easily led along; a word would do it. But he repeated himself a great deal. This seemed very dull at first, and then, not disagreeable – I found he could listen, too.

I have decided to return to Harrow, I told him. There is nothing to keep me here. It will please my mother but that cannot be helped. At least, it will *displease* no one else.

Lord Grey's sympathies were of the nodding kind. We sat together at the little work-table in the long hall, in front of a fire. Dusk was still in the air, and we needed no other light.

'Shall I make up your bed in the hall?' Alice said, clearing the plates away.

'There's no need of that,' Lord Grey said. 'We don't mind bed-fellows, do we?' and he pulled her on his lap and tried to kiss her. But she was too quick – and it occurred to me for the first time I was drunk when she evaded me, too.

'I shared a bed last night with Mr Becher,' I told Lord Grey, upon retiring to his room.

'I hate sleeping alone,' he said.

We undressed and got into bed and lay in the dark, for about ten or fifteen minutes, until I was certain Lord Grey was asleep. He breathed heavily and peacefully and gave out the still warmth of a body asleep. But I could not sleep, and after a while opened my eyes again and found him looking at me.

'One can't be always among women,' he said.

After a moment, he went on: 'At school we found other ways of amusing ourselves, but it is damnably difficult, away from school.'

We lay like this for another few minutes, and I had the strong impression of being again in the narrow boat with Mary, and the rock pressing heavily down upon me. He turned over abruptly on his side and rested his head on his hand. 'I should be happy to pretend we are at school – it makes little difference to me, being older.'

His face in the dark looked very large and soft.

'Are you cold?' he said, for I had really begun to shiver. 'Let me warm you.' But he stayed as he was when I made no reply. 'Perhaps you would find it easier if I showed you the way. It is easily done.'

I put my head against his neck and closed my eyes.

'There is nothing to cry about,' he said, sounding by this point perfectly sober and sensible. 'You will find it a great comfort. Look at me.' But I kept my eyes shut, and he continued to speak. 'We may please each other as much as we like. And there is none of that dressing up required by women. Though as for that, if you prefer it, I will send for Alice; it is sometimes simpler at first in the company of a third. But I think you have no need of her.'

Afterwards, I *did* sleep; and he slept, too. And then it was morning, with the green dull light of morning in my eyes. I lay very quietly, so as not to wake him.

2

Last August, my wife and I moved with our three-year-old daughter to Boston for the year. I had a fellowship from the Radcliffe Institute, which is a part of Harvard, to find out what I could about Peter Sullivan. This offered me a reprieve from the business of teaching, but of course it offered no reprieve from the business of Other People's Work. On the first day (of class, I want to say, but there were no classes) we met for a kind of assembly in the grand converted gymnasium of old Radcliffe College. The fellows introduced themselves to each other, standing up one at a time like alcoholics. When it was my turn, I said, 'I'm writing a book about a guy I used to teach high school with.'

'Tell us more,' the Dean called out. I had tried to sit down.

'By the time I knew him he had basically stopped talking. But he wrote novels, and after his death I managed to publish two of them. I think he might have slept with his students. Some of them; or one of them, anyway. I want to find out what you can learn about people from the books they write – how much is true. He grew up in Boston.'

We set up house in the bottom half of an old Victorian double-decker on the Cambridge side of Porter Square. A dark, cool, heavily windowed apartment with many of the built-in features you used to find in Ivy League dorm rooms: paneling and pillars, glass bookcases. The first two weeks were entirely taken up with settling in, finding a nanny for our daughter, a rug for the sitting-room floor. Buying a car. We drove down to my sister's house in New Haven, where I still kept a few things from the last time I had lived in America, a decade before – when I was teaching at Horatio Alger. The posters I had proudly framed for my first apartment had survived undampened in my sister's garage, and we hauled them back to Cambridge and hung them again on the rented walls. As if nothing much had happened in the past ten years, only marriage and the birth of a child.

In fact, what had happened was this. I ran into my future wife practically coming off the plane from New York. She was the daughter of the Hampstead couple whose basement I lived in. Was, is: her parents are friends of my parents, and we knew each other slightly as children. Caroline had just finished university when I got to London. She was interning at a documentary film company and 'squatting' in her parents' attic until she could afford a place of her own. My bedroom window underlooked the small front garden and the tops of the cars parked at street level. Every morning I saw her emerge from the house in a smart coal-grey coat and modest skirt, with a leather briefcase (a graduation gift) in hand, and walk downhill to catch the bus that would take her into Bloomsbury. This was an image to fall in love with if you were homesick, unemployed, and twenty-three years old. I fell in love.

On those rare occasions when I had the chance to speak to her, she laughed at my jokes because she didn't understand them, and her accent had the peculiar clarity and lightness of the English upper-middle classes – as if her tongue were a sharper instrument than mine. I loved most of all hearing her play the teenage daughter when her mother was home. The basement flat had no washing machine, so I had to use the one upstairs, which gave me an excuse to waste time in their kitchen. Not just to shove my clothes in but to hang them out afterwards to dry on the radiators; to come up again when they were dry and carry them stiffly downstairs. Caroline's mother always put the kettle on when she saw me and quietly laid out whatever was in the fridge; and I sat down, with a voice all thumbs, and tried to keep up with the brisk intimate patter of their family life.

For several years after leaving New York, I kept my apartment there, renting it out when I could. A symbol in brick and board of the fact that my roots were elsewhere. Caroline and I sometimes used it as a summer getaway, though she never slept well in it. The noise from 2nd Avenue sometimes woke her at night, and when she couldn't fall back asleep, her thoughts began to race, and everything, including me, began to seem alien to her: the traffic, the lights coming through the French blinds, the heavy, air-conditioned coolness of the city. I told her to wake me. Two in the morning in New York is a good time to feel the enormity of the years ahead of you, and we had nothing to do all day but recover from the night behind us and eat pancakes and wander the streets. But she was glad when I sold the place. Now my old bachelor posters were back on our walls, and we were back in America.

*

The Radcliffe Institute of Advanced Studies surrounds a green Oxford-style quad. Curving lanes run through it. There is an old New Englandish clapboard cottage, housing a part of the administration; a brick-fronted library with storey-high windows; a building with a turret; and several long-limbed oaks shading the grass and the little stone benches propped against their trunks. My office window overlooked the quad.

The first thing I did by way of real work was also what required the least effort – the least stepping out of my office. The Radcliffe paid one of the Harvard undergrads to take out library books for the Fellows, and I ordered copies of Byron's letters and journals and poems, and Marchand's *Portrait* (which Peter had access to himself) and MacCarthy's *Life* (which he didn't), and tested 'Fair Seed-Time' against them. The title, of course, comes from Wordsworth not Byron. It is the famous opening of *The Prelude*: 'Fair seed-time had my soul, and I grew up Fostered alike by beauty and by fear.' I found an odd echo of the word in one of Byron's journal entries: 'What a strange thing is the propagation of life! A bubble of seed which may be spilt in a whore's lap . . . might (for aught we know) have formed a Caesar or a Buonaparte.' But none of this was likely to yield much insight into Peter's private life. What I wanted was to find the parts of his story that *didn't* stand up to the history, which he might have invented himself or drawn on his own experience for. Peter had been accused at Beaumont Hill of improper sexual relations with a teenage boy. 'Fair Seed-Time' tells the story of the rape, or seduction, of a teenage boy. It struck me as unlikely that there was no connection between them.

I began by going over Byron's letters, sentence by sentence, and looking for anything Peter might have used. This turned out to be dispiriting. The letters are twelve volumes long. Any life, even a life as vivid as Byron's, contains a great deal of material unsuitable for fiction; and I waded through pages of description, in-jokes, plans, apologies, printers' corrections, and intimate references to people I had never heard of. But there were discoveries that made the task bearable. Throwaway lines from the letters would suddenly reverberate, because I had read them before in one of the novels. And I still remember the excitement I felt on coming across, in one of the later journals, the following entry:

When I was fifteen years of age – it happened that in a Cavern in Derbyshire – I had to cross in a boat – (in which two people only could lie down –) a stream which flows under a rock – with the rock so close upon the water – as to admit the boat only to be pushed on by a ferry-man (a sort of Charon) who wades at the stern stooping all the time. – The companion of my transit was M[ary] A. C[haworth] with whom I had been long in love and never told it – though she had discovered it without. – I recollect my sensations – but cannot describe them – and it is as well. – – We were a party – a Mr. W. – two Miss W's – Mr. & Mrs. Clarke – Miss R. and my M.A.C. – Alas! why do I say *My*? – our Union would have healed feuds in which blood had been shed by our fathers – it would have joined lands – broad and rich – it would have joined at least *one* heart and two persons not ill-matched in years (she is two years my

elder) and – and – and – what has been the result?
– She has married a man older than herself – been
wretched – and separated. – I have married – & am
separated. – and yet *we* are *not* united. –

At some point Peter had read this passage: I felt him almost looking over my shoulder. But the excitement didn't
last. I wanted discrepancies, not facts, and most of Peter's
discrepancies turned out to be trivial. He left Mrs Clarke
at home and widowed her; brought only one of the Miss
Wollastons, but all of the Pigots; and included John
Musters, whom Mary Chaworth eventually married. All
of this proved dispiriting in a different way. It's true that
I was getting closer to Peter, to the way he worked. I saw
him again and again take a line from a letter or biography
and spin it out into a scene or a piece of analysis. Mary,
for example, really did refuse to dance with Byron at
Matlock Bath; he was heartbroken. The line employed by
Peter to do the breaking – *What, do you think I could care
anything for that lame boy?* – was lifted almost verbatim
from Marchand's *Portrait*. But Byron didn't overhear her
saying it at the ball and she was probably speaking to
her maid, not John Musters. Novelists write shorthand, I
knew that already; but finding out the facts behind Peter's
story broke whatever spell, of truth or truthfulness, it had
cast on me.

Phrase after phrase, as I made my way through the
letters and *Lives*, bounced faintly off its echo in 'Fair Seed-
Time.' 'I have looked into the de Ruthyns,' Mrs Byron
declares in the opening scene, 'and cannot find their title
in the peerages of England, Ireland or Scotland. I suppose
he is a *new* peer.' Peter copied this from a note she wrote

to the family's financial adviser, John Hanson. But the change of context matters. She wasn't gossiping; she was looking into the credentials of a tenant. Peter played around with characters, too. Musters, for example, figures in Peter's story as 'quiet' and 'mysterious.' In fact, the best account of him we have comes from a hunting journal, which remembers him as someone who could have 'leaped, hopped, ridden, fought, danced and played tennis with any man in Europe.' Far from the sinister 'Man of Method' Peter has painted, Musters seems to have been the Regency equivalent of a frat boy: good-natured, good-looking, idle and a little stupid. The 'hunting' he wasted his time on was just the ordinary, innocent, violent kind of hunting.

The significance of that word 'mysterious' (which is the quality that makes Peter's Byron so 'uncomfortable' around Musters) may have been taken from Louis Crompton's book *Byron and Greek Love* – published in 1985, and the first to address the question of his homosexuality. Peter probably picked up all references to 'the Method' in it, too. This was the term Byron's college set used to describe their pursuit of boys; a necessary code, because homosexuality was still punishable by death. When Byron boasted to his friend Skinner Matthews, shortly before setting off for the Continent, about the pleasures to be had from the boys (or 'hyacinths') of Falmouth, Matthews congratulated him 'on the splendid success of your first efforts in *the mysterious*, that style in which more is meant than meets the Eye.' In the same letter, he requested that anyone 'who professes *ma methode*' should 'spell the term wch designates his calling with an e at the end of it – *methodiste*, not metho*dist*, and pronounce the word in the

French fashion. Everyone's taste must revolt at confounding ourselves with that sect of horrible, snivelling fanatics.'

Peter leaves out this e when Lord Grey describes John Musters as 'a Man of Method.' Maybe to avoid drawing attention to the phrase, which is already suggestive enough. But the word itself shows only that Peter had read Louis Crompton's book. I began to see how shallow the waters of his imagination were. Still visible beneath its surface: the junk or detritus of misplaced facts. Little details like the chicken-wire box also struck me in a new light – as the kind of rich 'effect' a writer strives for to suggest something real. 'All anybody wants to know about is how much is true,' I had complained to Steve Heinz. But once you figure out how much *is* true, I don't know what you're left with. 'Pure invention is but the talent of a liar,' Byron once wrote. But what should we make of the talent of impure invention?

*

Still, there was one incident that Peter dwelt on in greater detail and with greater certainty than any of Byron's biographers. The longer I looked at 'Fair Seed-Time' the more I came back to it. By this stage my desk was littered with opened books and loose papers; a real mess. A half-dozen cups of emptied tea were growing moldy, but some of them held down the papers and others propped open the books. To walk into an office like that, every morning, always suggested to me the outward expression of some internal disorder: an obsession here, an inattention there. But the truth is, I liked being there. October had come, and a few chilly mornings had pinched the blood back into the edges of the leaves – they stood out shyly against the green of the Radcliffe lawn.

Nothing I had read suggested that John Musters in real life was guilty of anything worse than attracting Mary Chaworth to him and making her unhappy in marriage. But something *did* happen between Byron and Lord Grey. On his return to Southwell in the spring of 1804, Byron refused to see him.

'I am not reconciled to Lord Grey, *and I never will,*' he wrote to his sister Augusta. 'My reasons for ceasing that Friendship are such as I cannot explain, not even to you my Dear Sister (although were they to be made known to any body, you would be the first,) but they will ever remain hidden in my own breast . . . He has forfeited all *title to my esteem*, but I hold him in too much *contempt* ever *to hate him.*' When they were reconciled, partly at least, in the summer of 1808 (they had some business to discuss together, as landlord and tenant), Byron wrote, 'I cannot conclude without adverting to circumstances, which though now long past, and indeed difficult for me to touch upon, have not yet ceased to be interesting. – Your Lordship must be perfectly aware of the very peculiar reasons that induced me to adopt a line of conduct, which however painful, and painful to me it certainly was, became unavoidable.'

Lord Grey in his reply pretended or professed to understand nothing of Byron's *peculiar reasons*. The only third-party reference to whatever it was that took place is a note written by Byron's university friend, John Hobhouse, in the margin of a copy of Thomas Moore's *Life of Byron* – which was published some ten years after his death and more than thirty since the incident in question. 'A circumstance occurred during this intimacy,' Hobhouse remarked, 'which certainly had much effect on his future morals.'

Almost all Byron's biographers agree that Lord Grey made a pass at Byron in the autumn of 1803. What's less clear is whether Byron reciprocated – whether his subsequent revulsion had something of the guilt of acquiescence in it. Lord Grey insisted to the end of his short life (he was dead by 1810) that he did not know why Byron had cut him off. Which suggests either that he was lying or that nothing had happened, or that something *had* happened which was perfectly mutual, or which he thought was perfectly mutual. Hobhouse's note is the best evidence we have. He didn't know Byron in his boyhood, but they traveled the Continent together after leaving Cambridge and became very intimate. During this tour, Byron allowed himself, for the first time, to indulge freely his homosexual inclinations – which Hobhouse neither shared nor sympathized with. But Hobhouse's comment is more suggestive than explanatory. A 'circumstance occurring' doesn't say much about agency; and the 'effect' of it could have been great even if Lord Grey did nothing more than give Byron ideas. In Peter's account, something *did* happen, and that something is pretty close to rape.

Rape scenes had featured in both of Peter's novels, scenes of sexual initiation, but this one struck me as a departure from the others: it was the only one involving a man and a boy. (Lord Grey was eight years older than Byron, which makes a difference, at twenty-three and fifteen.) I don't want to say a writer can't write a scene like that without drawing on personal experience. But if there has been some personal experience, I also don't see how he can leave it out entirely.

That said, the incident in 'Fair Seed-Time' poses a couple of problems. Peter has chosen to tell it from the point of view of the boy, and a boy who is more or less silent throughout the whole . . . transaction, which doesn't take more than a page. Some of the language belongs obviously to the period, to Byron's and not Peter's. And at the heart of the scene lies an image whose source is clearly Byron's own life: 'I had the strong impression of being again in the narrow boat with Mary, and the rock pressing heavily down upon me.' An image of such natural symbolic power that Byron himself continued to recur to it two decades later. It seems too suspiciously *literary* to be true, even for him: the sexual rite of passage made literal, in a boat, with darkness and wetness and Death ('a sort of Charon') conducting the whole experience. This is the stuff of fiction, not life; and yet it was life, too, and the whole point of my project, my fellowship, was that I could learn to distinguish between them.

In the end, I managed to make a few distinctions between Peter's treatment of the facts and the facts themselves. He downplayed the friendship between Byron and Lord Grey. Byron once referred to him as 'the best of Friends,' but in Peter's story, they didn't know each other well and never moved far beyond their practical relationship – of landlord and tenant, or host and guest. The mention of their school days struck me, too. Then there were all the little decisions Peter made about how to 'play' the scene. The boy is silent and unwilling, but not unresponsive. He looks for comfort from the source of his discomfort. Coldness seems important, physical coldness and the warmth of coercion. Most suggestively, Peter chose to tell 'Fair Seed-Time' from the victim's point of view, and not Lord Grey's. Maybe this was the purpose behind his fiction: to imagine, out of curiosity or remorse, what he had done to other people; to see himself through another's eyes. Or I needed to go farther back into his life than Beaumont Hill.

*

I suffer worse from jet lag than Caroline does, and on our first day in Boston, around six a.m., I put some clothes on my daughter and together we ventured out into the new world. A blue, later-summer morning, still drippy with dawn. Our apartment was in an upscale neighborhood only slightly over-run by student digs. There were American front yards and American front porches. We stopped sometimes on their steps, to jump down them, and glimpsed the evidence of American lives being lived behind the glass-fronted doors. On one end of our street was a bagel chain, where we sat together for half an hour along with the other early risers: commuters, shift-workers, and retirees, who have forgotten how to sleep in. Shared a bagel and a bottle of apple juice through a straw. Then we wandered to the other end and found the neighborhood park: a couple of basketball courts; a field already lined for little-league soccer; a fenced-in corner for the garden co-op; and a children's playground.

There was another young girl at the park that morning, who had flown in with her parents from London the day before – on our flight. Her mother and I talked about the strangeness of this coincidence, and the pleasantness of

middle-class American neighborhoods, which seemed to us equally strange. Especially at that time of the day, with the park sprinklers coming on, wetting the dew-wet grass, and the first joggers on foot. It feels like it would be a sin to be unhappy in a place like this, I said.

I spent a great deal of that year in children's playgrounds, sometimes with a book or a newspaper in hand. Sometimes with my daughter asleep in the stroller beside me, and my lunch in a bag. New England fall, which comes so highly recommended, lived up to its reputation; but the decline towards crisp bright November weather from heavy bright August weather was particularly gentle that year. As late as Thanksgiving, I could take my daughter to the park in nothing more than the wine-red jumper her dead great-aunt had knitted her. I could sit myself comfortably down on a bench, without chasing after her to get warm, for as long as it took me to read the opening section of the *New York Times*. The grave concerns of the newspaper print were spread out against a background of colored bars, loose leaves, and sand.

Occasionally I saw the little English girl again with her nanny, but never her mother. There were plenty of others though. My own mother is German, and I try to speak German to my daughter as much as I can. This tends to attract questions, and questioners. The neighborhood we lived in had a good supply of home-grown Germans, employed by the universities and the local tech industry. So I practiced my *Deutsch* on them, which is for me really the language of my childhood and calls up childish feelings and memories.

Another youthful association: one of the mothers I met was a woman named Kelly Kirkendoll, recently divorced, with two children. She looked familiar to me when I first saw her, lifting her boy off a slide he was climbing up, to let another kid go down. And I wondered if we'd been at college together. But Kirkendoll is a good Texan name, and her maiden name turned out to be even more familiar: Manz. The Manzes lived in the posh colonial house, red bricks and white columns, on the corner at the top of our road – a baseball throw from the house I grew up in. We used to get the bus to school together in the morning. But Kelly was pretty and fair and naturally sociable and unreserved, and I was none of those things and never said more to her than a few words. She seemed to me more approachable now.

'I'm a mess today,' she tended to announce when she saw me – as a matter of habit. A kind of apology for being thirty-three instead of thirteen. As if to say, what must you think of me, I've gotten older.

She had moved to Cambridge with her husband a few years before for the sake of his job. Which meant giving up her own job, as an elementary-school teacher. She wanted to get back to work, and Austin, Texas, but it was complicated for legal reasons, and her divorce had only just come through. So she was 'treading water' – her phrase, though it summed up what we both felt about those playground days. The first time I saw her she had both kids in tow. Later, once the older boy was settled in school, our three-year-olds learned to occupy each other. We could sit more or less peacefully on one of the park benches and let the afternoon go by.

Sometimes my work-thoughts carried over uncomfortably. My daughter was only three, but there were eight-, ten-, twelve-year-olds, who came to use the swings after school or climb up the more ambitious slides. Byron was said to have corrupted his page-boy, Robert Rushton, when he was not much older; and the subject of one of his most famous love poems, 'The Maid of Athens,' was hardly ten when Byron and Hobhouse lodged briefly with her mother on their first Continental tour. *Childe Harold* itself was dedicated publicly to a young girl, about whom he wrote, 'I should love her for ever if she could always be only eleven years old – and shall probably marry her when she is old enough & bad enough to be made into a modern wife.' By our own modern standards he was probably a pedophile and certainly a rapist, at least of the statutory kind; and it was hard not to imagine that Peter's interest in him contained an element of something unpleasant.

*

Caroline found work interning four days a week at a local public radio station, which suited her, she said, much better than TV. So we hired a nanny for three of them and split the other two days of childcare. Every morning I watched her leave the house in a smart professional jacket and modest skirt. The same leather briefcase clutched against her side. Then she got in the car and drove to WBNW, which was housed in an industrial park off the highway to Needham. The station she worked for had a books program, and she managed to get me an invitation to it. This made her very excited. (I used to tell her, in the first few years of our relationship, that she brought me luck.) So one morning we shared the commute and I saw her at work in the office. Thin false walls and stippled ceilings, a water keg, a few plants. Windows that couldn't be opened overlooking the parking lot, and the heating already on in October. She sounded to me much more efficient and English than she had sounded in years, and I was reminded again of the girl I used to know, whom I didn't know well. Afterwards, she forgot to give me a kiss, and I got in the taxi she had called for me and was driven away.

When she came home she wanted to talk about my impressions. We always had a lot to do, from about five thirty in the evening to half past seven, when our daughter went to sleep; and these sorts of conversations would be interrupted by cleaning up, making her dinner, running the bath and so on. If one of us had something we wanted to talk about we could be easily offended. The thing I said that pleased her most was: 'You seem really to like the job.' To her ears, this meant that she looked natural and happy in it. But when I asked her if there was any chance it could turn into something more than an internship, she became upset. 'I don't want to stay here,' she said.

Over our own dinner, when the house was quiet again, she asked me if I ever 'cared that our parents are friends. I mean,' she said, 'did it ever change what you feel about me?'

'I don't know what the right answer is. I think it probably did. It meant that I wanted to know more about you, because I liked your family. I wanted to know what it was like to be a member of your family. Is that the right answer?'

She nodded; to my surprise she was almost in tears. 'I feel a long way from anything I know here,' she said. 'But I know you.'

*

One of the benefits of the Harvard connection is that it allowed me to come into contact with the kind of people who might be useful to me professionally. These are all awful terms: connections, contacts, kinds of people. But a few weeks into my fellowship, I went to a reading at the Brattle Theater and ended up at dinner afterwards with several other writers and prominent editors – including the critic Henry Jeffries, who had recently taken a job at the *New Yorker*. A mild, handsome, balding, middle-aged Englishman. He had arrived in America ten years before, and we compared his first and my second impressions. 'You must have had the sense,' I remember saying to him, 'as an ambitious young man, of always leaning slightly forwards, if you know what I mean. An uncomfortable position, if you have to keep it up long.'

'Yes,' he said, kindly, 'I *do* know what you mean.' After a pause, he added, 'You must be happy to be home.'

'Well, I'm not really home,' I told him.

At one point, I succeeded in starting a more general conversation – on what was 'essentially the subject of my fellowship.' For a minute I held the table, feeling in my own voice something of the effect of my personality on others. What can we say about a writer from the way he writes? Or she writes? (Drink had made me fastidious about these things.) His moral qualities; his life. Jeffries had taught with Saul Bellow before his death and told a few stories about him. Mostly admiring; but after receiving the Nobel Prize, Bellow had turned to his son and whispered, This is why I was never around. For this. Or something like it.

'I don't even know what you win,' I broke in. 'Money, a plaque?'

'I couldn't say if they give you a plaque. But it's a lot of money.'

'And for that he ducks his duties as a father? When his writing is mostly about the big questions at stake in daily existence?'

'I suppose you blame him for his marriages, too?'

From the other end of the table, someone called out, 'You can't blame a writer for his marriages, God help us.' Sam Hess, I think his name was. Forty-something, square-shouldered and -jawed and careless of his appearance; he was losing his hair. 'A writer writes and sacrifices what he needs to.'

'This is only because he's been told it's okay,' I said, 'by a long line of shirkers and delusionals. Because it's a part of the culture that attracted him in the first place. But a guy like Bellow should have seen through it. The whole point of his work is the moral sympathies required to navigate your way through a decent life. He should have been great at marriage.'

'Are people good at marriage?' Hess asked.

'Sure they are. And Bellow should have been a first-rate husband and father. With his sensitivities, and patience for the long game, and powers of restraint. In *Herzog* he comes up with ideas for children's books, and these are great books: about the thinnest fat man, and the fattest thin man. And then he has to make excuses to his son? For the sake of a plaque, and money he doesn't need?'

Jeffries said, 'I'm afraid that writers have their vanities, too. But it wasn't the plaque, as you know very well. It was the work itself that drove him.'

'As if other people don't work. Who needs to work less than writers? Three hours a day is plenty. The rest of the time he can spend with his children, and cook and shop. Even if we don't hold him to a higher standard and forgive him a divorce or two, I still don't know what to make of five wives. Not every divorce is a failed marriage, okay; and people change. Life changes them. But I thought his special gift was character, I thought he was expert in the field of life-changes. Maybe what we should do is take another look at the work. Maybe that's where the fault lies: it wasn't profound enough. He needed to be deeper or greater. With more inner resources, he could have made it through ten years of dinner with children screaming and toys on the floor, like the rest of us.'

'This is crazy,' Hess said. 'What's it got to do with the work? A guy isn't a bad accountant if he splits on his wife.'

'But if he gets audited himself, you might think twice about leaving your returns in his hands.'

'My example was a bad example. But you have to admit writing poses special problems. Writing what you think has a tendency to hurt people. Also, there's a pressure to be open to new feelings and experiences, which isn't always helpful to a marriage.'

'That's a nice way of putting it. Maybe there should be more writers who write about what it's like *not* to experience very much, and *not* to feel new feelings. That sounds to me like the real human condition. Maybe this is what we need.'

'I'm not sure I understand you, but what you describe also seems to me a recipe for bad marriages.'

'Is this really the subject of your fellowship?' Jeffries asked me.

On the walk home, I cooled down a little, and the flush of high spirits turned into something else.

Steve Heinz had told me that Peter's mother was still alive, so I called him and got her name. Mary, he said. I would have preferred Orla or Clodagh, but there turned out to be only six Mary Sullivans in the Boston phone directory, and only two in Charlestown – which is where, I dimly remembered, Peter once told me he grew up. I tried both numbers and let them ring, twenty, thirty times each, imagining the hallways in which they echoed. Another week went by, with my head in Byronalia; when I was bored of it, I called. Once I got an answer from a woman who told me her husband was out, when I mentioned Peter to her, but I think it had little to do with the name itself. She was unused to the phone and suspicious of strangers.

'He's back this minute,' she said, 'if you don't mind ringing back.'

The addresses listed weren't more than seven or eight blocks apart – neither one far from the Navy Yard. So one afternoon, because it was sunny out, I put on my coat and caught the T to Haymarket.

Charlestown is huddled between river and highway; to reach it on foot, you have to cross a six-lane bridge. This is a good place to appreciate what the 1950s did to Boston. What you see is an architect's vision of human progress: the bright curves of access ramps; the strong splendid verticals of suspension bridges; billboards like movie screens. And between them, fragments of a low-slung Victorian terraced city: the North End. It's only the noise that's unbearable, and the nearer view of pot-holed roads and dirty cars. I came over on the wrong side of the bridge and had to chase a gap in the traffic to arrive at the relative quiet of Charlestown Square. From there, the old city emerges again: leafy streets, brick sidewalks and houses; steep hills.

This wasn't the neighborhood I imagined Peter growing up in, but Charlestown has suffered a sea-change since his childhood. It has become rich. The greasy spoons have been turned into coffee shops and the bars into restaurants. Most of the pretty row-houses have fresh facades; sometimes you can measure the effects of gentrification in the line of soot that separates one from the next. The first door I knocked on, after trying the bell and hearing nothing, had a basket of begonias hanging above it, still dripping from a spray. A tall narrow house with a dormer built on but in bad repair. Most of the other houses on the block, a side street that dipped then rose towards Bunker Hill, had been cleaned up and turned into flats. This was the only one with a single bell. About three o'clock in the afternoon, mid-October; I could see a dull light shining behind lace curtains on the second floor.

A short, elderly woman came to the door. There was a broad stairway behind her with a red tattered runner running down it, fringed in gold brocade. An umbrella stand, containing several tall umbrellas; a chandelier with little electric candles, colored by hand; and a row of old-fashioned mail slots hung against the wall.

'Are you Mary Sullivan?' I asked. 'I was a friend of Peter's.'

'I don't know what you're talking about.'

'Peter Sullivan. I used to teach high school with him.'

'He's dead now, why don't you let him alone.' And she closed the door in my face.

There was a coffee shop on the corner, but I walked on looking for a stationers and ended up at a pharmacy, which sold gift-cards and envelopes. At the coffee shop, I ordered tea and sat down with a borrowed pen and tried to explain myself. It took me half an hour to come up with something serviceable, but in the end, I lacked the patience for a waiting-game and simply knocked at the door with the card in my hand. She opened it soon enough. I guess old ladies can't afford to turn away too many opportunities for diversion. But she looked perfectly respectable and sober, in a flower-print dress and sandals, over thick ankle-socks. She had none of the whiskery, red, angry Irish quality Steve Heinz had described to me. Maybe she had cleaned herself up or was only drunk for the funeral. When she saw it was me again, she said, 'You think you're the first has come. On account of those books.'

'That's what I want to talk to you about. I've written you a card.'

'Why don't you just spit it out, since we're standing here.'

'Do you want me to read what I wrote?'

'What's a matter with you, there's nothing wrong with my eyes. Oh, give it me, give it me.' She took it out of my hands and squinted at it, while I fidgeted like a boy on the stoop. At last she said to me, 'So it's you I have to thank. You might as well come in.'

A little alcove had been carved out under the stairs, with a desk and a bell on it, beside a visitors' book. There was a small black-and-white TV, no bigger than a shoebox, showing a baseball game. The Red Sox were in the playoffs, and the voice of the commentators carried through the house, in spite of the soft carpeting, to the back of the long hall where the kitchen was. There were flies, and a few slices of cake left on the counter, on a stand, under a mesh hood – ornamented by daisies, the kind of thing I had seen only in antique shops. The window over the sink showed a tree in the garden in front of a chain-link fence, but no grass or sunlight. To let in air, the back door had been propped open by one of those dull wire crates Coke bottles used to come in.

'Did you always take lodgers?' I asked her. 'Even when Peter was a boy?'

'What do you think this is, a lodging house?'

'I assumed, because of the guest-book . . .'

'Of course it is. What did you expect us to do? A house this size and only one boy to show for it. Now would you like tea?'

By the time she had made a pot and set it down on the table with two hands, she had decided on the line to take with me. I showed her the copy of *A Quiet Adjustment* I had brought along, the hardback with the image of a woman's head in the oval of a picture-locket; and she said, 'You could put a vase on this and never worry. I suppose you get paid pretty well for your trouble. If you don't mind me asking.'

'What are you asking?'

'Don't be stupid. By rights this sort of thing should go to the mother.'

'Believe me, I wish it had, Mrs Sullivan.'

'So what do you get for it, a good thick book like this?'

'It depends on how many you sell.'

'Just look at it' – turning it over in her hands – 'at twenty-five dollars a go. You wouldn't need to sell many, at twenty-five dollars. Mind you, there can't be many'd go for it at that.'

'It's what people like to call a critical success.'

'What people?'

'Publicists. Authors.'

'I didn't know they were the same thing. So how do you make a living at it?'

'I don't. I have a job.'

'And what might that be?'

'At the moment I'm being paid to find out what I can about Peter.'

'Is that a good line of work, is it?' she said.

It went on like this for maybe another hour; halfway through Mrs Sullivan brought out the slices of cake. She didn't mind talking about Peter, she said, 'within reason,' but she didn't mean to be cheated out of her rights. As for looking over the house, or seeing his old room, there could be no question of that. She didn't deny she had some of his letters and books, and not a few of his things, but before she showed me anything I might make use of, she needed to get a fairer sense of the price. At one point she even asked me who to talk to, about an estimate; at her age, for this sort of thing, she didn't know the right people.

'There's nobody,' I told her. 'Nobody but me.'

I should forgive her if she exercised the right to her own opinion.

Much of what she told me I could have found out elsewhere. He was born 'in this house, in this kitchen,' in 1942 or 43. Mrs Sullivan was still sharp enough to resent, with a very natural anger, any slips or gaps of memory. His father died in the war, and afterwards she let it be known that anyone who was clean and sober was welcome to a bed in her house, and breakfast and dinner, for a dollar a week – it started out, a dollar a week. Mostly young Irish men from the Navy Yard, at first. She kept her own bedroom and a sitting room, on the top floor; but there was a bathroom and three other bedrooms beneath her, and Peter didn't need but one of them. It was good for him to have a few men in the house. Mrs Sullivan had three sisters in the neighborhood, and a mother (a widow herself), and it didn't do for a boy to be spoiled by women. Not that he needed company. The worst she could say of him, though he was her own son, is that he kept himself to himself. You couldn't get his face out of a book.

'He had a great head for books, when I knew him.'

The front door opened and closed, and someone went upstairs; but Mrs Sullivan didn't mind it, so I went on. 'Did he visit much? When he was out of school?'

'Was he ever out of schools, that one? But he lived here at college, too, if that's what you mean. And on his first job. And afterwards, again – when he had reason to. But who's paying you?' she asked me suddenly. 'You said somebody's paying you. Well, who?'

'It's something to do with Harvard.'

'I like that, when they wouldn't give *him* a penny.'

'Is that where he went to university?'

'I suppose they want you to ask me about that boy. What's his name – Pak or Chung or some business like that. We might as well get all of that over with now.'

'I wasn't sure if I'd ask you or not. But if you don't mind talking about it.'

'I don't mind setting the record straight. After all the foolishness people came out with, and not just in the papers. To my own face. This is what I have to say, and that's the end of it. There never was girlfriends and there never was boyfriends. He never gave me any trouble, he was that kind of a boy – the kind that wasn't much interested in anybody but himself. Some boys are like that, just as much as some girls. For myself, I never saw much use to the whole business. My husband liked it. But when he was dead, I can't say I missed it, and Peter was just the same.'

'Did he bring friends home sometimes?'

'That's what I'm telling you, he didn't have much use for visitors.'

'What about the lodgers?'

'I hope that's not what I'm hearing you saying. This wasn't that kind of a house.'

'I mean, did Peter make friends with any of the lodgers?'

'Oh, he sat down with them sometimes, to the radio. He was civil. But nobody could get a word out of him, that's how he was. Mind you, some of them tried.'

She dismissed me at last, saying: 'If you want more tea, you'll have to go out for it. That's all the cake and I can't be bothered to brew another pot. What I want right now is to sit in my chair and watch the end of the ballgame.'

'Can I come and see you again?'

'If you want anything else, you can pay for it, like everybody else.'

'Shall I leave you his book? I didn't know if you'd read them.'

'God help me, I tried,' she said. 'But it was Peter all over: the child couldn't utter a natural word. A great fuss about nothing. The things used to put him in a state, you wouldn't believe. But he was always nervous. He had it from his father. Now his father is dead and Peter is dead, and it's only me again. But they never was much company.'

On my way out, I looked in quickly at the sitting-room door. An electric heater in the fireplace was plugged in-

136

to a socket by the mantel. There was a coffee-table with magazines spread out across it: a public room, with a TV under the window and the blinds drawn above it. A few comfortable chairs under lamps. I couldn't imagine a boy feeling at home in it, with young men in the armchairs, smoking and watching television. No wonder he stayed in his room. Mrs Sullivan herself sat down to the little black-and-white box in the entrance hall.

'You can see yourself out,' she said.

'I'll come again.'

'I guess you can please yourself.'

A few things stuck in my thoughts on the long walk back, across the bridge again and into Boston, against the grain of traffic with the light in my eyes. A little colder now; the sun gave no more warmth than the glitter off moving cars. 'One can't be always among women,' Peter had written. 'It didn't do for a boy to be spoiled by women,' his mother had said. A half-echo. One of those phrases, probably, that knocked around his childhood and came to stand for a whole climate of feeling – for the awkward but necessary, almost formal relations of men and women in his mother's house. Maybe one day a lodger had used it to get him into bed.

It somehow consoled me to hear that he didn't talk much, even as a boy. That this was a fact of his personality, along with the nerves and the self-containment. The love of books. He was present to me also in the bones of his mother's face, in her natural pedantry. I reminded myself to look up where he'd gone to university. Boston College, it turns out, on a scholarship; but if Harvard had accepted him once, I don't know.

A few days later, I had an idea and got in touch with a guy I had met through the Byron Society in Cambridge, Paul Gerschon. Gerschon worked at the Houghton, Harvard's rare-books library. It occurred to me he might be useful in helping to prise Peter's papers out of his mother's grasp – that this is something certain librarians become skilled at.

We met downstairs at Café Pamplona, on the corner of a rather ugly side street off Harvard Square. I had seen him only once before, at a talk, with a few dozen people around, but he carried in his hand a copy of *A Quiet Adjustment*. I would have recognized him anyway, by his soft-skinned face and large lips; his pale hair and eyes. It seems too easy to call him *bookish*, yet it is strange, also, that this should be so recognizably human a quality. That the long association with books breeds a certain manner, formal, gentle, curious, hesitant. A tall man himself, he stooped under the low basement ceiling, and we carried our drinks upstairs to the patio garden, which was carved out of the sidewalk and crowded by wrought-iron chairs and tables. The weather was bright but windy, and we decided after a few minutes to drink our drinks and return to his office at the Houghton, where we could talk in peace and warmth. Also, he wanted to show me their collection of Byronalia – nothing first-rate, he said, but still, they had a few interesting pieces.

On the way, he told me stories about Peter. It turns out they knew each other pretty well. 'We were what my wife calls Society Friends,' he said. 'Which means there were large tracts of our lives that never came up for discussion.'

'Because you were sensitive to . . .'

'I would have used the word indifferent. We didn't get together to talk about our marriages. We talked about books. But you're right, maybe a part of the reason was the fact that a number of our members, what I would call an honorable minority, lead fairly eccentric lives. Isolated lives. Until recently you might say that I was one of them.'

He had married, rather late in life, and his wife had just given birth to their first child – a boy, now eleven months old. This also provided us with conversation.

'Then you never talked much with Peter about his private life,' I said eventually.

'By private life, I suppose you mean the incident at Beaumont Hill School. I don't want to give you the impression that we tolerate in our membership any indecency or unpleasantness. But I will say this. I had, I have, a lot of sympathy for men in Peter's situation – I mean, men who have more or less been denied . . . a sexual life. Or have denied themselves one. It doesn't make much difference. I wasn't around when Peter resigned from Beaumont Hill, or was forced out. But don't for a minute believe that the Byron Society, as a group of people, is free from the vice of gossiping, especially about sexual matters. It is the Byron Society, after all. We knew the story, we talked about it. Peter himself could be very . . . funny about himself. I read your preface to *Imposture*, and I must say, I did not recognize the man you described in it. The picture you drew in it annoyed me. Peter was not a silent man, especially on the subject of Horatio Alger. I suppose you know who Horatio Alger is?'

'I know a little about him; not much.'

'The author of a hundred-odd stories about the American dream. He had to resign his post at a church in

Brewster, Massachusetts, for committing the sin of paeder-
asty with two teenage boys. So he moved to New York
and set up a hostel – for impoverished children. And
began to write. Nobody reads him now, but Peter used
to. It tickled him pink to land a job at a school named
Horatio Alger. But I will say this for him. I don't think
Peter would have cracked jokes if he had anything to
feel guilty about. Anything that counted. You never know
what other people are capable of, but I think you sometimes know what they are capable of joking about. Peter
was sharp, but he was never cruel.'

'People seem to me to be capable of joking about anything.'

'You may be right; this is your line of work. As it happens, the Houghton has a pretty fair copy of Herbert
Mayes' book on Alger, *A Biography Without a Hero*. A
hoax, of course. He made up whatever he didn't know,
diaries, letters, etc. The Macy-Masius first edition, from
1928, a little worn at the edges. Not a rare volume, but
interesting to me.'

Interesting was one of his words. We were in his office
by this point, which was carpeted in soft institutional gray,
windowless and rather dark, with nothing but a lamp on
his desk to light the room. But there were several precious
things in it that daylight would have damaged. Paul had
made a selection of the Houghton archives for me, which
included a manuscript of *The Curse of Minerva*, Byron's
poem on the rape of the Elgin Marbles. It was bound in
red straight-grain Morocco and inscribed: 'This MS was
written by Henry Drury, the tutor of Lord Byron and was
made by him from one of the original nine copies which
were privately printed in 1812.' The two young men had

become friends, after a bad start, which plays a small part in the action of 'Fair Seed-Time.'

'Also not a first-rate piece,' Paul said, turning to the first page with its beautiful opening lines:

> Slow sinks, more lovely ere his race be run,
> Along Morea's hills the setting sun . . .

'But suggestive, don't you think? I don't know why he did it. It's usually the other way around: the student copies down the teacher's words. But by that stage, Byron was famous.'

We talked only briefly about the trouble I had had with Mrs Sullivan. Paul promised to do what he could. He didn't often make 'house calls.' Valuing private papers wasn't really in his field, but he knew enough to 'pretend a competence,' he said, 'which is all that matters in this case. I'll ask around for a sense of what such things are worth. I can't imagine she wants very much money, or that her idea of *much* is the same as yours.'

'I wouldn't be so sure,' I said. 'She's a canny old – woman.'

'What would you be willing to pay? Well, let's see what she's got first.'

Before I left he offered to show me something else. He'd been playing around with the library's scanner recently and had uploaded, if that was the word, a box of old photographs onto his computer. From some of the Society 'field trips.' There were pictures of Peter among them, from a visit to Missolonghi they'd undertaken together a few years before his death. Peter and Paul at sunset, standing in front of a still, clear body of water, with the sun behind them, a dot of intensity, and their eyes reddened by the flash. A thumbnail of Peter, among two or three others, leaning with his back against a wall. They were watching a couple of Greeks playing roundish stringed instruments; there was a hat on the gravel of the square and some coins in the hat. Another one of Peter, with his glasses in hand, resting his sandaled foot on a rock. A low undistinguished hill behind him, with a path slanting up it.

'Not far from where Byron died,' Paul said.

Apart from the sandals, Peter was wearing a pair of denim shorts and a loose T-shirt with a purple lion on it that looked familiar – the school logo. His legs and arms were skinny and muscular, and very brown; and you could see, in spite of the length of his uncombed beard, a broad smile stretching out the lines of his face. The kind of smile my father makes for the camera, to be friendly, without caring much about how he looks. And I saw Peter for the first time as one of your average American eccentrics: fond of hiking and group expeditions and nature; an old, popular high-school teacher on his summer holiday. I could imagine him coming back to class in the fall and talking about the wonders of 'Europe.'

'This is why the picture you gave of him got under my skin,' Paul said. 'He was a popular member of the Society. By our standards, very sociable and lively; good company. His Greek was terrible, much worse than mine, but he used it shamelessly and often made himself understood. While the rest of us counted over our declensions. Peter once said to me that when he was a child, he thought he hated people; it was only when he grew up that he realized he hated children. He qualified this, of course. There weren't many people he liked – maybe one per cent of the population, what he called the *literate* one per cent. But around them, he was a very happy man.'

'What did you say to this?'

'I remarked that he had made an odd choice of profession.'

'And to that?'

'Sometimes, he said, you can make them literate yourself.'

*

One of the things I liked about Kelly Kirkendoll, apart from her name, is that we could talk about Austin together. Even though her childhood, the bulk of which took place less than a hundred yards from mine up the curve of Wheeler Street, bore little resemblance to my own. Kelly was homecoming princess and captain of her high-school basketball team, facts I never knew about her till she told me, with the kind of ironic tone you employ towards younger siblings or past selves. Not that she was vain. Or as she said herself, 'I'm vain about the things I've got to be vain about, and modest about the things I've got to be modest about. And right now, there's more things I've got to be modest about than vain.'

For example, as she explained to me, she was captain of the basketball team but not its best player. The girls voted her captain because everybody could get along with her, which was mostly because the smart girls didn't think she was smarter than them, and the pretty girls didn't think she was prettier. This was also the reason she got elected homecoming princess, not queen. She was too tall to be really pretty, as she put it. She had big hips and shoulders that were good for playing the post and getting rebounds, but not so good for looking like Barbie. The reason I didn't know she was homecoming princess is that I didn't go to my high-school prom. We talked about this, too. Fifteen years after the fact, she liked me for it. 'I don't remember much about you, but I remember you were a weird kid. Too tall to talk to for one thing, though I tried sometimes, which you probably don't remember, either. You were shy with girls. I guess you've changed a lot?' she said, laughing.

We spent too much of our time together, which was often interrupted by children, discussing our high-school lives. Her life, I should say. I found myself becoming nostalgic over someone else's past. Only the setting was the same; everything else was unrecognizably different. But when she told me stories about getting drunk in the parking lot of Dan's Hamburgers, because one of her high-school buddies worked the counter there, on those summer nights in Texas which remain uncomfortably warm until one or two in the morning, but Dan's stayed open, and instead of the stars, you could see the trucks with their lights on coming along North Lamar, my heart contracted a little, as if I had ever been a part of those carefree good times now permanently out of my reach.

'That's what used to annoy me,' Kelly said, 'about those stories about high-school drinking. I don't want to say it was always innocent but compared with what? Compared with my life today? Mostly it was just sitting in cars and talking.' Then she laughed again. 'Which isn't much different from what we're doing now.'

One of the playground benches had a distant view,

across the soccer fields, of the basketball court. While the weather was warm enough, which it was until the second week of November, a handful of the same boys biked over every day after school and played. Even at a hundred yards I can tell who can shoot and who can't, by the way his off hand falls away from the ball, by the position of the wrist. When I was a kid I used to spend an hour or two a day in the backyard, regardless of weather, working on my jump shot; and nothing showed up the passage of twenty years more vividly than those hundred yards. This at least was a part of my childhood I could feel a decent nostalgia for. Eventually, I started bringing a ball to the park myself. When my daughter fell asleep in the stroller, I wheeled her into the shade of the oak trees that overlooked the court and worked on my jump shot. For as long as an hour, depending on how much she slept. Shooting, silently chasing the ball, planting my feet and shooting again, while the boys at the other basket screwed around and sometimes got under my feet.

Kelly joined me once. As it happens, she wasn't particularly good at basketball. Tall for a girl, she used her elbows well but had put on ten pounds since 'her prom dress last fit her' and hadn't played since senior year. Basketball was just another one of those things she picked up because of high school and forgot about as soon as she graduated, like the Bill of Rights. But her play didn't embarrass her. Even as a teenager she never worried much what other people thought of her. Once in a while she would 'pretty herself up,' as she put it, but most days she showed up at the bus stop wearing jeans and a T-shirt and no make-up, and even, if she was running very late, her glasses.

'You probably remember them. Like Coke bottles,' she said, squinting and lining up a shot.

Her blonde hair was straight and slightly reddish, and her complexion clear and pink. She never had a problem getting boys to like her, so why should she bother with all the 'other stuff'? High heels, powder, painted nails.

'I bother a little more now,' she told me, 'when I get a chance to go out, which is never. But most of the time you see me as I am. A mess.'

A low-hung October afternoon, warm rather than bright; and for a good hour, while our daughters slept, we passed a ball around and sometimes pretended to play in earnest. Kelly accused me of running around too much, like a kid brother, and eventually gave up chasing me and began chasing rebounds instead. Passing the ball back to me, talking as I shot. She was still confident of the fact that anyone she liked would like her too, and the rest didn't matter. Even at thirty-three, with a divorce behind her and two kids on her hands. No job, and the place she wanted to live a plane-flight away.

'I'm not very good at being unhappy,' she told me. 'So I don't try.'

She talked about her divorce, too, and there were times I had to wait with the ball in my hands to hear her out. Her husband was somebody she had known since high school, though they didn't begin dating till the summer after graduating college. He'd come back from a place out East and was working part-time at the donut shop on Guadalupe, which is where she ran into him again. For a while they 'hung out, with a few other friends, too. It was just a summer thing. But then Kevin got a good job, at Dell. And I started my teaching certificate. His apartment was nicer than mine, so I told him I was moving in, and that's what I did. He was kind of a good-time guy; maybe I bullied him into it. Even when we got married a few years later it didn't seem like a big deal. He always knew how to enjoy himself, let me put it that way – more than me. Basically, I never did anything I wouldn't tell my dad about, which included a little pot and a lot of beer but nothing worse. Kevin did many things he wouldn't even tell me, but then he'd get up in the morning and go to work, so he didn't see what I had to complain about. And until we had Matty I didn't complain, much. Don't get me wrong, he's a great dad, for the five minutes a day he wants to see his kids. But the rest of the time, he's either working or having fun, or thinking about work or about how to have fun. And you know what, I told him, I don't care if I'm your idea of fun or not, you're stuck with me. But I guess he wasn't,' she said.

'He walked out on you?'

'Not exactly. I'm the kind of girl, if you stand me up once, it's not a big deal. But after that, I don't hang around.'

'What does that mean, stand you up? Did he have affairs?'

'It depends on what you call an affair.'

'I don't understand.'

'My dad, who still likes Kevin, too much if you ask me, has a phrase for what he is. A befriender of women, my dad calls him. Kevin likes to make women like him. He thinks it makes him likeable. And he liked it even more after I stopped liking him, which I don't blame him for.'

We might have been back in high school, after class, only this time the girl I was talking to was Kelly Manz.

The rest of the illusion held up pretty well: that I was on my father's court, with all afternoon before us, and a lifetime, too, until my daughter woke up and I climbed the large-stoned wall to the shaded terrace with the picnic tables and consoled her. She always woke angry. The next time I saw Kelly she complained of spending the rest of that day in her own sweat. She didn't get a chance to shower until both kids were in bed, which was nine o'clock, and by that time she was too tired. Her excuse for not joining me again.

'Even if I don't care what I look like, I draw the line at smelling,' she said.

Something had made her uncomfortable, though she couldn't help herself afterwards and continued to talk about Kevin when we met, in the cooler intimacy of the children's playground. I was also aware of feeling in some way complicit. But I told myself, you've never confided in her about Caroline; there's nothing wrong with listening. And when she talked to me about divorce law, I talked about Peter.

Kelly surprised me by having nothing but sympathy for him. After ten years in the public school system, she said, you learn to distrust anything you hear about sexual harassment. Well, almost ten years, and even if it was only elementary school. Men had it harder. She had more or less decided from the beginning to ignore whatever the staff directives on the subject were, because if she got fired for cuddling a nine-year-old boy she wanted no part of the profession. But she had seen teachers with over thirty years experience in education practically in tears because they had kissed the top of a kid's head when she fell over in the playground. Just waiting for the other shoe to drop.

And it was worse in high school, she told me; she knew from first-hand experience that certain girls are asking for it.

'Don't think for a minute they don't know what they're doing. Compared to some bow-tied history teacher who probably had only two girlfriends in his life and married one of them.'

In Peter's case, I told her, there was a boy in question.

'Oh boys, girls. The boys are just as bad.'

She turned out to be useful to me in a practical way. I had driven over one afternoon to Beaumont Hill, a twenty-minute ride from our apartment along the highway towards Walden Pond. As soon as you leave the exit, you see nothing but green streets and shaded houses – one of those wonderful suburban American neighborhoods that conceal their riches under privately maintained natural scenery. But I got no deeper into campus than the school gates. No one without 'express and expressed permission,' I was told, could be admitted to the grounds – there was a pre-fab hut with a guard in it by the side of the road, checking names and passes. I could hardly mention the purpose of my visit as a ticket in, but Kelly knew one of the science teachers from Ed. School and offered to get me an invitation to lunch.

By this point I understood a little more about Peter's 'incident.' The archive on the *Boston Globe*'s website reaches back to the 1980s and a quick search of 'Peter Sullivan' and 'abuse' eventually turned up the right guy. There was a picture of Peter, beardless and loose-haired, above the headline – a staff photo, his pale, childish face sitting on top of a necktie striped with brown and green, the school colors. The same look he gave Paul's camera in

Missolonghi: a broad, embarrassing, unembarrassed smile. Nothing that had happened in the intervening thirty years had had any effect on the face he made for photographs. The headline itself read 'When Abuse Is Only Civil,' and the purpose of the article was to point out some of the oddities of Peter's case. This was clearly a follow-up to a previous piece, a short item I found a minute later, not more than a paragraph in a sidebar column devoted to court news: 'Prestigious Boston Prep-School on Trial.' The only other reference to the incident was an editorial that did not name Peter directly, though it referred to Beaumont Hill, among other schools, and addressed the question of settlement. 'How much can we blame a school for the misconduct of its teachers? How do we measure such blame? In dollars.' Etc.

Peter's case highlighted a number of interesting gaps in the law. In Massachusetts, the age of consent is sixteen for women and eighteen for men, but this applies only to heterosexual sex; there is no provision in the law for homosexual consent. There is, however, a separate clause regarding 'sexual inducement,' which appears to apply equally to men and women and to homosexual and heterosexual acts, and which sets the age of consent at eighteen. But it also requires that the victim be of 'chaste life,' which the law does not define and which is usually difficult to establish. In any case, parents tend to shy from exposing their children to the necessary parade of testimony. There was some talk early on of applying 'sexual inducement' laws to make a criminal case against Peter, but the plan was dropped. Apart from anything else, the proof of intercourse depended on the evidence of the boy, Lee Feldman, who eventually refused to testify – by this

150

stage he was a sophomore at Brown. Peter was never a defendant in the lawsuit, which was levied at Beaumont Hill; and, in fact, the evidence against him was slight enough that the Massachusetts Department of Education could find no grounds to refuse a renewal of his certification. Peter himself might have had a case to make against the school, for firing him, but he seems to have let the matter drop on accepting the job at Horatio Alger. The civil suit was settled out of court.

But a few suggestive facts emerged at the pre-trial hearing. Lee Feldman was adopted. The plaintiff, his father, owned a number of car-dealerships in the Boston area. He was also a 'prominent figure in the Brookline Jewish community' and a member of the board at Temple Ohabei Shalom. Mr Feldman had recently closed two of his shopfronts, in Newton and Watertown, and was under 'internal investigation' for his role in certain loans the temple had taken out to finance the construction of a new community center. According to defense lawyers, Lee's 'sexual inclinations' had been a subject of commentary in the Feldman family for several years before the incident at Beaumont Hill. They intended to establish that Mr Feldman had discussed it with Rabbi Mordecai Stern shortly before his son's confirmation in the spring of 1986, six months before he first attended a class taught by Peter Sullivan. Lee Feldman was an indifferent student, but his grades improved dramatically after taking Peter's course. The Feldmans had been delighted and surprised by their son's acceptance to Brown University, which they attributed largely to Peter's influence. They even invited him to Lee's graduation party, for which they rented out the ballroom of the Parker House Hotel in downtown Boston, an event costing 'upwards of thirty thousand dollars.'

The Feldmans, for their part, claimed they knew nothing of their son's sexual orientation until the summer after his freshman year in college, when he announced it to them. This announcement apparently included the phrase, 'What did you think Mr Sullivan and I were always doing, reading?' Lee Feldman first admitted and subsequently denied that intercourse between them had taken place. He said, in fact, that Mr Sullivan used to invite him to his office, where he would ask him to 'read out loud to him.' At the time, Peter was acting head of the Dramatic Society, which entitled him to a 'room of his own' a few doors down the corridor from the English office. The Feldmans alleged that Mr Sullivan used his 'position' to entice their son into his office on the pretense of considering him for a part in the school performance of A Winter's Tale. Since Beaumont Hill is a single-sex academy, boys are often forced to play female roles, and Mr Sullivan provided Lee with 'costumes for changing into.' It was also alleged that at least on one occasion, and possibly more, Peter Sullivan masturbated himself behind his desk while Lee Feldman read aloud to him. Lee refused to confirm this accusation to his father's lawyers, but he did not deny it either, even after recanting the rest of his story.

'I couldn't really see what was going on over there,' he said, when the Globe interviewed him by telephone from his college dorm room. (I've adapted the article to reflect the fact that what took place was a conversation, with questions and answers, and not a series of statements.)

'What were you reading?' he was asked.

'Byron, Swinburne, that kind of thing. Whatever he wanted me to.'

'And what kind of clothes did he ask you to wear?'

'Oh, most of what my parents said was bullshit. There was a wardrobe in the office with some costumes from other plays. Peter didn't care what I wore but he let me try stuff on. He didn't like it much, because some of the costumes went back as far as the 1930s, organza dresses and things like that, which were pretty easy to tear, but he let me anyway because otherwise I refused to come.'

'Did he watch you when you undressed?'

'Probably he did. Wouldn't you?'

'What made you decide to tell your parents about Peter Sullivan?'

'Look, he started calling me freshman year and wouldn't leave me alone. Beaumont Hill wasn't a specially happy place for me. I don't blame Peter for that – he tried to help. But my life is different now; I don't need any help. I thought if I told my parents about Peter, they could get him off my back. So I made a few things up. But I didn't expect my dad to go ballistic like he did. I mean, he knows what I'm like, that's all bullshit, too. The whole thing got out of hand. That's when I had to step in and tell the truth.'

'Do you think there was anything improper in your relationship with Peter Sullivan during your time at Beaumont Hill?'

'What do you want me to say? I'm not that into *proper* anyway.'

'Do you think there was anything the school should be held accountable for?'

'Oh, definitely blame the school,' he said.

The article also quoted the Beaumont superintendent of

police, which had made its own investigation. 'It is very unusual,' he said, 'in cases involving a male teacher and a male student that only one kid comes forward. Mostly you see this kind of pattern with a female teacher and a younger boy, where the teacher considers it a consensual relationship and believes herself to be in love. I'm talking about relationships lasting several years. Where the motive for abuse is primarily sexual, and not emotional, you usually find little clusters of incidents – periods of activity. In Sullivan's case you had a teacher who had been at an all-boys school for almost twenty years. It makes no sense to me that this is the only incident. For one thing, there's usually a lag between the crime itself and the moment it gets reported. And here we have a lag of three years. That's a long time for a sexual predator who has learned he can get away with something to remain inactive. What we do is put out little feelers in the community, to see if anything else comes up. But it takes time; it takes time.'

This was the note the story ended on, but if anything else subsequently 'came up,' the *Globe* failed to report it. A few weeks before Thanksgiving, on one of my 'child-care Fridays,' I put my daughter in her car seat and picked up Kelly from her apartment a few blocks away. (Caroline was researching a story in the Public Library and took the train.) Kelly also needed to bring her three-year-old and spent a few minutes transferring her own car seat and buckling her daughter in. By this stage our children knew each other fairly well, and their excitement at sitting side by side in the back of my dirty Corolla contributed in large part to the excitement Kelly and I felt at setting out together. Boston is a cold city but not a dark one and even in November sunshiny mornings outnumber the gloomy ones. Then there are the changing leaves, which seem to possess their own internal sources of light. By mid-November most of the leaves have fallen, it's true; but this only has the effect of reducing the ratio of leaf and twig to the natural proportions of a candle and its flame.

'There are times I don't mind not being in Austin,' Kelly said, as we drove through neighborhood streets to the highway.

At Beaumont Hill she gave her name to the guard in his hut, who checked it against a list and waved us through. And slowly the campus opened out before us – not one building or two, but at least a dozen, spread out against the kind of landscape, green and loosely wooded, always described by its acreage. Some of the buildings dated from the founding of the school, in the 1920s. They had soft red bricks and white pillars. But subsequent decades were also represented, and a dark glass structure, curiously angled and roofed, was still under scaffolding. It overlooked a wood, which fell away from the hillside; even from the road you could see across the tops of the trees the tops of the Boston skyline. We drove for several minutes to get our bearings. The place looked more like a college than a day-school, though a handful of students still boarded in the original clapboard mansion, gabled and dormered, that had occupied the land before the school moved in, and which was known as Founders. An extension had been built on at the back of it, which is also where the parking lot was. So we parked and got out and wondered where to go.

Kelly called her friend, who came to meet us. A bell rang somewhere, a proper church bell, clanging, and a few students emerged into the cold bright afternoon, carrying backpacks and trays of food. There were stone benches along some of the paths and circling some of the trees. Peter had landed a job at Beaumont Hill straight out of grad school and never taught anywhere else until they fired him twenty years later. At the time, he had lived among these scenes for almost half his life. The rest of the world seemed very far away. Kelly's friend, a slim southerner with a face roughened by acne scars, introduced himself to me and led us across several paths to one of the red-brick buildings where the cafeteria was. Bob Schiele, he said his name was, and the students who passed him called out *Schiely*. There was a dress code for most of them, which involved brown trousers and a green jacket, and a tie that depended on age and position in the school. Only the seniors could wear their own clothes, which made them stand out and also exaggerated their restless, intimate airs. I didn't have the sense that this was an unhappy place, but unhappiness is often difficult to spot, even in teenagers.

Bob had been at the school three years. He spoke sometimes too softly for me to hear him. His accent had the gentleness and gentlemanly ironies common to both certain gay men and privately educated southerners, and I couldn't decide at first which camp he belonged in. But he had once made a pass at Kelly in grad school, which went 'unreciprocated'; was married, to a venture capitalist who worked in Boston; and had a kid, a small boy, just six months old. All this came out in the first few minutes of conversation, while we were waiting in line at the faculty canteen. I had my daughter in my arms, but Kelly let her girl roam free among the Formica tables and metal-legged chairs. When Bob introduced us to his colleagues, who asked us what we were doing eating in the Holmes Hall Cafeteria on a Friday afternoon when we weren't contractually obliged to, Kelly said she was visiting Bob, and I said I used to teach at Horatio Alger and was trying to find out something about 'an old colleague of mine, who had once taught here.' By this point we were sitting around a round table. A handful of people had heard of Peter, a few of those remembered why they had heard of him, and one or two remembered the man himself.

'I suppose you're coming because of those books,' someone said. A fat-lipped old man with hanging cheeks and moles on his cheeks. 'Those novels.'

'Have you read any of them?'

'I picked one up out of curiosity. It may interest you to know, they had it on what's called the Beaumont table in the upper school library. Where they put books written by faculty and alums. But curiosity gets you only so far when you have as little time for spare reading as I do. Nothing much happens in them, isn't that right?'

'It seems to me quite a lot happens, incest, rape; a suicide. But I should tell you, I'm their editor. At least, I helped to get them published. It also depends which one we're talking about. They're quite different.'

'Yes, but you know what I mean. They're more about how people feel.'

'That sounds fair.'

'But you can't really know how people feel, can you? Especially real people and if they're dead.'

'What do you teach?'

'I should have told you, history. Also, a little economics.'

'Did you know Peter? How long have you been teaching here?'

'Sure, I knew Peter.'

'And did you like him?'

'Sure, I liked him. Didn't see any reason not to. Even when there turned out to be a reason, I still liked him. You don't stop liking people because of reasons.'

'Don't you?'

'I said, who knows what goes on behind closed doors. Also, don't have any illusions about these kids. They say all kinds of things. But this was not a popular opinion at the time. We were very sensitive to the issue, even before those priests made all this stuff public interest.'

'What was he like?'

'I thought you knew him. Very funny, when you could make him out, which wasn't all the time. A good colleague. Not somebody you got to know better or invited home, but somebody you didn't mind seeing in the hall coming your way.'

'Anything else?'

'Look, it's been a while. I once had a kid, a foreign kid, not a dumb kid, but couldn't write an essay to save his life. So I talk to his English teacher and Peter goes to work on him, and the kid does fine. Not great but fine. This is the kind of interaction we had together, but believe me, there are teachers out there who can turn even this kind of a discussion into a he said, she said.'

'Did he ever talk to you about his private life?'

'This is what I'm telling you. What do I care about people's private lives. All this scandal-mongering. Whenever I hear something like that, I think of what my mother used to say: unhappiness is mess.'

'Were there people who knew him better?'

'This is also not the kind of information I keep track of.'

I wasn't sure what I hoped to find out, but this conversation was representative. The people who still remembered him didn't remember him well. Mostly I wanted to get a sense of the life he had lived at Beaumont Hill, whether he had changed much by the time I knew him. One thing I learned: the school has some faculty accommodation on campus. These days it's restricted to teachers willing to take on pastoral responsibilities for the boarders, but while Peter was around, a few of the bachelors saved money by renting rooms in Founders and dining in Hall with the students. For most of his twenty years at Beaumont Hill, Peter occupied one of these 'suites' – a single room, large enough for a desk, attached to a private bathroom. If he wanted a shower he could use the communal showers. Twenty years was longer than usual but not unheard of. And part of the worry, part of the reason the school board reacted so harshly in the Feldman case, had to do with their nervousness about the possibilities entailed by this arrangement. Which also explained why the teachers' union failed to act in his defense.

There was only one woman at the table, who introduced herself to me as we waited by the kitchen doors to bus our trays. Another quiet talker, with soft red hair and not very much of it, and glasses. Beaumont Hill began hiring women a couple years before Peter left, and there was some controversy over it at the time. A few of the teachers made the women feel very uncomfortable. This lady wanted to tell me Peter wasn't one of them. She taught German and European literature; Medley was her married name, but she was born Katarina Wupperthal. One of the things she remembered about Peter was that he always called her Fräulein Wupperthal.

'I don't know if this is what you find interesting. It isn't very interesting, but it is what I remember.'

'Is there anything else?'

'Sometimes even then he discussed his writing.'

Katarina had a natural interest in children. She was one of those women who can't be around them without, for example, taking off her wristwatch and quietly setting it aside where they can reach it, then snatching it playfully from them until they ask her for it. This partly explains why she said little at lunch; she was amusing my daughter.

'That's interesting. He never discussed it with me.'

'Well, maybe I don't mean discussed. I didn't even know at the time he was writing anything, but I remember once he told me he had an idea for a story, or maybe it wasn't a story it was just an idea, *was man auf Deutsch ein Gedankenexperiment nennt.*' (She had heard me speaking German to my daughter.) 'I think you have the same word in English. A thought-experiment.'

We were sitting outside now, on the cold stone stairs leading down to the lawn where some of the seniors had taken their trays of food. My daughter, who likes steps of all kinds, was busy enough to let us finish this conversation in peace. There were leaves in the grass scattered loosely around the trees, in various colors, and my daughter had decided to place one leaf on top of each of the steps. But they kept blowing away. One of the students, who had noticed what she was trying to do, laughed at her; and she laughed back at him, much more loudly. She also began bringing him leaves.

'He had this idea of a doctor,' Katarina said, 'a family

doctor, someone who performs routine check-ups and physical examinations, who decides to tell a few of his patients, after these check-ups, that it is clear from the medical evidence that they are suffering really unusual amounts of pain. That nobody else suffers the way they are suffering and that they have simply become accustomed to it. He doesn't offer them any relief from this pain or go into any of the details. It was a part of Peter's idea that after this doctor tells his patients these things that none of them disagrees with him. That it more or less confirms what they had always suspected. At the same time, they don't expect any treatment or any relief and don't ask him any questions about the kind of pain they are suffering, which they take entirely on faith. And they leave his surgery feeling much better than they had before. I haven't read any of Peter's novels, because I take no pleasure from what is called contemporary literature, but when I heard he had published a book I remembered this conversation – maybe I had been complaining to him about my back, which sometimes gives me trouble, though the doctors can find nothing wrong. And I wondered if he had written about it in the book. Can you tell me if he did?'

'There may be something similar. But whether he used this specific story or not I would say it was very much in keeping with . . . the tone of the novels themselves.'

Afterwards, this conversation affected me more than it should have. I found it difficult to keep my mind on the necessary small talk while we sat on the steps and watched my daughter play. Kelly appeared behind us, with Bob in tow, carrying her own daughter, and Katarina had a class to teach and left us to prepare for it. We let the girls run around together, chasing leaves, and then I pushed myself up off my knees and chased the girls. It really was time to put them in the car and drive them to sleep, but Bob offered to get us into the room that Peter had lived in, or if not the same room exactly, something very much like it, and Kelly was sufficiently excited by the prospect and pleased with her friend's helpfulness that I couldn't refuse. So we went back to Founders and got a key from the secretary there, a big-permed woman with medical sunglasses she kept shifting on her nose. As it happens, one of the rooms was unoccupied, but she had no way of knowing if Mr Sullivan had lived in it or not.

'I suppose he was before your time,' I said.

'There's less that's before my time than you'd imagine. I've been here thirty years. I remember Mr Sullivan. I remember young Lee-Sung Feldman, too, if you want to know, who maybe wasn't the worst kid I ever saw come through Beaumont, but I can't think of anyone to beat him.'

'I didn't know his name was Lee-Sung.'

'I said to Mr Feldman once, before this whole thing blew up, what did you want to get a Korean kid for? If you're picking and choosing. It's not fair to the boy, to raise him like that, so he doesn't know what he is. But they figured that out eventually.'

'That's an ignorant thing to say,' Kelly said. 'I don't even know what you mean.'

But we took the keys from her and walked through the back door into a hallway that led to the main entrance. Founders, and the land around it, once belonged to a branch of the Holmes family, relatives of Oliver Wendell Holmes. The building still had something of the gloomy grandeur of a private wealthy residence, paneled walls and portraits in oil on the landings, combined with certain technological advances already out of date: a dirty air-conditioning unit propped inside one of the windows. Stippled false ceilings to hide the air vents. But the stairs still creaked underfoot. Kelly said, 'I don't know why I'm so excited, but I'm excited.' And she put her palms together so that you could hear them sticking lightly when she pulled them apart.

The room Bob let us into, on the second floor of the older wing of the house, overlooked the new parking lot at the back. Gray carpet on the floor; nails in the walls. It wasn't much bigger than my office at the Radcliffe. There was space for a single bed and a small desk and a chair, and a door to the bathroom, which was window-less and had a toilet in it and a kind of hip-bath squeezed between two walls. Probably carved out of the closet that used to be there. The place reminded me of the replica hut at Walden Pond, not more than fifteen minutes by car from Beaumont Hill, which had been built according to Thoreau's instructions in the book. I even said to Bob and Kelly, 'Self-sufficiency.' To live there for nearly twenty years and then be forced to leave. The window stood dir-ectly behind the bed but I don't know what it would have overlooked before the parking lot was poured in. Maybe a garden. Katarina's story was also on my mind, and it was hard not to imagine that the kind of pain Peter had in mind, in his case at least, was sexual in origin.

*

By this point the girls really were so tired we had to get them home. They fell asleep on the way, and Kelly and

I sat in the car outside her apartment for maybe half an hour, to let them nap. Talking about Peter but also other things. Her husband had filed a complaint against her, in the Probate and Family Court, to prevent her moving with the kids back to Austin. Most places had a presumption in favor of the right to relocate for the custodial parent but not the Commonwealth of Massachusetts. She had to show it was in the best interests of the children. It wasn't enough to say, my happiness is the best thing for them, even though it's what she believed.

'I *do* really believe it,' she said. 'I think I'd believe it even if it counted against me somehow. But it's hard to be sure of that.'

She didn't blame Kevin, she just hated arguing everything out in front of other people. And so far he'd been pretty honorable about certain facts he could mention that would help his case. Her lawyer said, You can't trust anybody when it comes to kids, especially not ex-husbands. But she didn't want to live like that, by suspicion. He said, Everybody uses everything they got.

'What kind of things?'

'Stupid things. I once slapped a child, not for any good reason, but because I was hardly thinking. Just because I'd had enough – of what, I don't know. The girl got over it in about a minute, but I cried by myself in a stall in the restroom for the whole of my lunch break and looked so red and ugly for the rest of the day I had to complain all the time about hay-fever and forgetting my pills. I was probably crying about other things, too. I'd had some trouble with this girl before, which really means that I'd had some trouble with her parents, and when the dad found out, he tried to get me suspended. The school didn't suspend me, but it's on my record. Then there's the fact that James has learning difficulties. He doesn't really, I don't believe in them, I know that's a stupid thing to say, but I don't. Still we registered him as attention deficit to get him into the school he's going to, which is a good school. And the court might want to know if the school he would go to in Austin is just as good, which it probably isn't. That kind of thing. But Kevin hasn't mentioned it, maybe because he's embarrassed.'

Part of the time we sat in silence, with the door resting open by its own weight, to let some air in. We could hear workmen working a few houses away and see a truck coming and going to the site, which was boarded up. Otherwise the street was quiet enough and almost unnaturally colorful, with leaves and parked cars and painted houses. When my daughter woke first, and woke Kelly's, I think we were both a little relieved that the spell of silence we were sitting in had been broken.

After Caroline came home (it was her turn to put the girl to bed), when I had a part of the evening to myself, I looked into the copy of *Walden* I had bought from the park store on our last visit to the lake. To find something consoling; this is how I put it to myself, thinking of Peter's narrow room. 'Most men appear never to have considered what a house is, and are actually though needlessly poor all their lives because they think they must have such a one as their neighbors have.' And: 'To have for the motto of my cabin those lines of Spenser which one of my visitors inscribed on a yellow walnut leaf for a card –

Arrivéd there, the little house they fill,

No look for entertainment where none was;
Rest is their feast, and all things at their will:
The noblest mind the best contentment has.'

There is plenty of this sort of thing in the book. I also looked over Peter's two published novels, to see if there was anything in them that resembled the story Katarina had told and which Peter had once brooded on. But the closest I came was a reference in *Imposture* to a tale about a doctor 'mysteriously in thrall to all the people he had inadvertently killed.'

*

Caroline and I had intended from the beginning to return to London for what she called 'the whole month of Christmas.' On the Tuesday before we left I got a call from Paul Gerschon at the Houghton Library. He said he had something to show me. Mrs Sullivan had entrusted him with several boxes of her son's old papers and books, which he had brought by taxi to the library to assess, and which were now sitting on his desk. Any time I liked I was welcome to come by. So the next morning I made my way through the carpeted internal corridors of the administrative offices, which even at that time of year felt oppressively air-conditioned, to Paul's door. He was looking over manuscript papers when I came in, blinking under the glare of his desk-lamp, and stood up rather slowly to take my hand.

'I get these head-rushes,' he said. 'Low blood pressure. It doesn't help that I slept not much last night. My son is teething. I said to my wife, at my age.'

'So what did you think of Mrs Sullivan?'

'I thought, it's wonderful the respect certain suspicious people feel for professional titles. I gave her my card and was in and out in fifteen minutes. Do you know how old she is?'

'I can guess.'

'Eighty-three, and still runs the place with some help from a cleaning woman. She told me all this herself in those fifteen minutes. Maybe suspicion is what keeps the brain alive. She also said, four or five different scholars have approached her about these papers. I liked the way she said scholar, as if it's one of the old professions, like priest or whore.'

'And you believed her?'

'I did not. She's trying to talk up the price.'

'Is there anything to talk up?'

'A few things, some of them more interesting to me than you. Peter had a first edition of Trelawny's *Recollections*, published by Edward Moxon in 1858. In fair condition; bookseller's notice tipped to front fly. Worth maybe a couple hundred dollars. Then there's Harriet Beecher Stowe's *Lady Byron Vindicated*. Another first edition, the English one – published by Sampson, Low, Son, and Marston. The binding's been repaired with brown paper, probably by him. It's not worth more than forty dollars, but Peter inscribed it and wrote the odd marginalia inside.' He began passing me books across the desk, and I took them from his soft hands and looked at them politely and afterwards couldn't think where to put them, so I put them on the floor by my chair. 'This is rather nice – the third canto of *Childe Harold*. Sadly rebound; a third edition, but from 1819. And my favorite of the lot: the war cantos of *Don Juan*, published by John Hunt in 1823 after Byron's famous split from Murray. In good condition it would fetch as much as five hundred dollars, and this is pretty fair.'

'Anything else?'

'Oh, just what you'd expect. Marchand's *Life*, in three volumes. Looks hardly touched. His *Portrait*, too, rather more dog-eared. The twelve-volume letters – actually, I think one or two are missing. *Byron and Greek Love*, by Louis Crompton. *My Dearest Augusta*, by Peter Gunn. Ethel Colburn Mayne's chatty little biography of Anna-bella. Grosskurth's silly book. A handsome deco edition of the poems, published by Bliss Sands & Co and originally priced at three and six.'

'I mean novels, other poets.'

'I haven't had a chance to go through everything yet. You mean, other than Byronalia. A few Penguin classics. *Cranford*, by Gaskell. A complete set of the *Waverley* nov-els, a show-piece edition, to look good on the shelf, but the bindings suggest he read them, too. Or somebody had. *The Heart of Mid-Lothian* is held together by rubber band. *Persuasion* and *Mansfield Park*. A dozen Jameses, from *The Aspern Papers* through to *The Wings of the Dove*. *David Copperfield*. *Moby Dick* – you know, the staple diet of a high-school English teacher. Many of these in the Norton school editions. *Twenty Years After*, by Dumas. Clough's *Amours de Voyage*. William Morris's *Defence of Guenevere*.'

'And nothing more modern?'

'It depends what you mean by modern,' Paul said, shift-ing boxes on his desk and putting his head in them. 'He owned a well-thumbed copy of *Goodbye to All That*.

Also, *The Bird of Dawning* by John Masefield. A few American things. *Goodbye, Columbus. The Adventures of Augie March.* Second or third editions, as if he read them in his youth. Nothing more recent than *A Girl in Winter*, by Larkin. No, I lie. I'm forgetting the O'Brian novels – you know, those sea-tales. A more or less complete set.'

By this point, there were books stacked like children's blocks on the desk and the empty chairs and on the floor.

'Not a terribly large collection,' Paul said. 'Just imagine them on the shelf – you wouldn't need but three or four. I would say, the collection of a book-lover who spent a great deal of his life moving between rented accommodations. A few favorite items mixed in with the necessaries. Did you ever see his place in New York?'

'No. I didn't know him particularly well. Sometimes we went for walks in the neighborhood – around the school. I heard from my old boss that maybe he lived in Washington Heights. A lot of the teachers did, since it's affordable and commutable to Riverdale.'

'His mailing address was somewhere in the one-eighties.'

'But this is not what you were looking at when I came in.'

'No.'

Paul stood up and moved delicately away from his desk, between the books.

'Why don't you sit down,' he said and began clearing off more space. There were a couple boxes of papers on the floor and he straightened the pile he'd been looking at and returned it to one of them. 'Excuse the mess. This is more or less how I live. I remember once going into the Strand bookstore with Peter, in New York. It was sunny when we went in and dark when we came out. For two or three hours we hardly said a word to each other, and didn't buy any books, either. A whole afternoon. Is this enough light for you? I'm used to reading in these little pockets of light.'

I edged around him, and we exchanged places. 'So what am I looking at,' I said.

'It depends what you want. His mother threw everything in together, but I've been busy rearranging. The bigger box holds drafts of the novels. In order, long hand. Not illegible, but a little crabbed. Arrows and clauses added between the lines. Sometimes he used an erasable pen – you can still see the rubber-shavings on the page. Sometimes Tipp-Ex. On those marbled composition notebooks you buy for school; he dated the pages occasionally, in the margins, when he sat down to write. The other box has a few stories and shorter pieces; also, what seem to be letters.'

'Letters people sent him?'

'Not that I can see, though I haven't made an inventory yet. From what I can tell, it's drafts of the letters he wrote, which he maybe typed up later when he was satisfied with them, to be sent off.'

'Who to? I didn't know he kept up correspondences.'

'Just look at them. This is the first part of the business that made me feel this is none of my business. But why don't I leave you alone for a minute, in peace. And you can judge for yourself.'

Paul left and for the next two hours I had his office to myself, until he tapped on the door again and put his head round and suggested we get some lunch. But until then everything was quiet, apart from the faint industrial breathing of the air-vents. You could think of the building itself as a kind of animal, with the motor left running, even in sleep. This isn't work I'm very good at. I haven't the patience for archives, or the curiosity. It seems to me that the bulk of what's interesting about a writer lies in the published material; there's a kind of perversity involved in digging up from the manuscript pages the half-dozen first intentions he later thought better of. Of course, in Peter's case, nothing was published until I published it, and maybe what I disliked was the idea that the versions we worked with were only provisional. Paul had left out copies of *Imposture* and *A Quiet Adjustment*, for comparison. I planted my elbow in the light of the desk lamp and lifted a marbled notebook from the box under his desk.

Turning the cardboard cover gave me my first little thrill. Peter had written down in block letters the word IMPOSTURE, and underneath it, this line: 'The opening and closing of Henry Colburn's large, red front door had produced in the course of the morning, as if by force of suction, a bright eddy of human traffic.' There was a date, written in red pen, which suggests it had been added later: *June 6th, 1983. Beaumont Hill.* The beginning of his summer holidays; Peter was forty. The school campus, on its fifty acres, would have been empty of everyone but a handful of janitors and administrators, and the odd live-in teacher with nowhere else to go. I thought of the desk in the room at Founders, which may or may not have been his desk, just as it might have been his room, pushed up against the bed so that if you were sitting down to write you could turn your head to look out the window. From that angle you'd likely see the back extension of the house. The paper he wrote on, frail to begin with and now curled slightly at the edges, had retained the Braille-like impressions of his pen – you could run your fingers over the lines and feel the words.

In my parents' house in Texas, in my old bedroom, there is still a box of legal pads that my father brought home for me to write on, and which are covered in poems and stories. Also, drafts of plays, few of them completed; ideas for poems and stories, and sometimes several versions of the same thing, written out fair or messy depending on the draft. Not a box exactly, but a seaman's chest, ribbed with wood and covered in pressed tin, which my father himself bought for me at an antique market and spent a month on, taking a piece of steel wool to the rust. My bedroom window overlooks the courtyard and sometimes I would sit on my bed and write while he was outside, not ten feet away, rubbing his hands raw against the rust. He had in mind already that I would keep my manuscripts in it, which I found flattering, as an indication of how seriously he took my schoolboy scribblings. It also suggested to me the idea that these are things to be preciously stored because no one will read them. The memory of that summer was very strong in me as I glanced through Peter's notebooks, and I felt again as I had not in years the atmospheric pressure of a writer's ambitions, 'like ten feet of cold water' on top of your head. Such pent-up, concentrated loneliness.

There was another date at the end of another book ('his arm stretched forth, his gesture expanding into an embrace.'), under which he had written the word *FINIS* and *December 29, 1985* – a week into his Christmas holidays, and a year and a half after he first put pen to page.

After an hour or so I shifted my attention to the second

box. There were five or six folders of loose-leaf paper – not just paper, but receipts with something scrawled on them, paper napkins, train tickets, torn-out pages of books. Several containing nothing more than a single phrase or observation. For example: *Greater and greater happiness, which like a small tea stain in wash after wash becomes more general.* Or, *Softly as spiders, descends.* The folders were labeled by content (ADMIN, MISCELLANEOUS WRITING, NOTES, LETTERS, etc.) and had on them the branch and leaf insignia of Harvard College Library; they belonged clearly to Gerschon's efforts at 'rearrangement.' I found a few stories and a few poems, as Paul had said, but I wanted to look at the letters, and this is the first one I came to:

Peter Sullivan
Beaumont Hill School

23rd of March, 1986

Dear Sir or Madam,
I am an upper-school English master at the Beaumont Hill School, a preparatory academy located in one of the wealthier suburbs of Boston. You may have heard of it. Several of our students have gone on to make names for themselves in various fields, and we boast also our share of famous parents. The school is very well-respected, both within the teaching community, and outside it; it is the kind of institution on which others model themselves.

For almost twenty years I have taught at this school and struggled against the declining interest my students show, not only in literature generally, but especially in the fields of poetry, and in whatever else strikes them as old-fashioned or out of date – a category that includes, of course, most of what we would call the classics of Western civilization. It occurred to me some time ago that what I needed, to bring these classics to life, is a story that would allow my students to treat the authors of these works as characters in their own right, and to appreciate the act of composition itself as a dramatic act.

If you want something done, there's nothing like doing it yourself. I have now written such a story, which touches on the life, not only of one of the most famous poets of his age, Lord Byron, but on scenes of composition which have themselves become a part of literary history. I am referring to the famous summer in which *Frankenstein* was written, by a nineteen-year-old girl intoxicated by the company of two great poets. This book, or novel, which I have called *Imposture*, would serve as a very useful commentary to any class on Romantic poetry, whether it was taught at the high-school or collegiate level.

I confess to knowing nothing about the business of publishing, but one thing I do know something about is the business of teaching. If a school like Beaumont Hill can be persuaded to adopt such a novel as one of its set texts, others would follow suit; and the sales possibilities among high schools alone would more than justify the expense of publication. I do not know if it is customary or not to send publishers unsolicited manuscripts in their entirety, but this is what

I have done. My novel is enclosed, and I look forward to hearing your response to it.

Yours sincerely,
Peter Sullivan

I leafed through the rest of the folder. There wasn't a single private letter in it; all of them seemed to begin Dear Sir or Madam. I had the impression of one of those after-school tasks assigned for the punishment of misbehaving kids. Copy down a hundred times the following words. Sometimes he mentioned recently published novels that had made the best-seller lists and seemed to him to bear some resemblance to his own. Mostly potboilers, from what I could tell, with titles like *Mistral's Daughter* or *The Sands of Time*. Sometimes he mentioned the name of a parent or colleague who had recommended him to a particular editor or house, because he or it 'would make a good fit for the kind of work I am doing, and I'm told it's important, right from the start of a career, to establish a relationship with a publisher sympathetic to your literary ambitions.' And so on.

There was another folder of materials, which Gerschon hadn't labeled yet, but just at that moment he knocked at the door and I didn't get a chance to look at them till after Christmas. I asked him if there was a Xerox nearby, and he let me photocopy a few pages, including the letter I have just quoted in full. 'Against the grain of my conscience,' he said. By rights they all belonged to Mrs Sullivan.

'Why Byron?' I asked him, on the way to lunch. 'And *only* Byron – he didn't write about anything else. You're probably the wrong person to talk to about this, but three novels looks a little like a fixation.'

'I've been thinking about that. Maybe for someone like Peter, who lived the way Peter lived, there was something about Byron, and the way *he* lived, that he couldn't get out of his head.'

'Did Peter ever talk to you about his writing?'

'No,' he said.

'Did he ever show you anything he had written?'

'No.'

'Did he ever show *anybody* anything he had written? I mean, someone he knew, who knew him, who wasn't a dear Sir or Madam.'

'They hardly look like the pleadings of a great writer, do they,' Peter said. 'Though maybe great men plead no better than anybody else.' Later, when the food arrived, he came back to this question. 'Maybe Lee Feldman, is what I wondered. Maybe he showed something to Lee Feldman. All of that business took place a couple of years after he finished *Imposture*. But nobody that I know of at the Byron Society, which would have been a natural starting point for friendly reactions, ever heard about his writing till you published it.'

'Why didn't he talk about it with you?'

'Let me ask you the same question,' he said. Then: 'I don't know. You look at these letters, and maybe you get a feeling for why. The same feeling you get reading them: embarrassment. I suppose writers have to sell themselves like anyone else; but not like that. As if he didn't trust anyone, or thought they were all idiots. But he only comes across as desperate himself, or completely out of touch, which amounts to the same thing. What are you smiling at?'

'Just that I used to write such letters myself.'

For fifteen months I lived in the basement of that Hampstead house and went quietly crazy. The only room with any natural light was the bedroom, so I put a desk in there, which meant that my commute to work in the morning was all of four and a half feet. I used to take a walk first thing just to get myself out of the house. On one of these walks, on a turning off the High Street, I discovered a charity second-hand shop with a steady supply of suits and dress shirts for six-foot-six men. Over time I acquired a closet full of these suits. (Not that they fit me – the guy shedding them was six inches bigger in the chest.) I bought ties, too, and spent a few minutes each morning picking out combinations of jacket, shirt and tie before sitting down to write.

It wasn't only in the mornings that I looked out for Caroline, hurrying to catch her bus. My desk was pushed under the window that gave onto the front stairwell. In the mornings, she never saw me, but coming home she faced the other way and sometimes glanced down 'just to see if I was really working,' as she said to me once, in her kitchen, while I was picking laundry off the radiators. Around six o'clock each day I became conscious of the fact that she might come home any minute and looked up occasionally into the last of the daylight to check. I wanted her to see me writing; the thought of her kept me going longer than I otherwise might have. Sometimes she waved, and once, after forgetting her key, she came down to use the back stairway, which gave me the chance of inviting her in to tea. I didn't mind being seen in jacket and tie at my desk, but sitting across from her at the kitchen table turned out to be different – a fact that struck me when I brought in the tea. I looked ridiculous; worse, I looked unhappy. '*Very* smart' was all that Caroline said.

From time to time, in the throes of some urgent feeling that might have been optimism or desperation, I took an afternoon off from my other 'work' to write letters – to agents and publishers and magazine editors. I had one of those books that list them. A soft-bound volume, thick as the yellow pages, with bright red lettering on the front and on the back stories of advances paid. After only three months, etc. So I wrote letters. Dear Sir or Madam, the whole business. I am a young American writer living in London. My first novel is about. I am writing to you because. In your last issue, I noticed a story, which I liked very much. It suggested to me that you might be the right . . . A few years ago you published a book. My own first novel. I have written a short story. Whether I could interest you in a poem or not. I don't know if you accept unsolicited submissions. A good friend of mine suggested I get in touch. Recommended you to me. Me to you. I am just at the stage where I am beginning to consider.

Every line of these letters was equally unnatural and dishonest, and I disliked myself for writing them and resented the need to. Though I never wrote anything as bad as Peter Sullivan. And there was no need to, because nothing ever came of them. Except rejections, which I kept in a shoebox under my bed, since even this contact with the literary world seemed better than nothing.

Maybe I would have given up if I hadn't come home one day from one of my walks and seen Caroline through the bedroom window, reading, licking her thumb and turning over the pages at my desk. I sat on the stairwell for two or three minutes watching her and then climbed up the stairs again to continue my walk. When I came back again, she was gone, and two weeks passed before she brought up the subject of my writing. I remember that for most of that time it struck me as some kind of dirty secret, which Caroline had stumbled upon but was too embarrassed to mention. It was a real relief to me when she did, and relief led to other things, but if Peter ever had any personal response to what seems to me the clearest and best expression of his character, I don't know.

A few days after my lunch with Gerschon, Caroline and I returned to her parents' house in London, which is the house she grew up in and where we had also fallen in love; and I didn't get back to Cambridge or Peter until the new year.

Behold Him Freshman!

I heard of her marriage from my mother, who seemed to take in the news that particular form of delight which is sometimes called sympathy. We were having tea at the Pigots. Since Kitty was occupied, in conversation with Mrs Pigot, I had retired to my chair by the window to read. Elizabeth and John were on the floor in front of the empty fireplace, tempting the dog with bones. But I was listening to my mother. I heard her say, 'That puts me in mind of something, I must tell Byron.'

Then she called over to me, 'Byron, I have some news for you.'

I said, 'Well, what is it?'

'Take out your handkerchief first, for you will want it.'

'Nonsense,' said Mrs Pigot, 'he isn't a boy.'

'You will see.' Then, more loudly: 'Mary Chaworth is married.'

'Is that all?' I said.

'To Mr Musters. I received a letter this morning from her aunt, Mrs Norris. What are you reading? I thought you would be more affected.'

In fact, it surprised me to suffer so little at the news – *Miss Chaworth married*. But I was then busy with preparations for entering upon college life. Our sentiments are not exhaustless, and divided amongst so many objects, they appear weak and colourless, and we begin to suspect ourselves of indifference. At least, this is what my mother accused me of, as I gave her my arm and we walked the short distance home.

She said, 'I preferred your childishness. These modest, patient airs become you very ill.'

All this to provoke me. She dreaded my going as much as I longed for it, and by a dozen little stratagems each day attempted to incite in me a violence of reaction to equal her own.

'I like what you call airs,' I said. 'You mean, I suppose, that you cannot reduce me to tears, as you used to.'

'You take everything coolly. For my part, I have ceased to take offence at it, but I thought Miss Chaworth would bring the blood to your cheeks.'

The next day, Elizabeth had engaged me to tea, and as the weather was fine we sat in their garden afterwards with books on our laps and read or pretended to read. The clouds in the sky were broken up into little pieces of clouds – it had been dry all week, and the earth had a contracted late summery look, so that even the lawn had need of a feather-duster.

After a silence of no great duration, Elizabeth said, 'I feel I must require you to write to me, and you must protest, in great earnestness, the impossibility of your neglecting me.'

'You think I will not.'

'I think you will find a great deal to amuse and distract you.'

At the bottom of the garden was a low stone wall, and on the other side of it, a field with sheep grazing. Beyond the sheep, a farmhouse made up of the same dry grey stone as the wall, and beyond the farmhouse the hills rose mildly to the heavens, and towards Annesley.

'I will not pretend any reluctance to leave Southwell, but I have no great desire to go to Cambridge.'

'This is because you may do as you please. So nothing pleases you.'

We continued to read, and the shade of the cherry tree, leaning across the bench, moved slowly across our faces. 'Now, this *will* please you,' she said after a minute and holding her book at arm's length, out of the glare of the sun. 'This more or less fits the case:

> Scenes of woe and scenes of pleasure
> Scenes that former thoughts renew,
> Scenes of woe and scenes of pleasure
> Now a sad and last adieu!'

She is a handsome girl, with a pleasant voice, but when she recites there is something that enters her face and gives her a very unnatural and insistent air. But I replied, 'No, do not say last. You do not mean to raise my hopes in this fashion.'

'I believe your mother is right. You have become very unfeeling. I thought you more soft-hearted, but you are spoiled by London women. They have taught you to be tender and cold.'

I took the book from her and opened it to the frontispiece: Robert Burns. Then, as I had a pencil in hand, I wrote something beneath his name and returned the volume to Elizabeth, saying, 'Perhaps that will satisfy you of my feelings,' and she looked at it closely and held it away again, and read back to me in the same loud voice:

Now no more, the hours beguiling,
Former favourite haunts I see,
Now no more my Mary smiling,
Makes ye seem a heaven to me.

'A very pretty sentiment,' she said, after a suitable pause, 'though I must confess, I did not believe till this moment you could feel so little for Miss Mary Chaworth as you have pretended to feel. But I believe you now.'

We parted soon afterwards, amicably enough; and a few days later, I sat on the London coach and looked out the window as it drove along King Street, having taken leave of my mother half an hour before – sitting on the steps, with her face in her hands. Consequently, I was much surprised to see her again through an opened door at Mrs Crawley's, the pastry-cook. She was waiting her turn and spoke to no one and I felt almost sorry for her.

* * *

After a month in London at Mrs Massingberd's, I went up to Cambridge. There was at first a slight difficulty about the rooms. The porter, having mistaken me for a commoner named Brown, sent me to the wrong stairwell, and I went up and down it a good quarter-hour, on a foot already sore from confinement, without finding my name above any of the doors. It was by this point nearly four o'clock in the afternoon – the sun rapidly descending over the college roof – damp rising between cold stones. For a minute I thought of going to an inn, but I found the porter again and was gratified by my display of temper, and he directed me at last to a very pleasant room off a stairwell wide enough for a coach and six. His name, the porter's I mean, is Cummings, and I think he shall remember me hereafter.

The next morning at chapel I met this Brown. He is short and freckled, with a reddish, chafed complexion. He had heard of Cummings' error and was rather pleased by it. He said to me, 'It is odd that our acquaintance should be launched in this fashion.' But I don't mean to confine my acquaintance to the sons of lawyers from Chorley. No one of any distinction, in name or appearance, rose early enough for chapel. I said to myself, this is the Southwell spirit; you must cure yourself of it.

My first task is to fit up my rooms, which are large and bright but unfortunately situated. On one side there is my tutor, and on the other an old Fellow of the college; he came out to see me directing the joiner, who was building a cabinet and two seats against the angle of the bay. The cabinet is for books. He said to me, 'You are tall enough, come here,' and led me into his room, where there was a small fire and a small rug in front of it. Then he invited me to a glass of 'right sherries', which stood warming on the hearth-stone. 'Do you know Henry Mortlock?' he asked. 'Do you know Frederick Toms? Do you know Richard Willoughby?' He had been at Harrow thirty years before, but I told him all the old masters have gone.

'No, I have got the names wrong,' he said, 'otherwise you would know them.'

Later, he knocked on my door with a knife in his hand. The window to his room had been painted shut; he could not reach the top edge. So I stood upon one of his chairs, while he fretted at my side, and scraped away until the window fell open.

The tutor I met on my way out. He introduced himself first to my servant, who introduced him to me. His name is Jones. His hand was damp when I shook it, and he called me 'milord'.

'I don't suppose we shall see you at any of the lectures,' he said and walked with me as far as the college gate.

'I wished really to go to Oxford,' I confided in him. 'But there were no rooms at Christ Church.'

'You may find your life here rather lonely in comparison. To school, I mean.'

'But at least I have escaped my mother.'

'I suppose your schoolmates are mostly at Christ Church.'

'Lord Clare. Delawarr. William Harkness.'

'Are there none at Trinity?'

'One or two.'

I saw him again at supper, which I ate in Hall, appearing for the first time in my state robes. The effect was superb, but uncomfortable to my diffidence. It seems I am the only nobleman admitted to the college this term. The result has been a flock of invitations, fluttering and vying for space upon my table. I have written to Hanson, who *dispenses* my inheritance, and requested him to order me down four dozen of wine – port, sherry, claret and Madeira, so that I may return in kind each *geste* of hospitality. The joiner's work is finished, and most of my furniture has arrived. In short, I begin to like a college life extremely. The wine was sent, and I am drunk most nights on retiring to bed, which is rarely before two or three in the morning. Meanwhile, I have brought and bought a great many books and read none of them.

The great question has been to determine in which set I hope to establish myself. William Bankes likes to say that one needs the shelter of a *reputation*. I think he is right – and Bankes at least 'recks his own rede' and has fashioned for himself the largest reputation in college. For his rooms, which are located not five minutes from my own, he has imported two high-backed, oak-carved pews from the chapel at Kingston Lacy, his father's seat, and positioned them on opposing walls. Against the chimney-breast hangs a replica of Christ crucified, from the Lady of Martyrs in Shelford – which he paid a carver's apprentice two pounds for, and painted himself. On Sunday afternoons, which is when I first visited him, he hires a 'moiety' of the college choir to serenade him, and we dined (there were a few others besides) on claret and stewed quail while the boys hallelujahed round us.

His taste in clothes is equally striking. He complains even on mild November afternoons of the cold and drapes across his shoulders a sort of table-cloth, of orient hues. But for all that, he is sensible and widely read, and guilty of nothing worse so far as I can tell than an appetite for feeding suspicion. The old Fellow across the hall once asked me, 'What the devil does he do with those singing boys?'

To which I had the quickness to reply, 'Gives them supper,' which amused him perhaps rather more than it ought. Later I heard him humming, as he made his slow way along the stairs,

Little Tommy Tucker
Sings for his supper;
What shall we give him?
White bread and butter.

How shall he cut it
Without a knife?
How will he be married
Without a wife?

They call this place the University, but any other appellation would have suited it much better, for study is the last pursuit of the society. The master eats, drinks and sleeps, the Fellows drink, dispute and pun, and the employments of the undergraduates are more easily conjectured than described. I have only supped at home three times since my arrival, and my table is constantly covered with invitations – though I am the most steady man in college, as Bankes himself admits. There is nothing to vex me but money-troubles, though these are vexing enough.

I have had a letter from Hanson, who complains of the *rate* of my expenditure. He does not understand what is expected of a man of rank. I wrote him an angry letter in return. Bankes refers to him as 'the solicitor' and thinks the whole exchange contemptible (I have shown him some of the letters), a sentiment I heartily agree with; yet somehow I cannot leave off. Hanson's interference has at least the advantage of keeping my mother at bay, for she depends upon him as a proxy. I have explained to him that we are now totally separated. The instant I hear of her arrival in Trinity, I will quit Cambridge, though rustication or expulsion be the consequence. She fears I have got into the hands of the money-lenders. Not yet; but Mrs Massingberd has promised to stand as guarantor, with a Jew of her acquaintance. Denied by a parent, I am forced to seek refuge with strangers.

A part of these first few weeks, when I was not dining out, I have passed with Edward Long, whom I knew at school. He was a great favourite at Harrow among the masters, and perhaps this prejudiced me against him. But here he is very unhappy and I like him more. When the weather is clear, we ride out towards the weir above Grantchester, and on one sunshiny day stripped and swam. Then lay on the bank sunning, and afterwards threw eggs and coins into the water and dived after them. He said to me, as we cantered home again, sober and cold, and head-achey from the cold, that he felt himself to be a very innocent young man.

I was rather puzzled for a reply, but he went on, 'Indeed, I envy you the freedom of your manner with William Bankes.'

'The freedoms and manner,' I said, 'are all his own. *He* talks, and we listen. But he is not so particular or strange as he first appears. And the rest of his set are good-natured enough: Rhodes and Milnes; MacNamara, Price and Gally Knight. When I am there, I never think twice about how we pass the time. It passes.'

'I assure you, there is nothing I dislike more than my own silence.'

'Oh, you talk well enough, when you wish.'

In the evenings Long sits sometimes in my rooms, with his 'cello on his knee, and plays. It gives me a kind of satisfaction to feel his music drifting through my window and across the college. Several hours might be wasted in this manner, while I revolve rhymes about my head and write some of them down. His face as he addresses the bow is almost as good as a painter's model, for it hardly moves. What with downcast eyes, concentrated lip, and fair cast of skin (which has never yet known the need of a razor), it serves me very well for any number of Carolines, Emmas and Marys.

Bankes, as it happens, expressed great interest in my 'old friend' and invited him to play in his rooms. But the experiment was not a success. The piece he had chosen, a cantata by Scarlatti, ran on tediously. Long felt this but having begun it could not bring himself to stop. Afterwards he made his excuses and retired very soberly at half past midnight, carrying his instrument awkwardly in hand and pushing his way out.

*

Bankes is the kind of man of whom stories are told. Sometimes he tells them himself. For example, once at Gronow's, gaming late into the night, he emerged at last with twenty guineas in coin and a single opera ticket. Dawn had dawned, but he was engaged to MacNamara's for breakfast and never likes to miss an engagement. At MacNamara's they ate eggs and fish and drank champagne, from ten in the morning until four in the afternoon, by which point he was perfectly steady, so long as Price held him up. At six o'clock he dined with his father, where they finished three bottles of claret between them, and ate roast mutton, and afterwards he went alone to the theatre with his ticket. There was no one he knew in the box, and as it was completely full, no space to fall down in, either.

His neighbours were all of them a little surprised to find him in their midst, having expected his companion of the night before, whose name he had forgotten. It so happens that at that time, which was shortly after the riots outside the Old Elizabeth, the theatre had stationed guards along the upper corridors, each with a musket, a high beaver hat, and a chair to sit in. There appeared to Bankes, as Lady Wishfort says, 'nothing more alluring than a couch' – separated as these were from the stalls by a thick curtain. After the first act he stood up and offered to exchange places with the guard outside his box, who agreed, for some portion of the twenty guineas he had won earlier in the day; so Bankes put on his hat and tucked the musket under his arm and fell asleep.

It may have been Price or Gally Knight who added something about the other terms of the exchange and the advantages of the little curtain. Bankes does not encourage such remarks but is never embarrassed by them. Among the choir-boys employed by him to 'lengthen our afternoons' are several who have become friendly with their *pastor*; they visit his rooms, even when they are not paid to. Boys of thirteen or fifteen, accustomed in their domestic lives to scenes of squalor and desolation, find amongst our friends a great deal to flatter and tempt them. They are given to eat and to drink and Bankes also has a passion for dressing some of the fairer specimens 'with as much modesty as cunning' – that is, very little of either. There is something in these exhibitions I dislike, a kind of forced good humour, but among the odd consequences of these odd displays is that they awake in me strong sympathies for the boys in question.

There is one in particular who has, with real modesty

and cunning, thus far resisted every attempt to *beautify* him, but continues to receive his 'Sunday fee' for singing in the little chapel. It was his voice that first attracted my notice, but his countenance fixed it. He is very fair, almost painfully so, and dark-eyed, and slight; and says little or nothing. When he *does* speak, it is almost impossible to hear him. Like certain birds, he must sing to be heard. His name is Edleston, and he is an orphan and lives in the low stone almost windowless house at the back of St Nicholas. I flatter myself that he makes some distinction between the interest I take in him, and that of Bankes, Price et al., for he continues to come each Sunday and, I have been told, takes his leave very early if he finds me absent.

*

Christmas I spent in London at Mrs Massingberd's. But even to London the influence of William Bankes extends, or rather, I should say, of Skinner Matthews, another of his set. Matthews has a passion for 'the fancy', and through him I have become acquainted with that class of idler to be found most mornings at number 13 Bond Street, in the rooms of Henry Angelo and 'Gentleman' Jackson. I have vowed to become *less* than I was, and to this end waste an hour of each day in sparring and fencing, under their tutelage, in the hope of being wasted away in turn.

Matthews is a very remarkable man, and a sceptic, but a principled upright character, nonetheless, in his narrow sphere. He has put me in the orbit of a famous French 'entremetteuse', who assists young gentlemen in their youthful pastimes. Something lately occurred in her line of business a little out of the ordinary, and when Matthews declined it, the refusal was offered to me. She sent me a letter couched in such English as a short residence of sixteen years in England has enabled her to acquire. But there was a postscript, which contained these words: – 'Remember, Milor, that *delicaci ensure everi succes.*' It appears the Regent had taken an interest, and was known to be jealous.

The object in question was a pretty Portuguese creature, not more than fourteen years of age. She is the daughter of a mussulman merchant, who had embarked with his family at Lisbon and escaped the French blockade only to be overtaken outside Gibraltar by pirates. These shot away one of the masts, killing meanwhile the captain and first lieutenant etc., and a few dozen sailors and passengers, including the girl's father, mother and brother, before storming the ship and driving her on to Tangier. The girl herself was largely unhurt except for a few splinters in her ankles and thighs. But the wounds became infected, gangrene set in, and the ship's surgeon was forced to amputate both legs above the knee. She survived otherwise unblemished and was eventually sold on to a trader making his way to Marrakesh.

A few months later she found herself in London under the stewardship of Madame DuReine. Madame presented her to me with an air of secrets penetrated, at the top of a narrow house, under the eaves, one wet low foggy January evening, with the damask curtains drawn – across the windows, across the four-poster bed – from which the maiden in question could do no more than sit up. The loss of her legs gave her an air of sweet dependency; she takes, at least, no *other* exercise. Her complexion is very pale, for a mussulwoman – that is, the shadow of pale, but her eyes are large and shining. And she is light enough to be lifted in one hand.

But such amusements cost money, especially if they are to be repeated. Since then I have confined my promiscuities to one of the actresses at Covent Garden, whose part is very small, and who visits me sometimes between the acts. Elizabeth complains of my neglect. It may be, indeed, when even the *conversions* of the Jews dry up, that I shall be forced to make a brief return to Southwell. But I had rather go back to college. And there are reasons besides my mother for keeping out of Southwell. On my last visit, I was deemed by several brothers to have been guilty of an advance, or several advances. And I mean to commemorate a few of these maidens in humble verse, to be privately printed by Ridge of Newark and circulated among friends. I have begun to sleep very poorly alone, and when I sleeps not, I scribbles.

*

In Cambridge, the weather improves, and Long and I have returned to the weir above Grantchester – on horseback only, though we speak of resuming our more strenuous exercises soon. He is becoming less unhappy; that is, he grows *lecturous*. He says that he does not think *me* happy and deprecates my association with William Bankes. Long's father knows Bankes *père* and says he is the kind of man of whom it is remarked, on a very slight acquaintance, what a good fellow he is, I should like to know more of him; and then one begins to wonder why he has not more friends.

'Bankes has a great many friends. I am only too conscious of how slight my claims to his attention are.'

We were sitting on the mossy roots of a willow, to which our horses were tethered, and smoking damply. The trees reflected in the water were mere sketches of trees, between blottings of clouds. An early March day. We were both cold, though I was conscious also of a strange reluctance to stand up and go.

'What claims has he on yours, I should like to know. There are stories told about him which do not bear repeating.'

'My dear Long, I am not so innocent as you believe. There is something very flattering in your concern. It supposes me to be what I am not and what I never was.'

'You are not so difficult to know as you would perhaps wish.'

But then, he has got in with the clerical set, which includes Hodgson and Burton-Smith. They attend Widmore's lecture on Church history and meet afterwards at the Crowne. His shelves are filled with volumes of Canon Ryman's *Reflections and Interpretations,* and when he brings his 'cello to my rooms, as he continues to do, he plays Purcell's fantasias or something from Croft's *Musica Sacra.* I believe his new friends discourage these visits, but Hodgson is not a bad sort and has besides this great inducement to sociability – he is short of cash.

I have been forced again to apply to Mrs Massingberd. Augusta refused to stand as security for another Jew-debt, and, which was worse, alerted Hanson to my predicament. It seems as easy to renounce a sister (whom, after all, one has hardly known) as disown a mother. Mrs Massingberd is more persuadable. It is a great vice to think about money at all, but without it, one thinks of nothing but money. A subscription was put round for a statue of Pitt, who was a frequent visitor of the college and died early this year. Hanson has said to me (several others have remarked the same) that they expect my true calling to be oratory. I gave some thirty pounds. It has also been necessary for me to maintain a carriage. Finding nothing that would satisfy, I went to the expense of having one built.

Bankes begins to quiz me about Edleston. It is perhaps his greatest vice that he interprets everything in the light of his own character. The truth is that I do not entirely disagree with Long. A few of his *Sunday* boys have become through his influence habitual drunks; one of them was even barred from chapel. Since he lived on the parish, this child (for he is little better than a child) has forfeited not only his position in the choir but his dwelling-place also. Edleston tells me it is not known where or how he lives. But Edleston himself, who has a great horror of drawing attention, is sober and modest and chaste. It is for his sake that I have bought the carriage, as he dislikes the *show* of appearing publicly with me. In this way we travel freely unobserved.

*

A few weeks ago, I took Edleston to the weir above Grantchester, where we swam from its banks. Or rather, I swam while he watched me, clutching his arms together – in spite of the warm May morning, full of motes and sunshine. I stripped and dived in and lay with my head on the water, but Edleston grew cold even before I did and wished to return to the carriage – a half-mile tramp through wet grass.

His father, who was in trade, died a few years before; his mother he never knew. There is a sister, too, a few years his elder, from whom he has jealously kept me. Perhaps they have other relations, but none has claimed them. Since his father's death, he has 'sung in the choir and made his bed' in the orphanage – he knows no persons of influence but Reverend Broughton and Mrs Carmichael, who runs the priory school. From them he has learned manners and a little Latin. His sister dislikes Mr Bankes, or dislikes his visiting him, which amounts to the same thing; but he has never before had a penny to call his own, and Mr Bankes is generous. Each Sunday he tells himself to keep away but cannot.

He was born almost to the day two years before me, a fact which affords us some astonishment and much pleasure; but he might from the look of him be three or four years my junior.

Bankes, as I say, quizzes me a great deal about him, and not only Bankes but Matthews, too. They talk of the Method and call me a very pious Methodist. But Edleston's modesty is infectious and, for his sake, I feel everything I ought. He dislikes my connections with women, even of the theatre. Between Long and Edleston I keep to a very narrow path, but in London I am free to do as I please, and a great deal pleases me. Then when I am sick of self and love return to Cambridge. But my money has run out, and there is nothing for it but a summer in Southwell to replenish the supply. I am almost glad of it. Edleston alone ties me to Cambridge, and sometimes he strikes me as a very good reason for going.

Several days I put off telling him, and then I could not put it off any longer. He had come to my room after chapel when I was still in bed. He sat at the head of it, as he sometimes did, and I said, 'I am glad you have come today, for I mean to go to Southwell tomorrow, to see my mother.' Adding, after a minute: 'The truth is, I am rather dipped at the moment and hope to persuade her to raise a loan on my behalf. Come here; you needn't take fright so.'

But he had retreated to a chair, somewhat encumbered with old clothes.

'I don't see why you should mind me,' he said.

'You know very well why I do.' I dislike this sort of talk, and being obliged to declare what everybody knows. Sitting in bed in this way made me feel foolish, so I began to dress in front of him.

'You have made a great change in my life,' he said. 'I am grateful for it.'

'I hope you are more than grateful, and less, too.'

'But you don't know what my life here is like without you. Since you don't like to know, I don't tell you.'

'I know well enough; you tell me often enough.'

But he can never keep angry at me long, and we parted for the morning on very good terms, only a little more tenderly and carefully than usual. In the afternoon, we rode out to Grantchester and bathed, diving for eggs, plates, shillings in the weir. There is at a corner in the Cam, about ten or twenty feet submerged, the root of an old tree, to which Long and I make a game of clinging; but as Edleston knew nothing of it, I dived down with a breast full of air and counted to a hundred, looking up all the time into the green sunshiny water to see if he would follow me. When I could breathe no longer I floated up. He was

197

sitting at the edge of the river, with his legs under him and his arms crossed. When he saw me he gave a shout and turned away; and when I had got my own breath back, I joined him on the bank. We lay like that, drying and warming ourselves in the sunshine.

In the morning Edleston met me very early at the door of my room. He could not be sure when I was leaving and had suffered from an anxious night at the thought of missing me. In his hand he held a little box and in the box, which he offered me at once (for he had a horror of farewells), was a little cornelian, attached to a ring, the stone itself no bigger than a suskin.

'It is very small,' he said. 'I am only sorry it is so small.'

'This matters to me not at all, except as I am more likely to lose it.'

'I wanted to give you something in remembrance. I like to think that, poor as my company is, it has kept you out of worse.'

'My dear child,' I said, much moved, 'you are only too good. You are everything I once was and am not. You keep me up to the mark. But this is all nonsense; it is only a month or two. I will see you very soon.'

It is a three-day journey to Southwell, and I spent the first day in a sort of fever of feeling, which could only be relieved by composition.

*

I arrived about four o'clock of a July afternoon. Mrs Pigot was taking tea at Burgage Manor, which I was grateful for as it put Kitty on her good behaviour. She welcomed me with one of her smiles – she does not know herself how ugly they make her. I sat down to a fresh pot and buttered bread. These were brought to me in the drawing room, a pretty enough room when the sun is out (which it was), with a view of the Green – and of my carriage in the road, and the groom attending the horses, and my valet staggering under the weight of my box. Presently he was heard on the stairs; then he showed his head in the doorway, a little breathlessly, and asked where to dispose of it.

'John is at home,' Mrs Pigot said, when he was gone. 'He is back from Edinburgh; I should think he will be very pleased to see you.'

'What have you been talking about?' I said. 'You have an interrupted air.'

'Our prodigal sons,' Kitty said.

But Mrs Pigot very slightly shook her head. She has grown still thinner since I saw her last; even Kitty looks well beside her, fat and well. Mrs Pigot for her part praised me for my slender and elegant appearance.

'You are no longer a boy,' she said. 'John still looks like a boy.'

'My clothes have been taken in twice since the new year. I dare say Elizabeth would pass me in the street, without stopping.'

When I had finished the tea, I retired to my room to change; then walked out, looking for John and his sister. They live in a prosperous sort of house, with two columns, at the edge of the Green. Elizabeth herself answered my knock, then called out behind her into the house, 'John, John! Guess who has come back when he said he wouldn't.'

We spent the afternoon in the garden, which overlooks on one side a series of fields, rising into the hills of Annesley. Another wall is shared with the Pigots' neighbour, a public house. As the weather was fine, and it was a Sunday afternoon, their gardens were crowded; and the noise of people carrying over the wall gave us a pleasant sense of seclusion. John had just come back from studying medicine. He was very amusing on the subject and has become acquainted with almost every class of human misery. But we also exchanged Southwell gossip. Julia Leacroft has got engaged to the son of Lady Hathwell's steward. It appears he has been boasting from Rainworth to Newark of having attracted the preference of Lord Byron's *established favourite*, and broken his heart. But Mr Leacroft is disappointed and hopes to take up his cause with me. All of which meant nothing more than that Elizabeth had decided to tease me. I was sorry to find she had so little news of her own.

Kitty, when I returned at last, was less sanguine than before. She had not known I was going out, she said. Mrs Pigot had left shortly after my arrival (this was not true), to allow her a decent period for the welcome of her own son. I could imagine her disappointment on finding me, etc. After supper, she began to inquire into my financial obligations, interrupting herself from time to time to exclaim, 'I promised myself to keep quiet on this point, this evening. But I cannot, I will not.' And beginning again. She discovered the coach and four stationed in the road and went out to inspect it with a lantern in her hand.

'I wonder I did not note it at once,' she cried.

'It is a gift, for you,' I said, following her out into the cool of the evening. 'The mother of Lord Byron should not be seen in such a thing as the little two-in-hand you go about in.'

'Go about! I like that, when I am confined to these four

walls, unless Mrs Pigot invites me to what she calls a *family supper*, because she is ashamed of me, too.'

But we bade our good-nights at last, and the house grew quiet.

***

I have now been here six weeks. Most afternoons I spend at the Pigots' house or riding with John or walking through town with Elizabeth. And in the evenings, when I am not engaged, I write. Ridge has agreed to print a collection of my verses for private distribution. The title gives me a great deal of trouble; Elizabeth and John and Mr Becher have all made suggestions. I gave them the poems in manuscript, after Elizabeth corrected and copied them in a fair hand. A few of the verses Mr Becher deems 'in advance of provincial life', and Elizabeth also expressed some fears of the *interpretations* that might be made on them. There is no one who has been more publicly associated with Lord Byron than herself; she still has some concern for her reputation. But this is only her teasing, and I do not mind it much.

The stanzas objected to belong, most of them, to a series of poems addressed 'To Mary'. Now this Mary is not one of your Southwell ladies. I met her in Newark at the printer's, at Ridge's office, which sits above the bank. There is a shop on the High Street as well, but he is mostly to be found beside his press, which he attends himself. Mary is one of his assistants, and took my hat when I came in – with chalky fingers – promised to clean it and forgot. She is a short shapely lively girl, not pretty but spirited, with a pock-marked face and small speckled eyes, like quails' eggs. On taking my leave, I saw her chasing after the carriage, hat in hand, with a bright eager look of apology in her face – and before we had gone five hundred yards on the road to Southwell, the business of our apology was finished, and she had scrambled out again.

I have sketched her as well as I can, but she refuses to *sit* long enough for a full study. Her father was a coachman who lost his leg under a horse; her mother is dead. For two or three years she has supplemented the small income of the printing-press with private clients. I believe she is sixteen or seventeen years old – she is sometimes vague. She remembers only the date of her mother's death four years ago. Her father, whom I have not met, hardly leaves his room, where she also sleeps, but he introduces her where he can among his former associates. When the room is required, he sits on the steps and waits. I have made it a point of honour to rescue her from these surroundings, which he tolerates, as I am a lord, and he believes there might be some profit in it to himself.

On the road from Newark to Southwell there is an old mill-house, which has fallen to ruin; but it has retained four walls and half a roof, which keeps one room dry (there are only two). It is used sometimes as a hunting-lodge. Mary sleeps there and I have gone to the expense of repairing the roof and two of the windows and providing a door. Once a day I ride out to her, unless it is wet; but then, she is only more eager the next day. Ridge, who knows nothing of these arrangements, complained to me of her disappearance, which has caused him some delay, as she was a very willing useful sort of girl, in this respect as well. But it is four miles on foot from the mill-house to Newark, and four miles to Southwell, which suits me perfectly and keeps her at home. Whenever I ride out to her, I tell Kitty I am going on printer's business.

But there are women enough in Southwell to occupy me. It appears that the rumour about Julia Leacroft's engagement is untrue. I had this from her father's own lips one evening, *a propos* of whatever you please, at a small dance given by Mr Buckleby. Mr Leacroft said to me, when I had taken a rest from dancing, 'There is nothing I dislike more than what is sometimes affectionately called a *little woman*.' (Julia is rather tall.) And then, 'It is all nonsense, of course, the stories about Mr Tuttle. This is what comes of living in a small town.' Now is such *paternal solicitude*, I asked myself, so very different from the consideration shown Mary by her own poor father? To be fair, Mr Leacroft expects a better price. I danced one dance with Miss Leacroft and afterwards we sat on a bench in the garden and ate an ice.

Elizabeth protests that I have become so lively she hardly knows me; and the truth is, she knows nothing of my arrangements about the miller's cottage, and I should be sorry if she did. I think she would be shocked, and she is not easily shocked. About a dozen times a day I consider the necessity of riding out to Newark. Mary has employed herself in my absence and swept the floors clean and pulled the rotten sodden remains of the mill-wheel out of the water, so that the stream flows past the cottage and does not flood it on rainy days. There are always picked flowers on the window ledge when I come and, if it is cold, a wet green smoking little fire in the grate – for she knows how I hate the cold. She calls me *Lordy*. Our bed is straw covered in sacking, and the stalks come through and tickle us until we scratch ourselves. We begin to stink of each other, and when the sun is out, before riding home, I bathe in the shallow water, stepping gingerly on stones and roots. Then dress with the clothes sticking to me. She stands cheerfully in the doorway as I ride away.

In the evenings, I dine at the Pigots, and afterwards go out, with John and Elizabeth, to a party at the Leacrofts or the Muswells, etc. where we might encounter Lady Hathwell or Mrs Burgage-Mainwaring, who lets the house to my mother. Mr Becher is often 'in attendance'. And I discuss with him the question of Reform and think of the brown hairs on Mary's legs.

*

I have had a letter from Edleston, and Kitty has one from Hanson. I don't know which gives me more pain. Edleston writes to say that his sister is to be married – to a clerk in a counting-house! And that among the inducements which persuaded her to accept his proposal (I would say *this young man's*, but it appears he is not a young man) was his conviction that he could obtain a place for his wife's brother, once she was his wife, at the same house. And this is what the world calls love. I have never met Miss Edleston but have seen a sketch of her, in pen and ink, done by her brother, who is very accomplished in this art; and if it is anything like, and if she is anything like *him*, she must be 'beauty's self', with or without her robes. And yet Nature's Coin has bought her nothing better than a middle-aged clerk in a mercantile house in the great city of London, who lives in two rooms off the Pentonville Road.

Edleston is in despair, on his own account as well. The truth is, he cannot bear to part from me and revives an old plan we have sometimes discussed of living together, like Nisus and Euryalus, or Lady Butler and Miss Ponsonby, in *retirement*.

Hanson writes about my debts – it is his great theme, and he returns to it as Cato to Carthage. Not only the four or five or seven thousands worth of debts contracted in London and due upon my majority, but the small accounts scattered about Cambridge, for which he himself is liable, as I tell Kitty, by deed of Crown. If the tradesmen go unpaid the shame is all his own. But Kitty seizes her opportunity and begins to lecture me about my father. Who was also a spendthrift, and a profligate, and a whore-monger, and what you please, though I tell her, we have nothing so much in common as a horror of *you*. She says that she does not believe me to be happy, that I was always a loving child, who defended her even from imaginary slights and would rather go without his dinner than suffer the least insult to his or his family's honour. But that I had got in with a disreputable set at college. Augusta (who knows nothing of the matter) has said something to her about Bankes's choristers, and Kitty has imagined the rest. The name of Byron is now a term of abuse, and fathers even in Southwell guard their daughters against me.

I gave her several instances to the contrary. To which she responded, inconsequently enough, that if they knew the true state of my affairs – Newstead and Rochdale hopelessly entangled, myself in debt and under bond to several Jew-lenders, etc. – they would keep their daughters to themselves and not parade them about in this shameless way. But a Byron can never resist *bidding* for what is *offered*.

She suspects me of the wildest improprieties and checks

my room each night, standing in the light of the hall in her night-gown, to re-assure herself. Elizabeth tells me it is true, she has made such a spectacle of herself no one in Southwell will return her card, unless I am at home; and she has no visitors but Mrs Pigot, who makes it a point of duty to call on her twice a week. Kitty talks a great deal of Aberdeen, where her cousin still lives in a large house on the river; and where she was known, it seems, to two or three good families, whose visits she received. But the fact is, people grow tired of hearing her complaints, accusations and regrets.

Mrs Crawley's macaroons, for which she sends daily, have made her dyspeptic; and she doses herself afterwards with pink pills from Stambridge, the apothecary. He sells her a notorious diuretic, which I have tried myself to no very pleasant effect. I have spoken to him confidentially about her – about these pills, and other things. I think they do her no good and some harm. He took me aside into a small room at the back, extended into the garden, with a sky-light, rather dusty, shedding a milky cloudy light over everything – phials liquids powders brass instruments books.

'If Mrs Byron comes to you asking for – this or that,' I said, 'complaining of slugs in the garden or difficulty sleeping, take care what you give her.' But he only smiled at me, and I felt a little foolish. 'I should not like to answer for the *use* she intends to make of it,' I said.

Later I learned the reason for his impertinence. It appears my mother had approached him on similar business, concerning *me*. Mr Stambridge told John Pigot, who was visiting his shop (and who knows how many besides); and John told me. We were riding out one day towards

Newstead, with a strong sunny breeze against us. John in his hesitant way delivered himself of the story, which he had been brooding on, like a hen laying its egg, and was much relieved to hear me laugh at it. We rode as far as Ravenshead, then south to Garden Lake, which took us the better part of the morning. Then rested our horses and let them drink. I could see the arch of the Abbey, and the trees blown this way and that behind it, through the ruins.

John said, 'Shall we go on? Is Lord Grey at home?'

But I dislike seeing the place in another man's possession, and Mrs Pigot anyway expected us to lunch. On our way back, I asked him (as a medical man), if he meant to kill himself, the method he should prefer. He could not resist this appeal to his professional opinion. Cyanide, he said, in solution, with a little magnesium – to mask its bitterness.

Meanwhile, my poesies accumulate. Elizabeth wonders greatly at the extent of them, if nothing else, for she never sees me with a pen in hand, and she sees me every day. But I write when no one else writes, at two in the morning, or at six; at breakfast or dinner; on sofa or lawn or bed, and in every *conceivable* position. Even at the mill-cottage, I have fitted up a table and furnished it with quill, ink, paper. Such is our appetite for contrast – after one kind of exertion, we delight in another. And while Mary sleeps, I write.

Elizabeth says to me, 'It is strange you so often profess such a passion for solitude, when you strike me now as the most *public* of men.'

'You used to consider me boyish and shy. I suppose I have changed.'

'No, you are shy still, in certain company, and boyish enough I think.'

'Then I don't know what you do mean.'

We were sitting on chairs at the edge of the Green, which we had carried ourselves from the Pigots' front room. About four o'clock on a Saturday afternoon, when the families of Southwell make their parade of the town – a few hundred yards each way. Elizabeth had sketch-book and pen on her lap, with an ink-pot at her foot, and considered the view with her fine narrow ironical eye. But she liked to talk as she worked and did not look at me.

'Your shyness,' she said, 'is only a sort of stage-fright. You hang back rehearsing your lines and preparing an entrance. It is nothing like real shyness, which wishes to be let alone. You wish to be brought out. John is shy.'

'It may be you do not understand me.'

'Oh, this is your great cry. You must have secrets, or something at least to confess to.'

'Now I do not understand *you*. But I am never alone, when I write. I think this is what you mean. For then I am also rehearsing my lines, as you put it.'

She looked at me sharply then and opened her mouth. But said only, with a kind of admiration, 'My dear Lord Byron . . .' The thought of what I could tell her, of what I might sincerely confess to, made me unhappy.

Most days around noon, if it is hot enough, John and I meet in a corner of Mr Buckleby's fields and play cricket. I wear seven waistcoats and sweat; John's bitch mastiff chases the balls. Mr Becher joins us occasionally, and a few others, Captain Leacroft included. Afterwards, we go to the Pigots' house, which is nearer, and I take nothing for lunch but biscuits and soda-water. Captain Leacroft has started the idea of putting on a play. His sister meets us there, with Elizabeth and one or two women, and we sit long hours in discussion. I have prevailed upon them to put on *The Wheel of Fortune* by Cumberland, as he was also a Trinity man, and I feel some affinity on that score. The part of Penruddock is very good, and I have picked it out for myself – the rest may dispose themselves as they please.

Mary grows sulky if I don't come till after tea. I find myself approaching the cottage, its plumes of smoke just visible from the road, reluctantly, and departing afterwards equally reluctant. Ridge said something odd to me once, that he had seen her in town going into the milliners, Mrs Michelson's. Mary has a distinctive burrowing gait, low-shouldered and sprightly; he could not be mistaken; but when he followed her into the shop, she was nowhere to be seen. It appears she owes him money.

Long has written to invite me to Littlehampton, where his father has taken a house. But I am still too much in the thick of Southwell affairs to think of leaving. Mary depends upon me entirely. I have passed more than two months in this desultory way, taking tea with the Pigots, walking out with Elizabeth and riding with John; cricketing swimming dancing; making love occasionally, and a few other things. Edleston complains that I have forgotten him, for I have not written above once or twice since departing the Cam. My head is so full of my rhymes (I wrote him at last) I have no words to spare for ordinary prosing. But perhaps I have been unfaithful, in my way – my heart always alights on the nearest perch.

* * *

It is all over, and very suddenly, too. One day in Newark, coming out of Ridge's, I thought I saw Mary's *shapeliness* exiting swiftly towards Friary Road; but a grocer's cart then overturning, with a confusion of bloody fruits, I could not follow in the carriage and gave her up. I made no mention of this to her in the afternoon (and she none to me), but drove away as usual, returning an hour later to find her in bed with one of the soldiers then stationed in Newark, from the Coldstream Guards; a fat pliable fair-haired gentleman, who seemed not at all sorry to see me, as he had *got what he paid for*. These were his words. It seems Mary had kept up a little of her old trade – 'which would not be put off,' she says to me, with the injured innocence of womankind. And though I was in rather a jealous passion at the time, I could not help laughing at this, which is always the death of me – one cannot be violent and amused. The guard and I parted on reasonable terms (for, after all, he meant me no harm), and Mary and I not much worse – though I could not help feeling a little shame-faced towards her, for imagining our affair to be anything but . . . what it was. But part we did, as we could not continue on the old terms and I had no intention of paying the new. This was at first a source of some heart-ache, which made the solitary ride afterwards to Newark appear very long, and the evening at home still longer (the Pigots had gone to Cheltenham for a week); but it declined into a fretfulness and died in the night, and I woke again the next morning feeling something like relief.

After two or three days, I had really begun to think very little about the whole business – when I was awoken one night, about two in the morning, by my mother. She had found Mary at a window attempting to steal in. How the 'poor lone woman' came by the house I do not know; perhaps she recognized the carriage. Kitty had seized her by the ear or throat or whatever else she could fasten on and taken her into the kitchen, where I met them. It appears Mary is with child; her father had discovered this fact, and beaten her; and she had walked or run at dead of night all the way from Newark (eight miles on a muddy road) to claim the protection of her – protector. That she had previously sacrificed all claim to this protection, it did not suit my dignity to reveal; for my mother raised up such a storm of protest and abuse one could only keep from capsizing by sailing into it. It needed only this, says she, for me to go one better than my father, for he at least did not *marry* his whores. And other similar reflections. In the end, taking advantage of a brief abatement, I escaped with Mary to the carriage, which my groom had prepared, and we drove away in the 'dead of night' but without its silence – for Kitty pursued us as far as George Street in her night-gown.

Mary was by this time considerably calmer; she is the kind to take this sort of farce with a laugh, which I like her for. But then in the moonlight I could see the marks on her cheeks and throat from her father's hands.

'You change your tune quick enough,' I said.

'What do you mean?'

'A minute ago you were beating your breast – all tears and threats. I suppose the story about the child is no truer than anything else.'

'You kept me like a whore; I don't see what you was surprised about.' Etc. Even then she could not entirely command herself and began to make her *appeal*.

I had already formed the resolution of driving on

towards London. But Mary must be deposited some-where. She was too large to be kept like a cat and too small to be ridden like a horse. After a few miles, the houses of Southwell gave way to trees and hedgerows, and the moonlight carried across them into the road; a fine wild scene, fit for the brush of Cozens. We had taken the way to Newark, and I thought, after all, I can do no better than return an errant child to her father; but at the mention of this proposal, Mary, who had grown quiet, began to grow loud again and I preferred her quiet. When it became clear I had no intention of taking her with me, she requested to be set down at the miller's cottage, which was, after all, in my way. I told her she could not stay there. As soon as the season began, it was used by hunters. She said she would not stay, but since I minded so little what became of her, she meant to ply her trade a few weeks longer, until it was exhausted (the regiment had already received its orders to decamp), whereupon she would decamp herself – to Nottingham probably, as it was nearest. And so I left her, almost without a pang, at the small ruined cottage above the quiet stream where we had known a great deal of pleasure, and some tenderness. I watched her out of the window turning the handle of the familiar low door and disappearing.

A few days later I arrived in London and drove straight to Mrs Massingberd's, who was not expecting me, but re-ceived me nevertheless with the kindness of a landlady, who loves lucre, which I prefer after all to the affections of a mother. Kitty, I thought, was unlikely to follow me, and then, the next day, she knocked at my door, a little red-faced, but by this stage (and she had travelled many stages) more sorrowful than angry. She sat down in the deep chair by the window, where I like to sit reading, and called for a glass of water, which I gave her.

After a minute she said, 'I do not mean always to be fighting with you, Byron.'

'It seems to me you have come too far, and in too much haste, *not* to fight. Peace is generally more patient.'

'The things you do that put me in a rage make me smile after. I cannot stay angry at a Byron very long.'

'In my estimation, which may not be exact, as there is too much feeling involved, you have been angry at a Byron for most of my life and at least half of yours.'

'Permit me to say, then, that I am not angry now.'

She finished the glass of water and closed her eyes a minute. I sat on my bed. There was, outside the window, the prospect of a very fair summer's day. The trees were green in Green Park and cast enough shade, even at ten in the morning, for the dogs to sleep in. I could hear the irregular hammering of a nail and looked out, above my mother's head, to see a man setting up a stall in the grass; an awning lay in a roll at his feet, striped red and white. Carriages made their way along Piccadilly.

'If you wish to lie down in my bed,' I began to say; and then, 'why don't you sleep a little, Kitty.'

'I'm very comfortable where I am,' she said, but I lifted her up under her arms and put her to bed. She was very heavy and hot; her head was damp.

This left the chair free for me to read in, and I sat down to read – and fell asleep. When I woke up, an hour or maybe a minute later, my mother was snoring, lying flat on her back with her nose in the air. I closed my eyes again and listened to her, a very regular soothing summer's day sort of noise. The light in the window had changed colour; the day was hotter. I stood up suddenly and went out, to see a man I know on Bury Street, with whom I had left a few articles I was now in a position to redeem. Afterwards I dined at Brooks'. There were two or three others at the club I was glad to see, including Matthews, whom I know less well than Bankes but would like to know *more*. We got a little drunk together, not very. When I returned to number 16, it was after seven o'clock. Kitty had sat up in bed with a plate beside her, Mrs Massingberd having sent out for something to eat; the room stank of fish. We fought rather furiously for two or three hours about everything and nothing (she was angry I had left her alone), until I told her, she had better find a hotel as she could not stay here.

'God knows what will become of you,' she said, on her way out. 'At this rate. You had better marry rich. I pity your poor wife.'

But in the morning she promised to return to Southwell, as I had no intention of remaining in London. Long had invited me to join him for a week's bathing in Littlehampton, where his father had taken a house – though once my mother had gone I tarried for a few days at Mrs Massingberd's, dining out, mostly with Matthews and others of that set, before travelling to the coast.

*

The house revealed itself to be a square, modern, comfortless dwelling, of the kind in which the bed-posts obscure the windows, so I established myself at the Dolphin Inn, a few hundred yards away and nearer the pier. On the first morning Long and I walked out to the end of it and fired at oyster shells. It transpires that he is a little encumbered with a young brother, named Henry, and very like the older but fatter and more inclined to laugh; though he turned out to be useful enough, in hunting out shells. The morning was cloudy and the sea sick-looking and grey, with a brisk breeze pushing reluctant waves up-river. The report of our gun-shots echoed dully off sky and water. But by the afternoon the wind had pushed the clouds away, too, and the sea cleared, turning a very pleasant blue. We stripped to our drawers and shirts and jumped off the end of the pier. Henry did not trust himself against the current, but after a few turns in the water I climbed out again, and carrying him on my back, a little unwilling, tumbled in. But since the tide was running out, we did not stay long; and dressed again on the pier and dined at the Dolphin, and afterwards Long sent his brother home, for he had begun to tire of him, and together we got drunk.

In this way, several days passed. In the morning we played cricket and Henry chased the balls. Then we lunched and swam or swam and lunched, or drank and did nothing. I met Long's parents, too – the father not at all resembling him, but small and round, with a small, round face. Fond of his own wit, too; Mrs Long more sober and square-headed. In her company, Long acquired again the pious miserable airs I disliked him for at Harrow.

One morning a letter arrived for me, from Elizabeth. It appears I am an author. Ridge has brought out a few hundred copies of *Fugitive Pieces*, which were sent to me in Southwell – from whence I had departed in too much haste to alert him. But Elizabeth kindly included one in her letter. I sat at breakfast perhaps a half-hour longer than usual (for I never eat much), putting it on the table and looking at it, then taking it up again, and opening some page and reading quietly to myself, for as long as I could bear. The first line of the first page (though the last I turned to), which should begin 'loud the winds whistle' had been changed to 'round the winds etc.', making a nonsense of the whole stanza – and after that I 'read no more', but devoted my attention to the letter.

Elizabeth congratulates me on the publication of my *Pieces*. It gives her great pleasure to disapprove of them. She disapproves of them several times a day, when she is stopped in the street, or run into at Mrs Crawley's, or invited to take tea. She has read them aloud to Mrs Pigot, and John, and even to Mr Becher without a blush, though hers perhaps was the only *unreddened* countenance. But (to drop for once her customary manner) she advises against an open publication. She is even a little sorry for poor Julia Leacroft, who is a stupid, vain, promiscuous flirt, but perfectly capable of feeling an insult if it is explained to her. And there will be women enough in Southwell to explain.

But it appears that only a handful of my verses give open offence. Becher has added a note to say, that with a few suppressions, there is nothing to prevent the publication of a 'fine slim volume'.

After breakfast, I made my way up to the house and showed Long a copy of the poems, which he turned in his hands admiringly and looked at glancingly. Indeed, it was handed around all the family, and stared at, as if it had been a baby or a piece of ambergris. I believe from that moment I began to go up in their estimation. But none of them allowed their admiration to tempt them into a *perusal*, which Long at least (who made the attempt) expressed himself grateful for, later in the day – as the book contained, he said, several passages he should not like his mother to see. There was something confidential about his manner I did not like, as if I knew very well which ones he meant; so I asked him what he meant. We were standing again among the stones of the beach, at the foot of the river at dirty low-tide, and firing intermittently at shells.

Instead of answering, after a long pause, he said, 'I am only a little surprised. I thought you more ambitious, that you wished to be something more than a little amusing. Of course, you will shock a few old ladies, but they are easily shocked.'

'Do you know, I believe you are a little shocked yourself.'

'I did not like your verses on the Cornelian,' he admitted. 'I know whom you intended by it. I should not like my mother to read them, under a mistake.'

On the last night of my visit, Henry, being told of this fact, burst into tears, a very remarkable display for a boy of thirteen. It appears that until my arrival Long had refused to do anything but read in his room, or walk out by himself along the harbour and up the coast as far as Goring. Mr Long did not think his son at all happy at Cambridge – he asked my opinion on this matter several times, when Long was out of the room.

I said, 'I have never known him particularly happy or high-spirited, even at school. But he is no less spirited *now* than formerly.'

After dinner, which we ate *en famille*, Long and I walked out alone to the end of the pier and threw bottles at the water. It was midnight, or near enough; a fine clear

217

starry evening, too warm for wind. The bottles splashed audibly and floated turning on their sides. Gleaming and rolling in the moonlight, they were rapidly borne away. After a while he said to me, 'It is just as well that you are leaving. Henry is at the age when he is especially attachable – and when attachments are most dangerous to him.'

'I have been attached, in one way or another, since the age of seven. I have never been shy of attaching myself.'

'We all know of your attachments.' Then, after another pause, 'I should deeply regret any constraint in our own relations, which might be occasioned by – which I might be forced to adopt, for the sake of – in the light of – certain rumours, which have reached me.' As I continued silent, he felt compelled to explain himself further: 'You assured me once yourself, *I am not so innocent as you suppose.* I have warned you about William Bankes. It is not just a matter of his reputation, or yours. There is a question of law.'

'You are a damned fool,' I said, and stripped off my shoes, trousers, etc. Long watched me with an odd expression, but when I was already in the water and calling out to him, he stooped to the ground and emerged again, pale-skinned, and jumped in beside me. The tide was very low, and the current consequently fast. It ran us out to sea in a heart-beat, and for several minutes it was all I could do to stay upright in the water with the pull of the tide against my legs. The town dissolved and the coast replaced it, curving away to either side, and for these few minutes I was really half-afraid – the fear of the water contributing to and increasing the flush of anger I had felt rising in me. But then, Long appeared again suddenly at my side, and we drifted together a half-mile along the coast until the shore was near enough we could splash our way towards it, then stumble heavy-legged onto sand. For a minute we stood leaning audibly recovering our breaths, laughing, too; but after a long walk over rough stones to the pier, we were both a little silent and out of temper.

The next day I travelled to London. I might have stayed longer (as there was plenty to amuse me), but felt a strange urge after all to return to Southwell. I wanted to see my book on someone's shelf. But I stayed long enough in town to visit Edleston. He was living for a few weeks with his sister in Camden, sleeping in the parlour in front of the fire and rising early to make way for his brother-in-law, who departs at dawn for his office in Greville Street. Edleston hardly knew me at the door. For a second, or half of one, he gave me a stranger's glance, taking me in with a cool eye, and then, and then, the transformation wrought upon his features was remarkable and highly gratifying to me. It was as if a lamp had been lit within – and *flared* before settling. His sister I met for the first time across his shoulder, appearing dimly in a dim hall, with a shawl about her neck to ward off the cold (though it was not cold).

Edleston declares I have been 'taken in' so much, he does not know me; and treats me with pretended shyness. His sister hardly left us alone for a minute. But he is proud of her, too, of her looks, for one thing, and kept bidding me to admire her. This I did, freely enough, for she is pretty as a locket and smiled at me as brightly as if a button had been pressed.

We walked as far as Bagnigge Wells, which was not far, and took a turn in the gardens. He held her hand, and I felt for an instant a pang of strong feeling at the sight of them – like children half-sleeping they dragged their feet through the gravel. They spoke humorously and affectionately of her husband; he might have been their uncle or schoolmaster. The day was intermittently fine but then a cloud blew over, with a little rain in it, and we took shelter under a sycamore. Her name is Anne; her married name is Ashdown. By the end of the day (we spent perhaps six hours together; after the gardens, I bought them lunch at a public-house) she had grown brave enough to take my arm in hers.

Generally I prefer tall women, but I was glad to make myself useful, buying her one or two things she liked, and not just to eat. She was particularly pleased by my interest in her brother, to whom I could be of immediate service. As I am driving to Southwell in a few days, I said, and Cambridge is in my way, there is no reason he should not take advantage of me. Oh, says she, clasping her hands together. In her presence he is solicitous and ironical. When the rains came he held his coat over her head. I stood somewhat apart, consoling myself with the thought of our journey to Cambridge.

Yet as the morning approached I found myself apprehensive. He was asleep when I called for him, and he tumbled into the carriage with his bag and continued sleeping. For an hour or two I watched him. As soon as he awoke he began talking. (When he is happy he talks, and I listen.) His sister is much less miserable than either of them had feared she would be. Mr Ashdown is decent and quiet; mostly he lets them alone. He is content to look at her. But when he does not let her alone it transpires she is perfectly content to be – and he blushed with such a childish air I could not help laughing. He laughed, too. He would lie in the parlour and listen to the noises they made. Like two doves squawking over a nut, he said.

Mr Ashdown had taken him to Greville Street and introduced him. The thought of working in such a House no longer filled him with horror – if he could be near his sister, and me.

'I was told I made a favourable impression,' he said. 'I believe I am good at making impressions. I made one on you.'

There was still no place for him and Mrs Carmichael expects to keep him 'at least another year'. But he had begun to see that a year is no very great term. For the next several hours we made plans together, until we reached Cambridge a little after two o'clock. (We dined at the Mitre and I deposited him afterwards at the Priory. There is a sort of garden in front of the orphanage, with a gate attached to it; we parted at the gate. I gave him a copy of my book, with the page folded back at the Cornelian; we both shed tears.) He could not live with his sister on the Pentonville Road, not in their parlour, not for more than a month. But he might live with me, if I meant to take up residence in the city. My rooms at Mrs Massingberd's were of course too small for a *brace* of occupants, 'even when one of them requires so little space'. He had really very few clothes, or wants, or needs; he wanted a bed, and a little company. He needed a roof. And in this way the hours passed quickly enough, with a great deal of enthusiasm on his part, and tenderness on mine.

*

It appears my poems have made a small sensation. I have

been stared at in Southwell, and with my own eyes seen a mother put her arm around her daughter (the girl not much more than eleven years old) and guide her to the safety of – the far side of the street. But the *women* have not taken fright; they all wondered at my sudden departure. Our play is to be resumed and I have recounted a half-dozen times already, between the acts, to every Tom, Julia and Eliza, the story of my flight from *Mrs Byron furiosa*.

Mary has gone. I drove one afternoon to the cottage – a late September afternoon, overcast and warm. How quickly nature reclaims her own. There had been a heavy warm rain in the night, and the stream had flooded again and made its bed in the parlour. A vine had climbed into the window, and flowered, and shed its flowers on the floor. There were *bees* in the grate, dead and bright. But no sign of Mary and Ridge had not seen her either, when I enquired of him; I suppose she is in Nottingham.

But the play's the thing. We began to rehearse at the Pigots', for their drawing room would do very nicely. There is a set of doors onto the balcony, which might serve for an entrance, and the room itself is large enough to accommodate ten or a dozen spectators and a few changes of scene. John, who cares little for acting, is nevertheless devoted to changes of scene; he has taken the carpentry in hand and with his sister begun work on a large canvas almost as big as a wall, on which they have daubed trees and woods, a moon, a ruined hovel. But Mrs Pigot looked at the play and would have none of it. It is altogether too loud, she says; she wants a quiet life. Elizabeth had been talked of for the part of Arabella (which I was not much in favour of, as it would be rather like kissing your sister), but this was also forbidden.

'I believe I am not very strict,' says Mrs Pigot to me, 'but I will not have you making love to my daughter in my own house before half the young women in Southwell. If you must make love to her, do it quietly; but if you wish only to put on a play, you may do it elsewhere. I have no objection to Elizabeth's acting either. She may take the part of Dame Dunckley. A mother could make no objection to *her*.'

The trouble is, it is a very good play, but there are not many parts in it for ladies. I am rather surprised it was agreed on, as the ladies always have their way in these matters. But Penruddock is an excellent role – Kemble took it at Drury Lane last year and was much admired. Miss Leacroft was so good as to tell me she had never seen Kemble perform in London, but she had 'no wish to any more'. For a while she was spoken of for Arabella, and would have made a fine Arabella. After Mrs Pigot threw us out, Miss Leacroft and her brother persuaded us to *shift the scene* to their own house, a few hundred yards away at the other end of the Green.

Captain Leacroft is to take the part of Woodville, my inveterate enemy. But Miss Leacroft has been disappointed. Her mother inquired of Elizabeth why Mrs Pigot refused to put the play on at her own house, and Elizabeth answered her, with as much mischief as honesty, *that she did not wish to see her daughter made love to by Lord Byron*. Now Mrs Leacroft refuses, unless Julia takes on another role, and she has been forced to accept the part of Miss Tempest, which is no part at all. Arabella is to go to Miss Bristoe. I have no objection to Miss Bristoe, who is only a little dark, to my taste, with strange wide cheeks and a rather foolish smile, which she turns upon me as if opening a purse; but what I cannot stand is to have Julia Leacroft and Charlotte Bristoe continually complaining at me about the wantonness of the other. Mr Becher was supposed to act as cicerone; Elizabeth persuaded him. But meanwhile he has accepted the role of Weazel and is too busy acquiring his lines to make any objection to the ladies' 'sweet behaviour'.

Elizabeth, of course, is an exception. She is really a very superior woman – clever, amusing, good. She is only too good for Southwell, which accounts in large measure for her sometimes lonely air. She has a sharp edge, but a little society might have rounded her out. I have begun to confide in her about Edleston, whom she longs to meet. It is a pleasure to me to talk of him to her.

'You are not so much changed after all,' she says to me. 'You had always a capacity for affection.'

'He certainly is perhaps more attached to me than even I am in return. During the whole of my first term at Cambridge we met every day summer and winter without passing one tiresome moment, and separated each time with increasing reluctance. He is the only being I esteem, though I like many.'

'My lord,' she said, for she saw me blushing, 'I am not so jealous of your liking as that; you needn't mind me.'

She delighted at first in referring to him as *my Cornelian*, which was a sort of code between us, for all this kind of talk. But she has lately added to it, and calls him the Edle*stone*.

Meanwhile, Becher talks to me about my verses, repeating at length his earlier advice, that with a few judicious excisions there is nothing to prevent their open publication. But he has no real ambitions for me in this respect; he considers it a useful step on the way to a parliamentary career. In two years I take my place in the House of Lords. The poems to Mary must go, and indeed I am not sorry to see them cut. It is like cutting away a part of me, and not the best part. Everything humorous, amorous, lecherous must be suppressed; what remains, what emerges, is a collection of very fine *sentiments* (it is Elizabeth who complains of this fact).

'You will please the ladies,' she says.

But this can't be helped. 'It is what we are all condemned to,' I tell her.

John Pigot and I drove down to Harrogate for a week, to catch the end of summer and *rehearse our lines*. He has perhaps seventeen of them, but they cause him a world of trouble. He marvels at my facility. It rained steadily. We had brought our dogs – his bitch mastiff Nelson, and Boatswain, my own Newfoundland, whom I have had from a puppy. As there was a sort of jealous feud between them, whenever one or the other came into the room, it took all three men, myself, John, and Frank the groom, and whatever waiters we could find, to separate them with a pair of pokers and tongs. This kept us busy enough. John returns to Edinburgh in a few weeks – as soon as our play is finished; and has been feeling a little painfully the preference of womankind against him (or rather, in my favour).

Becher is in an odd position. We meet to rehearse in the Leacrofts' drawing room every afternoon, and he appears among us, a little older, very sober, his face partly obscured by what Elizabeth calls a good *ancient* clerical beard, such as you find in the old prints. He looks, she says, like Pliny the Elder, of whom she knows nothing but that he died of his curiosity and wrote books – but she likes calling him the elder, this is what principally amuses her. He sits quietly among us, rehearsing his lines, while we all make love in our way. And he says nothing, or nothing publicly; he only *looks* a sermon.

He has one scene with Elizabeth, which is why to be sure he accepted the part. Elizabeth plays an old crone, who keeps house for me; and Weazel has come to apprehend me of my inheritance. Elizabeth tells him that I don't like to be disturbed at my books. Penruddock is supposed to be very fierce. She is got up in her mother's old crinoline skirts, which are so stiff and old, it requires of her no pretending to shuffle about the stage, bent almost double, with her face half concealed by a bonnet, mothy and large, that hangs over her cheeks and brows. But I am always a fool for such contrasts, and Becher is not much better. He says to her, *What am I to do then, who have come some hundred miles upon his business?* And she, by way of aside: *Go on, go on; by the living, my fine spark, I would not be in your place for a little.* The accent she gives to *My fine spark* is wonderful; it is a sort of teasing easy to feel but impossible to account for. Later, he says to me, as Dame Dunckley crosses the stage, *Ah, Sir, you surely can't forget there are such things in this world as beauty, love, irresistible woman* . . . But it is cruel to laugh at him.

Elizabeth *is* cruel. I wonder in fact what she is about – as she likes him well enough and has besides, at other times, a decent respect for him, which is perfectly mutual. And she is not so young and he not so old, and neither much in want of a fortune. In short, the match is eminently suitable. But though she is frank about most things and delights in all kinds of personal talk, she prefers to direct her inquiries *outwards*.

Miss Leacroft likes to quiz me about her; she has a quizzing manner. She has a way of tilting her head a little backwards and lowering her eyes and saying whatever comes to mind (which is not a great deal), as if no one had ever been so wicked. Such as, 'You go about with Miss Pigot, I believe; you are often seen together.' We were sitting at dinner, with one or two others, in the Leacrofts' fine hall with its portraits and panels. Captain Leacroft had got a ship; the dinner was in his honour. As I like him exceedingly, I am both glad of it and sorry to see him go, but he has determined to remain until the end of the play. He must see the play through to the end, he will not leave us 'in the lurch' – with the result that everything has been brought forward a week. For most of the evening, we hardly exchanged a word. He had stationed me beside his sister, and Miss Leacroft's confidential airs prevented our conversation from becoming general.

'We make no attempt to conceal the fact,' I told her. 'I am on good terms with all the family, especially John. But I expect to see still more of Elizabeth, when he returns to Edinburgh. Mrs Pigot is not very lively; she misses her son.'

'Oh, Elizabeth is it? That's very fine. I suppose you know she means to marry Mr Becher.'

'I know nothing of the kind, but I have my hopes. He certainly esteems her as a very excellent woman. And she likes him well enough. But if it is enough for *that*, I cannot say.'

'Mr Becher would do very well for her. But she thinks

herself terribly superior – nothing but a lord will do. I hope she is not disappointed.'

This is all very tiresome, but as she has bright blue eyes and soft gold hair, I do not mind it much. After dinner, Captain Leacroft took me by the elbow and walked me as far as King's Crescent, before turning back. A damp September night with the clouds still heavy in the air. There was a fire lit in the dining room and you could see the heat of it reflected in his cheeks. The ship he has got is called the *Diana*. A 22-gun frigate; she sails for the West Indies in convoy in a week's time. It is a great opportunity, he repeated, and expressed himself delighted to leave his family 'in every expectation of happy news'. But as it was late, and he sufficiently obscure, I did nothing to correct his impression.

***

The play is over. We gave three performances, one of them in the garden, as it was a mild dry evening, which went off very well. Everything went off well. Penruddock in particular was much admired, and there was talk of Kemble and Drury Lane among the spectators. Indeed, it was talked about for weeks and months afterwards. Even Kitty joined in the general applause. She loves a play (and any other kind of amusement) and saw us three times, sitting very properly upright on the Leacrofts' high-backed rosewood chairs. She never slept and laughed sometimes even when she was supposed to.

We have all felt painfully the want of occupation; there has been nothing to replace it. John is gone; Captain Leacroft, too. Kitty, at least, has become less unreasonable

– she is too grateful. I have decided not to take up my place at Trinity this autumn, and the presence of her *son* has allowed *Mrs* Byron to resume many of her old relations. But then, I have been too busy reading, reflecting, composing to think of returning to college, where these things are unheard of. The second volume of verse is under preparation. It is to be called *Poems on Various Occasions*, a fine, mild, meaningless title that can offend no one, not even Mr Becher. Ridge has spoken for it and I ride to Newark weekly, thinking of Mary, and my Cornelian, and – many other things.

Only Edleston regrets my absence. Long and I have hardly exchanged a letter. Bankes wrote to congratulate me on the volume of my *poesies* which Long had given him. He did not know I wrote, and underlined 'volume' twice as if the chief source of his wonder lay in the *quantity* of verse. It surprised me to find Bankes and Long in communication. I made Bankes a suitable reply and expressed my resentment to Long for distributing without my consent what was always intended for private circulation. Especially as I am in the midst of preparing a revised edition. But I have not heard from him. It is left to Edleston to wonder at and regret my absence. The truth is I wonder at it, too. But when the play was over I felt the need of some other occupation and was surprised at how well the task of revising answered. I have become as sociable as a wolf and see no one for whole days at a stretch, excepting Elizabeth and Mr Becher and sometimes Julia Leacroft.

*

It is quite shameful how the weeks go by, and nothing to show for them but a few bound volumes. *Poems on Various Occasions* appeared, fatter than its predecessor, but soberer, too – a good *burgher* of a book, Mrs Pigot calls it. It produced no great sensation, but then, I aimed at none. The daughters of Southwell may read it safely in their fathers' drawing rooms. Indeed, I have seen them do it, and the effect is gratifying. Elizabeth mocks me for becoming respectable, but (as I tell her) nothing but virtue will do in this damned world. I am already at work on a sequel, for public circulation; it is only in want of a title.

We have all become very dull and the worst of it is, we are too dull to mind it much. On St Stephen's Day, at least, we had a revival of the play. John was at home for Christmas and for two or three days we amused ourselves, in the sudden fever of rehearsal; but the performance itself fell rather flat. Captain Leacroft had been replaced with Miss Bristoe's brother, who is only fifteen. He forgot his lines and when he remembered them spoke so loudly no one could understand them. Afterwards it emerged that he had drunk a bottle of sherry beforehand; we were only lucky he was not sick. Mr Becher felt the awkwardness of his position. To be seen one day before an altar, and the next on a painted stage.

On New Year's Day, which was warmish and wet and consequently more muddy and miserable even than is usual for this miserable season, we rode out together towards Annesley, as far as Miskin Hill, and waited out a shower of rain under the elm trees. I could see through the rain the house itself bright and wet under a patch of clear sky. But Mary is gone, as far as Colwick Hall, which is not very far, though it might as well be the moon.

I said to Mr Becher, 'I am told she is not very happy. My mother has it from a cousin whose housekeeper knows Mrs Thomason, who has gone with Mary to Colwick Hall. There is no actual cruelty, she says, but a general indifference.'

'Who is not happy?'

'My cousin Mary – Mary Chaworth. For a summer at least I was very much in love with her. But she married John Musters, who was reckoned a great catch. He is perhaps five or six years my senior. I was rather afraid of him.'

And then, says he, after a decent silence: 'Do you think she will marry me?'

'Who will? Have you asked her?'

'I have. She wanted to consider the question, for the space of a night and a morning; and in the morning she told me, no. She said she could not.'

'When did you ask her?'

'At tea at Mrs Pigot's, on the day after our play. Mrs Pigot very kindly let us alone. John was out and Elizabeth sat quietly with her hands on her lap until I was finished.'

'Did she give you a reason?'

He shook his head; his beard was wet and dripped. There was a fine web of drops across his face, which he brushed away with his hand. 'Do you suppose,' he said, 'it is because she is in love with you?'

'She is not in love with me. I do not think she is. Elizabeth is good and kind and wise but not very loving. She has complained to me herself that her understanding is rather better developed than her affections. She says she has no *ear* for feeling.'

'Then she might marry me without feeling.'

'Would you like her to?'

'Very much. If she has no feelings, she must do without them.'

But the rain had stopped and we rode back to Southwell and separated by the Green. Kitty berated me for appearing in the hall in muddy boots; but I could not get them off without her, which forced us into a confederacy of sorts. Afterwards I ordered a hot bath and lay in it much of the afternoon – feeling very sorry for Mary and Mr Becher, Elizabeth and Edleston, and everything else.

*

I have had another letter from the *Edlestone*, as Elizabeth calls him. His voice is breaking. Bankes took him aside on one of his Sunday afternoons; he is rather more fastidious than the choir-master. It grates on his nerves, he said, to feel himself in the presence of that awful transformation, from boy into man. 'Do you wish me to keep away?' Edleston said. To which Bankes apparently replied: 'If you are willing to keep *quiet*, there are still one or two years of boyhood left to you.'

Perhaps he intends to trick me into returning. All that sort of thing used to disgust him, but he does not say that he means to give up Bankes's Sunday afternoons. In the round of his life there is little enough variety, to be sure, but I should be sorry to see him made use of as an object of pleasure.

This is what comes of a long separation. For several days after the receipt of this letter, I felt out of temper. I kept it in a book I was reading but found myself reading the letter instead of the book. But then, we are often drawn to what displeases us. At present, I am too dipped to appear at Cambridge in anything like my old splendour, but have a notion of returning after the publication of my poems – as a man of letters, who may be forgiven the holes in his shoes and the stains in his shirt. Kitty is presently attempting to raise a loan from her Scotch relations, who are comfortable enough themselves to give comfort to others. If that fails, I may have to sell the carriage and two or three of my horses.

As Elizabeth is the only person I speak to of my *Cornelian*, I thought she might confide in me about Mr Becher's proposal. But she keeps her counsel wonderfully. It occurred to me at last that the proposal was not made public (by her own *expressed* desire), and she might not have known I was in the secret of it. So one day I raised it directly. We were sitting in my own front room, overlooking the Green, which was a very rich green as the rain had been falling steadily since breakfast. Kitty and Mrs Pigot had gone out to inspect one of Kitty's improvements in the kitchen; they had just left. We had finished our tea, and I said something like, 'Mr Becher looks to me very unhappy.'

'He always looks unhappy,' she said. 'It is his beard. It is an unhappy beard.'

'No, he has generally a humourless look, which is not at all the same thing.'

'I thought he was a great friend of yours.'

'So he is, which is why I dislike seeing him miserable.'

After a minute, she said, 'You say that, as if you believed me capable – as if you believed me capable of improving his state of mind.'

'Yes, that is just what I do mean.'

'But I am not capable of *that*.'

There was a fire in the grate, which we both stared at. I was surprised at my feelings, of which resentment made up a large share; and it occurred to me that not all of it was on his behalf. She had done nothing to offend me – and yet, offence of a kind is just what I had taken.

'Then I have been misinformed,' I said. 'He told me that he had put his happiness in your hands.'

'Oh, if it were only my hands.'

'I don't understand you. I supposed you to admire him *as much as any man alive*. These are your own words; forgive me if I repeat them to you. Perhaps you had rather marry a dead man. His fortune is not great, but he has a respectable house, a good living, and the favour of a generous patroness. Of his attachment to you there can be no doubt. You have long been the object of his preference.'

'I don't intend to marry out of admiration. There is also the question of *my* preference.'

We looked at each other for a moment, and she continued in a different tone, 'But Byron this is no way for us to talk. This is not amusing to me, and we have determined always to be amusing. I hardly recognize you. You look as solemn as a penguin, and as for what you *sound* like . . .' She gave a kind of laugh. '*His fortune, his favour, his attachment*. I am not used to thinking you such a paragon of propriety.'

'It is odd you should say that, as I have just had a letter from my *Cornelian*. He complains as usual of my neglect, but not for the usual reason. It seems that in my absence he has become vulnerable to a kind of attention from which my presence alone might have protected him.

Such is the regard in which I am generally held – only you are willing to brave my disapproval.'

'And has he stood firm?'

But it was the old tone again, and I only looked at her.

'In spite of your neglect?'

'I believe he has.'

'It does not surprise me,' she suddenly broke out, 'that a young man should contract such a friendship. But that he should be proud of it!'

The rain had ceased and a soft light made its way through the softening clouds, which had the effect of making everything in the room a little harder to see – even Elizabeth looked rather faded in the glow. She sat in her chair, and I sat on the sofa stretching my legs, not very comfortably. I stood up to poke at the fire. I think we both had the feeling that whatever we had to talk about had been talked *out*. After a minute (to put an end to the discussion), I said, 'Indeed, I am not proud,' and shortly thereafter Kitty and Mrs Pigot returned.

*

Since then there has been a little coolness between us, which is just as well; it does us good to be sometimes apart. Miss Leacroft quizzes me interminably about Elizabeth, and wonders whether we are to have 'a proper Southwell wedding', which is all a nonsense on her part – the fact that she mentions it at all shows her fears in that direction somewhat abated. I should be happy to give up the Leacrofts altogether, and the Pigots, too, now that John is away. My solitude is busy enough. The latest 'slim volume' is nearly ready for the press, though it wants a title, and there is nothing to detain me here but Ridge and Kitty's loan. I am waiting only on one or the other to return to Cambridge.

Edleston says he has forgotten me. I am sure he will not recognize me, as I am slimmer even than I was, which is saying a good deal.

Miss Leacroft tells me her brother is expected daily. The family are in a constant state of *news-readiness* about him. He was stationed off Martinique, when he was attacked or boarded or sunk or put in chains or stays (in any case, made to endure some species of nautical torment), in what I have no doubt was a very gallant action, involving two French frigates and a privateer. It is the privateer who comes in for their particular condemnation; it is what *Tom had not reckoned on*. Anyway, he was captured and subsequently re-captured – all in the space of a rather breathless week (the news came three days apart) and is now to be sent home again till he has got a new ship. The *Diana* was stove in.

I have had one other piece of news. A few days ago a rather tall bearded stiff and painful-looking man appeared at our door, wishing to speak to his lordship. About fifty years of age, shabbily and dirtily dressed, but with an air of effort – a man meaning to look respectable. His lordship was duly summoned. I did not recognize him at first (which is no great surprise, as I had never met him), not even his name when he gave it. But after a minute, during which time he kept up a steady stream of embarrassment, under his breath and beard, and never once looking me in the eye, but *talking* all the time, it struck me just who it was and what he had made himself respectable *for*.

He was none other than Mary's father. It seems she has

lately given birth, to some unfeathered, two-legged thing, and he wanted me to pay the interest on my paternity. I cannot exactly remember the terms he put to me, as I was so enraged: that if I did not pay a certain sum of moneys, for the care etc. of this same child – but before he could finish, I had beaten him about his ears so that he fell to his knees. I helped him to his feet and boxed his ears again. Then he limped away. At least the child (whoever he belongs to) has brought about a reconciliation of sorts between father and daughter; for when I last saw Mary she was black and blue with his *interest in her situation*, this being one of his phrases.

For several hours afterwards I was too angry to write and went out shooting with Boatswain, firing at coins and birds. And it has been three days now. Somehow this anger has transmuted itself into something else and I have half a mind to ride over to Nottingham and inspect the brat. After all, it would be something to have a son. And my father never suffered much for the raising of me. His part of the business was over quickly enough. All this came over me in a kind of fever, and I relieved it, as I usually do, by scribbling. There was pleasure to be had in giving the boy my own blue eyes and imagining its mother dead. I felt for Mary a great deal more tenderly, laying her in the lowly turf, than I should at the sight of her, reclining amidst the luxuries of her trade in a second-floor room on a Nottingham side street. Besides, I should never be sure the child was my own, which counts against it; and the poem itself has somewhat exhausted the sentiments that inspired it. I rode over to Newark afterwards to give the page to Ridge in case there was time to include it in the new edition. There was not. Oh, but we have got a title for my book. Ridge himself suggested it. What do you say to *Hours of Idleness*, he said.

***

I am back in Cambridge, though it was neither the publication of the *Hours* nor Kitty's loan, which at last came through (in spirit, at least, if not in its material form; I have begged an advance off Hanson), that precipitated my immediate removal. It is almost fair to say I have been *chased* out. Mary's noble father, after his reception at Burgage Manor, applied himself more successfully to blackening my name amongst the citizens of Southwell – by putting it abroad that I had promised to marry a poor innocent girl, his daughter, fitting up a house for her to be mistress of; afterwards getting her with child and abandoning both child and mother to their fate among the streets of Nottingham, etc. etc. The character of the informer was sufficiently obvious to any impartial judge that his lies were mostly ignored; but they had their effect on one party with a more particular interest in my reputation – that is, Mr Leacroft, who had been dangling his daughter before my eyes for the better part of a year, in a way that could only inspire in him strong sympathies for Mary's father.

All of this coincided with the return of Captain Leacroft, who sent me a rather shame-faced letter, as we get on very well together, that stopped just short of calling me out. As I wish him no harm, and he is an excellent shot, I interpreted this letter in the manner most favourable to his good sense. Miss Leacroft, meanwhile, has been forbidden to so much as speak to me. She saw me once as she was coming out of church and gave me a look (to do her justice) that suggested she felt everything she *ought*, and a good deal more than I had supposed. Her brother, at their father's urging, then sent me a second letter, and we met, not at dawn exactly, but at the Coach and Horses, around four o'clock in the afternoon.

He explained to me that his father's sense of Julia's honour would be perfectly satisfied by my extended absence from Southwell; but that if I remained, the family must demand some other satisfaction. Mr Leacroft hopes to rekindle the interest of Lady Hathwell's steward, who is a good man, with some prospects; and was much in love. Julia meanwhile has lost all her colour – she has grown quite pale, not from weeping, but from its suppression, as Mr Leacroft finds her misery provoking. John, who is sick of the whole business, wishes for nothing but another ship to carry him into *more peaceful waters*. At least I could put his mind at rest. Since there is nothing to keep me in Southwell, I promised to leave; at which he, in a different tone, and with an air almost of disappointment, asked me if I had a message for his sister.

I thought of answering *Crede Byron*, the family motto, but it seemed not exactly to meet the case. So I gave him instead a copy of my book, which I had about me, and wrote under my name on the fly-leaf, *To Julia*. Then, after considering a moment: *Vixi puellis nuper idoneus*.

*

Edleston in fact did *not* recognize me but passed by me twice while I was staring at hats in the window of Kettler's on Charles Street. I caught his reflection in the glass and said nothing, though why it gives me such pleasure *to go unrecognized* is more than I can say. I have heard my name spoken at Fawlkes the Booksellers, on the steps of the Corn Exchange, in a chop-house, at the Mitre, and once, even, in chapel (there is a new boy in the choir Bankes wanted me to look at). As the author of *Hours of Idleness*, a nobleman, and a member of the University. It occurs to me at last what fame is: a kind of concealment, which permits me to eavesdrop on conversations regarding myself. Bankes has determined to act as a corrective. He likes to quote from the book, especially from the preface, which requires on my part a certain muscular rigour of expression.

The second time Edleston passed me I called after him. He turned and looked at me and then – embraced me in the street, a cause for wonder, as he used to dislike extremely attracting attention. But he is much improved, in temper and character, and not so shy as he was, or vain, which is perhaps the same thing. His voice cracks occasionally and his face, which had never known a razor, bristles now unless he shaves it. There was some awkwardness at the beginning, as there always is in such cases, polite inquiries made and repetition of sentiments, but afterwards we walked along the Backs as far as Clare Bridge, and got along very well. We both indeed had the sense of possessing *a great deal of news*. The river was high (it had rained all week; this was the first sunshiny day), and the fields long in grass, and rich-smelling. The cows dined contentedly, and we sat down against the dry roots of a tree and watched them.

Mr Ashdown has obtained a place for him as clerk in his own firm. The position is available from October, at which point Edleston will remove to London. And as I mean to go down in a fortnight, with no intention of returning until the beginning of term, we have but two weeks left. At present he has nowhere to live in London and means to sleep in his sister's parlour until he finds lodgings. This produced a slight embarrassment, as it raised again the question of our residing together, which we had talked of as a solution. Of course, he knows me to be a creature of strong habits, and a weak will; and it may well be, in October, that I choose to remain in London, and we can pursue our original plan. But he does not depend on it, which is all that I ask.

When he asked me why at last I had decided to return to Cambridge (it could not be on his account, as I had kept away so long), I told him. Later he reverted to the subject of women and spoke lightly of making his fortune in London by a great match. Then the rain returned briefly, in spite of the heat. It was too hot to sit still, and since I did not feel like swimming, we walked back along the river to Trinity and agreed to meet again in the evening after chapel, which Edleston is obliged to attend.

*

We have met since, almost every morning and evening, for a week. I certainly love him more than any human being, and neither time or distance have had the least effect on my (in general) changeable disposition. After mattins Edleston comes to my room and wakes me and watches me dress – in boot and spur most days, as he hopes to become a gentleman and I am teaching him to ride. Then we ride out past Grantchester, as far as Hauxton church sometimes, or Harston, returning to dine at Grantchester. He used to have a strong aversion to drink, but he has given it up (his aversion, I mean), and we get drunk together. Indeed, I have not been *very* sober for a week, but as I touch no meat, nothing but fish, soup and vegetables, it does me no harm. Edleston gets drunk quickly, becoming first silent, then silly, then sleepy; then he falls asleep altogether. But I wake him again and we ride home. He does not sing in the choir, as his voice has broken, but is still expected to Evensong, to which he dutifully makes an appearance. More dutifully than decently, I should guess. So far no one has remarked on his condition. But this state of affairs cannot last, and will not – in a week I shall be gone.

Edleston pretends not to understand the necessity of this, as I have just returned to Cambridge (after a year's absence) and there is nothing to keep me in London but the pleasure of staring at my book in the shops. I tell him, this is exactly my reason for going. Pretends, I say, for the truth is, we both feel the necessity of it. We cannot go on as we have been going on. No happiness is so perfect that it does not demand more happiness. The weather itself has been as quiet as winter, and as hot as Africa. Not a cloud stirs. What we talk about together, I hardly know – for we never stop talking, and I never think twice what I am saying, before or after, which accounts perhaps for my imperfect recollection. Women sometimes; it is a relief to me to be able to talk to him of women. He has developed a humorous sort of ambition, in this respect, and means to set himself up as a *modern beau*. I have offered to introduce him to Madame DuReine when he arrives in London, and he is full of curiosity about her. A very childish curiosity, which is not unlike fear. But I have seen him kissing his sister and taking her by the arm affectionately. He need have no doubts of his *propensity* in that direction.

What we do *not* talk about is much clearer to me. One morning, as he did not find me at home, he left a note. We had arranged to go riding together, but the Marquis of Tavistock had come down the night before. I had supped with him at his Tutor's, which was entirely a Whig party; and having got drunk, fell asleep afterwards on the settee and was later removed to the servant's bed. I woke up in a very understandable state of confusion and could not find my shoes. When I found them (the Marquis was still asleep, or had gone out; his servant did not answer my call), I wandered across the courtyard, feeling ghostly, and discovered the note from Edleston under the door. What was in it I cannot here repeat. He had been – excessively disappointed by my absence. He had been angry.

I sat down, a little angry myself, and not very clear-headed, and began to make him a reply, in which the passion of anger eventually gave way to other strong feelings, which I was too ashamed afterwards to look at. But I sent it him regardless. When I saw him again in the after-noon, everything was forgotten or forgiven; at least, no mention was made of the note. But since then we have kept up a kind of correspondence by these means, which is never discussed between us, but contains a great deal of what . . . we choose to leave unsaid. I find this manner of *carrying-on* almost unbearable, but every morning or evening, as soon as he is gone, I sit down to write. When I see him again the thought of what he must know makes my head burn.

*

It is all over – he is gone; or rather, I have left him. On the last night, we took supper in my rooms with a bottle or two of claret, which we got through quickly enough. Afterwards he lay down on my bed and I read to him from the *Hours*. There was a great deal of tears on both sides. He declared the Highlander to be his favourite, or next favourite, apart of course from the Cornelian; which showed I think some acuteness on his part. He liked its sentiment and force and *felt* the verse flowing freely and naturally beneath my pen. He liked the lines *Yet the day may arrive when the mountains once more shall rise to my sight in their mantles of snow*, which struck him as hopeful in spite of the hopelessness of the rest. 'Thoughts on a college examination' pleased him less; he does not admire my ironical vein. It is the face I present to everyone else, which is the very reason he dislikes it.

Whenever St Bene't's tolled the hour, he said he must go, and remained.

We talked also about his apprenticeship. He did not much relish the thought of living with his sister's husband, especially as they had a son, who cried at the sight of him; and she was carrying a second and consequently continually out of temper. He had seen them at Easter and was obliged to make himself useful; but he could not help it, he had a horror of small children. Especially boys. The child had entirely destroyed what was left of their former intimacy, after his sister's marriage. Her colouring was poor; and the weight of her belly made her flat-footed and slow, when she had always been boyish and graceful. They had liked to run races together. It was on the tip of my tongue to say, In October, when you come down – but I don't know what I could have said, and I did not say it.

At two or three o'clock, he said he really must go, and I suggested we meet again for a final parting at breakfast. He said he would return after mattins. Then he said he had a sort of confession to make, which accounted partly for his ill-humour. He was always first dissatisfied with everyone else when he had something to be guilty over. He was sitting up in bed with his chin on his elbow; I had pushed the easy-chair to the side of the bed. His head was just above my knee and I sometimes stroked his hair. He confessed to me that he had kissed a girl, the daughter of one of his schoolteachers, a little older than himself. He had not told me before for fear of offending.

'Why should I mind it,' I said.

He had kissed her for the first time on midsummer's night, and a few times since; but on my return from Southwell, he had purposely avoided her. But then a few days ago he had kissed her again. He told himself, there was nothing he need be ashamed of, he had done me no harm, and after all, I had spent the better part of the year consorting with every variety of womankind, to use my own phrase for it, but then, in spite of everything, he felt ashamed. After a minute, for I had said nothing to break the silence, he broke it himself by asking, 'Do you mean to get married?' It was a strange turn his thoughts had taken.

'I suppose we all marry in the end,' I said.

'It seems an odd sort of life,' he said. 'To spend it among women.'

'I believe in most marriages a husband and wife are very seldom together.'

'Then why marry at all?' he asked.

'To be apart from them.'

He could not deny there was something pleasant in it, he continued. The girl in question was slight and pretty – quite unlike her father. Her face was very warm, but then, they had been dancing, in the heat of the May-pole fire. Afterwards, he meant the next day, they were very strange with each other; and indeed they had been strange enough before. It was all very strange. He could not get used to it. It seemed not at all natural. A few days ago he had kissed her again, perhaps I could recall his reason for it; she, not at all willingly at first, for he had come across her in the Priory gardens, on her way to her father. He took advantage of the coincidence and darkness (it was almost ten o'clock), and she resisted him a little, but as he was angry he did not much mind. And soon she did not mind it either. They parted at last rather suddenly when Mrs Carmichael appeared in the kitchen door with a bucket in hand. And he had not seen her since; but he had begun to think about her, thinking of me as well, and whether I liked to amuse myself in this manner with women.

'One can't be always among women,' I said.

He looked up at me (for he was still in the bed beside me), but something about the whole business disgusted me, his innocence and his *air* of innocence, and after a long embrace, which was tender enough in its way, I sent him to bed. In the morning he came again, as he had promised to do, both of us a little head-achey and yellow-eyed; and we had a second parting, a *breakfast-parting*, which is always at least nine tenths an affair of the stomach, and not of the heart. But after all I may see him again in London.

3

Among the most vivid memories of my childhood: arriving late at night in Austin, at the end of another summer, after a long flight, after one of our years abroad. A wall of evening heat meets you outside the airport. Dozy and underslept, confused by jet lag, a little sick from the plane. You squeeze at last into the car among the boxes, suitcases, bags and other children. Fall asleep again on the short journey, and then emerge into wakefulness and the deep almost oppressive familiarity of home: the hedgerow running along the front porch; the broad southern house, white and ghostly in the street-lamp light; the cool tiled steps leading up to the front door. The noise of crickets, not the nostalgia conjured by that phrase, but the real insistent sound of something too loud and too near and everywhere invisible. The slash of a sprinkler cutting through it, silent then suddenly flicking its tail against the grass. The voice of your mother: 'Do you want to eat something? Let's get you into pajamas. You can watch TV while I make the beds.' The creak and smell of the house.

We returned to Boston on the first wet day of the New Year. When we got out of the cab, the rain was cold enough you could see it falling through the air in stretching lines. There wasn't anywhere to pull over. Twenty inches of snow had fallen in our absence, and since everyone shoveled it off the sidewalks, the curbs were guarded by five-foot piles of ice. The only way through was along the sides of parked cars. I carried our bags up the front steps, slick in the half-thaw, then came back down for my daughter. Caroline had found a blanket to wrap her in; she wasn't wearing much, she'd been sick on the plane. But she was awake now and watching her breath in the air.

'Daddy, I'm cold,' she said. 'Why am I cold?'

'Because it's winter and partly because you're tired. But you keep me warm.'

I carried her one-armed against my side and held on to the banister. During the night, the temperature dropped and, before the skies cleared, another few inches of snow fell. Caroline slept through the early morning light reflected off it, but my daughter and I couldn't. I dressed her quietly and took her outside and let her sit on the porch while I shoveled the pavement clear. The snow lay gently unevenly and sparkled whitely. The noise of iron on brick rang out loudly into the dawn. Meanwhile I talked, continuously explaining, 'It's easier to shovel before everyone steps on it, because snow is softer than ice. The reason snow is white and water is not' etc. – to keep her interested, and she from time to time said, 'Tell me again.' Caroline woke up from the cold of an empty bed and came out at last in her slippers, bathrobe and overcoat and warmed herself against our daughter, sitting down beside her on the top of the steps. By this point the sun had risen over the rooftops and the sunshine was brilliant enough she could only squint down at me, sleepily, quizzically.

*

One of the things we had planned to do during our year in Boston, besides visiting Walden and Cape Cod, seeing the whales in the harbor, going to a ballgame and the Symphony Hall, was conceive again. We wanted another kid; that much we could agree on. What we disagreed about was when to start 'trying' – maybe the strangest of all the strange euphemisms for sex. Caroline felt strongly that we should have the second child at home, in London, with all her family near. I didn't disagree in principle, but babies don't always come when wished for, and I figured we might as well 'try' as soon as we got to America in September. But my fellowship was a ten-month fellowship, and Caroline worried that if she got pregnant too soon, she might have to give birth in Boston – either because it hadn't finished yet or because by the time it had she'd be too pregnant to fly.

This struck me as a totally unreasonable anxiety. It had nothing to do with her perfectly understandable preference for being near her mother at a difficult time. Her mother could easily fly out to Boston, if it came to that. Besides, the university health plan was likely to provide her with much better care than the NHS. Her objection to giving birth in America seemed to me more symbolic than practical – a rejection not only of my own childhood and former way of life but of the shadow of a possibility that our children might share in it. The idea that having a baby in America and spending a few extra months in Boston before flying back was so terrible a fate we had to eliminate even the faintest possibility of it struck me as frankly insulting. Insulting to her as well – to all of us, as a family. As if I were always plotting to lure her to the States, because I was so unhappy in England; as if she made me so

249

unhappy. This was pure craziness, but calling it craziness only made Caroline dig her heels in more. Pretty soon we started repeating ourselves. I said, it's just a practical question or should be, and she said, it might be practical for *you*.

The truth is, she was probably right and maybe I even knew it at the time. Somehow I had got it into my head that having a kid in Boston might make a difference to us, to Caroline as well; and that this small difference could lead to greater changes. Even though I had never lived in Boston before that year and realized fairly early on that I wouldn't be any happier in Boston than I was anywhere else. Somehow I had got it into my head that whatever was going wrong in my life could be attributed to the distance I had traveled from home. For all I know, this is a common delusion. We think the problem with adulthood is that we betrayed our childhoods to reach it; and having children, and giving them the childhoods we grew up with, seems like the only way of making amends.

In theory at least, neither of us won the argument. Conception is always a strange business; for us it was a little stranger, that's all. Sometimes Caroline gave in to me and sometimes I gave in to her. More often, we didn't bother to fight it out. But by the time we landed in Boston, one week into the New Year, it was pretty clear that Caroline had won in practice. She wasn't pregnant and even if she got pregnant immediately she still had plenty of time to move back to London in the summer. This thought occurred to me for the first time on the seven-hour flight from Heathrow to Logan, and when I saw her looking down at me from the front stoop, on that snowy morning in January, and warming herself against our daughter – I wondered if it had occurred to her, too.

*

I began the New Year, as I often do, full of ambitious resolutions. One of these was to invite Henry Jeffries to lunch. I hoped to plant an excerpt from Peter's unpublished novel in the *New Yorker*; Jeffries was my only connection at the magazine. So alongside an invitation to lunch I sent him the three long chapters from Peter's unfinished manuscript – explaining my purpose, that I was writing a kind of biography about him, to fill in the gaps between these Byronic interludes. Could he give me his opinion of their quality? I was too close to judge.

For a week I heard nothing, and I thought of Peter and his letters, to publishers, editors, and agents, and the waiting around he must have gone through before he realized there'd be no reply. The calculations he must have made: about the postal service, and the time it takes to read two hundred pages; the time it takes to respond to them; the time it takes to get a second opinion or convene an editorial meeting; the time it takes for a manuscript to disappear irrevocably under the weight of subsequent manuscripts. Of course, sometimes he probably did get an answer and quickly enough, but it's the silence that stretches your nerves, more than disappointment. Then Jeffries emailed me, in his characteristic way – as if the condescension were all on my side. What a lovely idea, etc., and thank you very much for 'the pages. While you're at it why don't you send me the biographical bits. Have you been to Sandrines? It's a typically Harvard sort of place, not very expensive, though it looks it; near my office and rather better than the sandwich shops. I didn't spend seven years in higher education to eat sandwiches when I grew up.' So we had a date, two weeks off, and for two weeks I enjoyed the feeling of belonging to a 'world' that included Harvard University, the *New Yorker*, and lunch at Sandrines.

Meanwhile I got back to work, in the stacks of the Widener – the library on Harvard Yard that sits behind pillars on top of those famous steps. The steps themselves are as tall as a house and as wide as a tennis court, but the stacks are less impressive: windowless institutional corridors, one after another, lit by hanging bulbs. The books lined up like prisoners; there's nothing to sit on but those rolling stools. I spent a week in front of the shelf of Byron biographies, looking into the facts of his relationship with Edleston. Wearing hat and gloves (which made a nuisance of page-turning), since the stacks are unheated. Books don't need much warmth, but I could see my breath rising under the electric lights.

There aren't many facts. Edleston *was* a choirboy in the Trinity chapel, though whether Byron met him there or in Bankes's rooms is unclear. Bankes's Sunday afternoons at home were not only the stuff of college legend but facts of college life. 'It was constantly asked, "What the devil does Mr Bankes do with those singing boys?"' Peter puts these words into the mouth of the 'old Fellow' who lives across the hall from the young lord. He also lifts more or less verbatim one of the few descriptions we have of Edleston, from a letter Byron wrote to Elizabeth Pigot on the 5th of July, 1807 – 'with a *bottle* of *Claret* in my *Head*, & *tears* in my *eyes*, for I have just parted from "my Cornelian" who spent the evening with me.' This is the scene Peter's chapter ends on, but he places Byron's description of the boy much earlier in the episode: 'his *voice* first attracted my notice, his *countenance* fixed it, & his *manners* attached me to him for ever.' A few months later Edleston followed Byron to London to take up his position as a clerk in a 'mercantile house.' But they never lived together, as they frequently talked of doing. It isn't quite clear why not.

Did they ever sleep together? Byron later referred to their affair as 'a violent, though *pure* love and passion.' He talks about a 'friendship' that gave him just 'as much trouble as love.' In the poems he wrote to Edleston, and sometimes read to him, their kisses were always 'chaste.' His friend Hobhouse, however, continued to worry about the relationship, and Peter in his story foists those worries on to Long. Byron, after he left Cambridge and before he embarked with Hobhouse on their tour of the Continent, refers cryptically to his reasons for going. 'If the consequences of my leaving England were ten times as ruinous as you describe,' he writes to his financial adviser, John Hanson, 'I have no alternative, there are circumstances which render it absolutely indispensable, and quit the country I must immediately.' Most of his biographers attribute his hurry to a fear of being caught up in a sexual scandal – the kind of scandal that drove him out of England for good after the breakdown of his marriage in 1816. And Edleston is the likeliest culprit. There's an entry in Hobhouse's diary from the 6th of June, 1810, shortly before his solitary return to England, which reads (or may read; there's some dispute over the orthography): 'tales spread – the *Edleston* accused of indecency.' Hobhouse disapproved of 'the Edleston.' He disapproved generally on their tour of what Byron got up to with the natives, which is one of the reasons he went home early.

If Byron did *not* sleep with Edleston, it's hard to say why not. The likelihood is that either Lord Grey or one of his Harrow bedfellows had already initiated him in homosexual intercourse. Byron may have slept with his pageboy from Newstead, Robert Rushton, who was younger than Edleston and equally 'innocent.' He certainly had sex with a number of boys in Greece and Turkey, though these affairs came later, and after he had cast off the shackles of British respectability – what Peter has him refer to, in *A Quiet Adjustment*, as Hobhouse's 'scruples.' One of the things the Romantics liked to romanticize is male friendship, but it's clear from Byron's letters that his passion for Edleston included an ingredient missing in his love for Edward Long or Hobhouse. It's just possible that Edleston did not reciprocate Byron's obvious attraction. We know nothing about his feelings that Byron has not told us, and Byron doesn't tell us much, apart from boasting of his 'attachment' – which can be explained easily enough by the gratitude of an orphan towards an aristocrat who showers him with gifts and promises. The only evidence we have of Edleston's homosexual inclinations is that disputed reference in Hobhouse's diary. But even if he felt no desire for the young lord who took him under his wing, Edleston might have felt the pressure of Byron's towards *him*, and given in to it. In spite of all this, the biographers tend to agree that Byron did not sleep with Edleston, and the best account they can give for this fact is that he – forbore to. This is certainly the story that Peter decided to tell.

Byron came back from Greece in the summer of 1811

to find a number of the people he had cared for in England, and some of the ones he hadn't, dead. Long, who quit Cambridge to join the Coldstream Guards, drowned en route to Lisbon in 1809; he was on his way to fight Napoleon. Charles Skinner Matthews drowned, too, caught in the reeds of the Cam, where Byron, Long and Edleston used to bathe. 'I would have risked my paltry existence to have preserved his,' he wrote to a friend. He was staying at Newstead when he heard the news, and presiding over his mother's dead body. She had died a few months after his return but before he'd taken the trouble to see her. 'Oh Mrs By,' he said to her maid, 'I had but one friend in the world, and she is gone!' Later he wrote to Hobhouse a little more coolly or coldly: 'Indeed when I looked on the Mass of Corruption, which was the being from whence I sprang, I doubted within myself whether I *was*, or She *was not*.' Edleston was dead already – had died of consumption a few months before. 'It seems,' Byron wrote, 'as though I were to experience in my youth the greatest misery of age. My friends fall around me, and I shall be left a lonely tree before I am withered.' The following spring John Murray brought out the first edition of *Childe Harold's Pilgrimage*, and Byron became famous – his grief had suddenly stepped onto a larger stage.

Edleston died in May, but the news didn't reach Byron until October. After the sexual freedom of his Continental travels, he let three months go by without looking up the young man he had once described to Elizabeth Pigot as 'the only being I esteem.' There's an echo of that phrase in his response to Edleston's death. He wrote to Francis Hodgson, an old Cambridge friend, who had known both Matthews and Long, 'I heard of a death the other day that shocked me more than any of the preceding, of one whom I once loved more than I ever loved a living thing, & one who I believe loved me to the last, yet I had not a tear left for an event which five years ago would have bowed me to the dust; still it sits heavy on my heart & calls back what I wish to forget, in many a feverish dream.' In spite of his shock, he manages to avoid any pronouns. Hodgson was about to take orders and used to argue with Byron about religion.

A few days later, in a letter to Hobhouse, Byron gave an account of his feelings for Edleston that was both less guarded and more equivocal: 'At present I am rather low, & dont know how to tell you the reason – you remember E at Cambridge – he is *dead* – last May – his Sister sent me the account lately – now though I never should have seen him again, (& it is very proper that I should not) I have been more affected than I should care to own elsewhere.' He can't leave the subject alone and a week later, from Cambridge this time, writes again: 'I am very low-spirited on many accounts, & wine, which however I do not quaff as formerly, has lost it's power over me. – We all wish you here, & well wherever you are, but surely better with us . . . The event I mentioned in my last has had an effect on me, I am ashamed to think of, but there is no arguing on these points. I could "have better spared a better being." – Wherever I turn, particularly in this place, the idea goes with me, I say all this at the risk of incurring your contempt, but you cannot despise me more than I do myself. – I am indeed very wretched, & like all complaining persons I can't help telling you so.'

Something has happened to his 'esteem' for Edleston, which he formerly boasted of; his own self-esteem has suffered in the drop. Part of the poignancy of this last letter lies in the fact that the only person he can talk to about his grief disapproves of it. Hobhouse had traveled through Turkey and Greece with him, understood his inclination for boys, and 'despised' him for it. And Byron, hearing of Edleston's death, can open his heart to no one else; he is desperate to see him.

As I worked my way cold-fingered along the stacks, I wondered why Peter had chosen the Cambridge choirboy – picked him out of the hundreds of Byron's lovers, to tell his story. Was it because they *didn't* sleep together? Edleston himself emerges from Peter's account with a very definite character: petulant, shy, vain, soft-hearted, manipulative. None of these qualities can be found in the rather blank young man described by the letters and biographies. 'He is nearly my height,' Byron wrote, 'very thin, very fair complexion, dark eyes, & light locks. My opinion of his mind, you already know, I hope I shall never have reason to change it.' But he changed it quickly enough after Edleston died.

*

The last time I saw Henry Jeffries was at a reading he gave in November at the Harvard Book Store. He was reading from his new book, *The Art of Fiction*, which was more or less a collection of essays about novels he liked and the way they 'worked' – Jeffries' word for it, by which he meant the negotiation a novel makes between the formally satisfying artificiality of art and the unshaped reality of the world. Jeffries read very well. He wore a jacket but no tie, spoke in audible ordinary tones and told lots of jokes.

The bookstore had set up a dozen rows of chairs in one of the side rooms, but it turned out that there weren't enough seats. A number of people (I was one of them) squatted beneath the shelves or crouched under the low ceiling of the staff exit. Someone even rigged up a TV in the front room to broadcast his talk to the rest of the store. Afterwards I bought one of the books and joined the queue of people lining up for his signature. I waited maybe fifteen minutes. When my turn came to approach him, he very gallantly shook my hand and pulled me aside for a brief conversation.

Over the weekend before we had lunch I finally got around to reading *The Art of Fiction,* and I brought my copy along with me to Sandrines. Jeffries was late, and as I sat at a table in the window, waiting, I felt the need of something to read; but somehow I couldn't bring myself to take out his book. It would look too pushy. He came in a few minutes afterwards, with an air of mild hurry, which was really just his air of apology. I had met him two or three times, but the impression he makes in my memory always differs a little from the effect of his presence. For one thing, he generally turns out to be better groomed: clean-shaven; expensively and modestly dressed. Sitting down, he crossed his legs and I noticed his shoes – a pair of brown brogues without laces.

Sandrines, as Jeffries promised, *looks* like a Harvard institution, at least from the inside. The building it belongs to is unprepossessing, flat-faced, vaguely modern, but the restaurant has taken over the ground floor and fronts the street with an elegant wall of glass. There is a curved bar in a corner of the room, backed by a mirror that reflects the irregularities of the bottles lined up against it. The barman wears an apron. White table-cloths heavily cover the small scattered tables. Women in pearls lunch there; retired men in suits. Jeffries ordered the special without looking at the menu, said he 'felt like a beer,' and asked me if I'd join him. 'What a lovely idea,' he repeated, as we waited for our food. I told him I had been reading his book.

'That's one of those phrases, isn't it,' he said. 'Like *I couldn't possibly eat another bite.*'

Jeffries was maybe five years older than me, but I couldn't help feeling around him, as I often felt towards successful people, that he had thought more seriously than I had on certain important questions, and that this was the reason for his success. (While I was so out of it I didn't even know what the questions were.) The few times we had met before, I had the sense of some affinity between us, which was partly just the effect of his charm – the charm of the modest, famous man. But it was also the effect of shared tastes. Jeffries grew up in York, a pretty, provincial middle-class English city. His father was a civil servant; his mother painted watercolors and organized events for the local chapter of the WI. They scraped enough together to send him to Winchester, pushing him 'bottom first' (his own phrase for it), and with some difficulty, one or two rungs up the class ladder. My childhood was Texan, Jewish, classless. I grew up playing basketball in the backyard. But we had read the same books and that fact counted for more than the other differences.

When the food arrived, he pushed back his chair to make room for the waiter. After he had gone, Jeffries said, 'Although, as it happens, I have been reading yours. In some ways they're not dissimilar, though I must say I've never taken the idea . . . quite as far as you.'

'What idea is that?'

'All this business about Peter's life, and what you can read into it from the novels. I'm sympathetic, but has it occurred to you what it will look like to people who aren't?'

'How will it look?'

He didn't answer at first, so I went on. 'Maybe you're right about the critics. But most readers assume automatically that writers write novels to write about themselves. It's harder to persuade them that something in a book *isn't* true than that it is.'

'It's almost a relief to hear you say that,' he said. 'You make me feel very reasonable. Even so, I would hesitate to do what you're doing. Deciding, for example, on the strength of three novels whether twenty years ago a high-school teacher slept with one of his students. I'm also not sure why you care.'

'I don't care much if he did or not,' I said. 'I just want to know.'

'But what does it matter, at this stage.'

This was an argument I'd been waiting to have, so I gave him the answer that I had ready. That Byron himself treated fiction as a kind of code, which allowed him to refer more or less openly to the facts of his life: to his divorce, for example, in the opening canto of *Don Juan*. Everybody knew what he meant, and what's moving about the poetry isn't the story it tells but the real history it refers to. He could be surprisingly even-handed and forgiving. This is how *his* fiction works, I said. 'It seems natural to apply the same standard to Peter.'

'That sounds to me more clever than honest.'

'Let me put it another way then. What I know about Peter Sullivan is that he grew up in Charlestown in the lodging house run by his mother. Never had girlfriends or boyfriends, never took anyone home. Went to BU though maybe he got into Harvard. Landed a job at a private school outside Boston and lived in a dorm room on campus, until he was kicked out for allegedly improper relations with one of his students. Moved to New York, where he got another job at a private school, which is where I met him. Never talked to any of his colleagues. His only friends seem to have been members of the Byron Society, which meets up maybe once a month. Sometimes he went on holiday with them. In his spare time, which he must have had plenty of, he writes these novels, which aren't published until he is dead. This is why I'm curious about what happened at Beaumont Hill, because nothing else seems to have happened to him at all.'

There was a silence; I had the feeling I was talking too much. Outside, across the shadows of the street, a typical college-town figure made his way: either a bum or a professor. Uncut beard, untied shoelaces – leather boots. In spite of the cold he wore only dirty chinos and a tweed jacket. Jeffries pointed him out to me. We watched his progress through the large restaurant window. 'One of your vivid types,' Jeffries said. And then, 'Memoir seems to be the form your thoughts are taking these days.'

'Probably because of Peter. I find it disheartening, going through these stories and working out what he made up and what he didn't.'

'I've told you already I don't think there's any need to.'

'Whenever I give a reading of Peter's work, this is what everyone wants to know.'

Jeffries called for coffee and while we were waiting for it, he said, 'I rather enjoyed seeing myself as a character, by the way. Even if the role was small. *Balding* I particularly liked.'

'I should have warned you. I never remember what I put in these books.'

'I wondered about that, after *Playing Days*. If anybody was offended. I was wondering if your wife has seen what you've written here? Forgive me. I'm being presumptuous.'

'Presumptuous?'

'Personal, I suppose, is what an American would say. You seem to be writing a book about yourself.'

After a moment I said, 'I don't understand what you're getting at.'

'When we met at dinner, I remember you felt quite strongly that writing was not a profession that should compromise any of one's other duties . . .'

'I don't see that it has.'

'Then, she doesn't mind?'

'Being in a book? I can't say she likes it, but it doesn't matter much. It's only a book. Byron liked to say that going naked was the best disguise.'

'Not Byron, someone else. Congreve maybe; Walter Scott. But being in a book isn't what I meant.'

Suddenly I saw what he *did* mean. 'Oh, that's just because you read too much into everything. You'd be surprised how many women I meet and don't have affairs with. Kelly's just one of a crowd.' He didn't say anything, and for some reason I kept talking. 'People tend to overstate the importance of sex. They want to persuade everyone else how much they're having. In fact, our culture has

262

to work pretty hard just to get us to have sex at all. The technology keeps getting better. Movies and magazines replace pictures and dirty novels. Along comes the Internet. The trouble is these things only make us consume more sexual substitutes, because we don't really want the real thing. But you think I'm saying all this for your amusement.'

'No,' he said, because he had been smiling unhappily, 'I was only thinking what an odd pair you are, you and Peter, to be writing about Lord Byron. Because he quite liked sex.'

When the bill came, Jeffries paid it, making the excuse of a company card. Afterwards, on our way out, I told him, 'I've gone about this in a very odd way. I wanted to persuade you to publish an excerpt from Peter's new book. But I don't think that's what I've persuaded you of.'

He rested his hand on my shoulder. 'If I can't it isn't because I don't want to. It will only go to show how much my voice counts for at the magazine. Not much, I'm afraid. The fiction crowd are really running the show.'

We walked together as far as Harvard Square, against the stream of tourists and students. 'I think we part company here,' he said and shook my hand. 'What an excellent idea this was. We must do it again.' From the steps of the station a man stopped to ask us for change. He needed to get back to his sister in Needham. She had called him to say that she'd been in a car accident, but then his phone ran out. When he tried to buy a train-ticket he discovered his credit card had just expired. He didn't have any money on him; he was stuck. A youngish black man with an educated voice – he wore a collared shirt and jeans. Only his shoes gave him away, a pair of dirty sneakers with holes in the toes and the rubber soles pushing out the seams. Jeffries dug out a dollar bill from his pocket. 'You poor man,' he kept repeating; afterwards he gave me a look. I had waited awkwardly a few steps ahead of them until the transaction was complete, then I shook Jeffries' hand again and said goodbye.

*

Snow lay so thick over the public parks, over the sand-boxes and the slides (where it had turned to ice), that I more or less gave up on taking my daughter to the play-ground. Only the swings were free of ice, but it was too cold to swing. Sometimes I carried a sled the necessary six blocks and pushed my daughter down the half-slope lead-ing to the soccer field. From start to finish no more than fifteen yards – you could see by the time you went home the tracks she had made. The blades burned the snow into water, which froze and gleamed. But I liked watching her more than she liked sledding, and we didn't go often. There was never anyone around when we did.

I hadn't seen Kelly since returning to Boston after Christmas. But a few days after the lunch at Sandrines, there was a knock on my office door. Almost no one came to my office. When I opened the door, Kelly stood there, wet-haired and red-faced and smiling. 'I bet you didn't ex-pect me,' she said. Her daughter was asleep in the buggy. I told her to push it inside, which didn't leave much room for anyone else, so she pulled it out again, with some dif-ficulty, and left it in the hall. 'I don't care if she does wake up,' she said, 'so long as I can have a pee. That's what I really came in for. I was walking back along Brattle Street and saw the sign on the college wall and thought, you work here. I bet they have bathrooms. And here I am.'

'There's a bathroom through the door at the end of the hall.' But she stayed where she was.

'Well, how are you doing,' she said.

'I'm fine, working.'

'I bet you didn't expect me,' she repeated.

'I didn't know who to expect. Nobody ever knocks on my door.'

'Until I did,' she said. I had the sense for the first time that she was nervous, or high-spirited for some reason; or both. She took off her duffel coat and hung it on the back of the opened door. But she was over-heated from walking, and a minute later she took off her sweater, too, and sat there in jeans and T-shirt, still very red in the face. Her blonde reddish damp hair fell into her eyes and she pushed it away. 'I bet I look something,' she said, 'don't I? I went up to the guy at the desk and suddenly I couldn't remember your last name. I always call you Ben, and I thought, here I am pretending to know the famous writer and I can't even remember his name. So I just said, Is Ben around, and the guy said second floor. Elevator at the end of the hall. I'm glad they put your names on the door. I wouldn't have had the guts to ask anyone else.'

I said, 'What do you mean, pretending.'

She stood up and went to the window behind me. This involved pushing past me a little and standing with her back towards me; the office wasn't large. Her presence made a perceptible change in the warmth of the room. 'So this is one of those famous Harvard views,' she said. Outside bright sunlight fell across the snow of the quad. Icicles hung from the eaves of the college library; a birch tree bent its snowy head. While we watched a mainten-ance truck backed its way along one of the paths, beeping. There was no one else around. 'I practically walked the whole way from Lechmere,' she went on. 'We had one of those court meetings, and afterwards, I thought, I better get this kid to sleep and she never sleeps on the train. It's too exciting. But by the time we got to Mount Auburn I really needed a pee. I haven't seen you in months.'

Maybe because of Jeffries' warning, I felt unusually awkward around her; awkward and a little excited. 'I'm flying to Austin next week,' I said. This was true. A friend of mine at the university had arranged a reading – the Eng-lish faculty was paying for my flight. The Harry Ransom Center had an interest in my visit, too. They have a large holding of contemporary manuscripts, and money to pay for them. One of the curators wanted to talk to me about Peter's papers; I told her I was just going over them myself but could discuss it with her when I came through town. Really, the whole trip was just an excuse for me to go home for a few days. For some reason I felt the need of it.

'To Wheeler Street?' Kelly asked. This was the street we both grew up on.

'Yes, I'm staying in my old bedroom.'

'Will you do something for me,' she said. 'Will you knock on my parents' door and tell them I'm okay. You know the house I mean, the red-brick house. Tell them you've seen me recently and that I look fine. I do look fine, don't I? That's what I keep telling myself. I look in the mir-ror and say, you look pretty normal to me.'

She didn't stay long. Shortly afterwards her daughter woke up and I sat with her for a minute while Kelly used the bathroom. Then she came back and wrapped them both up again. I saw them out as far as the elevator. Before the doors closed on her, she said, by way of goodbye, 'You'll have to watch out now. I know where you live.' The doors didn't close immediately and we stood there for a few seconds looking at each other until they did.

*

For several weeks, before my trip to Austin and after it, too, every time I sat down to work, I half expected Kelly to turn up. My solitude had a crack in it. I could feel the difference like you feel a drafty window. Whenever there was a knock at the door, my heart began to race a little, but it was never Kelly, who didn't repeat her visit until the spring.

I began to think about her unwillingly. Steve Heinz's comment came back to me. 'I thought maybe something had happened to you after ten years in England.' He meant, repression, lovelessness. Meanwhile, Caroline and I continued to 'try.' A few times a month she spent ten dollars on a stick to pee on, and I lay in bed in the morning, waiting to hear some noise of reaction from her, good or bad. But she was always quiet and this was always bad. One of the side effects of our arguments about sex had been that even when we could agree to it I found myself sometimes in the awkward position of desiring to desire, and failing. Even now, when there was nothing to argue about, the problem persisted – not always, but enough to worry me. Eight hours alone in an office leaves a lot of time for worrying. And then there'd be a knock at the door, and I could feel my heart quicken, and a phrase from Byron or Peter (I wasn't sure which yet) would come into my head: 'That I should live again impassioned days.' It seemed to me perfectly reasonable to believe there would be no problem with Kelly. I couldn't be certain, of course, but somehow this cast a different light on the problem itself.

Before I flew to Austin, I needed to look over the second batch of letters. Gerschon, a little unwillingly, had made copies and sent them by university post to the Radcliffe. They were waiting for me on my return from London, an innocent brown envelope in my office mailbox. After the lunch with Jeffries I finally got around to reading them. It occurred to me at last why none of Peter's personal letters had survived – if he ever wrote any. Peter was a Luddite. He wrote everything out longhand, including the novels. Presumably it was only the business letters he bothered to type up on an actual typewriter. (So far as I know, he never owned a computer.) There may have been other letters, but no drafts survived their sending, and whatever there was remained with his correspondents, whoever they were.

What *had* survived was more amusing than informative. Amusing isn't the right word, either. He finished a first draft of *A Quiet Adjustment* sometime in July 2001 – that is, two years after I met him and a month or two into his summer holidays. We know this from a date in one of his marbled notebooks. Probably he spent the rest of that summer at his Remington, turning the novel into something he could show to strangers. In October of that year, with the school term in full swing, he began to send out letters to editors, agents and publishers, as he had before. (On a whim, I called up Random House, Penguin, Little, Brown, etc., to see what they did with old manuscript submissions. None of them had any record of Peter's.) These letters more or less closely resembled the ones he had written over a decade earlier, on behalf of *Imposture*. Maybe one reason he kept the drafts was to keep track of whom he had written to – I know from first-hand experience how easy it is to forget. But he also began to write directly to other authors, the writers of the day, to enlist their help. These included John Updike, Norman Mailer, John Irving, Philip Roth, James Michener, J.D. Salinger, Thomas Pynchon and Saul Bellow.

Some of these letters were no more revealing than the ones he wrote to agents and editors. *Dear Mr. J.D. Salinger, I am an upper-school English master at Horatio Alger.* But sometimes he broke out of his role for a minute and lost his pleading tone. He became intimate and confessional. To Bellow he wrote about the effect on him of his unpublished manuscripts, sitting in his desk drawer year after year – 'emitting their rays at me.' He went on to say:

> On all sides there are forces at work on me. In *More Die of Heartbreak* (not your best book, by the way), Mrs. Bedell cries out, What am I to do about my sexuality? A very moving cry, but forgive me, in her case, the answer seems obvious enough. Let it go. This is what I have done myself and with much greater temptation. Maybe you don't see the connection between these two things. But writing is like a sexual act in which it becomes clear only later whether anyone else was involved. You have had a regular orgy – I congratulate you.

To Roth, he strikes the same note.

> I was disappointed by *Sabbath's Theater*. Maybe I
> came to it too late, after the others – after the
> *Communist* and the *Pastoral*, which are very fine.
> (Now that my novel is finished I read a great deal.
> One of the luxuries of a bachelor life, as you know.)
> But it seems to me your argument in those books was
> that living without sex or sexuality was the only way
> to remain decent. This is not the argument of Mickey
> Sabbath. I wonder, should we trust the moral of the
> better book, because it is better? (*Sabbath's Theater*
> is full of inferior passages.) Or does this have noth-
> ing to do with it? As for the morality of the author,
> that is another matter. I used to have a great respect
> for writers, but now that I have written a few novels
> myself (one of them, at least, what you might call a
> work of literature) I have lost a little of my admira-
> tion. No one could have managed his life any worse
> than I have, but I can shuffle my characters around.
> It turns out this is very easy, compared to the real
> thing. I wonder if you agree.

Updike comes in for another little lecture, on Byron.

> He felt very strongly that what qualified him to write
> *Don Juan* (a poem, I would guess, you have an affin-
> ity for) is that he liked to put it about, as my mother
> would say. Probably you know the letter. Could any
> man have written it, he wrote, who has not lived in
> the world, and tooled in a post-chaise, in a hackney-
> coach, in a gondola, against a wall, etc. I wonder if

you agree with him – if you consider this one of your qualifications. As for me, I have been very little in the world and by my own reckoning wonderfully chaste. But I write. You might almost say, I write in lieu of all the rest.

So many of his letters come back to this phrase: 'I wonder if you agree.' The cry of the lonely man who wants an audience and hopes to provoke one into existence. He didn't really expect their help and he didn't get it. He wanted to shout out, I'm one of you, too. (To Norman Mailer he wrote, 'Success seems to have made you angry. I wonder what failure would have made you.') Updike and Bellow are dead, and Pynchon and Salinger hard to get hold of, but I emailed Roth's agent to see if Peter's letter ever reached him. An assistant wrote back to say that they had no record of Mr Sullivan's letter. Mr Roth was at work on a novel and could not be interrupted. I tried his publisher. Another assistant explained to me that it was not their policy to archive any of their writers' correspondence. What was not passed on was thrown away.

*

I flew to Austin out of New York because I wanted an excuse to look up Peter's old apartment. It's about four hours by train to Grand Central. The landscape outside the train window was draped in white like summerhouse furniture out of season. Only the sea, which occasionally glittered into sight, had any life or color in it. White clapboard houses, some of them new; factories; car lots; mansions. Harbors almost empty of boats. A few islands.

Bare trees. My daughter begins shouting at six most mornings, and I had gotten up with her to make the early train. All the way to New York waves of suspended sleep kept breaking in me. Nocturnal rhythms persisted. I woke up at Harlem-125th Street with the uncomfortable sense that I had been dreaming of Kelly – that something had happened that shouldn't have, or that I had done something I shouldn't. Muddled with sleep and guilt I was too slow to make the platform and had to wait until Grand Central to get out and catch the subway uptown.

Nothing much came of this excursion. The last address Gerschon had for Peter was W. 189th Street between Wadsworth and Gorman Park. I got off at 191st Street and walked slowly through the strange shadowy quiet of Washington Heights. By this point it was a few minutes after noon, but very little light made its way to the pavement between the tall apartment blocks – although the sky above me was a clear winter blue. What was strange was just the contrast between the size of the buildings (suggesting a high density of lived life) and the absence of people. I had an impression of privacy and obscurity *in quantity*. Wadsworth Avenue was a little livelier: sunlight fell on it, and there was plenty of traffic. But 189th Street was very quiet indeed. The entrance to his building was set back between two pillars, and I went up to the locked doors and rang the buzzer of his old apartment, eight floors up, and waited a few minutes in the cold. When no one answered I went for a walk.

Gorman Park was just at the end of the road. It turned out to be one of these small stately New York spaces, surrounded by thick walls, gloomily paved, and shaded by high trees. Not much room to kick a ball around in but good for an hour's green cool in summer. As it was winter there was almost no one there: just a man in an overcoat on one of the long benches, warming his hands in a newspaper. I imagined Peter himself coming there after school to stretch his legs and work out a few ideas. Deciding whether or not to walk on to Fort Tryon, for a larger view, which is what I eventually did. But I couldn't find my way up the hill – the rock-face kept interposing itself.

Twenty minutes later, carrying my luggage with me (only a backpack filled with papers and clothes), I discovered the funny elevator at the A-train stop. The attendant wore a warden's jacket and sat down for the journey on a wooden chair, the kind of chair people leave out on the street when they move house. We rode together (it was just the two of us) above the city, and when I got out it seemed twice as cold as it had below. The wind blew through me, but I walked along Fort Washington and into the park until I could see where it was blowing from: south down the Hudson from New England. Since the café was closed, I had to walk back almost as far as I had come to find somewhere to eat – a grocery store and taqueria on the corner of 190th Street, with a few chairs and a table pushed together behind the shop door. After lunch I tried Peter's bell again and this time somebody answered.

I explained myself through the entry-phone – that a friend of mine once rented the apartment. He had died a few years ago, and I wanted to see for myself where he used to live.

'Listen, I've just gotten in,' a woman said. 'I have to pick up my daughter from school in an hour. I want to have lunch. I want to sit down for a minute.'

'I won't be much more than a minute.'

'This is the kind of thing they tell you not to do in New York,' she said, and buzzed me in.

The lobby, which might have been grand, was empty and dark; several of the marbled tiles needed replacing. But still the building had charm – the charm of something on which money had once been lavished. Each of the brass-fronted mailboxes had its own little window and a slot for names above it. It gave me a shock to see 'P Sullivan' picked out in rubber lettering on one of the boxes. He'd been dead only four years; nobody had bothered to change the name. The elevator itself was narrow and badly lit. Soft quilted padding hung from three of its walls, covering the mirrors. On the way up I tried to calculate how often Peter must have stood where I was standing. Twice a day at least every day of the year; and sometimes double that, if he went out for a shop or a walk. About a thousand times a year. Unless he stayed at home on weekends, when he wasn't teaching, and in the summer – on the days he had no reason for getting out of the house.

These buildings weren't designed for visitors. They were designed to make visitors lose their way. I had come up the wrong elevator and had to go back down again to the lobby – there was another elevator for Peter's side of the building. Eventually I found his apartment at the end of a long pink-walled corridor covered in brown carpeting. Little scalloped lights, set into the walls and spaced a dozen feet apart, cast shadows against the ceiling. The numbers on the doors climbed into the thousands: Peter lived at eight hundred and seventy something. The woman who answered his door was frizzy-haired and large-breasted and short. She wore a red button-down shirt and a blue cardigan with shoulder pads. I could see behind her a chaos of toys, books, washing, and a wide sliding window with a view of the brown apartment block on the other side of the street. She had a cup of coffee in her hand and a little smear of jam on her mouth.

'So who was this friend of yours anyway?' she said, letting me in.

'His name's still on your mailbox slot. Peter Sullivan.'

'P Sullivan, the great P Sullivan!' This put her in a good mood and she offered me some coffee.

The apartment was small. One wall of the living room was the kitchen; there was just about room for a sofa, a small breakfast table, and a television set. She showed me her bedroom, too, which was covered in more toys and books and had a child's colorful duvet falling off the double bed. This is where her daughter slept. The bedroom had a window, but it gave on to the air-shaft and was always closed. They kept the blinds drawn over it, because it used to scare her daughter, who didn't like the thought of something climbing through. Probably she wouldn't care now, but it didn't let in much light and they never bothered putting her to the test. Her husband and she made do with the sofa-bed; it's the only way they could go to sleep when they wanted to, and he came home late and liked to watch a little TV.

'He needs to get in his TV time,' she said.

I asked her how long ago they moved in.

Four years, she said. Their daughter was one when they moved.

'What did it look like when you moved in?'

'It looked like all these places look. Empty and not very clean. They cleaned the floors and the top of the oven, but

275

the inside was disgusting. And the windows haven't been touched in years. But there wasn't anything left if that's what you mean.'

'Do you mind if I look round for a minute by myself?'

'Go ahead. He must have been a pretty good friend.'

'I didn't know him that well. That's why I want to look.'

So I went in the bathroom and opened an unexplained door, to a cupboard containing a vacuum cleaner and an ironing board. I looked at the sliding mirror over the sink. I stood at the wide living-room window and stared at the brown building opposite. Then pushed it open, with some difficulty, and leaned my head into the cold air: you could just catch a glimpse of the green of Gorman Park. In the bedroom I pulled up the blinds to the air-shaft and looked at that. For some reason the phrase came into my head again: 'That I should live again impassioned days.' Somewhere between these walls he had written that line or transcribed it from of one of Byron's letters. And it occurred to me that, whatever else he felt, the loneliness he felt must have been passionate enough.

*

Afterwards, I caught the red line to Penn Station and then the shuttle to JFK. It always amazes me, when I make these trips on my own, how close at hand is the solitude in which I spent the first half of my twenties. As soon as I go away, it comes back; there it is, waiting. I stare at my reflection in the window of the airport bus. I mumble my destination to the woman at the check-in counter, because I haven't said a word to anyone in three hours. I buy a root beer and a *Sports Illustrated* and turn the pages in peace and quiet till my row number is called at the gate.

On the flight to Austin, I took out some of the papers Gerschon had copied for me and read them over. To prepare for my meeting at the Ransom Center. One of the reasons I thought Peter's third novel was incomplete was the gap in time between the second and final sections. There is plenty of other material he might have used, which would have borne out his general theme – including the homosexual experiments of Byron's first Continental tour, and after it, his affairs with Augusta and Caroline Lamb. (His general theme I took to be the uncomfortable relationship between innocence and sexual attraction.) But for some reason he chose to write the ending first, and he died or killed himself before he could finish the rest. Gerschon's papers showed that Peter once intended to flesh out Byron's middle years.

For example, Peter had written out longhand a few paragraphs from what might have turned into a chapter of its own, relating to Byron's exile in Italy. This is what he wrote, in Byron's voice:

My school friendships were with me passions (for I was always violent), but I do not know that there is one which has endured (to be sure, some have been cut short by death) till now. That with Lord Clare began one of the earliest and lasted longest, being only interrupted by distance, that I know of. I never hear the word Clare without a beating of the heart, even now.

About a week or two ago I met him on the road between Imola and Bologna, after not having met him for seven or eight years. He was abroad in 1814 and came home just as I set out in 1816. This meeting annihilated for a moment all the years between the present time and the days of Harrow. It was a new and inexplicable feeling like rising from the grave to me. Clare, too, was much agitated, more *in appearance* than even myself, for I could feel his heart beat to the fingers' ends, unless indeed it was the pulse of my own which made me think so. He told me that I should find a note from him left at Bologna. I did. We were obliged to part for our different journeys, he for Rome, I for Pisa, but with the promise to meet again in spring. We were but five minutes together, and in the public road, but I hardly recollect an hour of my existence which could be weighed against them.

There were details in this I wanted to check against the history, but I had no books with me, apart from Marchand's edition of the *Selected Letters* – which was in my backpack in the overhead locker. The man sitting next to me in the aisle had fallen asleep with his elbow on my armrest. After a half-hour I began to feel trapped and pretended to need the bathroom. He made a noise like an animal and shifted in his seat. So I went to the bathroom. I wanted a minute to myself anyway and crouched in the narrow cubicle and washed my face, wondering if Peter had seen Lee Feldman again before he died. You need to find Lee Feldman, I thought. Instead of wasting your time on whatever it is you're wasting your time on.

*

What I remember most vividly from this short trip is the feeling building up inside me on the four-hour flight that I had something important to talk about with my parents, maybe even something to confess to, and my total inability to talk about it when I arrived. My father met me at the airport in the old Volvo and said, Nice to see you, how're you doing. But what we talked about on the drive home was the economy. He's an economist as well as a law professor and was still caught up in post-election news. He had strong fiscal feelings. My plane was a little delayed and we didn't get home till after ten o'clock. There was food on the table waiting for me, but my mother and father and I took our plates into the TV room and ate in front of the Jim Lehrer *NewsHour*. Afterwards my father turned on a basketball game and fell asleep on the couch, and my mother 'showed me to my room' (she wanted to know if I needed a duvet; the weather in Austin, even at night, was somewhere in the 60s). She sat at the foot of my bed, as she used to; and instead of wishing me goodnight, she said to me, as she always used to say, *Bessere dich*. For nostalgic reasons. It means, better yourself.

My father had two hours of lectures in the morning, but I saw him for lunch at Ruby's, the barbecue joint behind our house. The smoker was near enough to our backyard we could smell it from the basketball court on windy afternoons. The restaurant itself isn't much to look at. A typical Texas shack, the kind that looks like it was built in two days to last a few months and which lasts thirty years. Dirty pine walls with old posters nailed into them. A courtyard fenced in by corrugated metal. The waitress called out our names, and we picked up our trays – there were squares of greaseproof paper on them, covered in meat and onion shavings, with bowls of beans, sauce and potato salad on the side. We carried them to the courtyard. My father, a New Yorker by birth, wore the loose-laced leather shoes he always teaches in, chinos and a dress-jacket. I noticed for the first time the small nub of plastic in his ear, a hearing aid, which upset me more than it should have. Not that it bothered him much, except that he couldn't figure out if it was turned on.

Mid-February overcast mild Austin weather, the temperature of left-out milk. As we sat down to eat I told him about the meeting I had that afternoon with a woman from the Ransom Center. She wanted to buy Peter Sullivan's papers, I said.

What do you get for that kind of thing, he wanted to know.

'I have no idea. A few thousand dollars. More than he deserves.'

'What have you done with your own papers?' he said.

'Which ones do you mean?'

'For example, what you used to keep in that chest I gave you.'

'They're still there. Still in my room.'

'Maybe you should bring along a sample.'

'Dad, I don't think she's interested in my high-school poems. I didn't come here to talk about me. That's not why they flew me in.'

He looked up from his food. 'It can't hurt to ask. What did they fly you in for.'

'To talk about Peter.'

On the walk home, through straight narrow back streets, the houses smaller than the houses on our block, with narrower plots, many of them overgrown, the bamboo grasses growing through the chain-link fencing that separates one garden from the next, he said, 'One of these is for sale, I can't remember which. I thought, maybe I'll buy it, for you kids. There's always more kids coming along.' And then, when I didn't answer: 'What's happening with that book about me.' This is often how he referred to *Playing Days*, my memoir about the year I spent in Germany after college. Fulfilling his old childhood dream of playing pro basketball. He flew out to visit me in Landshut, the small town outside Munich where I lived, and this visit takes up several chapters. *Playing Days* had come out in England a few summers ago, but my American publishers were still on the fence about it.

'They want to see what happens with this thing I'm working on first.'

'What thing is that?'

'The book about Peter.'

'Listen,' he said, 'I've got to get back to the office, but not yet. Let's take another turn around the block.'

A few hundred yards from our house, there's a small park with a creek running through it. Houses overlook it, some grand and new, some old and poky. A turn around the block usually means a walk from one end of the park to the other.

'You remember my old friend Tom Vance,' my father said. An active seventy-something southerner, he had once joined us for the all-you-can-eat at my father's favorite Thai place. One of the friends my parents had picked up after the kids left home. 'He used to be a lawyer in Houston then came in from the cold as he says. Now he teaches a semester a year at the law school – mostly corporate law. He bought a big house out by Mount Bonnell. One of those concrete boxes with a view. But this is not my point. He's part of the poetry reading group, along with John Robertson, Philip Bobbitt, Steven Wiseman and the rest of the university bigwigs. They take it in turns to host. Bill Bradley sometimes comes along. He's given a few lectures at the law school. When I mentioned the trouble you were having to Tom Vance, he offered to show the book to Bill.'

'What can Bill Bradley do?'

My father gave me a look. 'What do you think a man like Bill Bradley can do? Bill Bradley can do whatever he wants to do. All these Washington types have connections in publishing. It doesn't hurt he won a championship with the Knicks.'

'I once got stopped in the street in New York. A homeless guy told me I looked like him.'

'I met him once myself. Sometimes Tom invites me to these shindigs and your mother makes me go. A very pleasant man; large hands. I told him, do you want to know an interesting fact. My son broke all your scoring records at Oxford.'

'That's just not true. What did he say?'

'I didn't know I had any scoring records at Oxford. As I said, a very pleasant man. But I don't know him well enough to ask a favor. Tom says he does.'

'I don't need favors,' I said. At the age of thirty-five, married, with a daughter and three published books to my name, I thought I had outgrown this sort of conversation with my father. This was the conversation I spent my twenties having. 'This isn't what I feel like talking about,' I said.

'What do you feel like talking about?'

But we had come to the end of the block, and I could easily put him off a little longer, as we walked together up the bend in the road to our front yard.

*

I had promised Kelly to knock on her parents' door, and after lunch, with the house to myself and nothing to do until three o'clock, I wondered if I should get it over with. Instead I wandered from room to room with the lights off, looking out windows, sitting in all the chairs. Remembering what it was like to be at home. Kelly had said she would tell her parents to come to my talk. I could meet them there, though I didn't much like the thought of introducing them to mine and explaining the connection. This is what I told myself as I put on jacket and tie and walked out: Get it over with; but I didn't get farther than her front yard. I looked at her house, the house Kelly grew up in. Pretty Georgian façade, red bricks and white pillars. Green lawn sloping into the street, with the heads of sprinklers poking out of the grass. The kind of house, I vaguely remembered thinking as a kid, in which a real American family would live. But time on my hands always makes me late, and in the end I had to hurry, sweating into my undershirt, to make my appointment at the Ransom Center.

Ms Niemetz met me at the museum lobby then took me to the student canteen. She was hardly more than a student herself and wore her pale hair short; her glasses had bright red rims. This was her first year out – she had just finished a PhD on Middleton Murry. Originally she came from Jamaica Plain, but she liked Austin and had recently bought her first pair of cowboy boots. Still, the Boston connection is part of what attracted her to Sullivan; her brother had friends who went to Beaumont Hill. The novels themselves she could take or leave. Historical fiction left her cold; her interests were more political. But she had a passion for obscurity – 'for its own sake,' she said, 'like art.' Over the plastic cafeteria table, between salt-cellars and napkin-dispensers, I showed her my copies of Peter's letters. These she loved, especially his letters to famous writers. Already whatever was private about them had disappeared. They were objects, and she handled them (even the Xeroxes) as if they were frail as lace.

She told me it was a good time to be selling manuscripts. Their budgets were set at the beginning of the academic year, and whatever they didn't spend, they lost. Around February the sense of urgency began to set in. Even without consulting her boss, she felt comfortable offering two thousand dollars – just for the manuscripts. She was interested in the books, too, but buying books wasn't her department. Besides with books there were other market considerations; the process was more complex. I told her that a friend of mine at the Houghton in Harvard was also interested in the manuscripts. Well, she would talk to her boss. Maybe they could go as high as five.

Then she looked at me and said, 'Of course, part of what they're worth depends on you. You're writing a biography of him, aren't you?'

'Not really a biography,' I said. 'I don't know that it will help his reputation.'

After coffee, she led me back across campus to the museum and up several stairs to a conference room. Then left me alone for a few minutes to prepare my talk. Blinds covered the windows; there were too many lights on. The air conditioning seemed to be running, too. Folding chairs had been arranged in rows in front of a lectern, but the rest of the furniture, a seminar table and several upholstered chairs, was expensively made. They looked like they belonged in the dining hall of a newly built stately home. I had a headache; I sat down on one of the chairs and waited. Eventually people started to wander in. I counted them from the lectern: about a dozen. All but three I could account for – my parents and their colleagues, my sister and her friends. Ms Niemetz had made two stacks of Peter's novels on the table. Not a single one was bought and none of the three unknowns was related to Kelly. Two were an Asian couple who came late and left early. The third was a man in his thirties who took notes and had trouble gathering all his loose-leaf papers, his water bottle, his paperbacks and notebooks together, in his various bags, after the talk was over.

I had chosen several passages from the new book: the bit about Mike Lowenthal and his Society, the opening few pages of 'Fair Seed-Time.' It surprised me how uncomfortable I felt. Mostly the questions had to do with Peter's Byron, but on the ride home, my mother, who was sitting in the front seat, said without turning, 'I liked what you wrote, but it's odd, I never like you as much as a character in one of your books as I do in life. You seem to me nicer in life. You seem to me happier.'

My sister said, 'That's an awful thing to say. I can't believe you said that. What a terrible thing to say.' She was sitting next to me in the back seat, as we used to. The only one of us to settle in Austin, she had kept up something of the old childish intensity of her relations with my mother.

'It's not an awful thing to say. I don't even think it's a *critical* thing to say. I like the books very much. Whether I like the narrator as much doesn't matter one way or another. When I said it was odd, that's really what I meant. I meant that I find it curious.'

'You find it curious that you dislike your son.'

'That's not what I meant or what I said.' My mother was very upset by this point. I could see her in the rear-view mirror. Her round face, with its top of silver hair, looked flushed with suppressed feeling. 'Ben, tell me *du bist nicht beleidigt*,' she said, switching halfway into German, as she often did. It is the language of her childhood and ours, and she uses it to express the old deep sympathy. Tell me you are not offended.

'Leave me out of this,' I said. 'This is between you two.'

*

My father planned on taking us out for dinner, to celebrate he said, but I wanted to go home first to change out of my jacket and tie. I never feel at ease in formal clothes; I never feel like myself. The bedroom I moved into when I was seven years old is outside the main house, under the stretch of roofing where the garden tools used to be kept. My parents decided to incorporate it after my mother found out, at the age of forty-four, that she was having twins. This meant that for most of my childhood I went to bed two locked doors away from the rest of my family. What I looked out on each night was the darkened garden and the short concrete stairway to the back entrance. After changing into jeans and T-shirt, I walked along the side of the house to the front yard. My flight was early in the morning and we probably wouldn't get back from the restaurant till after ten o'clock. Too late to knock on the door of an old retired couple. If I wanted to look up Kelly's parents I had to go now.

It's less than a hundred yards from my front door to hers, but by the time I reached the Manzes' house my heart was beating as fast as it would have if I were back in high school and going to visit a girl. Though the truth is, when I *was* in high school, I never had the courage to do anything more than eavesdrop on her conversations at the school bus stop. I stood under the pillared portico and rang the bell and wished I had kept on my jacket and tie. The doorbell made a deep artificial bell sound; it echoed through the house. After a minute I heard steps and then I saw, through the clouded glass panes running either side of the doorway, a hesitant beige figure in beige skirts approaching under a bright hall light. Refractions in the glass made her slip suddenly from one pane to the next. But when the door opened a man stood in the doorway, with his shirt unbuttoned and his shirt tails hanging out of his trousers. He had a tie in his hand.

'Hi,' I said. 'My name is – I used to live down the road from you. Probably you don't remember me. My name is Ben Markovits. I'm a friend of Kelly's. From Boston; I didn't know her well in high school. I told her I was coming to Austin and she said I should look you up.'

'I'd invite you in for a drink,' he said, 'but as you can see, we're just on our way out.' He was small-featured and well-groomed, with a short brown beard, though his hair was thinning on top and the hand in which he held the tie was veined and liver-spotted. The way he rested on the edge of the door also suggested a little the weakness of

287

age. Behind him the hallway led in beige tiles to a well-lit kitchen – by the looks of it, recently installed. An expensive, comfortable, not particularly attractive house.

'That's kind of you, but I'm on my way out to dinner myself. But I gave her my word. I said I would knock on your door and now I have.'

'What a shame. She should have warned us.' For a moment he looked at me, shrewdly enough. His face had none of the cheerful softness and vagueness of Kelly's face, which must have come from her mother. His accent was gently southern. 'Is there anything she wanted you to tell me? I spoke to her on the telephone yesterday.'

'She wanted you to hear from someone who had seen her that she's doing fine.'

'I'm glad,' he said.

And that was that. I walked back down the hill, under the light of the street lamps, full of some strong feeling that was partly embarrassment and partly something worse. My father was watching television, half-asleep, when I came in the back door; but I woke him, and the four of us climbed into the car and drove to dinner. We went to a place we had been going to since I was a kid, one of the first true Mexican restaurants in Austin, and were seated in a corner of the grand old-fashioned dining hall, which was more like a courtyard than a room, with tiled floors and potted trees and tables lit by lanterns. At dinner my mother wanted to return to her argument with my sister. She felt guilty; she wanted to make herself understood. She wanted to understand herself, she said.

'I don't know what it is. I have been trying to work it out. And then I thought of course I don't like to hear that you're miserable. That's only natural. But you're not, are you? Do you remember when you were thirteen or fourteen, you wrote those terrible poems. I only remember their titles, the blood and the pounding, the city of sorrow. From reading too much Edgar Allan Poe. For a while I used to worry about you, but then I thought, it's only dressing up. And that's all this is. Dressing up in ordinary clothes. You don't look unhappy to me.'

'How do you know how unhappy he is,' my sister said.

I never sleep well before a flight and I made the mistake after dinner of going to bed too early. Then I woke up at one o'clock, wide awake, with the light of the back porch in my eyes. I could see from the window-blinds that my father was still watching television. A flickering private glow. Or at least that the TV was on while he slept on the couch. Around two or three I drifted off, very shallowly, and woke again at six in the middle of a dream, perfectly aware of what it was I had been dreaming. I had been dreaming about Kelly – a knock at my door. She had come to my office again, but without her daughter. I invited her in, and she sat down in the office armchair and took off her shirt. Her bra looked white and uncomfortable against her white skin. What are you doing, what do you want, I said angrily and woke up. Probably I was angry about the embarrassment of meeting her father, and when my heart stopped racing, I felt relieved to have done nothing wrong, even in my dreams. But not only relieved – it seemed a little strange to me, as I made my sleepless way to the airport (my father drove me) and waited in all the places you wait in an airport, that even in my dreams I had undressed her and turned her away.

*

When I got back to Boston I called up an old college roommate of mine whose father works at the *Globe*. I wanted to find Mike Scanlon, the reporter who covered the story of Peter's dismissal from Beaumont Hill. Maybe he could give me some clue about how to get in touch with Lee Feldman. The *Globe* was just then going through a difficult time. There were cuts and strikes; Scanlon, it turned out, was one of the people who had taken early retirement. The first address they gave me for him was an apartment on Mass Ave, somewhere in Back Bay. But the woman who answered his phone had never heard of Mike Scanlon. She had moved in a few months ago and didn't know anything about the previous tenant except that he left his grey sports socks behind one of the radiators. I called my friend's father, who asked around the newsroom and came back with an address in Winthrop where, someone said, Scanlon grew up and used to spend his summers.

There was no phone number for this place, so I got in the car one Saturday afternoon and drove out to find him. It's a half-hour drive from Cambridge to Winthrop and it took me two hours. Two hours untangling the knots of Boston's highways. Winthrop itself is on a spit of land on the far side of Logan airport. It has beaches out to the Sound and beaches towards the harbor where you can watch the planes fly in so low and loud it's hard to suppress an instinct to duck. In parts the land isn't much wider than a mile, and the ugly 50s clapboard houses built on the one road running through it have views to either side of water – of ocean out the front, and bay out back, with its piers and private boats. There's a little hill to the north where the houses pile up more colorfully, and to the south an old cemetery and a new industrial complex. Scanlon had one of the houses between shore and shore. Most of these are summer places, boarded up in winter against storms. Their front porches are stacked with chairs and boating equipment. Scanlon's house had a car in front and dirty boots on the steps.

He came to the door in his socks when I rang the bell. A shabbily bearded man in his late fifties, one of those beards where the grain of the hair runs constantly into little knots and looks painful to shave.

'Yes,' he said.

I told him that Don MacGillis from the *Globe* gave me his address; I wanted to follow up on a story he wrote some twenty years ago.

'Come in,' he said.

The house was in better shape than I expected, dirty and cluttered, but arranged with some taste. Shakerish furniture; William Morris wallpaper and curtains. Old-fashioned dark green linoleum floors in the kitchen and painted wooden boards in the sitting room. There were views to either side of water and sand and drifts of snow on the sand. It *was* the house he grew up in, he said. When his mother died he used it as a summerhouse. After quitting the *Globe* he couldn't afford to keep up the apartment in town, so he moved in full-time. That's why he had too much stuff: too many bookcases and rugs and side tables and chairs. It was cold inside and he wore a thick button-down shirt and Boston College sweatshirt on top of jeans.

The radio was tuned to NPR when I came in and he left it on the whole time I was there, about an hour. Every few minutes an airplane landed or took off, loud enough to make the radio unintelligible. He made coffee and we sat down at the kitchen table.

'I hope I'm not stopping you from doing anything.'

'This is mostly what I do,' he said. 'What story?'

So we started talking about Lee Feldman. He remembered Lee Feldman perfectly well. He interviewed him first over the phone and afterwards they met up several times in person, first at a coffee shop in Providence, a few minutes' walk from his dorm room, and afterwards in Boston. Feldman got stir-crazy in Providence, where there wasn't much to do outside the university, and liked to take the bus into Boston on the weekends. These subsequent meetings had nothing to do with the original story. Scanlon liked the sound of the kid over the phone and met up with him for personal reasons. They had a brief sexual relationship. Brief wasn't really the word. It lasted on and off for almost a year, but in that time they probably got together no more than six or seven times. Basically, Scanlon waited for Lee to call and then cleared his weekend whenever the kid wanted to come into town. He realized that any pressure he put on the kid himself would have made him look ridiculous. The affair ended when Lee stopped calling. Scanlon wasn't particularly happy about it, but then again, he hadn't been very happy at any point in the relationship. 'Apart from the odd moment,' he said. All in all he was better off out of the business and realized as much after a few months.

'What was he like?' I asked.

'This is what I'm telling you. He had the strongest sexual presence I've ever been in the same room with. Aside from that, I couldn't really tell you. He struck me as a deeply untrustworthy human being. This was no innocent kid, but to be fair to him, he never pretended to be innocent. That wasn't his game.'

'Did you ever talk about his relationship with Peter Sullivan?'

'A little, at the beginning. Not much. Mostly what we talked about was Lee Feldman, and I'm sorry to say Sullivan didn't have a very significant part in his autobiography. We talked about his father some. We talked about other boys. The truth is, I never believed anything he told me anyway.'

'Not even when you were in love with him.'

'I was never in love with him. But yes, I looked forward probably too much to seeing him and when I was with him I didn't spend much time disagreeing, let me put it that way.'

From the kitchen you could see through the window above the sink the airplanes sliding down the air with their tails down – first the sight of them, and then the sound of them approaching the house after they had already gone. We had finished our coffee but I felt he didn't object to me wasting his afternoon. I liked him. He didn't seem to me, in his own words, particularly happy, but he also didn't seem to care much about his state of mind. And I wondered if maybe he had something in common with Peter Sullivan. If Lee Feldman had a type, and this was it: the older reserved unsocial unhappy educated Irish American.

'Are you still in touch with him?' I said.

'Six or seven years ago I got a letter from him. Something to do with AA. I know he was changing his name – to the name he was born with, he said. Lee Sung Ho. He was also going through a religious process. Finding God. I held on to the letter for a week and then I threw it away. I thought, this I don't need. But he shouldn't be hard to find. The church he mentioned was in the Boston area. Lincoln maybe.'

'How about Sullivan? Do you know what happened to him?'

'I know he died. The *Globe* ran a paragraph on him in the obits, and I did a little extra digging around. An overdose of Plaquenil, which he was taking for his arthritis. Strong stuff; there are also some links to depression. We'd run a story a few years earlier about a woman who killed her mother with these pills, ground them up and put them in her coffee. And then of course those books came out. I think I've even got one of them in the house, but I read them both. I thought they were pretty good.'

*

Meanwhile ordinary life went on. Winter turned into somewhat milder winter; March into April. The snow had melted and frozen again but more compactly. Parking meant driving up ramps of ice. Caroline and I talked less and less of impractical things, which wasn't particularly noticeable as we always had plenty of practical things to discuss. How to persuade our daughter to sleep through the night. Who was picking her up when. What should we do on the weekend to get out of the house. I began to have fantasies of breaking down in tears in front of her (I thought about this a lot lying in bed beside her) but the closest I ever came was in front of our daughter.

Our nanny, an old Cantabrigian, had a child of her own and on Wednesday afternoons, unless her sister could do it, she needed to leave early to pick up her son from school and drop him at swimming. This meant in practice putting our daughter down for a nap and sneaking out around three o'clock, while one of us came home early. Mostly me. My daughter at this time had a strong preference for her mother. When she woke up, she called out first for her nanny (since her nanny had put her to bed), and then for Caroline. Sometimes she didn't complain when I came into the darkened room, but sometimes she did. Then began a process of negotiation. She could be very stubborn when she wanted. If I tried to lift her up she would writhe out of my arms. If I tried to talk to her she would jump up and down in her cot screaming. It was best to leave her alone but sometimes I couldn't help myself. 'What do you want from me,' I would shout at her, matching her repetition for repetition. 'Not you, not you.'

It was possible sometimes to trick her out of her misery by offering treats. Usually cookies or candy, but I remember once, when we had run out of both, sitting on the floor of her room beneath the cot and sharing a bowl of cherries with her. I had to pick out the pits with my teeth before giving them to her through the bars. Her face was soon covered in red juice and I had the taste of the cherries on my lips and tongue. She had been screaming for ten minutes straight but was now very quiet. Just the noise alone was enough to set me on edge. When I stood up to get more cherries from the kitchen, she said to me, in her calm patient reasonable voice, Don't go, and I sat back down in tears and had to compose myself in the dark so she wouldn't notice.

*

Mike Scanlon had said it wouldn't be hard to find Lee Feldman, and he was right. In fact, Lee found me. One of my duties at the Radcliffe was to give a talk on the subject of my project. These were public lectures; the college advertised them in the *Harvard Gazette* and put up fliers by the exits to Garden Street and Brattle. My turn came at the beginning of April. About thirty or forty people showed, most of them other Radcliffe fellows. They filled the first four or five rows of folding chairs lined up in front of what would have been the home-court basket in the days when the Radcliffe Gym was still a gym. Henry Jeffries couldn't make it and sent his apologies. I half expected one of Peter's old colleagues or classmates to ask a question or introduce himself, but no one approached me afterwards by the cheese and wine. Mostly I felt relieved to have the whole thing done with. It had occurred to me that someone who knew Peter wouldn't like what I was doing to his life.

A week later I got a note in my box, a proper note, written on Basildon Bond stationery and sent by the US Postal Service, from someone claiming to be Peter's English teacher at Central Catholic High. Peter was, he wrote, 'a good, quiet sort of student. I believe I have the distinction, if no other, of introducing him to the beauties of *Palgrave's Golden Treasury* – a copy of which (one of the old small blue-bound Oxford editions, containing, I am rather ashamed to say, those "additional poems" that brought the anthology up to J.D.C. Pellow!) was my gift to him on graduation day.' The note had a signature, which was illegible, but no return address or phone number. I phoned Gerschon to see if Peter had left behind any copies of *Palgrave's Treasury*, and Gerschon promised to 'rummage around.' A few minutes later he called back, having found what I was looking for: a blue-bound edition from 1933 brought out in London by the Humphrey Milford Press ('publisher to the university'). There was an inscription, he said, which he read out to me:

> For Peter,
> On Graduation Day –
> Imagination, intellectual curiosity, and a sense of humanity – essentials for a creative life. I wish you a creative future.
>
> > Fondly,
> > Malcolm Longmann
> > English Department
> > Central Catholic High

I looked up Malcolm Longmann in various Boston-area directories and found him at last somewhere in Alewife, a few Charlie stops from Porter Square. When I called him, though, he was reluctant to speak to me; he seemed quite shocked that I had tracked him down. He was retired, he said; he had no business with the school any more. It was only by chance he came across that flier for my talk. He had gone to sell a few old books to the Harvard Book Store, which his wife made him do at least once a year (and mostly in the spring), and seen it pasted in the window. The truth is, he said, his memory was not what it was. He remembered all sorts of things that had never happened and very little of what actually had. And then he had had so many students. 'You have no idea how many.' Lately he had tried to count them up. Several thousand at least. Probably I should have pushed him further, but a few days afterwards I got an email from Lee Sung Ho and forgot all about Malcolm Longmann, who must in any case have been close to ninety – I would have hesitated to push him hard.

Lee's note was perfectly pleasant. He had heard I was writing about Peter Sullivan and found my address on the Radcliffe website. He thought I might want to know 'what Peter was like, at that time of his life. I suppose you know who I am.' At the moment, he was lodging 'temporarily, until he could get fixed up elsewhere,' at his pastor's house, which was a very nice house with a large garden but a long way from anywhere. If I wanted to see him I'd have to come to him. He didn't have access to a car – he was taking one of his 'sabbaticals from driving.' I wrote back to say that of course I would come to see him and we fixed a time and he sent me an address: in Lincoln, as Mike Scanlon had said, not far from Walden Pond. So on another Saturday afternoon, one of the first warm days of spring, I drove with Caroline and my daughter out to Walden, parked on pine-needles by the side of the road, and helped them carry a bucket, spade, spare trousers and a Thermos of tea down to Thoreau's muddy beach. Then I left them there, in the mild sunshine.

'I won't be long. I'll be back by lunchtime,' I said.

Feldman was staying with a family called Ogilvy, who lived on one of those large plots of land off the Old Concord Road. The house was a colonial salt-box, recently painted, with a porch built on at the back, jutting out into an English-style garden. Daffodils had sprung up in the long grass; there were still humps of snow under the trees. I parked in a lane of dirt; there were no other cars in the drive. Two modest steps led up to the front door, but the bell made no sound when I rang it, and I had to wander round to the back of the house and enter through the screened-in porch before I found anyone at home – a maid, who spoke no English, and called out very suddenly and loudly, 'Lee Sung, Lee Sung,' in the general direction of the stairway.

Before anyone came down I had a chance to look around me. A quaint, pretty country house, low-ceilinged and dark, though the window-panes glowed green with sunshine. There was a seat in one of the windows, with a dirty flowered cushion; and an upright piano beside it, where the family propped its photographs. The only one I noticed was of a broad-shouldered young man with a moustache standing helmetless in his football uniform. Through an open door, the kitchen appeared brighter and more modern, and then Lee came out of it with a cup of coffee in his hand.

He stank of cigarettes. I don't know what I expected him to look like, but this is what he was: a short, fortyish Asian man, with close-cut black hair, and a fattening face still a little vague from acne around the mouth and chin. 'There's nobody here,' he said, 'but we might as well go to my room. That way we won't be interrupted.' His accent was finicky, educated and naturally ironic. Mike Scanlon's phrase came back to me, about the strongest sexual presence etc., a description that seemed to me laughable, though I have to admit I was reluctant to go to his room.

His bedroom had a view of the garden, which ended in a birch-wood, with a mud track running through it. I asked him where 'his family' was.

'Where every respectable American family is, with two girls, on a Saturday afternoon. At soccer.'

'A nice place to live, I would have thought.'

'Very nice, if you like trees.'

He sat down on the bed and I pulled out the chair underneath his desk and sat on that. Not a large room, and Lee had put nothing on the walls. There was only a row of books on a wide shelf nailed into the plastering. Mostly religious; a Bible. *The Good Earth*. A paperback, as thick as a textbook, titled *God of Healing*.

'What's your relationship with them like?'

'One of gratitude and dependence. If they hadn't taken me in, I don't know who would have. But I do what I can for them. I used to babysit sometimes, though Caitlin is old enough to look after herself.' He smiled at me. 'I mow the lawn.'

'How long have you been here?'

'About five years, off and on.'

'You wrote me that this was temporary.'

'That's why I say off and on.'

This is how we talked. He said very little unless I asked him a question, but he answered me happily enough. He sat on his bed with his shoes off and his feet folded underneath him. Not that he stayed still long. It occurred to me that I didn't like him much, that I had decided not to like him even before we met, and that I had begun the interview with adversarial feelings. Every few minutes we both fell silent, and then I started again on a new line of questions.

'How did you meet the Ogilvies?'

'Gene is pastor at St Mary-in-the-Fields. During one of my stints at rehab, I came out to a place called the Self-Reliance Center, which isn't in Walden exactly, but isn't far off. A sort of halfway house. The idea is to get us to fend for ourselves. So we chop wood, and darn socks, and pick berries, that kind of thing. There's a strong connection between the Center and St Mary's. Every Sunday afternoon you have to go to church. I told them I was Jewish. You can imagine what they said to that. That's how I met Gene.'

'How old were the girls when you moved in? Do you pay them any rent?'

'That's not Gene's idea of Christian charity.'

'What a wonderful thing to do for someone.'

'Oh, the Ogilvies are all extraordinary. Everybody who knows them says so.'

'But you can't stay here for ever, I suppose.'

'You seem very concerned. At the moment, I'm applying to law schools. That's my latest idea.'

After a minute, I said, 'I don't mean this to sound like an interrogation. I feel like I'm asking you all the questions. Is there a reason you got in touch with me?'

For the first time he hesitated. 'This is the kind of thing I do,' he told me. 'I think too much about everything. You can imagine I've got time on my hands.'

'Is there something you wanted to tell me?'

Downstairs I could hear the maid in the sitting room, shifting furniture, pushing a vacuum cleaner around. For some reason I felt there wasn't much time. If I wanted to find out anything, I had to find it out before the Ogilvies came home. Also, my wife and daughter were on the beach at Walden, getting hungry and cold. I suddenly thought of Steven Lowenthal's room at Flushing, my reluctance to sit on his bed, the bowling trophies and VHSs on the shelf above his desk. His father's voice rising up the stairwell.

'I don't know. Maybe I wanted to talk about Peter.'

'Have you read his books?'

'The first one.'

'And did you like it?'

'It's more a question of how I found it. I found it upsetting.'

'Why did you find it upsetting?'

'Did you not? I think it's an upsetting book.'

'Because Polidori kills himself?'

'Yes, because Polidori kills himself and because many years later Peter killed himself.'

'Did he show you any part of the book when you were in high school?'

He thought about this, and then said, 'My response to his writing is not what he was interested in.'

'What was he interested in?'

But Lee only smiled, and we began again. 'What drugs?' I suddenly asked him.

'I started with alcohol when I was fifteen or sixteen, and I kept that up even when I let some of my other addictions slide. Well into my thirties. I smoked marijuana in college though I didn't much like being stoned. A little cocaine. After college I began to experiment with heroin and crystal meth. Crystal meth was a problem. I really liked crystal meth, though I found I could stay off crystal meth as long as I was sober. But I wasn't very good at being sober.'

'How did you pay for these habits?'

'The usual way. I stole money from my parents. But then my mother divorced and remarried and her second husband refused to let me in the house. My father went bankrupt and was almost as broke as me. I worked shifts at a 7-Eleven. I shoplifted. I did a little dealing on the side.

Sometimes people paid me to have sex with them, and then I used the money to get high, and when I was high I didn't mind who fucked me, and so the habit more or less paid for itself.'

'How long have you been clean?'

'Six years.'

'I'm sorry for asking these questions. You seem uncomfortable.'

'It's not that,' he said sweetly. 'It's just that I'm dying for a cigarette, and Gene doesn't like me smoking in the house.'

'Do you want to go outside?'

'Maybe we could go for a walk,' he said. 'Do you have any other shoes?'

'I've got boots in the car.'

In the sun-porch, where the shoes and coats were kept, he sat down on a deckchair and pulled on a pair of wellingtons. Then he took a leather jacket from the hook. 'The first time this year it's been warm enough,' he said. I got my boots from the car, and we walked through the garden to the lane running into the woods. Lee lit a cigarette and blew out smoke. In the sunshine the day was pleasant enough, but in the shade of the trees the air was like the air of a cellar you get to by going down stone steps. Lee found a bag of mini-chocolates in the pocket of his leather jacket ('from Halloween, I suppose') and began to eat them, smoking and eating as he walked.

'I hope my daughter isn't cold,' I said.

'What did you say?'

'I left my wife and daughter on the beach at Walden. I hope they're not getting cold.'

The path was rutted and the ruts were full of water.

Patches of snow under the trees had turned to ice, and the ice dripped. But the woods themselves were beautiful and ghostly; and sunlight in the leaves overhead caught the dust off the leaves and glinted.

'This doesn't look to me like your kind of scene.'

'I wonder what you mean by that,' Lee said.

'Six years seems like a long time.'

'I get through years very quickly. I got through my twenties in no time at all.'

We walked on another hundred yards and opened a gate in the lane, which was fixed by rope to a wooden post in the ground. You had to lift it to pull it over the mud. Lee waited while I let him through. A few minutes later, I said to him, 'What happened in your twenties.'

'I dropped out of Brown after sophomore year and moved to New York. I told people I was a photographer and waited tables between relationships. It's one of my curses that there have always been people willing to pay for my style of life. When I was twenty-eight I met a movie producer with a house in Hollywood, an apartment on Columbus Circle, another apartment in Monaco and a hunting lodge in Scotland. For three years I followed him around; we did a lot of drugs together. I had a very good time. I got used to Egyptian cotton and heated bathroom floors, sea-views, first-class cabins, Pol Roger and guns. When he decided to get clean, he kicked me out and I began to go downhill. I moved back to New York for a while, then followed someone to Chicago and someone else to Boston and ended up, after several forgettable and mostly forgotten years, at the Walden clinic. Then I met Gene.'

'Can I ask you another question?' I said. 'I don't understand why a man with two young girls would take you into his house.'

'There's a very simple answer to that question, but you won't believe it. The answer is that he believes in Christ.'

'I don't know that I do believe it.'

'You think he has another reason for wanting me around.'

'There are a lot of other people he could have helped.'

'Oh, but I'm very good at being helped. I need it so much.'

'Is that what happened with Peter? That he tried to help you?'

'You have a funny idea of helping. But maybe you're right.' The lane opened out ahead of us into the road, and he stopped and caught his breath, but instead of walking on, he said, 'The other boys had decided I was gay long before I decided I was gay, but it was Peter who broke it to me. I used to come by his office just to sit there. I told him I was homesick and he let me sit there while he worked. But I wasn't homesick. I hated home. He could see I was unhappy and tried to explain it to me. Do you know why the other boys don't like you? It isn't your fault. They're just suspicious, that's all. I can't remember exactly what he said, but I can imagine it. He found my unhappiness exciting, though that wasn't the word he used. He said it made him think of everything he went through when he was my age, that it reminded him of what it meant to be sixteen years old. He wanted me to understand that everything I felt he felt, too. What did you expect me to do? My favorite teacher and the only adult I had any kind of trusting relationship with wanted me to touch his penis. So I touched his penis. At the time I didn't mind that he wanted to touch my penis, too. Up until that point my penis had never made me very happy. What he wanted to do to it didn't seem any worse than the other things people were doing to me, mostly my parents. It was almost a relief, when I got to college and could live like I wanted to live for the first time, to dump all the blame on him. Peter got my parents off my back. But it took me a while to realize that maybe he *did* do something to me. If nothing else, he turned me into a pretty secretive kid. Gene says I have to stop blaming myself, but that's not what you care about. That's not what you came here to talk to me about.'

'How did you know he wanted you to –'

'Oh for God's sake, he put my hand on his crotch and said, Look at me! Look at me!'

We walked on in silence. The road wasn't particularly busy, but sometimes we had to step onto the verge together while a car went by. One of the cars was the Ogilvies' station wagon. First they honked, and then they pulled over thirty yards ahead of us. The girls in the back had their kneepads and cleats still on. Two blonde girls with the flat pointy faces of adolescence: all bones and eyes. Mrs Ogilvy leaned out the window and Lee introduced me to her. A skinny, anxious, friendly, fair-haired woman. She told me to come for lunch, but I said that I'd left my family on the beach at Walden Pond.

'I think I'm already in trouble,' I said.

Her husband, who was leaning over his wife, stretching the seat belt, smiled. The man from the photograph; he had a moustache and a red cheerful face. Lee had opened the backseat door and was talking to the girls.

'Did you win?' he said, in a different voice. 'You both look too clean to me.'

Then they left us, with another honk, and we followed them into the road. A few minutes later the house came into sight, and I said to Lee, 'I met one of your old friends recently. Mike Scanlon, from the *Boston Globe*. He said that you sent him a letter. Something to do with AA. And I've been wondering if you ever got in touch with Peter.'

We walked up the drive together, and he stopped by my car and took out another cigarette. 'Yes,' he said, after lighting it. 'I saw Peter again.'

'When was this?'

'Around the same time. Maybe five years ago. Shortly after I moved in here.'

'Did he stay long?'

'No. He met Gene and the girls, and Mary told him to stay for supper. Maybe they're not your kind of people but they believe in forgiveness. Peter declined.'

'How did he look?'

'I think I was more worried at the time about how I looked to him. I was very nervous.'

'How do you think you looked to him?'

He sat on this question for a while. 'Oh, I can imagine,' he said at last. 'What's the word people like you like to use. Pretty depressing.'

As I backed into the road, he stayed in the garden finishing his cigarette. And I remembered something I had all but forgotten, I remembered coming back with Peter to the high-school cafeteria, after one of our walks, and finding the faculty canteen full of parents. Once a year the middle school had a parents' day and since their canteen wasn't big enough or grand enough to host them, they took over ours. Fifty-odd fathers in suit and tie; a hundred mothers making noise. On one side of the canteen, on a few cafeteria tables, teachers had laid out the school photographs. Most of the parents were crowding around them trying to find the envelope with their kid's name on it. Then they had to work out which pictures they wanted to keep before paying the middle-school secretary, who had a table to herself in another corner of the room. Peter hated all contact with parents and resented having to eat his lunch with the students. But the photographs amused him, the touched-up smiles of the kids, the cooing of the adults. As if we were running some kind of modeling agency. 'Innocence porn,' he called it, standing next to me and muttering in my ear. Driving back to Walden, I thought, you son of a bitch.

* * *

A few days later I found an email in my Radcliffe inbox from one of Peter's old students. One of *my* old students, too, she reminded me. I taught her freshman year at Horatio Alger and vaguely remembered a long-haired girl who nodded too violently to show she agreed with her teachers and never talked much to the other kids. She was working her way through grad school, she told me. An Internet service had alerted her to my lecture, which she was sorry to miss. 'I'm another one of these Romanticists,' she confessed. Partly because of Peter. ('Isn't it funny? I can't stop thinking of him as Mr. Pattieson.') This was really the point of her email. She wanted to tell me what she had never dared to say to Peter's face: that he was an inspirational teacher. He didn't play up to the boys in class, and since he had a passion for 'minor' writers, he was particularly good on women. Mary Shelley, of course, but Radcliffe and Inchbald, too. He could quote Felicia Hemans at length, and not just 'The boy stood on the burning deck.' Laetitia Barbauld.

'I wouldn't be doing what I am doing if it wasn't for him,' she wrote. 'Probably even you could tell I wasn't very happy at school. But then you come across a teacher like Peter, and you think, Ah, grown-ups! There's a whole world of people like you. You can't imagine what that means to a weird teenage girl. But of course there isn't – I mean, anyone like him. At least I haven't come across anyone yet. He supervised my senior essay on *Frankenstein*. Once every two weeks we met in that little office for an hour during lunch. He treated me like a colleague, he asked *me* questions. I used to look forward to that hour from the minute I woke up in the morning. I worried about what to wear, what to say, the whole thing made me nervous, until I stepped in that room and realized I had nothing at all to be embarrassed about. It was okay, I could talk as much as I wanted about books.'

Maybe it was this exchange that made me go back to Gerschon. I had almost washed my hands of Peter. But something had occurred to me on the drive back from Walden, and I wanted another look at the manuscript pages. Gerschon said he was knocking off early on Friday afternoon and offered to give me the run of his office. I spent the rest of the week re-reading Peter's last story and checking up on the facts.

'Behold Him Freshman!' follows more or less on the heels of 'Fair Seed-Time.' 'A Soldier's Grave' skips ahead almost two decades – a period that includes the years of Byron's fame, his marriage and the separation that pushed him into exile. When the story opens, he's living in Genoa with Teresa Guiccioli, the young wife of an old count from Ravenna. He has spent the past four years with her, 'confined to the strictest adultery.' The Pope won't give her a divorce, and the scandal of their relationship, besides a few other more political scandals, has forced Byron to take up residence in Genoa, where the government doesn't much mind them. Teresa has brought her brother Pietro and her father (another count) along. The whole family is living together at the Casa Saluzzo, though Byron has his own apartment.

By this point Shelley has been dead for a year. He drowned in a storm in the Bay of Lerici while sailing with a friend. Byron had kept up sporadically intense relations with Shelley since they spent the summer together near Lake Geneva in 1816. (The summer of the ghost stories, when Mary wrote *Frankenstein*.) Before he died, Shelley persuaded him to contribute to a new journal, *The Liberal*, to be edited and published by the Hunt brothers. Byron even invited Leigh Hunt – and his endless family – to Italy to talk over the details; and when Shelley drowned he had to deal with them, and pay for their upkeep, by himself. When Peter's story begins the Hunts have established themselves, at Byron's expense, a few minutes' ride from the Casa Saluzzo. Mary is living with them.

Shelley has left his old friend with one more entanglement: Edward Trelawny. Trelawny was a sort of professional adventurer, who fancied himself the real Byronic hero – the kind of man Byron could only write about. Trelawny eventually published a memoir of his acquaintance with the two poets. Its purpose was to glorify Shelley (also at Byron's expense), and it went some way towards creating the image later made famous by Matthew Arnold:

of the ineffectual angel, beating in the void his luminous wings in vain. Byron comes across as both self-absorbed and unsure of himself; easily deflected from his purpose.

This was one of the books I spent the week looking over – Peter had obviously referred to it while writing 'A Soldier's Grave.' But what I wanted to check the notebooks for was a date. Lee had said that Peter came to see him about five years ago, which must have been only months before his death. It had occurred to me that the two were related, that the reason Peter wrote the end of his book before the middle had something to do with his visit to Lee Feldman.

I stayed in Gerschon's office till about ten o'clock. There wasn't any window or natural light. Libraries, like casinos, are designed to make you lose track of time – to forget there's a world outside. I started with the letters and notes, the old receipts, before moving on to the manuscript itself, running my finger sentence by sentence across the pages. Peter's handwriting was always bad. It looked like frustration made visible, and probably to relieve it he used to scribble patterns in the margins. There were doodles of boats and suns. Trees and flowers. The zodiac. I had the sense that I was saying goodbye to him, in the air-conditioned quiet of the Houghton library. Surrounded by old books. That this was the reason I was skipping dinner (everyone else had gone home). But I didn't find any dates or anything more suggestive than a complicated little sketch, all gables and dormers, of a rambling old house thinly lined by clapboard.

A Soldier's Grave

I am almost ashamed to admit it, but it was Trelawny who gave me, if not the first idea then the final push, which amounts to the same thing. Trelawny, whom I hold in no very high regard, though he is tall and handsome enough and wants only clean hands and trousers to give him the appearance of a gentleman. But he was a friend of Shelley and is valuable to me on that account. Besides, it flatters my vanity to see the hero of Conrad, Lara, Manfred, et al. parading before me in the flesh, though he insists rather too violently on the resemblance and somewhat to the detriment of my own. He had come to the Casa Saluzzo on some business about a boat, which I had ordered to be built and subsequently tired of (my taste for that particular form of amusement considerably abated by Shelley's drowning). I was at this point, for various reasons, in a process of retrenchment; Trelawny offered to see it put up for the winter.

For several weeks he stayed with us but was not much in the way as he spent most of his days at Casa Negroto, where the Hunts were living with their brood of Hottentots – and Mary. I had foolishly given Shelley my word and consigned several innocent poems (and some not so innocent) to Leigh Hunt for a new publication, to be named the Liberal, as he meant to be liberal in it with other people's poems, and purses. Shelley's death left him totally dependent, and Trelawny made himself useful, as a messenger if nothing else, for Mr Hunt is either impudent or obsequious, and nothing between, and I had much rather give him my moneys than my time. Mary was displeased with me because she was displeased with everything, but I did what I could for her, which was very little, as she would not accept it. I was at work on *Don Juan* and gave her the manuscript pages to copy. For this I paid her a little money, which she *did* accept. Once a day, if the weather was fine, I walked in the garden with Teresa; her brother Pietro and their father Count Gamba had the apartment below my own, and kept her company when I would not.

'This is an odd Cicisbeo sort of existence,' Trelawny remarked to me one day at breakfast. It was my custom to take tea in the garden a little before noon, and sometimes he joined me. There was a fig tree that cast a pleasant shade, and even in October the sun was bright enough to make a few feet of shade desirable. 'I wonder you can stand it. Do you know what Mary says about you? That you are hen-pecked to your heart's content.'

'Teresa has a great affection for Mary. I am sorry to find it unreciprocated.' When he said nothing, I went on: 'But Italians feel everything more strongly. Do you know, that if *her* husband were to die (I mean the Count Guiccioli), Teresa would dress herself in mourning from head to toe and maybe even feel a little sorry for herself. Though he is a savage officious old man, who tore her from the convent at seventeen; and since the Pope will not grant them a divorce, his death would be a great practical relief to us.'

Trelawny can never sit still, unless he is eating; and as

there was nothing left to eat, he stood up and looked over the wall, to see who was passing. After a few moments he sat down again and said: 'You tolerate what no other Englishman of spirit *could*. It is one thing for an Italian to surround himself like this, with women and brothers. But I believe you are not very pleased with yourself, and Shelley might have forced you into a consciousness of it. If you will forgive me for saying so, I think you feel his absence as much as anyone.'

'You are wrong to think us so very attached to each other. Our friendship began after the age of reason; I have never loved anyone *sensibly*. But you are right to say that I am restless. I mean in the spring to buy an island, in Greece; or a principality, in Peru, and set myself up on a large scale.'

We were presently confined to Genoa, where the government ignored us, but I had a fancy of playing at governments myself. After a few weeks, when he saw no sign of it, Trelawny accepted an invitation to go hunting in the Maremma, and borrowed a horse, and left us. And so we passed the winter, and I wrote four more cantos of *Don Juan*, and saw no one but Teresa, and her brother, and their father. And the Hunts, when I could not avoid it, and Mary, when she could not avoid *me*. She always looked at me as if I had only to open the door, to let Shelley in; as if it was perfectly wilful of me, not to open the door.

*

In March, we had a notable addition to our society. Lady Blessington arrived in Genoa and, claiming a mutual acquaintance in Lady Hardy, I called on her the next day.

Besides, I had heard of her portrait by Lawrence, which made a sensation at the Royal Exhibition; she was supposed to be a great beauty – and I found her, at least, beautiful *enough*. We talked for an hour in the gardens of the Albergo della Villa, and the next morning, riding by the Corso Romano, which was only a little out of my way, I met her as she was returning from a ride herself. We stood in the lane at the foot of the Albergo, under the slope of an old Italian wall, with a vine growing up it. There were loose stones in the road, which the horses shifted on.

'You have been a great disappointment to me,' she said, as soon as I had dismounted. 'There is none of that scorn, that hatred of human-kind, which I had half feared on making your acquaintance; but which I had partly looked forward to. Do you know, I really believe you are the *least* unhappy of men.'

'I should hesitate to say as much for myself,' I replied. 'But then, I know a little more of the general condition of men, of this country or any other, than you perhaps have had the opportunity to observe. Besides, I defy anyone to be *very* miserable in your presence.'

She is a tall striking female, pale in the throat and rosy in the cheek, with fine brown large sympathetic eyes. If she were ten years younger, or if I were – what I was, there might have been some mischief; but she was reasonable enough not to mind much *not* being made love to. Her husband is no fool, though he sometimes appears it; and they maintain, besides the usual appurtenances of an Englishman's retinue, what Lady Blessington calls 'their voluntary Frenchman', a young count with the name of d'Orsay and the air of a *Cupidon déchaîné*. Her disappointment in me had this advantage, that it gave us a great deal to talk about; and from that day we instituted a regular habit of riding out together when the weather was fine, as far as Sestri.

These rides made Teresa very jealous, as she is no horsewoman and speaks abominable English, so that she always suspects me of a flirtation when I practise my native tongue. (Although it is the least conducive, of any of the languages at my disposal, for that purpose.) We had two small scenes together and one large one, and I managed to console her at last by assuring her that I had much rather fall into the sea than in love any day of the week. Lady Blessington met her once at Lady Hardy's, but Teresa does not show to advantage in English society, as it brings out her airs, which are quite ridiculous in a girl of some twenty years, and encourages her to treat me coolly, which she conceives to be the English manner (she is not far wrong), so that even her affection for me, which is genuine enough, appears in a very clouded light. All of which embarrassed me considerably, though their meeting had at least this good effect – it persuaded Teresa that she had nothing to fear from a woman so old and creased-looking. Lady Blessington is thirty-four. The next afternoon, when we met as usual for one of our rides, I tried to explain myself to her.

'I am sincerely attached to Madame Guiccioli,' I began. (This is the name by which the custom of Italian society, which cares much more about the word than about the *thing*, requires me to call my *Amante*.) 'But the truth is my habits are not those requisite to form the happiness of any woman.' We were riding along the Moro, with the sea very dark and troubled-looking though the heavens were clear enough. When we wanted to talk, we stopped; we had stopped now and sat resting on our horses' necks. 'I am worn out in feelings, for though only thirty-five, I feel sixty in mind, and am less capable than ever of those nameless attentions that all women, but above all Italian women, require. I like solitude, which has become absolutely necessary to me.'

'And yet every day when it is not raining you ride out with me to the Villa Lomellina, talking all the way.'

'Oh, I only go out to get a fresh appetite for being alone.'

'Are you so very much alone? It is an odd kind of solitude, which has room in it for a lover, and her brother, and their father.'

We arrived afterwards at a little square, with a fountain in its middle; there was a boy to take our horses from us and a few tables and chairs beside it, where we sat down.

'This is one of the virtues of the Italian system,' I said at last. 'They have a natural respect for adultery, and adulterers – and welcome us into the family. But unless I request their company, they leave me alone. Madame Guiccioli is in the habit of seeing me only once or twice a day; and in the night, according to requirements.'

'I never know when you are in earnest,' she said. 'You have the oddest way of attracting sympathy, and as soon as you get it, shocking it away again.'

'Are you very much shocked? I believe the wife of Lord Blessington, and the friend of Count d'Orsay, will find very little to shock her.' She said nothing, only smiling, and after a while I continued. 'There are only two principles to which I am entirely consistent: a love of liberty and a hatred of cant, which amounts to the same thing, as there is no liberty dearer to me than the freedom of *mind*. But I intend to make something of myself before I die. I don't mean more scribbling, which I am perfectly aware makes me nothing at all. I have half a mind to go to Greece – and play at governments, like Washington. I have a presentiment I shall die in Greece. Now is not this the sort of thing you hoped to hear from the poet of *Childe Harold*?'

But whether she hoped it or not, it mattered little, for a few days later she informed me that her husband meant to 'carry them both' (she meant herself and d'Orsay) on to Naples at the end of May. We were sitting in the gardens at the Albergo, which had a fine view of the terraces beneath us, all grey in the spring sunshine, with the green of the vineyards and the blue of the bay beyond them. 'Now I have offended *you*,' she said. 'For you look very gloomily at me.'

'I am perfectly prepared to be abandoned. It is exactly what I expect.'

'There can be no question of abandonment. We have stayed much longer than we intended – mostly on your account.'

'Only, it does me good sometimes to speak a little English.'

'Oh, if it is only on that account,' she said.

'And where will you go after Naples? One cannot be always living in hotels.'

'I do not know where his lordship means to take us, and do not much mind, so long as he returns me in the end to number 10 St James's Square.'

'St James's Square,' I repeated. 'It sounds to me now as mythical as Marathon used to.'

'I assure you it is not in the least mythical. It may even be visited, without the aid of Bruton's and a Greek grammar.'

'There are obstacles still more formidable.'

'You mean Madame Guiccioli.'

Eventually, I said: 'She had influence enough to prevent my return a few years ago and she may not be less successful now.'

'This is a most unaccountable life you lead!' she declared. 'I wonder you can stand it.'

We sat for a minute awkwardly in silence, but before I took my leave, she expressed more gently a wish to have 'something of mine as a remembrancer'.

'In that case,' I told her, still a little put out, 'I should like to sell you my boat.'

It rather surprised me when she agreed, and falling in line with the proposal myself, which was by no means a bad one, I offered her this inducement. 'I will ask my friend Trelawny to take you around, as he handles entirely that side of my affairs. I think you will not be sorry to meet him – perhaps he will live up to your idea of Childe Harold.'

'That is exactly what I *would* like,' she said. 'For you know, it was to see Childe Harold, as you call it, that we came to Genoa.'

*

Trelawny came, and Lady Blessington went, but Trelawny did not go. One day, while we were at breakfast, Fletcher announced that there were two gentlemen to see me. 'At least, one of them is an Englishman,' Fletcher said and gave me his card: Captain Edward Blaquiere. The other gentleman was a Greek named Luriottis. They had both come from London, where they had met with Hobhouse. Blaquiere seemed good-natured enough, if enthusiastic; Luriottis was something better. Hobhouse had lately joined the London Greek Committee, and Luriottis had been sent from the new government in the Morea to enlist their aid. Hobhouse had told them to apply to me. Fletcher returned with a pot of coffee and a plate of fruits; and then Pietro followed him, heavy with sleep, for we had gone to a party at Lady Hardy's the night before, and there had been dancing. Teresa's brother is a small, handsome, large-headed young man, and as brown as a Turk. Sometimes, to tease him, I call him the onion-eater, a term of abuse he taught me himself and native to Ravenna. It means peasant.

Pietro was delighted with Luriottis and practised his Greek upon him, which he reads a little of and speaks not at all. All of this put me unaccountably in very good spirits. It was a fine spring morning, the sky perfectly blue and the sun not very hot, unless you sat in it directly. I had broken a little biscuit and thrown it underfoot, and the sparrows pecked at it. Blaquiere wanted me to come with him to the Morea. Nothing could be nobler than their intentions, but somehow the Greeks had got themselves into a habit of disagreement under the Turks, which they could not break. What they wanted was someone or something to unite them; I had only to 'show myself', and they would 'rise up of their own accord'.

'Now what do you think of this, Trelawny?' I said. 'This would be something better than scribbling verses.'

'It would indeed, my lord.'

'And yet you take it all very coolly.'

'I don't for a minute suppose you will go.'

'Perhaps I may, if only on that account.'

'You could do nothing that would please me better.'

'Well, I have sold my boat, but I suppose we can buy another.'

He really is very provoking and sat there eating one after another the chocolates Blaquiere had brought me from Gunters in Berkeley Square. He said, 'If Madame Guiccioli will permit you.'

'What do you think, Pietro,' I said. 'Will your sister let us go?'

'Do you really think of going? But we cannot go as we are – to fight. We must have a new set of clothes. I will go to Giacomo Aspe and tell him what we need. We will certainly need helmets, if there is to be any fighting.'

We parted all on very good terms and saw them again in the evening, though I told the captain not to a mention a word of any of this, as we were dining with Teresa. And a few days later they left us – Blaquiere for London, to make the arrangements with the Committee, and Luriottis for Cephalonia, where Colocotroni was then stationed. He is one of the wildest and bravest of all the tribal chiefs, and wants taming. Teresa at least suspected nothing and we could continue as before. Trelawny, who has an unpleasant way of doing nothing but eat, sleep and drink, as if it was a great imposition to himself and a favour to everyone else, eventually betook himself to Rome, where he had an invitation from the Williamses. He meant, he said, to put a stone on Shelley's grave. But I wrote to Kinnaird in London and asked him to clear two thousand pounds for immediate release and prepare the way for more; and to

Charles Barry, my banker in Genoa, to arrange the purchase of a ship. On the recommendation of Dr Alexander, I hired a young Italian to accompany us – a man named Bruno, who reminded me of poor Polidori on account of his youth, but seemed otherwise sensible enough, in the Italian fashion. At twenty-one he believes to have seen a little of everything. I ordered him to procure sufficient medical stores for a thousand men, for two years. And every day I wait for news, of one thing or another, and feel for the first time in many months – I do not know what I feel.

*

Aspe's helmets have arrived; they are very fine. Pietro's is made of brass and black leather and green cloth, with a figure of Athene on the front. For Trelawny and myself I ordered two, on a grander scale, with plumes as high as the ceiling of the sitting room at the Casa Saluzzo; beneath which, on my own, I have had inscribed my coat of arms and the motto 'Crede Byron'. But Trelawny has not yet arrived. He is still in Rome, though I have sent for him. The boat arranged by Barry floats in the harbour, where it is being repainted from stem to stern and re-christened, too: the *Hercules*.

Teresa has been told; we could not keep it from her any longer. Pietro told her. I said to him (he had come into my room, where I was writing, about eleven o'clock at night; he could not sleep, for thinking of Greece, and because of the night heat, and went for a walk in the street, under the large Italian summer moon, and came back at last a little cooler and saw that my light was burning, and came in), I said to him, 'Do *you* tell her, Pietro. After all, you are her brother and she has only one brother. Lovers are easily replaced.'

He sat down in a chair, after setting a few books on the floor, and looked at me humorously. 'I feel I should give you a little advice,' he said.

'You may give me as much as you please, if only you tell her.'

'What are you writing there?' – leaning towards me.

'A letter.'

'And to whom do you write this letter?'

'You are very inquisitive. To an American, who has written me on behalf of his countrymen. He speaks very confidently of their good opinion, and I wish to return it.'

'Oh,' said he, a little disappointed. 'I thought you might be composing – verses.'

'Will you tell her?'

He crossed his legs at the foot and rested his weight on his hands on his thighs. 'Are you so frightened of her?' he said at last. 'I think she is a good quiet girl.'

'I am frightened of – myself. When I was younger (when I was as young as you) I did not much mind giving pain, or disappointment. But I like it less now. I am squeamish in this respect and had rather not see it given.' After a minute: 'Will you tell her? I think she knows. I think she is only waiting to be told.'

'Will she mind it so much?' When I did not answer, he went on, 'Perhaps you could put it in a poem, you write so prettily.' Then, in Italian, 'What is it good for if not for that?'

'She does not like my verses. She thinks they are indecent, so I have stopped writing them – for her. And then she reads so abominably, in English. And in Italian, I write even worse. There would be some misunderstanding.'

'No, she would understand the main.'

As the night was so warm, I had opened window and shutters and from time to time a breeze blew in. The moonlight fell coldly across the floor. There was also the noise of the cicadas, which seemed very loud in the general stillness, and underneath that noise, distant and quiet but not to be silenced, the noise of the sea. 'Will you tell her?' I said again.

'I feel I have not yet given you my advice,' he replied, his large handsome head leaning a little to one side. 'But I will tell her.' He did not move and a moment later added, 'She is not yet asleep; she has been sleeping very badly. At least, when I came in a moment ago, there was a light in her room. If I tell her, I will tell her now.'

'If you tell her you may tell her when you please.'

When he left me, to go downstairs, I blew out my own lamp and sat in the darkness, listening. I could hear his footsteps at first on the tiles, and then nothing, and then the various noises I have already accounted for, besides the hundred vague sounds of an old house at night. I do not know what I expected to hear afterwards; I counted the minutes. Perhaps she is already asleep, I thought, when I continued to hear nothing, or he has changed his mind. But I did not think he would change his mind. Eventually I lay down on my bed without undressing. The first time I met her, at the Countess Benzoni's in Venice (no, it was the second time; I forget, I met her before at the Countess Albrizzi's – we had all come to the Countess Albrizzi's to admire her Canova, and I took the arm of the young girl with the long name, and admired), she was but nineteen years old; she is not much older now. She had been married scarcely twelve months then and is now *not* unmarried. I thought, you are a weak, vain, foolish old man, to let your heart run on like this over a girl; but I had not felt it beat so violently in years. At midnight the bells of Santa Maria rang out, and I sat up and with some difficulty lit the lamp at my table and finished my letter to the American.

*

In the morning, Teresa greeted me with the words, 'You are taking my brother away.' Sometimes she came to my room before breakfast (at which I eat very little and rarely before noon), and we would talk of the night past and the day to come, and make plans. For these interviews she dressed as if she meant to go out, in dress and corset, and tied her hair in ribbons, and presented herself generally as Madame Guiccioli, which is what I always call her in front of strangers.

'I don't know who is taking *whom*,' I said. 'He is quite carried away by the idea.'

'Forgive me, if I do not understand what the idea is.'

'Why, a free Greece.'

She hesitated a moment over the next question; she had sat down at the foot of my bed with her hands in her lap. 'Does Pietro expect to make himself useful?' she said at last.

'I don't know what he expects.'

'I think he expects to fight. He showed me his helmet, which looks very foolish, and when I mocked him for it, he showed me yours. Do you expect it, too?'

'Mostly I mean to give away my money.'

'And when your money is given away, you will come back?'

'Maybe even before it is all given away.' And I added, sitting up, 'You take it very calmly.'

'It seems to me I take nothing,' she said, 'you make off with it all,' which made me at last raise my voice: 'You cannot expect me to continue living this way.'

'Excuse me, I expect nothing' – this with the natural inflection of the Italian *Dama*, which they acquire at birth and spend the rest of their lives perfecting; and which even in a twenty-three-year-old girl is something formidable. I had feared a scene, but this was not quite a scene – it got no worse. She left me shortly after, and I dressed and came down. And in the weeks to come (we had only a few weeks left, while the *Hercules* was fitting; and waited only on a word from Blaquiere, to tell us where to go), she uttered no reproaches beyond the quiet reproach of her manner, which was correct and gentle and only a little cooler than her usual. It may be that she hoped to provoke me, by this insufferable suffering air, into an outburst, which would produce a scene and be followed by tears, reconciliations and capitulations; but in fact I was only glad to be given no occasion for explaining myself further.

*

It occurs to me reading over these pages that I appear to be a stupid vacillating creature while Trelawny is a model of good sense; but this is not the case. He likes to boast that he has fought a hundred duels and a dozen sea-battles, and twice escaped imprisonment. Once at the hands of a Turkish sultan, who meant to 'cut off his head', for marrying an Arab girl, who died – he was discovered standing over her remains, which he had cast across a pile of burning logs on the beach at Naxos 'according to custom'. Then he gives himself airs about Shelley, who saw through him clearly enough and tolerated his vanities for the sake of his praise, for Shelley was not above indulging himself in a little flattery. But he could not help himself and mercilessly teased Trelawny (who only sometimes suspected it) by pretending to hold any number of theories, which no man of sense could submit to. I don't know who *attached* him first, the Williamses, I believe. Trelawny follows them everywhere, when he is not following me. At least he makes himself useful upon occasion, for which I meant to thank him by the gift from Aspe's. However, I was a little ashamed when I showed him the helmet, with its ostrich plume three feet high in the air – at which he stared, until I put it away again.

He is not pleased with the *Hercules*, which he says is a collier-built tub, and not a boat, and perfectly unsuited to anything but getting drowned in. But the stores have arrived, along with nine thousand pounds in cash and banker's credits; and there is nothing to keep us here but a south-east wind. There has been a final piece of awkwardness with the Hunts, who reproach me for abandoning Mary. But Mary won't speak to me or write to me, and accepts my 'cold charities' only if they come from Hunt, which I resent in part because it forces me into more of his negotiations. He takes a special sort of pride in abasing himself for money. Teresa, who visits Mary sometimes (her notion of duty is beautifully Italian), tells me that Hunt has poisoned her against me, and talks of my antipathies, which extend even to Shelley, 'whose memory I constantly attack'. This is a lie, as I have defended him to Murray, Hobhouse, Moore, etc. repeatedly, even where he is indefensible, that is, in regard to religion, and the inconvenience he made of his first wife. I know what this means, having suffered similarly at the hands of Lady Byron and her mother. But it does not matter. In a week I will be in Greece.

Teresa is going, too, with her father – to Ravenna. His passport has arrived and he has managed to persuade her to accompany him. He says he is too old to adapt himself and does not want to die 'looking at the Mar Ligure – his heart is Adriatic'. Teresa at first refused and vowed never to leave the house where we had been happy and the shore from which she had seen me sail; but it was borne upon her at last that the separation might be less painful if she forestalled it, and with this in mind she has been as busy packing her two small cases and one large box as I have been victualling, watering and fitting out with stores and crew a vessel of some hundred tons. But it could not last, her cheerful efficient spirits, and a few nights ago we had tears, in which I joined her, as we really are very attached to each other (by time if nothing else), and to part with her is to part with four years of my life in which I have been reasonably content – more, I have never *expected*. 'Let me come with you,' she said, tearing at my shirt, and when I refused her she promised to stay at the Casa Saluzzo until my return. On her own, if need be. She had a strong premonition that if she once departed for Ravenna she would never see me again. 'You know me too well to doubt my *presagi*,' she said. This shook me, as she knew it would, and we clung to each other passionately enough, which was perhaps the best course, as afterwards we were both calm and she did not mention again her going or my staying.

At five o'clock on the afternoon of the 13th of July, I kissed her goodbye, with Pietro and their father standing by. It was very hot and she watched us go from the shade of the door; in the passage behind her stood several boxes and cases, some of them open, in preparation for their own journey. Her father walked with us to the harbour, but Teresa stayed behind. Mary had promised to sit with her. I half expected to see Mary myself, and would have been glad of it, I think, as I dislike parting on bad terms, but she did not come until we were gone. On the pier, we met Dr Bruno, Trelawny, Charles Barry, and another gentleman, a Greek by the name of Skilitzy, to whom I had offered a passage. There were also Trelawny's bull-dog (who was called, but did not answer to, Moretto) and Lion, a Newfoundland, which I had accepted as a gift from a sea-officer of slight acquaintance to whom I had once spoken lovingly of Boatswain, now dead these fifteen years and buried in the garden at Newstead. Teresa had given me a silver knife, pearl-handled and engraved with the phrase, in Italian, *I kiss your eyes*. It was seldom out of my hand. Around my neck I wore a locket, with a few of his hairs in it, that had been given me (a long time ago) by Edleston – who is dead now, and died young, but knew me when I was almost as young as he.

We slept on board, but in the morning there was a dead calm, so we decided to row to shore. It occurred to me that Teresa might not have left; that I might see her again. She had promised that she would never leave the Casa Saluzzo until I returned to it, but though I had made her afterwards promise other things, she is a woman, and Italian, and might have disobeyed me. But on the way to the house I met Barry, who had just come from it; Teresa and her father were gone, the house was empty, so we proceeded to Sestri, where Lady Blessington and I used to ride, and sat in the garden at Lomellina and ate cheese and figs, which were still a little green. At sunset we returned to the ship, and in the morning, under a freshening breeze, made some way along the coast, as far as Spezia, before becalming again, so we dropped anchor and spent another night. In the night the wind increased; we began rolling, and the horses, in a fright, kicked down the walls of their stable, so that we had to return and make repairs. I slept on board but in the morning ventured ashore again, and giving way to a sudden urge, climbed the hill with Pietro to the Casa Saluzzo. The door was locked, but we found the key where it always is and went inside – where it was at least tolerably cool, though otherwise dispiriting enough. There was nowhere to sit that was not covered in sheets.

'Where shall we be in a year?' I said to Pietro. He looked at me but did not answer, and I went on, 'Even now, I might give up on this plan, which is a foolish one, were it not for the fact that Trelawny and Hobhouse and the rest of them would laugh at me.'

'In a year you will be king of Greece,' Pietro told me.

We returned to the ship and that same evening, with the breeze blowing steadily against us, set off.

* * *

When I awoke, I was instantly made aware, by the angle

of the bed, of our rapid continual progress and climbed on deck to see Spezia glittering in sunshine a few miles away. The wind had shifted in the night. It now blew against the shore and sent the waves racing. I felt happier than I had in several months. The motion of a ship under sail is incomparably superior to that of a vessel at anchor, and this fact alone produced in me a surge of spirits. I have always liked being at sea, though I pretend to know nothing about such deep matters as stud-sails, lanyards, spanker booms, deadeyes and *lignum vitae*. It is enough for me to sit where I am not in the way, and to be left alone in turn.

Our captain was John Scott, engaged by Barry and approved by Trelawny; a large stupid Englishman, who nevertheless knew his business (and nothing else). It was possible to have a certain amount of fun at his expense. He dressed for dinner in a bright scarlet waistcoat, and spoke no Greek and little Italian. Since most of his passengers were conversant in both, we mocked him freely at his own table, but he laughed at what he did not understand good-naturedly. At Leghorn, which we reached in less than a week, we stopped two days, and I went ashore to a very gratifying reception. The news of our intention had preceded us, and we took on, in addition to gunpowder and macaronis, toothpowder from Waite's and brushes from Smith's (besides other English goods to be had there), letters of introduction from the Archbishop of Ignatius to several of the revolutionary chiefs, including Prince Mavrocordatos and Marco Botsaris, who was even then engaging the Turks a little north of Missolonghi. Also, two passengers: a Scot named Hamilton Browne and George Vitali, another vague Greek to whom I had promised a passage home.

Vitali, who was handsome in his way and looked half Albanian, dark-browed and white-toothed, became an object of fascination for Captain Scott – especially as he spoke no English. I told Scott (which may have been true; I certainly had no information to the contrary) that Vitali was addicted to certain horrible propensities, too common in the Levant; and that he (Scott) should keep a weather-eye on his ship's boy, who was a fair-haired child of some thirteen years. Scott, who was greatly shocked, said to me, 'I wonder how such a scoundrel can look any honest man in the face,' which was exactly what Vitali did a great deal of. He had no other means of making himself understood and was, for the same reason, quite incapable of correcting Scott's impression – of which he had no notion, except such as might be acquired by the following incident.

It was Vitali's custom, like most Greeks, to take a short siesta after lunch; and as he had none of our English scruples, he used to strip down to his drawers when the meal was finished and cleared away, and lie on the table. Spying him once through the skylight, Scott could not resist emptying a bucket of dirty water over him. Vitali, who was thoroughly drenched, gave a shout of surprise, but afterwards said nothing; and the captain, who was decent enough in his stupid way, 'forgave him' (so he told me) for being the victim of his own joke.

But Trelawny and I took our revenge upon him. We persuaded the ship's boy one day, when Scott was taking his own siesta, to bring up the scarlet waistcoat. It was large enough to fit us both, even buttoned up; and putting each of us an arm inside it, I said to Trelawny, 'Let's see if we can take the shine out of it,' and we jumped overboard. We swam until it came loose in the water and dragged it back at last like a dead dog. This was unkind of me, and I was really almost ashamed, for Captain Scott (who had been wakened by this point and greeted us as we climbed up the side) has such a respect for rank that he could only force a laugh at his own expense. Yet he was very much attached to the waistcoat, which had been tailored by Weston of Old Bond Street and was thoroughly ruined.

In this way we reached the straits of Messina, passing within sight of Elba, Corsica and the Lipari islands. I had hoped to see Stromboli erupting but was disappointed in this; though afterwards, from the shores of Sicily, I saw the clouds of Etna rolling towards us on a sunshiny day, the bright blue of the sea darkening beneath them. In the mornings I fenced with Pietro on deck until we were hot enough to swim; and sometimes, in the afternoons, Trelawny and I boxed together or shot at birds – which, however, I have a horror of eating. I confined myself throughout to a diet of ship's biscuit, Cheshire cheese and pickled onions. On the 2nd of August, we came in view of Cephalonia, with Zante beside it; the mountains of the Morea stood up faintly against the horizon. It was a sobering sight. Most of us had gathered on the quarterdeck to watch their approach: Pietro and Trelawny; Dr Bruno; Vitali and Hamilton Browne. Browne and I had been thrown a great deal together, as he is a Scotsman, and I *was* one. He is a sensible man, with some poetry in his compound, sufficient to have him dismissed from service in the Ionian Islands, because he loves Greece – and likes Greeks, which is by no means a corollary of the first.

The ship made its own quiet current of conversation and he said to me, above the noise of the water, 'I believe you have come this way before.' I looked at him and he repeated, in his gentle sombre Scots:

> Slow sinks, more lovely ere his race be run,
> Along Morea's hills the setting sun;
> Not, as in Northern climes, obscurely bright,
> But one unclouded blaze of living light!

'This is flattery indeed,' I said. 'I don't know why it is, but I feel as if the eleven long years of bitterness I have passed through since I was here were taken off my shoulders, and I was scudding along with old Bathurst in his frigate, and Hobhouse at my side.'

Cephalonia presents to the eyes a series of low green curves; Zante, a white face. As we drew nearer the colours and shapes resolved themselves into trees and cliffs, low stony dwellings, and a line of empty beaches. Eventually Browne said, 'I remember to this day seeing a copy of *The Corsair*, which my sister had bought and not read, on a side-table in the hall of my father's house, where I had come for the new year, being then in school; picking it up and beginning to read, and sitting down again, I hardly remember where, it may have been on the stairs in the hall or at the dining-table, until I had finished, and taking the book up with me at night and reading it again.'

'Well, well, as I say, this is a very fine vein of flattery; it is very becoming in you.' But I was more affected than I cared to show, for reasons that remain to me mysterious (as I have suffered in my life praise and abuse in sufficient quantities to be indifferent to both), and turned away from him to stand alone at the taffrail, until Trelawny, moving between us, put an end to the conversation.

We anchored the next morning outside Argostoli, the chief harbour of Cephalonia. Here I had some expectation of hearing from Captain Blaquiere but rather to my surprise learned that he was on his way home. Colonel Napier was also absent from the island; and we were met at last by his secretary, Captain John Kennedy, who rowed out to welcome us. Kennedy is a fat pink (in the face; the rest of him is lean enough) amiable young man, who, it transpired, had made the acquaintance of Hamilton Browne more than a year ago, when he was forced to put in for port while cruising off Cape Matapan in heavy weather. Browne was stationed in Coron and they spent an evening together, drinking and gaming; Kennedy was relieved, he said, to be able to make good on a debt of some fifty piastres he had contracted to him then. Colonel Napier, the captain added, was expected daily in port. Kennedy had been entrusted to say, on his behalf, that they would do everything in their power to serve us that did not violate the terms of their neutrality. Their *sympathies* (he was perfectly aware, they were not so valuable as guns) were all on the Greek side of the question.

We slept on board the first night, as the wind was too strong for rowing, and we could not carry the stores ashore; and I began a letter to Captain Blaquiere: 'Dear Sir, – Here I am – but where are *you*?' I wrote also to Marco Botsaris, chief of the Suliotes, to determine the progress of his campaign.

Kennedy had confirmed for us what we already suspected, that the Greeks are in a state of political dissension amongst themselves. Prince Mavrocordatos is their chief diplomat and legislator, and speaks for the civilian mass in this revolutionary chaos (which has no power or authority, but a great deal of right on its side). He was proclaimed President of Greece at the national assembly two years before, but was subsequently demoted to Secretary of State. Kennedy informed us that he had just been dismissed, or had resigned (*l'un vaut bien l'autre*) and fled to Hydra. Which leaves Colocotroni, with I know not what or whose party, paramount in the Morea. This is bad, and even a little worse than I expected, as by all accounts the Prince is both reasonable and reasonably just (one by no means follows on the other) – and, apart from anything else, decently corruptible; whereas Colocotroni is reckoned neither corruptible nor persuadable. In short, everything is in a state of confusion: the Turks in force in Acarnania, and their fleet blockading the coast from Missolonghi to Charienza; while the Greek fleet from want of means or other causes remains in port in Hydra, Ipsara and Spezas. The Greeks themselves are divided, between statesmen, warriors and chieftains (who have been badly compromised by Turkish rule); and the British are not much better, fomenting against their own neutrality and forced to restrain with one hand what they offer with the other.

In the morning it struck me as both desirable and convenient to remain on board, to spare Colonel Napier any embarrassment; but I sent my horses ashore. In fact, for much of that second day a steady traffic passed between harbour and ship, including several boat-loads of Suliote warriors, who had heard that I was on board and wished to pay their respects. The sight of them gladdened my heart and brought back memories of Epirus, and the Veli

Pasha, and – a great many other things. After all, no cause is lost, which has such defenders. They are a fine wild race, as passionate as the Scots and as brown as Mussulmen, which, however, they are *not*. Captain Scott greeted them with less enthusiasm when he saw them swarming up the side, a few dozen at a time and talking all at once. I said to him, we must tolerate what we cannot resist. It occurred to me also that I could do worse than accept the protection of such men. This they themselves proposed, and before the end of the day, I had acquired a retinue of some forty warriors, the fiercest in Greece.

I would probably have increased the number, but I found them not quite united amongst themselves in anything except raising their demands on *me*. Trelawny disapproved of them, as they had no great respect for Trelawny. He accused me of playing at soldiering, which, of course, as I said to him, is exactly what I believed we *were* doing. The next day I went ashore, with Aspe's helmet under my arm, and summoning my men and taking a few of the horses, we rode as far as Guardini island; Trelawny and Hamilton Browne and the Suliote chiefs on horseback, and the rest of the men keeping pace on foot. They really are fine creatures, to be pitied and admired. I had heard of their defence against the Turks, which was much talked about at the time, but though defeat may be glorious in its way the destitution that follows on its heels is rarely salutary: homes burned and destroyed; food scarce; cunning and beggary, among women and children, supplying the place of honour and innocence.

Colonel Napier met us on our return, and I dismounted, leaving my horse, and walked with him as far as Government House, though we did not go in. It overlooks a square with a fountain plashing in its middle. Around the fountain several stalls are arranged, and behind the stalls there is a row of coffee-houses and tavernas. We sat down outside one of the former at a table with a view of the harbour (the *Hercules* being just visible above a stand of trees). Coffee was brought to us. Napier is a tall gentlemanly-looking man, only a little scarred by weathers and wars. He has read widely, and with discrimination; and is himself the author of *an historical romance* (which he mentioned blushingly but could not resist offering for my perusal). What is more to the point, he takes a reasonable view of the Greeks and never expected to find the Peloponnesus filled with Plutarch's men. He knows that allowances must be made for emancipated slaves, though the Suliotes give him some trouble, as they are all in debt and inclined to be violent when they cannot be honest. He thinks I may come to regret involving myself with them.

Argostoli is a pleasant enough town, and pretty in the Venetian style; there is a certain amount of good society to be had, most of it English. 'We all rather depend upon each other,' he said.

I told him I only wanted to look about me; that I considered myself an agent of the London Greek Committee, and had no desire to give any offence to the Ionian Government. 'I intend to make free,' I said, 'mostly with my own money.' He promised, within the limits of his neutrality, to do what he could for us; and repeated Captain Kennedy's assurance, that our cause had, if nothing else, his *sympathy*.

The next day we came ashore again, riding out in the opposite direction; Trelawny, who is fretful, stayed on board and wrote letters. When we passed through the main square, seeing my men, the shopkeepers began to follow us (as the Suliotes owe everyone money), so that we soon acquired a train of some twenty or thirty hangers-on, together with boys, children, beggars, etc., all scrambling beside the steady warriors and trying to keep pace. They made a great noise, and discovering who it was at the front of this caravan (by the plume on my helmet), began to call out, with almost one voice, milord, milord, milord – and did not altogether desert us until we climbed at last into the hills over the bay, where the path narrows and the fall on one side becomes precipitous. I decided to ride back more quietly, with only Dr Bruno and Hamilton Browne. Since Browne wished to be introduced to Colonel Napier, we left our horses at one of the coffee-shops and made our way into Government House.

It is newer than the buildings to either side, and narrower, too, being rather squeezed between them. Tall windows overlook the square, with a view of the bay behind it, and Lixuri on the opposite side. The Colonel's office is on the second floor; he sits between two of these windows at a great mahogany desk. There was a gentleman with him, but as he wished to be introduced to me, this made no difficulty – a Dr Henry Muir, the health officer, with whom Bruno had in any case a certain amount to discuss. When they were finished, after a few minutes, Dr Muir turned to me (he has a mild palsy in one of his hands, which expresses itself also in his voice) and said, 'We are in the habit of making do with each other here. I hope this excuses my presumption.' What he meant, in fact, was to introduce me to a young friend of his, another doctor, who had invited a few of the officers, and other like-minded Britishers, to his house for *a discussion of Christian faith*.

At which I could only smile (though I promised to go). There is really nothing for me to do until Blaquiere returns or the situation in the Morea resolves itself.

*

The young doctor is a Scot, also by the name of Kennedy, a rather forlorn young man who attempted to persuade us all (there were perhaps a dozen present) of miracles, the Apocalypse, and the honour of Pope Pius VII. At his house, which was very dirty (there was only one servant, who also cooked), I met another Scot – and another Colonel; they are all Scots and colonels – Duffie of the 8th King's Regiment, who invited me to dine at his mess. And so I begin to get about in *society*.

I believe this dinner was a great success. Duffie raised a very gallant toast, to the health of our glorious cause, which I returned with a little speech, to the honour of the service, which Duffie was afterwards good enough to tell me *did very well*. And we got drunk. I have not got drunk at your English dinner-table in almost ten years – though it was a mess-table at that, and in Greece; and half of the officers were Scots – even so. Dr Kennedy was also there, and anxious to pursue a few of the lines of opposition I had put up on the earlier occasion. 'I consider myself a student of your works,' he said. 'There is nothing in them to which I would make any serious objection – at least, where *you* are serious. Perhaps this surprises you. But the Pope himself has said, there can be no doubt without faith.'

'I like his holiness very much,' I answered. 'Particularly since an order, which I understand he has lately given, that *no more miracles* shall be performed.'

'Oh, you are mocking us again. It is too sad.'

This brought me up rather short, and I stared at him. He went on: 'I wonder what there is that you would *not* sacrifice to this desire to shock. But I will not be shocked, indeed I will not. You will find me a better friend than that.'

'I meant no disrespect. In fact, I am a great admirer of tangible religion and bred one of my daughters a Catholic, that she might have her hands full. She died in her convent a little over a year ago, though she was buried in the Anglican faith – at Harrow Church, in a pretty churchyard where I was sometimes happy while I was at school, and I was not often happy at school. She was buried among such good Christians that they refused to allow any inscription on her headstone, as they considered her a child of sin – she, who was but five years old when she died, and had scarcely left the convent in which I placed her.'

'Forgive me,' he said, bowing slightly. 'Your lordship's fame tempts us into believing that we have understood you.'

After this a sort of friendship sprang up between us, and I sometimes visited him, after one of our rides, and allowed him to exert himself in persuasion – for he is really a serious young man, to use his own word, and that quality is not often to be met with. And he exerted himself and I . . . kept back as much as possible my amusement. Though these discussions had an effect on me, which I did not much care for, as I left him always with the conviction that I liked him rather better than I liked myself.

*

Trelawny has been urging me into some course of action; he does not mind *which*, he says. Towards Missolonghi or Negropont, 'wherever there are Turks to be shot at'. But I am still awaiting advice from the Peloponnesus, and a letter from the Committee, and have determined to remain for the interim in the Ionian islands, especially as it is difficult to land on the opposite coast without risking the confiscation of the *Hercules* and her contents – which Captain Scott naturally enough declines to do, unless I insure him to the full amount of his possible damage.

To pass the time we have made a little excursion over the mountains to Saint Euphemia, by worse roads than I ever saw in the course of some years of travel in rough places of many countries. Trelawny came, along with Pietro, Dr Bruno, Hamilton Browne, and Tita, besides a few other servants. We left at dawn, climbing into the mountains on several mules, who began to stink in the hot sun, which was, to be fair to them, very hot; and their passengers fared not much better. But the sea at Saint Euphemia was as blue as the sun was hot; and we embarked in an open boat for Ithaca, arriving at sunset on that rocky shore, where, as there was no one to greet us, I suggested spending the night in one of the caves which open their mouths to the sea along that coast. 'You are thinking of your wonderful poem,' Browne said to me. 'But I believe it will not be comfortable, and here there is no Haidée to

342

awaken us.' He begins to grow a little tiresome; Trelawny was smiling, too.

Pietro, meanwhile, who had ventured further inland, came back to say he had found a house, and a host, who, being an Italian (from Trieste), understood somewhat of the obligations of that word. In fact, as he was an olive merchant, and a wealthy one, which was more to the point, he gave all of us an excellent welcome and to me at least a bed and a room of my own. Which I was grateful for, having bathed in the sea while waiting for Pietro to return. The sun had gone down, and though the waves were still warm, and the night air not much cooler, I had begun to shiver helplessly. But I slept soundly and woke early, in the white hot dawn, and woke the others, for I was eager to be going. (I felt this eagerness all day, and for much of the rest of the week; it was very little abated by anything we saw or said or did.)

We rode on to Vathy, which we reached about lunchtime; it is a pretty town with white walls, lying in the arm of a blue bay. The English Resident, a Captain Knox, who adds to his many virtues only the faults of a large family, received us warmly, and rearranged several of his children and offered besides the use of the prison, to which he had the key and which he assured us was very comfortable and nearly always empty. Browne and Pietro, both young men, slept there. In the morning, Knox and his wife, who is a large simpering sort of English woman, who blushed whenever I looked at her, conducted us to the fountain of Arethusa, which made me think of poor Shelley, and *his* Arethusa and her couch of snows. But there were no snows, and Lewis, who had been Trelawny's servant and is now mine, declared (he is a negro), that it was as hot as

343

the West Indies. But I had left our thermometer on board the *Hercules*, and so could not ascertain the precise degree.

Captain Knox had had the foresight to bring a picnic, which was spread out on a handsome cloth under the trees; with the grotto of Arethusa behind us, and before us, across the sea, the Gulf of Corinth, Lepanto, and the mountains of Epirus. 'If you look under that cloth, milord, you will find a good English cheddar,' Knox said; and, to do him justice, I found myself unwrapping a rather sweaty piece of yellow cheese. 'But as for the view,' he went on, 'I believe you will find nothing like it in England.'

He is a very amiable man; a good head shorter than his wife, whom he dotes on, and of a disposition generally to be pleased with what he has. But I could not help teasing him a little. The grotto behind us was little more than a cavern, and put me in mind of another. I said, 'I was once in a cave in Derbyshire that a great deal resembled this one. It was known as the Devil's Peak, and when I was still a schoolboy, we made up a large party and travelled some distance to see it.'

'I have not been to Derbyshire,' Captain Knox said. 'I am sure it is very fine country.'

'They make excellent cheese there,' I said, but he takes everything so agreeably, it is impossible to mock him. After a minute, I added, 'I was then in love with one of the party, who was engaged to another. And we lay side by side at the bottom of a narrow boat, and were *pushed* through the dark together.'

'And what has become of her?' It was Mrs Knox who asked.

'She married, and subsequently unmarried herself. A

few years later she began to write me letters. She wished to see me, but it could have done neither of us good, and I did not answer them.'

That night we dined at the Governor's House, where I met several more Englishmen. It is very gratifying, I have been welcomed everywhere by my own countrymen as if I had *not* been forced into exile a decade ago.

We passed a pleasant few days at Vathy, touring the north of the island as well and visiting the 'School of Homer'. The beauties of nature, at least, have been nothing diminished by the passage of centuries. The arts and traditions I leave to the antiquaries, and so well have those gentlemen contrived to settle such questions, that – as the existence of Troy is disputed – so that of Ithaca (of *Homer's* Ithaca) is not yet admitted. But scholars will one day stand upon the ruins of Watier's and doubt that *London* was.

Man, it must be admitted, has suffered rather more from the effects of time. Particularly in these last few years. On the streets of Vathy, you may see (once you have left the square and strayed into the narrower alleyways) children hissing at dogs to claim for themselves the scraps thrown out by the cook. The beggars are mostly young men; a distressing sight. Women of fifty sit darkly in doorways and lift their skirts above the knee as you pass by. Captain Knox, whom I really begin to admire, offered to take me on a tour of this wretchedness – he has done what he can to relieve the worst of the suffering but has never deluded himself into thinking it enough. To refresh his sense of it, he says, he used to walk with a pocketful of coins among the destitute; but has lately suspended the habit, as the children of the poor swarm so quickly and thickly around him he cannot pass more than a hundred feet before turning back. But for my sake he renewed the practice; and as it was the heat of the day, we made our way relatively unmolested.

I was never more affected by anything in my life, and I have known a great deal of squalor. On our return, I was half inclined to retreat to my room and call for pen, ink etc.; but my appetite for this particular form of diversion . . . is not what it was. Mrs Knox, who takes a great interest in the situation of the women, has introduced me to one of the families – a widow of Patras, named Chalandritsanos (her husband was killed in the Morea); she is the mother of three daughters, all of them exceedingly pretty and the oldest not more than eleven. Her two sons are away fighting with Colocotroni. The girls reminded me of the widow Macri and her three daughters; and the house in Athens where we stayed, with the courtyard and its lemon-trees, and Hobhouse, almost fifteen years ago. I offered to have them removed to Argostoli at my expense, and cared for, also at my expense; all of which was gratefully accepted, and my last day in Vathy was partly occupied with these arrangements.

On the morning of our departure, Captain Knox, his wife and five of his children (the two youngest were still asleep) accompanied us to the harbour and remained standing against the walls of the jetty for as long as we stayed in sight. Mrs Knox said to me, as I took my leave, 'They were all rather afraid of you when you came.' Knox has asked me to be god-father to his youngest son, but it will not do, and I refused. Whatever I care for dies; I have lost one child already.

We dined that night at St Euphemia and rode back

to Argostoli a different way, climbing the hills of Samos and sleeping at a monastery there. I was told afterwards that I behaved very strangely in the evening – that when the Abbot, who had greeted us, attempted to give me the benediction, I began to shout at him and would not cease shouting until he had removed himself, which is apparently what I had (in the midst of my ravings) demanded of him. Then, calling Fletcher to me, I attempted to run away. But Fletcher resisted, and Dr Bruno at last persuaded me to accept one of his pills, which he had hastily prepared. I afterwards fell asleep and awoke the next morning, a little weak and head-achey, and with no recollection at all of the events of the preceding night. Trelawny (who takes a humorous view of the episode) tells me I called out repeatedly that I was in hell – a delusion which may be partly accounted for by the torches lining the walls of the monastery. But as I say I have no recollection, and we reached Argostoli the following afternoon, on much better roads than those we set out on.

*

Botsaris is dead. We had this news on our arrival. It was Napier who told me; he saw us marching down from the hills (as we always attract a considerable following) and walked out to greet us. The story spread quickly among the Suliotes, who had gathered around me. They began instantly to beat their breasts and pull their hair, which is a thing I had read about but never seen; and which in the event made a great impression on me. He died at Karpenisi, leading a troop of two hundred men against a force of some fifteen thousand. But there was nothing we could do, and we managed at last to escape into one of the boats and make our way out to the *Hercules*, where the first sight that greeted me, on my cabin-table, was a letter from Botsaris. It was sent two weeks before and urged me to come on to Missolonghi. 'Your Excellency is exactly the person of whom we stand in need,' he wrote.

Blaquiere has not returned and I am still awaiting word from Hobhouse and the Committee. But I have written *to* him and explained myself, and my situation, which in fact is only gradually becoming clear to me. I have no intention of going to the mainland until I can avoid being considered a favourer of one party or another. As I did not come here to join a faction but a *nation*, and to deal with honest men and not with speculators or peculators (charges bandied about daily by the Greeks of each other), it will require much circumspection for me to avoid the character of a partisan. I have already received invitations from more than one of the contending parties, always under the pretext that they are the 'real Simon Pure'.

It was my idea that by staying on board I would spare myself a certain amount of useless annoyance, but the rumour of Lord Byron's arrival (and his moneys) has spread very far, and the boats ply themselves like so many ducks around us. When once they have got their foot upon the ladder, we can hardly push back into the water the men we have come so far to liberate. The worst of them is that (to use a coarse expression, but the only one that will not fall short of the truth) they are such damned liars. Whoever goes into Greece at present should do it as Mrs Fry went into Newgate – not in the expectation of meeting with any special indication of existing probity, but in the hope that time and better treatment may rehabilitate its inmates. When the limbs of the Greeks are a little less stiff from the shackles of four centuries, they will not march so 'as if they had gyves on their legs'.

I have come at least to one decision, which is to move ashore, to a small villa in Metaxata a few miles to the south of Argostoli. The Suliotes have really become impossible, and I have had the additional vexation of putting Trelawny in the right. Probably I should not have paid them in advance (which was at their own request) for this has had the consequence that the shopkeepers, who were in the habit of dealing with them on credit, have extorted from them the entirety at once. I have offered them another month's pay and the price of their passage to Acarnania (where they can easily go, as the Turkish blockade is over) just to be rid of them; and this a part of them have accepted. Though, after all, I am not sorry to see a few remaining, and we continue to ride out together when the roads permit – September has come and gone, but I am still here.

*

The house is very pretty, though small; set amidst vineyards and groves, with the castle of San Giorgio sitting on the hill above its shoulder. On the first floor there is a balcony, with a view (if you lean out of it) of the Morea. But our party is somewhat diminished. Aside from the servants, only Pietro and Dr Bruno remain. Captain Scott has taken the *Hercules* to England, freighted with currants; and Trelawny and Browne (they have lately become very thick) have proceeded to Tripolitza, where they intend to join the party of Ulysses, who commands a wild rabble of men in Eastern Greece. Trelawny is rather enamoured of him and calls him a 'second Bolivar', though this was perhaps on my account, as he wished me to 'bestir myself'.

I am not sorry to see him gone, though I am a little grieved at the manner of our parting. It was already decided he should go, as there was no room for either of them at Metaxata, and he had no wish to join me on shore. 'If you ever stop for six days in one place,' he said, 'you cannot be made to shift for six months. This is your own maxim, and I have found it to be true.'

On the eve of his departure, he came for the first time to the villa, to take his leave. We had only removed that morning; there was still a great deal to be done. I led him around the rooms and showed him the view from the balcony: of the island of Zante, and the Morea. It was a clear late-summery day, not very warm, but bright and pale at once; and the house, which was cool and still very sparsely furnished, had a kind of ghostly calm. We could see Pietro and Tita some way below, pulling the mules up a track to the front door, each of them loaded with several cases. But we could not hear them; they looked no bigger than children.

I said to Trelawny, 'The chief charm of the place is that it is out of the way. We were too exposed in the *Hercules* and could be seen from all sides, which was rather an invitation, to anyone and everyone, who wanted anything. But it is quieter here; perhaps it is even quiet enough for me to write.'

'Have you not been writing?' he said.

'You have seen for yourself how I have been occupied.'

He waited a minute, and then he said, 'Excuse me, I have seen very clearly what you have *not* been doing.'

'And what is that?'

'Why, anything at all; anything to the purpose, that is. You have listened to a great deal of flattery, I grant you that. And written many letters. And gone out riding, with a troop of bandits to whom you gave so little occupation, as you call it, that they themselves had nothing to do but take your money. You have made a tour of Ithaca, and explored the hills above Argostoli, and swum in the bay in the heat of the sun, till your head ached and you were sick in the night; but to the best of my knowledge, you have not taken a single step towards the liberation of Greece.'

'It is not my idea to do anything until I know what is to be done.'

'It is not your idea, and never has been, to do anything at all.'

The balcony was not very large, and we stood not more than a few steps apart; he had squared himself to face me, with his somewhat foolish good looks (like a gallant cutpurse's), as if for all the world he meant to push me off it. I said, 'I don't understand you.'

'Forgive me, I believe I express myself plainly enough.'

'No, I don't understand why you are angry at me.'

'I am not at all angry. I have given you up.'

'Oh,' I could not keep back a smile, 'then at least you had hopes?'

'Certainly I did, or I would not have come. I thought if I could once get you away from your *relations* in Genoa, you might begin to act the part you have always pretended to play. You are fond of saying that a man should have something better to do than write verses; well, you have found something better, but you are not doing it.'

'I have not written a line of verse since coming to Greece. I write nothing but government letters.'

'If that is true, then I am sorry for it, for at least you have a talent for writing verses.'

It is always left to Bruno, wherever we are (since he is a young man, and an Italian, and thinks of nothing but his stomach) to find us good things to eat; and we could see him leading several boys into the courtyard below us, where there was a table set out, and depositing on it what they carried in their arms, bread, cheese, olives, fish and wine. Meanwhile, Pietro and Tita had arrived, and got in everyone's way.

'Where will you sleep tonight?' I said.

'It does not much matter to me.' And then, 'On board, I believe. Captain Scott has promised to carry us as far as Pyrgos, though we must make our own way ashore. But you are not even angry at me; I had hoped to make you angry.'

'Then you have gone about it in the very worst way. Whenever anyone is angry at me, I wish only to placate them. I could never *keep* a grudge.'

'Well, shall we go down to eat?' he said.

'I don't like to part on these terms. I don't know if we shall see each other again. Whenever I take my leave, I feel it is for the last time; that everything is being taken from me.'

'As for that,' he said, 'I don't believe we were ever so fond of each other.'

We ate our lunch together, in the usual way; he, speaking very little and eating a great deal. Afterwards, he shook my hand, and I said, 'Let me hear from you often. If things are farcical, they will do for *Don Juan*; if heroical, you shall have another canto of *Childe Harold*. Come back soon.'

'I think your Harold days are done,' he said and rode off on one of Pietro's mules.

*

There is always a tax upon kindness, which is paid in further kindness. Mrs Chalandritsanos, whom, along with her three daughters, I had rescued from the squalor of Vathy and set up in some comfort here, is also the possessor of two sons. Both were fighting with Colocotroni in the Morea, when one of them, hearing that his mother had found a patron, immediately took leave of his chief and applied to *me*. This came at no bad time, as Trelawny had just left me, and I wanted someone to keep the Suliotes in order. Chalandritsanos *fils* is a boy of some fifteen or sixteen years, dark-skinned (though no darker than some Italians), with an oriental cast of eyes, through which he looks at you with a sort of fierce boredom. His manner was very little appeasing, for one who had come in search of charity; though this is rather the Greek method – to beg haughtily.

But the others have found me out, too, and I am no safer at Metaxata than I was at Argostoli. Here are arrived English, Germans, Greeks, all kinds of people, proceeding to or coming from Greece, and all with something to say to me. It appears that if I mean to have any quiet, I must make up my mind to join the fighting; it is the only way. Every day there are two or three or half a dozen visitors, who come to plead, stare, gawp, advise, in as many languages; and I receive them all and listen to their case or cause; and every day it grows harder for me to act. I believe Trelawny was right. When once I am settled, nothing can *un*settle me; but perhaps I am unsettled enough. The house at least is too small to admit guests. Even as it is, Pietro and Bruno share a room, and the servants make do in the kitchen.

I have begun to write again, a little at night, when everyone is in bed; but this was always my way. Another canto of *Don Juan*, the seventeenth – will I live to see it finished? From the window of my apartment, I can see the village below me, in transparent moonlight, which shows beyond it the islands, the mountains, the sea, with a distant outline of the Morea traced between the double azure of the waves and skies. I have put the Don at an English country house, with several ladies of the party, some of them married (though none of them to the purpose). In short, amidst scenes which were once well-known to me; but like Mr Hume's *ideas*, they grow dim, dim. And the lines come slowly and painfully. Teresa has complained that I do not write to *her*. This is untrue; only, I do not write her *at length* and mostly add a post-script to the letters Pietro sends her, for he is a dutiful brother.

At present, I am rather plagued with doctors: there are Bruno, Kennedy, Muir *inter alia*. The Committee has sent a young man, a Dr Millingen, who wishes to see the world and do some good in it. He has this merit, that he listens and does not talk much. But I believe he begins to chafe at our existence (*this* is not the world he has come to see) and soothes his restlessness by doctoring *me*. He says he is concerned at my drinking, and I have no reason to disbelieve him: he seems an honest man. But then, I drink mostly at night, when I sleep very little, and since I never get drunk . . . I tell him, that I drink rather than sleep, but that it comes to the same thing. He has asked Bruno the receipt for the little pills I take, as purgatives, besides doses of Epsom salts. I said to him, 'There are two things in this world that I especially dread, and to which I am equally predisposed – growing fat, and growing mad. Indeed, I should not like to choose between them.' But I asked him to examine my teeth; they feel loose in my head.

The Chalandritsanos boy is an odd mixture. I have seen him playing with the children, no more than ten years old, who sling stones at the trees that grow into the path at the foot of our house; but the Suliotes respect him, and every day he rides out at the head of some dozen men barking commands. His name is Lukas. I have made him my page, since he loves fine clothes and lets me dress him as I please, which is all that I require. He speaks Italian (of a sort), and has attached himself already to Bruno and Pietro, hoping to learn more. But they do not mind him much. To me he says very little, though he is not shy.

A few days ago we had an earthquake. There have been several on the island in recent weeks, but this was sufficiently powerful to make it a question of prudence to leave the house. I was one of the last to remain, and on my way down the narrow stairs opened the door to the other bedroom, where Lukas sometimes sleeps in the afternoon – I should not like to give the news to his mother, in the event of an accident befalling him. But the room was empty; I put my hand on both of the beds myself to make sure, and then sat down for a minute, heedless of the disturbance around me, before continuing downstairs.

*

It appears I may really be going. Hobhouse has sent me another colonel, this one by the name of Stanhope, a black-haired though by no means youthful officer of the Committtee, who arrived already in a hurry and with a great many good intentions. He is a rabid Benthamite and believes that the human machine may be easily regulated, with a little pressure here and there; to which end, he has carried with him from England (it weighs not much less than a ton) *a printing press*, as the best means of applying it. I think he means to *persuade* the Greeks of their liberty, and to reason the Turks into granting it. In person, he is pleasant enough, brisk and neatly attired, but you have only to say the word, and he cannot resist explaining himself, and it is always the same explanation.

Millingen is gone already, on to Missolonghi, where the suffering is intensest and direction most needed after the death of Botsaris. Stanhope intends to join him shortly. And I have committed myself to the Morea, the seat of the provisional government, of which I have received several favourable accounts from Browne and Trelawny. But I mean to judge for myself. Browne, meanwhile, has gone back to England with two Greek deputies, seeking an additional loan. And Trelawny has sent me a very amusing letter, quite in my old vein – he has decided to accompany Ulysses on to Negropont, where they will 'pass the winter, there being excellent sport', he says, 'between Turk and woodcock shooting.' He has been made a kind of aide-camp, with fifty men under his command, and never leaves the General's side – being accoutred exactly like him, in red and gold vest with sheepskin capote. With gun pistols sabre etc. All this he writes in his letter. There is also some talk (but this I have through other sources) of his being given Ulysses' daughter or niece or some such relation to marry, as the Greeks have a passion for kinship and press upon perfect strangers, as a sign of their hospitality, their precious women!

*

No, it is all off. Browne came first to Argostoli on his way home, where I met with him, and his account of the Provisional Government does not command in me sufficient confidence to give it the stamp of my approval, which is, after all, what my visit would suggest. He means to ask the Committee for a steamboat – he believes a great deal may be accomplished with an armoured steamboat. And this is also the opinion of several of the naval officers he has consulted with. The two Greek Deputies – Luriottis is one of them, and asked after Madame Guiccioli; he is a gentleman – have been authorized by the Provisional Government to beg another loan of me, of some three hundred thousand piastres, which is no more than what is required, he says, to activate the fleet. I agreed to give two hundred thousand, for the Greeks always expect some negotiation and have been so conditioned by the distrust that usually meets them that even honest Greeks (of which there are very few) begin to exaggerate a little, in anticipation.

It is now December. The fire in my apartment (which is always burning) smokes terribly, as the wood we had put aside was most of it stolen, and what remains is damp and green. I have been here almost five months. Yesterday I had a letter from Augusta, concerning my daughter. It appears that Ada suffers terribly from headaches, which begin to affect her sight. I was subject to the same complaint, but not at so early an age nor in so great a degree. Besides, it never affected my eyes but rather my hearing. This last news has left me more miserable than I can at all account for, as I was not fond of her mother and have not seen the child herself (who is now eight) since she lay sucking in that woman's arms. Perhaps she will get quite well when she arrives at *womanhood*, but that is some time to look forward to, especially where the climate is cold. In Italy and the East, it sometimes occurs at twelve or even earlier. (I knew an instance in an Italian house, at *ten*, though this was considered uncommon.) But Ada, Ada – I have been writing the word in the margins of the page, when I am meant to be writing my poem; and it is more suggestive to me than . . . anything else that I write. I find the idea that my peculiar habit of suffering is shared by another human creature almost inexpressibly moving. Poor girl, if she is at all like her father she will not be very happy. It occurs to me that if I once get this business over, I might return to England – if only to report to the Committee.

*

Well, it is settled; tomorrow we sail. In two boats – to Missolonghi. Stanhope is there already and has seen Prince Mavrocordatos, from whom he has sent this very handsome appeal. He tells me that I will be 'received as a saviour', and that it depends 'only on myself to secure the destiny of Greece'. They expect my presence will 'electrify the troops!'. There has been a kind of contest of inaction on both sides, Greek and Mussulman, but the Turks have at length come down in force (sixteen thousand they say) on Missolonghi, which however is stronger than it was last year, when they repulsed the attempt. And their blood is up at last. The Greek fleet has lately crushed a much smaller Turkish squadron (it was fourteen ships against four), driving one ashore onto the coast of Ithaca, to which they pursued it, in spite of the island's neutrality, murdering every survivor. For the sake of the treasure on board – they would not have been so forward over a question of honour. It was a cowardly business, but then, the *pretence* of neutrality, when there is a war, is equally shameful.

On Christmas Day (or the day after, it is not much minded here), I left Metaxata, and am staying at my banker's in Argostoli, while the boats are fitted out. The first, which is called a 'mistico', being designed for speed, will take us to Missolonghi; the second will transport supplies. I have asked Pietro to accompany it.

Bruno and Fletcher come with me, along with the dog Lion and the page-boy Lukas. Today I took him to pay his respects to his mother, to see that they were paid. She is a large-breasted comfortable-looking woman, who does not often stand up. At least, she was sitting when we came, and sent one of her daughters to open the door; and did not leave her sofa once in the course of our visit. It was another daughter who served us tea and dates. But she wept freely, and under this provocation, the boy wept, too. 'You will see that he does not dishonour us,' she said. (They are after all a fierce people!) 'If he dies, he should die as his father did.' His sisters clung to him and kissed his face and lips.

I promised to present myself foremost to every danger.

Afterwards, we went to inspect the boats, and he stood by my shoulder, a little behind, to escape showing his eyes to the crew.

It is imagined that we shall attempt either Patras or the castles on the Straits; and it seems, by most accounts, that the Greeks, or at any rate, the Suliotes, expect that I should march with them. I have been running in my mind through the ranks of poets who have died in battle (or its consequences): there are Kleist, Korner, Kutoffski and Thersander; Garcilasso de la Vega. If the wind is favourable, we sail tomorrow – it wants but two days until the new year. God knows why I am going, though after all, it is better to be playing at nations than gaming at Almacks or Newmarket or piecing or dinnering. I have hopes that the cause will triumph, but whether it does or no, still 'Honour must be minded as strictly as a milk diet.' I trust to observe both.

* * *

Our passage was not uneventful. We set sail a little after sunset. The air was fresh but not sharp, and the sailors' voices (for they were most of them singing) rang faintly against the clear sky. The mistico was the fastest and soon out-paced Pietro's 'bombard'. Until the waves separated us, we fired pistols and *carabines* into the night, calling out, 'Tomorrow we meet at Missolonghi – tomorrow.'

At two in the morning, we came in sight of a frigate, which I took at first to be Greek (it was within pistol shot), until the captain assured me it was not. But we kept very still and the dogs (who had been barking all night) were equally quiet, and managed to evade them. At dawn, we stood out a little way from the coast and saw two large ships – one of them chasing Pietro's bombard (which, after all, is the more valuable vessel, containing not only my horses, negro, steward and *Stanhope's press*, but eight thousand dollars of mine, with which I meant to make up the arrears of the soldiers' pay), and the other lying wait in front of the port. It appears (though I learned this only later) that several of the Greek ships, which had been guarding the entrance, had turned tail at the sight of the Turks *in protest, because they could not wait* – to be paid, that is.

By this stage I had begun to have serious concerns for the safety (not of myself, which matters little to me), but of my page, who would be most in danger in the event of our capture, *morally* as well as physically. The Turkish treatment of their prisoners of war, especially of young boys, is rather to be avoided. I would sooner cut him in pieces than have him taken by those barbarians. Besides, I had promised his mother to do everything in my power; so we ran up a creek (the Scrofes, I believe) and landed Lukas and one of the crew, with some money for themselves and a letter for Stanhope, and sent them up the country to Missolonghi. Lukas was at first very unwilling to leave the boat, until I explained to him the nature of the danger he faced – that was particular to *him*; at which he said very little but agreed to go.

In less than an hour, the vessel in chase neared us, and we dashed out again (showing our stern) and got in before night to Dragomestre. There we were welcomed by the Primates and officers of the town, who invited me into their several homes, each praising the excellence of his cook; but I preferred to stay on board, where I generally sleep very well, and my diet in any case is not various. A boiled potato, well-soaked in vinegar, or failing that, a little ship's biscuit and hard cheese, for I had got fatter again in Metaxata, on indecision, and mean to grow slim.

We stayed two nights in Dragomestre, for the wind was against us. The weather has turned wintry in the new year, and the rocks along the coast send up a fine cold spray. On the second day, three gunboats arrived from Missolonghi, which had been sent by Prince Mavrocordatos by way of convoy. (The mistico was practically undefended. We had taken with us only a few small arms. Whatever munitions we possessed were in the bombard with Pietro.) Lukas was in one of the gunboats. I was both glad and sorry to see him, as the danger was by no means past; but, after all, he is a brave child and shows a proper sense of duty to his *benefactor*. On the third day, the wind had turned sufficiently to allow us to progress into the straits, where we were twice driven on to the rocks at Scrofes (the sea being considerably fiercer than a few days previously, and the waves churning around us in such an ecstasy, that the spray reached a patch of sail *three feet* above my head). To Fletcher, who has a horror of drowning, I gave up my bunk and slept on deck, which enabled me to take this measurement. We were in constant danger, not only of splitting against the rocks, but of foundering in the open sea. I asked Lukas, who was on deck with me and observing very coolly the chaos of wind and wave, whether he could swim. He replied in the negative, but I assured him not to mind this, as I was an excellent swimmer and capable of saving both myself and him; for though the water was rough, the shore was not very distant. Meanwhile, we kept a look-out for the Turkish ships, but they had lost patience or tired of striving with the wind, and we reached at last the quiet of the lagoon outside Missolonghi.

I was in very good spirits throughout (as I love *necessity*) though a little *obscured* by five days and nights without ablution or change of clothes. The shortest way to kill fleas is to strip and take a swim, which is what I did. At Argostoli, I had ordered a scarlet coat, cut square on top and short below, in the naval manner, with golden epaulettes, as these suited the plume of Aspe's helmet – which however I had not got with me, as Pietro had taken it in the bombard. But I put on the coat and around eleven o'clock – on a cool unsettled morning, with the sea calmer, but the clouds being driven through a blue sky – we made our first appearance at Missolonghi. The inhabitants had gathered to greet us: Prince Mavrocordatos, Colonel Stanhope, Dr Missingen, etc. beside several other officers and citizens of the town, together with soldiers, priests, banditti, women and children, arranged in two rows, all screaming or singing, while we stepped ashore and the canons at a nearby fort fired off a *royal* salute.

*

Pietro was there, too; I was very relieved to see him. It appears he has had an escape no less miraculous than our own. The bombard succumbed to capture, and though Pietro had taken the precaution of loading all my letters in a sack, together with a five-pound shot, and dropping it overboard, there was nevertheless sufficient evidence of our preparations – shot, cannons, helmets, press, etc. – to convict them of war-like intentions. In fact, the Turkish commander was on the point of ordering the execution of the bombard's master, and the sinking of his boat, when he recognized Pietro, who had saved him once from shipwreck (with a half-dozen Turks) in the Black Sea a few years ago. After which they were treated very handsomely. Pietro was invited on board, to share a bottle of rum with him, and they were dispatched unmolested to Missolonghi.

We were taken directly to the house prepared for me, which sits on stilts on a narrow spit of land protruding into the lagoon; with a view on one side of the water, and on the other, of outhouses, stables, sties. It is a low damp dispiriting town, which I had visited once before, with Hobhouse fifteen years ago, and time and war have not improved it. There are a few government buildings, arranged around the landing, and then a scattering of huts and some more substantial dwellings further inland. Even in winter, the air is bad and dank as a cellar. But we have been given the finest private house, or at least, the tallest, which amounts to the same thing; and my rooms are on the second floor, with a view of the sea and dimly beyond it (in that dim air) of the mountains of the Morea. (Stanhope has installed himself on the first.) When it rains for any length of time, the house becomes unapproachable on foot – even after a morning's drizzle; but it was dry on our arrival, and not more than three minutes' walk from the jetty.

This was my first meeting with Prince Mavrocordatos, who is 'fair, fat and forty' (or looks it), and wears little round spectacles and a large moustache. Napier, who is a good judge of men, speaks highly of him, and my impressions were favourable. There is always an element of flattery, when I am introduced to a stranger, particularly if he is a Greek, and this obscures for a while his better and soberer qualities; but I believe, when once we have got through the dross, there will be a vein of ore. Stanhope was present, too; I was almost happy to see him. There was a great deal of excitement at the house, soldiers milling, civilians arguing, women cooking and shouting, but comparatively little furniture, so we sat on the floor, on cushions, around a little table, and made plans. I felt my old eagerness returning, which I had felt at Vathy, but this time better directed.

Our first object is Lepanto, which the Prince believes, with a small sacrifice of men and moneys, might be re-taken. And what an object! to be a second Santa Cruz! An expedition of about two thousand men is planned for an attack. For reasons of policy with regard to the native *capitani*, the Prince suggested assigning the command to *me*. The artillery corps is made up of such fragments as might combine to form a second tower of Babel: there are German, English, American, Swiss, Swedish officers, all offering their services. There is no one else, the Prince said, who could unite such divergent loyalties. Besides, he does not want the nomination himself (which is considered no sinecure), and can think of nobody who will take it; and so the responsibility falls to me. I did not decline it, as I had just arrived and was tired in any case of hearing nothing but talk at Argostoli – of constitutions, and Sunday Schools and what not. All excellent things in their time and place, and *here* also, but not much use until we have the means, money, leisure and freedom to try the experiment.

In practical terms, I agreed to give a hundred pounds

towards the artillery corps; and Stanhope has won from me another subscription to support his *press*, on the subject of which he is incapable of keeping silent for more than an afternoon. Well, we spent the afternoon together, and I promised him fifty pounds. It appears he has found a Swiss doctor, a Mr Meyer, to run it; another Benthamite. The first issue is expected in a couple of weeks.

At sundown the party broke up, as Lukas, who does not leave my side and was tired and hungry, began to chafe at his confinement; and it was determined that there was nothing to be decided today that could not be put off until the morning. We can in any case *do* nothing until the firemaster arrives, who has been sent by the Committee, and is expected daily with a supply of materials and men, for the manufacture of Congreve rockets and every other sort of incendiary fire. His name is Parry, and our future depends to a large extent on him and on the foresight of the Committee. He set out from England more than a month ago, on the *Ann*, but there have been unaccountable delays. The Prince has explained to me the state of our preparations: a few cannon, in very poor condition; almost no powder; a regiment of disunited foreigners, who speak no Greek and are (many of them) without the least experience of warfare, together with an equal rabble of native soldiers, who speak nothing else, and have no intention of fighting until they are paid.

I retired at last to bed with a good deal of mail (as we were expected much sooner), including several letters from Teresa. She writes very prettily and properly. I mean that the script is legible and correct, though her spelling even in Italian is often out. But her situation improves. Her father, in spite of promises made, was stopped outside

366

Ravenna and sent to Ferrara, where he lies imprisoned. This I knew before, but Teresa, who has had nowhere to turn, has found someone to turn to. Her old tutor (a very clever and liberal man, by the name of Paolo Costa, with whom I was briefly acquainted) has given her a room in his house, in Bologna, and it is from there she writes, not very happily but at least resignedly. But she never pretends to be happy when I am not with her, and in this respect, one place to her is as good as another, so long as she is not *here*.

What a contradiction she is – or rather my love for her, for she is consistent enough (and not least towards me). But I have always maintained that I am the *easiest* of men to manage, and she had the art of it: which is, to let me do exactly as I please in the few matters on which I have an opinion, and in all other affairs to decide everything for herself. There is no other way to account for how I have spent the last four years of my life, except to say, that they went *smoothly*; although there were passages (at the time) which seemed to me sufficiently rough. In her last letter, which was dated Christmas Eve, she could not resist complaining of my neglect, so that I made a final effort, and before snuffing my candle, wrote her a short note to be included in a package from her brother. For the first time I have something to tell her of which I am not ashamed, and which in a measure justifies my decision to leave her. 'It appears we may be really about to fight,' I began to write, when it struck me that this was *not* the news to relieve her anxiety, and that she cared after all very little for my justifications. So I contented myself with old assurances: that we are well, and that all here is well, and that I would write soon at greater length.

*

Lukas is no longer shy of me; that is, he begins to presume on my indulgence. The other morning I found him admiring a brace of pistols, which had been given me several years before by an American officer, on behalf of his ship and country, for which reason I had always valued them – as the respect of Americans means more to me, perhaps, than that of any other nation, since my rank counts for nothing with them, and they are not very practised dissemblers. What they admire, they admire *honestly*. Lukas told me he would like to have them 'for himself'. So I said, 'This is what I suggest. We will go into the courtyard and set a bottle on the stable-wall. If you strike it at twenty paces with one of these pistols before I do (you may have the honour), I will give you the brace.'

He jumped up readily at this, and we went outside. It was a dry day and the courtyard was not muddy. I called through a window into the kitchen, asking for a bottle, and presently one was brought out. Then I set it on the wall and paced out twenty steps in the direction of the house (so as not to fire into it, but towards the lagoon); but Lukas protested that it was too far, and together we counted out twenty steps again, with my hand on his shoulder. Lukas fired first, but too quickly and closed his eyes a little against the smoke. There was only the sound of the gun, and no other, and afterwards the bottle was still standing on the wall.

'The pistol is no good,' he said.

'Well, I will show you what may be done with it.'

He watched me with one of his smiles (as my hand is

not very steady), but after my shot rang out, there was another sound, and the bottle lay splintered in the mud.

'No, no, it was the wind,' he said, still smiling.

'Why do you say that?' (We spoke together mostly in Italian.)

'Because your hand is like this,' he answered, holding up his own and allowing it to shake like a leaf. 'Like an old man.'

'I wonder how old you think I am. I was once as young as you.'

But he called for another bottle to be brought out and set it on the wall again and counted the steps. But he counted too few, and we stood a little closer. All this with an air as if he thought me easily made a fool of. I believe it never occurred to him that he would miss. But again he misfired into the wind, and my own first shot knocked the bottle into pieces.

'The pistol is no good,' he repeated, but without a smile, and this time a little disgusted. 'Otherwise I would not be beaten by an old man.'

'I wonder how old you think I am,' I said again.

He looked me up and down, standing very straight and proud, as he always stands, and with his head a little to the side. After a minute: 'At least thirty.'

'You see, you have made me laugh, and for that you will get your desire. (It is the Italian phrase.) I will give you the pistols.'

'No, no,' says he, 'I would like something finer than that, something of my own. These pistols are no good.'

And, fool that I am (for I could never resist an appeal), I asked Pietro that afternoon to have a pair made up, at any expense, with an inscription I would furnish later; but he came back to me (and this is what struck me truly as absurd) saying there was no one on the island capable of executing my commission, until Parry's arrival – this at a military base in the midst of its preparations against an *empire*. The best we could do (it was his own suggestion) was have an inscription added to a pair of guns already existing; and he offered to inquire of Prince Mavrocordatos if he knew where one was to be found. I was reluctant to involve the Prince in an affair that had, after all, no relation to our mission, especially as my position in Missolonghi depended to a certain extent on his continuing esteem. But it occurred to me at last that Lukas might easily be called to defend himself, and his *patron*, against attack, and that there could be nothing ridiculous in giving him the means to do so. The Prince replied, very handsomely, with a brace of unadorned but beautifully made weapons, which I had gilded for Lukas and inscribed with a couplet from Thomson:

> Delightful task! to rear the tender thought,
> To teach the young idea *how to shoot*.

Which Lukas, who, when he likes, has the manners of a proper little boy, received very sweetly – gratitude at least is one of the emotions of which he is capable.

*

For several years past I have been accustomed to waking in low spirits, regardless of how I spent the night – or *would* spend the day. This melancholy (for which my name is a bye-word) is of no duration and signifies after all little enough. It is a sort of dew, which gathers and settles at dawn, but is easily burned away; a few hours will do it. Nevertheless, it is a prospect to be reckoned with at night, before going to sleep; and in the morning, of course. But lately . . . It is not as if I have slept well. There are nights when I hardly sleep at all. But I cannot recall a time, since leaving Venice, when I have *woken* better. I watch the window greying and brightening, and hear the animals in the yard being let out and the soldiers stirring in the kitchen below (several of the Suliotes sleep there); and then I sit up and call for Lukas to bring me tea.

There is a great deal to be done, and the house is constantly occupied, with soldiers, sailors, foreigners, Greeks, merchants, petitioners, officials, Princes and colonels, all talking, planning, arguing, chaffing and drinking at once; only we can do nothing until Parry arrives. But there are some things we *have* done. Stanhope has brought out the first issue of his *Hellenica Chronica*, with a motto from Bentham: *The greatest good of the greatest number*. It lies in stacks on the landing outside his room, and when anyone comes to the house, he presses a copy into his hands. Meyer, the editor, is a ridiculous person and brings out the worst in Stanhope. They spend hours together discussing the principles of education (for schools that have not been built), and the nature of the new constitution (for a government that does not exist). But at least they occupy each other, and are confined mostly to Stanhope's quarters, on the first floor.

It has been decided (I have decided it) that until the expeditionary force is assembled, and equipped, we can do no better than organize the force at our disposal, of some six hundred men with serviceable weapons, into a troop of irregulars. No General has ever before had such an army. My corps outdoes Falstaff's: there are English, Germans, French, Maltese, Ragusians, Italians, Neapolitans, Transylvanians, Russians, Suliotes, Moreotes, and Western Greeks, in front, and to bring up the rear, the tailor's wife with her troop of negresses, to wash, sew, cook and otherwise provide for the rest. Once a day we exercise in the yard, presenting arms, etc. and *firing* at straws; and in the afternoon, I ride out with the rest of the Suliotes (there are about a hundred), who form my personal bodyguard, with Pietro and Lukas, to each of whom I have entrusted a division of some twenty men. At night, we talk and drink and make plans, which rarely however survive the sobering of the morning, but nobody minds this, as we get drunk again the next night and make new plans; and in this way we have spent the better part of two weeks.

That there is something absurd about this manner of proceeding, I am perfectly aware. Pietro has spent five hundred dollars, which had been better spent elsewhere, on materials for fitting out his brigade. But this is what comes of letting boys play the man; all his patriotism diminishes into the desire for a sky blue uniform. Nor is Lukas, who is naturally emulous, to be restrained. He has begged off me (who have never had very great powers of resistance), in addition to the pistols, a gold jacket, a new riding coat, and a new saddle and saddlecloth with silk cording. But the prospect of Parry's arrival gives a decent margin to this foolishness.

In addition to our regular rides, I have instituted the habit of reading Greek with him for half an hour each day. The charge of a young man's life is one that I take seriously, and my promise to his mother, to defend and promote his honour, extends also to her son's education. The custom has this advantage, which is, that it benefits my own; and we sit together after breakfast on the sofa in my sitting room with a book shared between us that we puzzle out together. Besides, there is a certain charm in imagining, with the plume of Aspe's helmet drooping from the wall, and the mountains of the Morea showing faintly in the window, that Homer was no fabulist, and that freedom, honour, glory etc. are not only words but things, that may be fought for and won. Only think, a free Greece! It is the very poetry of politics. Nor is Lukas immune to the romance of association, and I believe that for him also this quiet hour gives a colouring to the rest of the day.

What a strange compound he is! His father was a school-master, a profession that is still reverenced in Greece. And Lukas must have acquired from him, before he died, a dutiful habit of instruction, for he takes his lesson, as Sir Toby took his drink, *meekly* enough. He reminds me in some respects of the choir-boy Edleston, in the symmetry of his face and the extreme innocence of his *appearance*; but where Edleston was modest, Lukas is brazen; where Edleston was hesitant, Lukas is ironical; where Edleston was warm, Lukas is – less warm. We have sat for twenty minutes together, with my head peering over his shoulder and my hand upon his knee, considering a few lines of verse, and when Stanhope came in to discuss (without knocking) some business to do with the arrears, I have watched the boy without the least sign of embarrassment or reluctance stand up to leave.

It is clear to me that I am nothing to him, except as a

source of some amusement and . . . many fine things. But at the moment it strikes me still as something to be grateful for – that I should live again impassioned days. If he is curious about me at all (and he is not much), it is only in this respect: that I have, without looks, youth or valour to recommend me, managed to acquire a *name* and the admiration of people he knows. Though he can hardly bring himself to believe that my fame depends entirely on what I have written; on books. He said to me once, in some wonder, as we sat on the sofa, 'They tell me you are a great man and say that I should show you respect and do what you ask.'

'Who tells you? However, what I wish for most is that you do for me what I *don't* ask.'

'Pietro. Tita. My mother, before we left.'

'And will you?'

'Well, you do not seem to me very different from other men.'

'And what do you know of men?'

'I am not a child, which is what you sometimes call me.'

'I do not think of you as a child.'

'But if you are a great man, it is not what I expected. Your hair is grey and not very thick, and your teeth are brown. And then, your foot makes you limp, which no one remarks on; indeed, people often say to you what they know to be false, as if you were a woman or a child. And you do what *I* ask, which I would not in your situation.' A little later he said, 'Have strangers often been disappointed in you?'

'You mean, when they meet me?'

'Yes.'

'They expect me to be less *lively* than I am.' The Italian

word, in this case, naturally suggests its opposite, and he replied, 'Does this disappoint them? You seem to me rather dolorous.'

I am not much used to making love where it was not wanted – I don't have the *art*. If Hobhouse were here, he would make me heartily sick of myself; but he is not here. Sometimes, however, I am a little sick. And wonder not only at my devotions, as the churchmen say, but at their object. For I *see* him clearly enough. Lukas is proud, without being sensitive; and free, without being generous; and honest, without being faithful. In short, he possesses exactly one half of those qualities that have made a joy and a misery of my life, but not the other. Yet whenever he leaves me (which however I don't often permit), I begin to 'cast mine eyes' about until I see him again. And every morning I awake eagerly, with a quickening heart.

*

I have managed at least to conduct one good piece of business, which is: to release four Mussulman prisoners to the care of Yussuf Pasha, in return for their treatment of Pietro Gamba and the crew of the bombard. In my experience it is generally a matter of practical self-interest to deal *gallantly*, even with one's enemies. Besides, the horrors of war are sufficient in themselves without adding cold-blooded ruthlessness on either side. The rest of my time is taken up with money-matters, for which I have only lately acquired a taste.

Pietro himself wonders at it, and reproaches me for it, as I have decided in the end to put a stop to his foolishness about the uniforms. The cloth, which he has ordered at ridiculous expense (the cost might have equipped, or at least maintained, three hundred men for a month!) will be put up at auction; for I would rather incur the dead loss of *part* than be encumbered with a quantity of things at present superfluous or useless in themselves. Pietro, who hates being in the wrong, has apologized in a fashion. This is the form his apology took. He came in one day to see me writing letters – to Charles Hancock of the Committee, in a request for funds; to a Mr Stevens, the customs officer in Argostoli, to deal with the sale of the cloth; to Yussuf Pasha, and Samuel Barff, and Captain Yorke, all regarding one kind or another of revolutionary business – and stood at my shoulder, and watched me in silence for several minutes, before reproaching me that I no longer write poetry!

It appears, however, that we may shortly have something better to do. The Turks have sailed out of the gulf again, and the five Speziot ships, which had been guarding the harbour at Missolonghi, turned tail at once. This comes at a particularly bad time, as Parry is expected any moment in the *Ann*, besides several other dispatches from the Committee, bearing funds, arms, men and mail. The Turkish fleet, finding no resistance, has since reinforced itself; and as I write, through the window of my sitting room, I have counted ten ships (of twenty guns or more) anchored in the waters outside of town. Everyone is in a fever, and there is a great deal of talk, of capitulation on the one hand, and resistance on the other. A scheme has been devised, of setting out at a night in a number of small boats, and cutting away rigging and anchor-cables, in the hope of driving several of these vessels onto the rocks. But for this we need a new moon (which is only two days away) and a strong wind, whereas the weather since Sunday last has been cold grey and settled. I am determined to be foremost in this assault, as it comes at my suggestion (or at my command, which amounts to the same thing), and I would sooner expose myself than any-one else; though Stanhope, Pietro, and the Prince are each of them, and for very different reasons, reluctant to permit this. But I intend to persuade them – as there is no one else who can unite the volunteers, which they admit; and they are under my authority.

Yesterday was my birthday, my thirty-sixth; and we had a breakfast-party in my apartments to celebrate the fact, an occasion I commemorated with a new poem, which I had finished the night before – my first in several months. Stanhope and Meyer (who never leaves his side); Pietro and the Prince; Bruno and Dr Millingen; Fletcher, Lukas and Tita were all assembled, when I came in carrying the fresh draft. I said to Pietro, 'You were complaining the other day that I never write poetry now. I have just finished something which, I think, is better than what I usually write.'

'Will you read it?' he said.

'There are reasons that make me reluctant to do so.'

'Then I will read it,' he answered, taking the draft from my hands. And he began:

> 'Tis time this heart should be unmoved,
>   Since others it hath ceased to move,
> Yet though I cannot be beloved
>   Still let me love.

> My days are in the yellow leaf.
>> The flowers and fruits of love are gone –
> The worm, the canker and the grief
>> Are mine alone.

Then he read on silently for a few minutes. The others began to clamour for him to continue, and Pietro and I exchanged a look, at which I shrugged my shoulders, and finally Pietro said, 'I think you are right, brother (which he sometimes called me). It is a little better than what you usually write; and it ends very prettily, but not very truthfully, I hope.' And he read:

> Seek out – less often sought than found,
>> A soldier's grave – for thee the best,
> Then look around and choose thy ground
>> And take thy rest.

Adding, when he was finished, 'But this of course we cannot allow.' And the discussion turned again to the proposed attack, and the poem was mentioned no more. Lukas understood not a word of anything.

*

The Turks have departed again, no one knows why or whither; and we will not fight. I awoke one morning to find the sea empty of anything, but a few fishing smacks, and was almost sorry.

*

As I write, Lukas sleeps in my bed. There is a lamp lit in the room, as (in his fever) he is afraid of the dark, and I have left the door open, which communicates between it and the sitting room. I am not very tired, and when I am, I will sleep on the sofa, which is no hardship to a seasoned campaigner. His cheeks are red and hot to touch, as if he had been running. Indeed, in his fever he looks very much like the boy he is, and not at all like the man he sometimes pretends to be. He is kinder in sickness than in health; that is, he wants kindness more, and when he could not sleep, asked me to sit by him. I sang to him (I could think of nothing else to do) one of the songs I remembered Lady Byron sometimes singing to our daughter, who slept very poorly, at least in the first weeks of her life (I never saw her after), but he asked me not to sing; so I began to tell him a story, but he asked me not to talk at all. And so I sat with my hand on his hair on the pillow (he did not want me to touch his skin) until he fell asleep.

All this is the result of another foolish expedition, to Anatolikon, for the purpose of persuading them of my . . . existence, which had the customary effect: a great deal of mutual congratulation. There was a violent salute of muskets and discharge of cannon to celebrate the removal of the Turks, who had lately been encamped there; and I shook hands with several dozen officers, officials and citizens of the town, who argued amongst themselves over precedence, which put them so out of humour they could only smile in a pinched sort of way on their being introduced. I was shown a very pretty church, dedicated to St Michael, which was supposed very recently to be the site of a miracle. A mortar had lately fallen, killing the curate's mother (this was not the miracle) and exposing a hidden spring, on which, during the worst of the siege, the townspeople had depended for their survival. This kind of superstition always dispirits me. It is the very cowardice of hope, and these same men who talk invincibly of omens will, when their harvest is ruined by two days of rain, call it a visitation of God and lay down their arms. But the visit ended in expressions of good health, which have already been answered in the usual way: Pietro, prostrate with fever and sweating in his own bed; and Lukas not much better and sweating in mine. (The doctor insisted on this, as he generally sleeps on the floor.) Our boat was caught in a shower on the journey home; we were all as thoroughly soaked as if it had sank. It appears at least that my constitution is not completely ruined, for I have nothing but a headache to complain of.

*

The assault on Lepanto has been abandoned. We have not the men, nor the money, nor (as it seems to me) the inclination. Parry has arrived at last, with eight mechanics, sent by the Committee, but much less in the way of materials than we had hoped. He tells me it will take at least two months to build the Congreve rockets, which are absolutely essential to any attack on occupied fortifications; consequently, the Prince and I have put off even the discussion of an attempt on Lepanto until it is practicable. The difficulty is, that if we confine ourselves to the *practicable*, our case is hopeless – we can only continue in the present manner, doing nothing, which takes up all of my time and is becoming increasingly intolerable.

I have lost all patience with the Suliotes. Having tried

in vain at every expense, considerable trouble, and some danger to unite them for the good of Greece, and their own, I have come to the following resolution: I will have nothing more to do with them. They may go to the Turks or the devil. The *Ann* arrived on the 5th and deposited its stores on the shore, which, though they fell far short of our expectation, and some way below our needs, are nevertheless vital to our continuing defence, and any hope we still cherish of striking a blow for the freedom of Greece. The Suliotes refused to transport these stores, of cannon, powder, shot, mechanical tools, etc. – all of which we not only lack ourselves, but which, should they fall to the Turks, which is not unlikely, as we are surrounded by sympathizers and profiteers, would furnish our own destruction – from the beach to the fort, owing to the fact that it was a public holiday! Not until I began myself, in a frenzy of rage, to carry what I could up the sand, did they relent; and afterwards they approached me, in a spirit of conciliation, with a request that some hundred or more of their number (out of a force of three hundred and fifty!) should be promoted, on the strength of these efforts, to colonel, captain, private etc. – which they care about not at all, as there can be no rank where there is no order, except as it relates to their *pay*.

Parry at least is an excellent soldier, in the good English fashion: that is, he cares nothing for Greeks, and less for their liberation, but a good deal about his men and his guns. I had expected him to be a little disheartened by the conditions he found here but was not prepared for the violence of his reaction. He tells me that the fort, which was badly built twenty years ago, and has been worse repaired, should never have been built at all: as it is situated in such a way that it defends nothing but itself. It appears moreover that the force, such as it is, of which I am commander, refuses to serve under him – because he is an Englishman, and not a lord, and a soldier, and not a poet! We suffer every day, and every day a little more, from desertion. The Germans, French, Italians, etc. who come to Missolonghi, because they have read Homer, depart again, because they have seen Greece; and many that choose to remain are simply too dispirited to undertake the effort of going home. A state of mind that too much resembles my own for me to condemn it.

Our society at least has lately had an addition, a little Turkish girl named Hato (this is what I have decided to call her, as her real name is unpronounceable) discovered by Millingen, who brings her twice a week to visit me and sit on my lap. She is a child of some eight or nine years. Her father was killed three years before, her two brothers also, in the burst of brutality that followed Missolonghi's declaration of independence. She lives with her mother, in some squalor, but in spite of the misery of her life has remained – pretty, spirited, charming and agreeable. She saw her brothers' murder (their brains were dashed against a wall by *hand*) and cried out against their murderers, who spared her only because she made them laugh. This is the famous quality of mercy. I have written to Lady Byron in the hope of persuading her to adopt the child, as a sister to our daughter; for she really cannot continue where she is. She is growing too beautiful by the day, with the dark *pure* oriental complexion and modesty of feature, together with large black eyes; and the Greeks in this respect are not to be trusted. If Lady Byron does not want her, I will send her to Teresa, who *will* – as the child comes from me, and has seen me, and her face has been touched by my hand and kissed by my lips.

Lukas is jealous of her, and for this reason alone I should be sorry to see her go – because I gave her a sequinned necklace, and sent Tita out to buy her sweets, indulgences which he considers his by right. Lately it has become a question with me whether he is at all conscious of what might be considered his provocation. That is, what he provokes me *into*. He certainly is not shy in my presence, and makes himself free with everything that is mine, in a most suggestive way. The Greeks are not known to be squeamish in these matters, and a boy of his appearance is unlikely to have reached the age of fifteen without some experience of its effects. That he likes to be admired, I can have no doubt, but his preening, from what I have seen of it, is rather innocent; he responds most powerfully to his own charms.

*

Two days ago I had a strong shock of a convulsive description, but whether epileptic, paralytic, or apoplectic is not yet decided by the doctors (Bruno and Millingen) who attend me; or whether it be of some other nature (if such there be). It was very painful and had it lasted a moment longer must have extinguished my mortality, if I can judge by sensations. I was speechless, with the features much distorted, but not foaming at the mouth (they say), and my struggles so violent that several persons, including Parry and Tita, who are both strong men, could not hold me. It lasted about ten minutes and came on immediately after drinking a tumbler of cider mixed with cold water in

Stanhope's apartments. This is the first attack that I have had of this kind to the best of my belief. I never heard that any of my family were liable to the same, though my mother was subject to *hysterical* affections.

Yesterday leeches were applied to my temples. I had previously recovered a good deal, but with some feverish and variable symptoms. I bled profusely and (as they went too near the temporal artery) there was some difficulty in stopping the blood, even with the *lunar caustic*. This however after some hours was accomplished, about eleven o'clock at night, and today, though weakly, I feel tolerably convalescent.

With regard to the presumed cause of this attack – as far as I know there might be several. Millingen conjectures that it was the result of the same sudden drenching that put Lukas and Pietro to bed, but which, owing to the de-bilitation of my constitution, has had a less immediate but more profound effect. There are besides this a number of general causes. The state of the place and the weather per-mits little exercise at present. It is possible that I have not been uniformly so temperate as I may generally affirm that I was wont to be. How far any or all of these may have acted on the mind or body of one who had already under-gone many previous changes of place and passion during a life of thirty-six years I cannot tell, nor – but I am inter-rupted by the arrival of a report from a party returned from reconnoitring a Turkish brig of war just stranded on the coast, and which is to be attacked the moment we can get some guns to bear upon her. I shall hear what Parry says about it; here he comes.

*

The Turks burned their ship, departing from it in the boats before we could reach her; there was nothing left but a hundred feet of cordage, and a little spare canvas, which survived the blaze. Afterwards there was more trouble with the Suliotes. One of their number, a man named Yiotes, had taken Botsaris's son (who is not more than ten years old) along – whether to participate in the action, or witness the end of it, is not clear. He was stopped by a guard, a Swede, for reasons that are still obscure, and will not become clearer; he is dead now. Yiotes was also wounded in the conflict, and believed dead; and the Suliotes, hearing that one of their number had been killed by a foreign soldier, surrounded the arsenal and threatened to overrun it and attack the town. I gave orders that the cannon should be pointed at the gate. As I was still too feverish to stand, I summoned several of the Suliote chiefs to my bedside. They raged at me, shouting their reasons (of which they always have a great many), to which I listened as calmly as I could – I was too weak to do anything else. After an hour or more of listening, and saying little, I *stood up* – which occasioned in them a sort of shiver of horror, as they are a superstitious people, with a great belief in revenging spirits – and by these means persuaded them to break up their siege. Since then we have settled again into the old unhappy alliance. And I have returned to my bed.

*

I have lately been thinking over something my mother once said to me on my return from Harrow one summer, now a very long time ago. Odd how a word or phrase recalls to us (even when we have little enough cause to cherish the remembrance) the dead, but I have several fresh reasons for the association. Outside my window I see a dirty square and a dirty island morning beginning, with its dogs and its restless children. It is never properly cold here, in the good old Scottish manner, but what cold there is has a wet way of entering the bones. My mother said to me, provoked no doubt by some foolishness on my part, of vanity either wounded or inflamed, that it is only children who love themselves. A phrase intended chiefly as a rebuke. She meant that I was a child still, and that my *amour-propre* was the proof of it. What occurred to me the other day was that in this case I am a child no longer.

Lukas and I have quarrelled, without reconciling; and somehow this has made no difference and we continue exactly as before.

This is what happened. I had summoned him to my room on account of some moneys that I kept in a drawer, and which had gone missing. (I noticed their absence when I was once more in a state to notice anything.) Stanhope, who dislikes the boy's manner with me, had accused him before of stealing; but as I always gave the child whatever he asked for, and am not particular about possessions, I never saw any evidence for the charge. But I am particular about money. He came in, with a red face, as if he had lately been crying, which made me suspect that he meant to forestall me. I asked him what the matter was. He said that his mother and one of his sisters had heard that he was ill, and had promised to visit him; but that someone had told them he was fully recovered, and they had just written to say they would not come. He asked me very coolly then if I had written to them. I told him that I had not, but that it was just as well, as any journey between Cephalonia and the mainland at the present time would put his family in unnecessary danger.

He said, 'That is not why. That is not why you wish to keep them apart from me.'

I asked him to explain himself.

'It does not matter. You always get your way.'

'It seems to me,' I said, 'that that is exactly what I never get. Indeed, you do what you like with me, to which I make no objection. I ask only that what you take from me you take openly.'

It was his turn to stare a little.

Then, for I hate insinuation, I said, 'Someone has taken from me, while I was ill in bed, several hundred piastres. I had counted them out for a purpose; there can be no mistake. They were in the turtle-shell box on my desk, and the box is now almost empty. I have summoned you to ask you if you took them.'

'I take nothing from you,' he declared. And then, a moment later, in the same tone, 'Maybe Pietro gave them to me. But I know nothing about the box.'

'What do you mean, that Pietro gave them to you? For what reason?'

But he would not look me in the eyes. Eventually, he said, 'You can ask him yourself.'

So I rang the bell, and when Fletcher came, I told him to bring Mr Gamba to me. While we waited, Lukas said, 'As this is nothing to do with me, I suppose I may go' – but without much hope, and he made no attempt to leave. When Pietro came, I put to him directly what Lukas had told me. Lukas began to laugh strangely; Pietro looked uncomfortable. After a minute, he said, 'Yes, it's true, I gave him the money.'

'Why did you give it to him? And if you gave it, why did you not tell me?'

Both young men had refused to sit down. I alone was seated, as I dislike standing; and Pietro went to the window before replying, 'You forget you were very ill. The doctors were always sending for something or other. We did not know what to do. We thought you would die.'

'And what did you send Lukas out for?'

Lukas was not laughing, but he was still smiling, when Pietro said, 'I did not send him out. I gave him the money so that he would stay.' He added, 'I would have given him my own, but I haven't any.'

The truth of all this (and a great deal more than was said) came home to me, as I glanced from one to the other: the boy with his bright eye looking directly into mine, and Pietro, who bears me no malice and a great deal of love, ashamed of something or someone and staring at his shoes. I said nothing for a long while, and then I asked Pietro to leave me alone with the boy.

When he was gone, I said to Lukas, 'Come, sit next to me. I am not angry any more.'

'Of course not, why should you be angry?' he replied, without coming nearer.

I said gently, 'For two nights, when you could not sleep, I sat by your bed.'

'I never asked you.'

Then, losing my temper: 'If my service is unpleasant to you, you may go.'

My blood was up, and I was tired of all this foolishness;

but he continued to provoke me. 'But you do not want me to go,' he said.

I stood up and walked towards him; saying, 'Oh, if it's a question of what *I* want,' – and attempted to seize him, but he, being younger, was quicker and stronger, too, and easily escaped. I might have followed, but for this damned foot. He stood in the doorway, panting and grinning, and I said to him, 'Look at me! Look at me!' with the tears suddenly streaming down my face. After he was gone, I went to the window, to see if he went out. To be surrounded on all sides by nothing! Nothing but watery swamp, and swampy water; but he so little felt the importunities of my presence, he must have stayed below, for I did not see him go out. After a minute of this watching, I grew thoroughly sick of myself, and then another kind of feeling rising up in me, I sat down at the table and for the first time in almost a month began to write.

Afterword

It seems fairly clear that this is the poem Peter had in mind, which Byron at the end of 'A Soldier's Grave' 'began to write':

> I watched thee when the foe was at our side,
>   Ready to strike at him – or thee and me,
> Were safety hopeless – rather than divide
>   Aught with one loved save love and liberty.
>
> I watched thee on the breakers, when the rock
>   Received our prow and all was storm and fear,
> And bade thee cling to me through every shock;
>   This arm would be thy bark, or breast thy bier.
>
> I watched thee when the fever glazed thine eyes,
>   Yielding my couch and stretched me on the ground,
> When overworn with watching, ne'er to rise
>   From thence if thou an early grave hadst found.
>
> The earthquake came, and rocked the quivering wall,
>   And men and nature reeled as if with wine.
> Whom did I seek around the tottering hall?
>   For thee. Whose safety first provide for? Thine.

And when convulsive throes denied my breath
  The faintest utterance to my fading thought,
To thee – to thee – e'en in the gasp of death
  My spirit turned, oh! oftener than it ought.

Thus much and more; and yet thou lov'st me not,
  And never wilt! Love dwells not in our will.
Nor can I blame thee, though it be my lot
  To strongly, wrongly, vainly love thee still.

It was the last he ever completed. He died a few weeks later of some illness connected to the fit he had suffered earlier; his doctors more or less bled him to death. Afterwards his body was shipped to England. The Dean of Westminster refused to bury it at the Abbey, on moral grounds, though it lay on view for a week at a house on Great George Street. Hobhouse made the arrangements, seeing his old friend in the flesh for the first time in several years. 'It did not seem to be Byron,' he wrote. 'The mouth was distorted & half open showing those teeth in which poor fellow he once so prided himself quite discoloured . . . I was not moved so much scarcely as at the sight of his hand writing.' The streets of London were lined with spectators for the funeral procession, which carried the coffin through Oxford Street and Tottenham Court Road, past St Pancras Church and out of London. After a journey of several days, it reached the family vaults at Hucknall Torkard, a few miles from Newstead Abbey.

Hobhouse was also behind the other more famous arrangement made by Byron's friends for his posterity. He presided, along with the poet's old editor John Murray, over the burning of his memoirs. Hobhouse and Murray thought they would ruin his reputation; neither had read them. The papers were destroyed less than a month after Byron's death at Murray's office on Albemarle Street, which Byron himself used to visit in his London heyday.

What happened to Lukas is less clear. Byron left him and his family some money, to be paid out of the debts owed him by the city of Missolonghi. It appears that the money was never paid, and Lukas himself, like Edleston and Lord Grey before him, died young.

***

About Peter and me, there isn't much left to tell. Paul Gerschon agreed to match the Ransom Center's offer for his papers and eventually I settled with Ms Niemetz on a price – five thousand dollars. Gerschon then offered to buy the books himself for his private collection. Another two thousand dollars. So I went down to Charlestown one morning to give Mary Sullivan the news. I wasn't sure how she'd take it. Seven thousand dollars, on the one hand, seems like a lot of money for a few boxes of books and papers. On the other, it doesn't look like nearly enough. She invited me into her kitchen and gave me tea.

'I suppose you'll be wanting your ten per cent,' she said.

But I shook my head and after that she cheered up. 'You've been a good friend to him. God knows, he didn't have many.'

As I was leaving, she said to me, standing in her own doorway while I stood in the street, 'Do you know what I mind most about all this? I saw that review in the *New York Times* a few years ago. Of the second book. A neighbor pointed it out to me; we get all kinds of neighbors now. Some of them even take the *New York Times*. I've got nothing to say against that review but I thought at the time, if only Peter had been alive to see it. It would have been something, to take a seat on the subway, minding your own business, and read *that* in the newspaper on your way to work.'

A few weeks after my visit to Walden, Kelly came to my office again. She was in tears when I opened the door and she sat down in tears. 'As soon as I started to knock I started to cry,' she said. 'Just the thought of what I was going to tell you set me off.' Her soft pink cheerful face looked red and childish. I went to the bathroom to get her toilet paper for blowing her nose. The judge had ruled against her. He had decided there was no compelling reason for her to relocate to Austin. It wasn't in the interests of the children, and her husband had a right to enforce the terms of their custodial agreement. Now she was stuck here, with no prospects of a job and her family one thousand nine hundred and fifty-two miles away. (She had looked it up on Google Maps.) Then she stopped crying and said, 'And you're leaving too this summer.' When I didn't answer, into a slowly changing silence, she added, 'This is hard for me. I have feelings for you. I don't know if you have feelings for me.'

She was sitting in the armchair with her hands on her lap, like a good girl, sitting up straight and composed, in spite of her red eyes and streaked face, and staring back at me.

'I'm sorry,' I told her, standing up. 'I don't feel much about anything at the moment.'

'That must be a real bitch for you,' she said.

I don't know how I got her out of my office, but I remember thinking that something had happened which I needed to tell Caroline about. Something that wasn't just my imagination. That evening, after our daughter was in bed, I began to try. 'Do you remember Kelly? The woman with the two kids I've mentioned to you. She's had some bad news and she came to my office today to cry about it.' And so on. 'I feel like I need you to forgive me,' I said, 'but I didn't do anything wrong.'

Caroline was silent at first, but when she started talking, this is the form her anger took. 'It's her I feel sorry for,' she said. 'I know the way you come on. As if you're tremendously interested and caring, when really you don't give a fuck about anyone else.'

We went to bed together that night, as we always do, reading for ten minutes in silence and then turning off the light. But after the lights were off the silence continued. In the morning our daughter woke us, by climbing over me into the middle of the bed, and we talked and played with her and breakfasted more or less as usual, and went to work. And after work we gave her dinner and put her to bed and ordered in and sat up a little later than normal watching TV. I thought the whole thing would blow over, but a few days later I came back from the office to find Caroline at home, sitting at the desk in the entrance hall where we kept our papers, reading. It's my habit, at the end of every week, to print out whatever I've written and put it in a drawer, where I mostly forget it, unless there's some reason for resorting to a hard copy. Caroline had been reading my book, and this time the argument lasted much deeper into the night and covered more ground, and when we went to bed at the end of it we clung together as we hadn't in years – as we used to in New York before we were married, when Caroline was woken by the traffic on 2nd Avenue and saw with horror our whole strange lives stretching in front of us.

One of the things we agreed on before falling asleep is that I would make no attempt to publish this book. At least, the sections of the book I had written; what Peter had written she didn't care about either way. So I stopped working on it. (I had just come to the end of my visit to Walden.) The first thing I felt was relief. I sat in my office every day and followed the news on the Internet. I took long lunches. I went to the gym. The image I had was of a runner, who, having worked through other resources, begins to draw on his own tissues for energy. This is what I had been doing, and when I stopped writing, I felt my energy for other things coming back to me. I slept better; my sexual anxieties declined. The weather was improving daily, and all but the last of the snow had disappeared from the public parks. My daughter and I spent hours wandering through the Mount Auburn cemetery, climbing on gravestones, which she particularly loved, getting lost among the endless indistinguishable lanes that curve between the hills and fields of the dead.

But after a few weeks the thought of those manuscript pages began to worry me. Peter's phrase kept running through my head – they were 'emitting their rays.' This was a subject, of course, in which he was expert: what it's like to have all those public thoughts stay private. I would see him sometimes in the faces of strangers: a man with an uncut beard, wearing out his best suit and waiting for the public library to open; or maybe sitting on a street bench over the lunch hour, reading. And Caroline relented. We were getting on much better by this point, and the marriage described in this memoir seemed to her almost as fictional as anything else that's out of date. 'Just don't do it again,' she said. She didn't want me or her or any of our children to appear in anything else that I wrote, because by that point she knew she was pregnant; and as for me I was relieved to get the book off my hands, and out of the desk drawer, and more than willing to exchange the pleasures of this kind of writing, such as they are, for the happiness that writes white.

ff

Faber and Faber is one of the great independent publishing houses. We were established in 1929 by Geoffrey Faber with T. S. Eliot as one of our first editors. We are proud to publish award-winning fiction and non-fiction, as well as an unrivalled list of poets and playwrights. Among our list of writers we have five Booker Prize winners and twelve Nobel Laureates, and we continue to seek out the most exciting and innovative writers at work today.

Find out more about our authors and books
faber.co.uk

Read our blog for insight and opinion on books and the arts
thethoughtfox.co.uk

Follow news and conversation
twitter.com/faberbooks

Watch readings and interviews
youtube.com/faberandfaber

Connect with other readers
facebook.com/faberandfaber

Explore our archive
flickr.com/faberandfaber